WOLF OF
WESSEX

BY MATTHEW HARFFY

The Bernicia Chronicles

The Serpent Sword
The Cross and the Curse
Blood and Blade
Killer of Kings
Warrior of Woden
Storm of Steel
Fortress of Fury
Kin of Cain (short story)

Wolf of Wessex

W(OF)LF
WESSEX

MATTHEW HARFFY

HEAD
ZEUS

An Aries Book

First published in 2019 by Head of Zeus Ltd
This Aries paperback edition first published in 2020 by Head of Zeus Ltd

9 7 5 3 2 4 6 8

A catalogue record for this book is available from
the British Library.

ISBN (PB): 9781838932831
ISBN (E): 9781838932848

Front cover: Axe engraved and carved by Chris Bailey, following
a design by Matthew Harffy and Chris Bailey. Photo by Iona Harffy.
Front cover background image: © Shutterstock

MIX
Paper from
responsible sources
FSC
www.fsc.org   FSC® C020471

Printed and bound by CPI Group (UK) Ltd, Croydon, CR0 4YY

Head of Zeus Ltd
First Floor East
5–8 Hardwick Street
London ECIR 4RG

WWW.HEADOFZEUS.COM

For Elora and Iona,
daughters of a dreamer.

Place Names

Place names in Dark Ages Britain vary according to time, language, dialect and the scribe. I have not followed a strict convention when choosing the spelling to use for a given place. In most cases, I have chosen the name I believe to be the closest to that used in the ninth century, but like the scribes of all those centuries ago, I have taken artistic licence at times, and, when unsure, merely selected the one I liked most.

Bathum	Bath
Briuuetone	Bruton, Somerset
Briw	River Brue, Somerset
Cantmael	Queen Camel, Somerset
Carrum	Carhampton, Somerset
Centingas	Kent
Ceorleah Hill	Chorley Hill, Bruton, Somerset
Cernemude	Charmouth, Dorset
Cornwalum	Cornwall. The westernmost part of the older kingdom of Dumnonia. The people of Cornwalum were known as the Westwalas (West Welsh) by the men of Wessex.

Defnascire	Devon. The people of Devon were known as the Defnas.
Denemearc	Denmark
Dyfelin	Dublin, Ireland
Éastseaxe	Essex
Ellandun	Wroughton, Wiltshire
Exanceaster	Exeter, Devon
Frama	River Frome, Somerset
Hengestdūn	Hingston Down
Íraland	Ireland
Langtun	Langton Herring, Dorset
Mercia	One of the kingdoms of the Anglo-Saxon Heptarchy. It centred on the Trent valley in what is now known as the English Midlands.
Scirburne	Sherborne, Dorset
Sealhwudu	Selwood Forest. An ancient forest that ran approximately between Chippenham in Wiltshire and Gillingham in Dorset.
Somersæte	Somerset
Spercheforde	Sparkford, Somerset
Súpseaxe	Sussex
Súþríeg	Surrey
Tantun	Taunton, Somerset
Tweoxneam	Twynham (modern-day Christchurch, Dorset)
Wessex (Westseaxna rīce)	Kingdom of the West Saxons. In the ninth century, Wessex covered much of southern Britain, including modern-day Wiltshire, Somerset, Dorset and Hampshire. During the reign of King Ecgberht, Wessex conquered Surrey,

Sussex, Kent, Essex and Mercia, along with parts of Dumnonia. Ecgberht also obtained the overlordship of the Northumbrians. Supremacy over Mercia was brief however, with Mercian independence being restored in 830.

Wincaletone	Wincanton, Somerset
Witanceastre	Winchester

THE BRITISH ISLES
AD 838

WESTSEAXNARICE

WESSEX

R. Frama
Hwudu
Sæla

incaletone

○ Ellandun

○ Witanceastre

Tweoxneam

NORÞHYMBRA

ÍRALAND

Dyfelin ○

MERCIA

ÉASTSEAXE
CENTINGAS
WESSEX
SUÞSEAXE
DEFNASCIRE
SUÞRÍEG
CORNWALUM

Anno Domini Nostri Iesu Christi
In the Year of Our Lord Jesus Christ
838

One

It had been a good morning until Dunston found the corpse.

When he'd left the hut, there had been nothing to suggest the grisly secret that was hiding deep within the forest. The weather was fine. A misty haze lingered in the folds of the land and along the winding course of the River Frama. There was a crisp bite to the air, but Dunston knew from the experience of many years that the mist would burn off as the sun climbed into the summer sky.

Sparrows scattered, bursting forth from the bracken as Odin, Dunston's rangy merle hound, sped off into the undergrowth. To see the dog run always lifted Dunston's spirits. The dog was close to seven years old, but seemed to think it was still a pup, such was its vigour and energy.

Dunston stretched his right leg and grimaced. Straightening, he winced as his back popped and cracked. He wished he could forget that he was no longer a young man, but his body would allow him no such fantasy. He'd suffered too many injuries, pushed his frame to the limits of endurance too many times for his muscles and joints not to protest. He ran his thick fingers through his beard and sighed. Sometimes he almost forgot the passing of the years. Each day was similar to the countless days before. But then he would catch a glimpse of himself in the polished plate that Eawynn had hung on the wall of his home and he would see that where his beard had once been as black as a winter's night, now it was streaked with silver frost. And the hair that had grown so thick and wavy was now thinning, receding back from his weather-lined brow.

Still, he was yet hale and strong and he strode off along the path, listening absently to the muffled crackle of Odin's passage through the leaf litter and undergrowth. After a few moments, silence fell on the forest and Dunston wondered whether the dog had picked up the scent of a deer. More than likely he would be rolling in some unspeakable dung. By God, if that dog returned covered in shit as he so often did, the stupid animal would be taking a dip in the river before heading home. And he'd be sleeping outside the hut until the stench abated. Christ alone knew what pleasure the hound took in lathering himself in excrement. Perhaps his instincts told him that in that way he would find it easier to stalk prey. Dunston thought it would be hard for any wild animal not to smell the dog's approach after he'd smeared himself liberally with manure. And yet, no matter how often he rebuked the beast, it never stopped him.

Dunston pursed his lips, meaning to whistle for Odin, but he paused before making a sound. Something was amiss.

He halted in a small glade, shaded beneath the surrounding trees and listened. He had lived with nobody but Odin for company for long enough to know better than to ignore his feelings. Breathing silently through his opened mouth, he noted his steaming breath billowing momentarily. There was no wind. He listened to the forest, straining to hear any indication of what might have unsettled him.

Silence. As absolute as a tomb.

Gone was the sound of Odin's bounding gait through the wood. No trees rustled their leaves. The birds, usually filling the forest with their twittering songs, had all hushed. The stillness was disquieting.

Alert now, Dunston moved stealthily into the brush beside the trail. With barely a glance he made out where Odin had passed. The fresh white wood of a broken twig. A bent fern. There, in the muddy earth between the boles of two gnarled oaks, a fresh paw print, claws dug in deeply where the dog had been running fast.

With scarcely a sound, the aches in his knee and back forgotten, Dunston followed Odin's trail. He stepped lithely and as quietly as a shade. He did not hurry, for to do so would be to make noise when he knew that the surprise of silence would serve him well against man and beast.

There were creatures that dwelt in these lands that it would do well to respect. He sometimes saw the spoor of bears and at times in winter, wolves would cause him trouble, ripping the flesh from the animals he snared. But he was not unduly concerned about bears or wolves. He was more worried that Odin might have stumbled upon one of the old boars that roamed the woodland. To face one openly could well spell death for a dog, no matter how strong. The larger boars had great, dagger-like tusks and he had seen hounds and once even an unlucky man, disembowelled by the furious wild pigs.

Dunston placed his hand on the large seax that was scabbarded at his belt. He had no spear, and if he was charged by a big boar, he knew the knife would do him little good. But the touch of its antler hilt reassured him. Barely breathing, he stalked forward, as silent as any woodland animal. He paused again, listening and sniffing the air. There was no sound. Surely if Odin had stumbled upon a boar, there would have been a cacophony of grunts and growls as the animals fought. Even the largest boar would not slay Odin without a fight. And yet, there was just the unnerving hush.

Light sliced through the leafy canopy, dappling the loam and leaf mould. Dunston dropped to one knee, the joint letting out a sharp report. He winced at the sudden sound, loud in the unnatural stillness. He peered at the ground, unsure for a moment what it was he saw. And then, the shapes of the trampled leaves and the scuffed mark on the moss-covered rock by the root of a linden tree all made sense in an instant of clarity. Odin had passed this way, but so too had several men. Large, heavy men, to judge from their tracks. Three of them. No, four. They had been travelling northward. Dunston examined the tracks closely. They were fresh. He did not recognise them. These were not the prints left by any of the men who came to the wood from Briuuetone. He would never mistake the tracks of the charcoal burners, the woodsmen or the swineherd leading his pigs in search of mast under the trees. No, these were strangers, he was sure of it. But what would four men be doing creeping around in his forest? Perhaps they were wolf-heads; men outside of the law, whose oaths were worthless. Such men could be dangerous. They had nothing to lose.

He pushed himself up and before setting off once more after Odin, he listened again. There was a whisper of a sound and an instant later, the grey, white and black hound loped into the lancing sunlight.

Odin, tongue lolling, panted. His chest heaved.

"Where have you been, boy?" asked Dunston in a hushed hiss. His heart soared at the animal's safe return and he let out a pent up breath, surprised at his own worry for the hound. He reached out a hand and Odin nudged it with his snout, licking his fingers. The dog's nose was wet and cool. Dunston rubbed absently at the dog's ear and was surprised to see a smudge of crimson on the beast's fur.

Blood.

He looked down at his hand and saw that it was slick with the stuff. Pushing Odin's head to one side so that it caught a ray of sunlight, he saw that the hound's mouth and muzzle were drenched in gore.

By Christ's bones, what had Odin discovered? Had he perhaps brought down a fawn? Odin was a good hunter and would often chase and slay animals. But somehow Dunston knew that this blood did not belong to any animal. The fresh prints of the men told him that much. That, and the unnerving quiet of the wood.

For the merest of instants Dunston considered turning away and walking back to his hut. A small voice whispered to him that he wanted no part of whatever it was Odin had found.

Later, on more than one occasion, he would regret not listening to that voice.

Yet as surely as he knew he wanted nothing to do with the strangers that were in his forest, nor to discover where the blood had come from, so he understood that it was not in his nature to walk away.

He sighed, blowing out air slowly so that his breath billowed about him for a moment in the early morning cool.

"Stay close, boy," he whispered. "Show me what you've found."

Odin looked up at him, its one eye dark and thoughtful, bearded mouth red and straggled. And then the dog spun around and padded silently back into the undergrowth. Dunston hurried behind, less concerned now with remaining silent as with finding the source of that blood.

It was closer than he had imagined. A few heartbeats later, Odin led him into a clearing surrounded by densely leafed linden trees. In the centre of the glade lay a corpse. He did not need to approach the body to know the man was dead.

The clearing was awash with blood. The man had been slain atop a fallen oak, the wood long dead and crumbling. The tree trunk was slimed with gore. The delicate white flowers of the dog rose that grew along the edge of the rotting tree were splattered with crimson. The moss that clung to the wood glistened darkly. Blood had spattered and smeared much of the clearing's green carpet of snakeweed and ivy. The corpse had been stripped to the waist. Where his skin was not daubed with his lifeblood, it was pallid; the blue-tinge of death. Dunston could not see the dead man's face. He had been left face down on the log. His greying hair dangled down, lank and blood-streaked, brushing the earth beneath his hanging head.

Dunston had seen death before. But the savagery of this man's slaughter made his breath catch in his throat. This was more than a murder, or a robbery of an unlucky traveller. There was evil here.

Dunston shuddered.

Odin padded forward into the glade.

"Stay," Dunston ordered, his voice harsh; a knife cut in the stillness of the forest.

The dog whimpered, but halted and sat on its haunches. Absently, Dunston reached out and placed a hand on the hound's head. The dog's warmth was comforting.

Dunston stroked the soft, warm fur behind Odin's ears, but all the while, his gaze remained fixed on the scene of slaughter before him.

The slain man's back had been split open. His ribs had been pried apart and his offal pulled from his flesh and splayed upon his back. Dunston did not need to get any closer to know that the bloody mess either side of the great wound in the centre of his back was made up of the man's lungs. They had been draped like crude, blood-drenched wings on the man's shoulder blades.

Dunston had heard of such things, but he had thought them the tales of scops to frighten children. Though why they felt the need to make the Norsemen any more terrifying than they were, he had never understood. In his experience, the men who came from the sea aboard the beast-prowed sea-dragons, oars beating as the wings of some giant bird, were fearsome enough. There was no need to invent stories of human sacrifice and ritual killings in the name of their one-eyed god.

Could it be that the tales were true? Had raiders landed nearby in their sleek ships, on the Frama perhaps? Surely the river was not large enough here to carry fighting ships? Were Norsemen even now creeping through the forest in search of prey?

And yet he had only seen the tracks of four men. And it was not the way of those heathen Norse to sneak around murdering men in the dark of the woodland. The people of the coast lived in constant fear of the coming of the dragon ships, he knew, but here? And why so few of them?

Whatever the truth of it, the remains of the poor man told him one thing. Danger was close.

Dunston dragged his gaze from the gory spectacle and cast around the clearing. Clothing was strewn about. A tawny-coloured cape. A ripped kirtle, tattered and flecked with dark stains. A single leather shoe. Dunston flicked his gaze back to the dead man and noted his left foot was bare.

An unusual shadow caught his attention. There was something large just beyond the clearing. He took a couple of steps towards it. His hand rested on his seax handle and once again he was moving with the silent stealth of a woodland hunter. Two more steps and he was able to discern what the object was. A handcart. A simple, two-wheeled affair that could be pulled by one person. Walking to the cart, he tugged back the greased leather that covered its contents. He was surprised to find several sacks, a wooden box and a couple of small iron-hooped kegs, nestling safely and seemingly untouched beneath the cover. Teasing open one of the sacks he found long white goose feathers inside. A second, smaller bag held leather pouches. Each of the pouches was tightly tied, but they were not sealed well enough to disguise the heady aroma of pepper, cinnamon and mace. Dunston's head swam with the powerful scents of the spices. These were not the things that would bring Norse warriors battle-fame and have their names sung of in the halls of their northern lands, but the stuff was valuable enough. Pulling the leather back over the cart, he looked about him.

A light wind rustled the leaves high above. The summer sun was warming the land. Somewhere far off a wood pigeon called. The forest was returning to normal, breathing once again after the sudden violence that had happened within its depths.

Dunston sighed. When he had awoken that morning, he had meant to check his snares, and then return to his hut and the forge. The knife he was making for Oswold, the leatherworker from Briuuetone, was taking shape and it would easily have been finished by midsummer's eve. But now that would have to wait. He could not leave the man here. The easiest thing would be to bury him and just keep what was on the cart. He could sell the items over time, and some of the things might be of use to him.

Shaking his head, he returned to the clearing. He knew he would do no such thing. He was no thief, and besides, there were killers on the loose. Perhaps even Norsemen. No, he would take the cart and the man down to Briuuetone. Let Rothulf decide what must be done. Perhaps the reeve would know who the corpse was. Maybe the dead man had kin.

Dunston took in a deep breath and spat, readying himself for the task of wrestling the man's gore-slick remains onto the small cart. He once more searched the ground, as much to put off the task as anything else.

The same four men. They had all been here. He could clearly see where they had confronted the man with the cart and then dragged him to the fallen oak. The spray of the man's blood showed Dunston where they had first tortured him and then, with a great gouting fountain of dark arterial blood, they had taken his life. Dunston reached out to touch a bramble, pulling a small red woollen thread from a thorn. His hand shook. He could almost hear the screams of the dying man, the laughter and shouts of the men who had butchered him. Dunston was no stranger to death and he was accustomed to slaughtering, gutting and skinning animals small and large. But this torn tragedy, a mass of ripped flesh and offal, this was no way for a man to die.

Twisting the piece of wool between his forefinger and thumb, Dunston steeled himself for what he needed to do. But just as he pushed himself up, he noticed the slightest of prints in the soft earth in the shade of the dog rose. This was something else. No, someone else. Judging from the size and depth of the track, this belonged to a child or perhaps a woman. Had the four men taken her?

Dunston's heart pounded. Was there even now a defenceless child at the mercy of the brutes who had committed this act of savagery? He searched frantically about the glade for more sign, but the area was trampled. Flies and insects droned and hummed now about the corpse, gorging themselves on its blood and cooling flesh.

He could find no more tracks. Perhaps he should follow the clear trail of the killers in order to see whether they had carried the child off with them. He did not like the prospect. There were four of them and he wanted nothing to do with men capable of such atrocities. And yet, without a backward glance, he hitched up his belt and walked into the forest after them. He would have to come back for the poor man's body later.

Just as he stepped into the gloom beneath the linden trees, Odin let out a piercing bark. By the rood and all the saints, the stupid dog would get him killed. Dunston hissed at the hound for silence, but Odin ignored him, raising his snout as if scenting something on the breeze, and then bounding off into the undergrowth in the opposite direction to the killers' tracks.

Unsure for a moment, Dunston hesitated. Then, with a curse, he turned and ran after the dog.

Two

Aedwen tried not to breathe. She strained to hear any sign that the men had returned. But the wood was silent now. Gone was the terrible screaming. Before the inhuman shrieking that had come later, she had been able to recognise the sound of her father's voice. He had spoken in that infuriatingly calm manner of his; the tone that mother had said drove her mad.

Walking back from the stream, Aedwen had paused for a moment when she'd heard him speaking, wondering whether he was calling something to her. But then she had heard the other voices, hard and jagged, as different from father's tone as a flint is to silk. Absently wondering who the voices belonged to, she had started up the trail again. The bucket she carried was full and heavy, and she had wanted to relinquish its weight.

That was when the shouting had started. It had quickly been followed by screaming. For a moment she had stood there on the path, the forest still cold and gloomy in the dawn. The chill water from the bucket sloshed her hand, starting her into motion. She heard several coarse voices, and laughter.

And her father had let out a piteous wailing cry. Tears flooded down her cheeks at the sound, but she knew what he would have wanted her to do. They had talked about what to do if they were ever attacked by brigands on the road.

"If you can get away, you run, girl," he had said to her, as he had stirred the pot of stew over the smoking fire. That was on the first day after they had left the home she had known all her life. When this was still an adventure.

Father had often berated Aedwen for not obeying him, but that morning she did as she had been told. She spun on her heel and sprinted away. She had run without thought for her destination or direction. Branches whipped at her face, snagging her dress. Brambles scratched at her skin. All the while, father's screams echoed around the wood. His dying cries followed her until she was panting and breathless, sweat plastering her hair to her scalp.

At last, his screams ceased. Aedwen flung herself down in the lee of a broad-trunked old tree. She lay there, chest heaving and her face awash with great sheets of tears. She wondered whether she had merely run far enough not to hear him any longer, but deep down she knew the reason for his silence.

She tried to remember that first night when father had told her to run in the event of an attack. What had he said she should do after that? She could not recall any more of the conversation. The memory of his smile was clear though, his teeth shining in the firelight. Like all of his plans and schemes, there had been no thought to what happened next. By the Blessed Virgin, how she wished they had never embarked on this foolish escapade. But father had seemed so sure of himself. Wasn't he always?

If only she could have talked him out of it. But he was so assured, so convincing. Mother would have put a stop to his madness. She always did.

Aedwen sniffed and her tears fell as great sobs shook her body. How she missed her. And now she would miss him too.

Aedwen allowed herself to weep for a while, before wiping her nose and face on her sleeve. She was alone now. She needed to think. Holding the face of her mother in her mind's eye, she took stock. All she had with her were her clothes, the eating knife that hung from her belt, and the bucket that she yet gripped tightly. Most of the water had spilt from it as she had sprinted through the forest, but there were a couple of mouthfuls yet swilling at the bottom. She upended the pail and drank.

She had no idea who the men were who had attacked father, but everyone knew the forests were filled with those cast out from the law: wolf-heads. Men and women who had fled justice and could never return to their homes. They had no qualms in slaying innocent travellers. Their lives were already forfeit, and they could be killed like animals. And so they became as animals, savaging those who passed through their wooded home, eking out a living from robbery and murder.

If such men had killed her father, they might already be coming for her. She forced herself to breathe shallowly, listening intently for any sound of pursuit. But the forest was silent and calm once more. A bird cooed somewhere in the depth of the forest. The sound startled her.

It's just a bird, she told herself.

Think!

Could her father yet live? She scarcely believed that it could be so. Surely those screams were those of a dying man. And yet she could not flee, leaving him to God knew what fate. Perhaps even now, the outlaws had stolen the goods from their cart and had abandoned her father, allowing him to bleed to death, slowly succumbing to his wounds. The thought filled her with horror. Could he truly be lying in the clearing in need of her help?

She would have to find out. And if she found him alive, how could she help him? She was no healer. Perhaps with the help of the cart she could get him back to Briuuetone, the last village they had passed through. If she could find the clearing where they had camped, she thought she would be able to trace their steps back from there to the road and the village.

But what if the men were still there? She shuddered. Aedwen was no fool. She knew what would befall her at the hands of such brigands. Once more she listened. The sun had risen higher into the sky and spears of light stabbed through the leaf canopy. A wind whispered through the trees, sighing and making the branches shiver. The green-tinged light danced and dappled the earth around her. Far away the bird called again. But there was no sound of pursuit. No yelling and snapping of twigs and rustle of undergrowth. She let out her breath and drew in a great lungful of air. The woodland was redolent of growth, verdant and vigorous. Summer had brought bountiful life to the land. And yet, she feared that in a small glade surrounded by pale-leafed trees her only kin lay dead.

She had to know for sure.

She would creep back towards the glade where she had left her father. If she suspected the men who had attacked him were approaching, she would hide and slip away. She was fleet of foot and fast. She trembled, the light from the sun offered little warmth down here under the trees. And the ground was yet cold and wet from the rain that had fallen these last weeks. They had slept without a fire last night, cold and shivering, huddled together for warmth, as the woods creaked and murmured about them. She pulled her thin cloak about her shoulders. The wool was old and fraying and the garment offered little protection. Whether her father lived or not, she would need to find shelter before nightfall.

Much of the morning had already passed and the sun would soon be at its zenith. There was no time to waste. She would be cautious, but she must move.

Aedwen pushed herself to her feet, brushing ineffectually at the leaves and mud that clung to her dress. After a moment's hesitation she decided to carry the bucket. It could prove useful and she was not sure she would ever be able to find this spot in the forest again. Taking another deep breath of the heavy, rich air, she started north.

Scarcely had she taken five paces, than a dog's piercing bark sliced through the sylvan stillness. Aedwen stifled a cry of fear, but was unable to prevent her feet from carrying her back at a run to the bole of the tree where she had been hidden until moments before. She pressed her back against the rough bark, her breath coming as ragged and fast as when she had first arrived here after running for a long while.

Another bark. Was that a man's voice she heard too? She could not be certain. Sounds of passage through the brush grew louder.

"*Hal Wes ðu, Maria, mid gyfe gefylled, Drihten mid ðe. Ðu eart gebletsod on wifum and gebletsod ðines innoðes wæstm, se Hæland.*"

She began to whisper the words of the prayer urgently. All her brave ideas of returning to help her father, or fleeing from any pursuit, had vanished like smoke on the wind. She could not move. Fresh tears brimmed in her eyes, then fell unnoticed down her already streaked cheeks.

"*Halige Maria, Godes modor, gebide for us synfullum, nu and on ðære tide ures forðsiðes.*"

The movements in the forest were growing louder. There was no more barking, but she was sure that at least one hound and several men were crashing through the ferns and brambles, unerringly closing in on her.

What should she do? What could she do?

Her mind raced, the words of the prayer blurring into nonsense as her fear engulfed her.

She must move. Run or perhaps climb a tree. But she did nothing; paralysed by fear and the fresh memories of her father's echoing death-wails.

A huge mottled hound rounded the trunk of a tree. It halted, straight-legged, tongue flopping and hackles raised. Its teeth were white and very large. The dog fixed her with a baleful stare and she noticed it only had one eye. Was this a strange creature of the forest? Some devil hound of the Wild Hunt perhaps? It looked more wolf than dog, and its size was terrifying. It looked at her for a moment, as if it was as surprised as she was, and then it let out a peal of barking howls.

Someway off, Aedwen heard renewed sounds of people approaching. She could barely breathe now. The hound was still barking, but it had not attacked her yet. Her hand fell to the tiny eating knife at her belt. Perhaps, she would be able to halt the beast with the small blade. It only had one eye, so maybe she could blind it.

She pulled the knife from its worn leather sheath. The blade was scarcely the length of her finger. Still, it would take an eye out, if she could find her mark. She readied herself for the animal to launch at her. Gripping the knife tightly, she pressed her back to the tree's bark and prepared for the attack.

Before the beast could pounce, a man strode into sight. He was not tall, but he was broad of shoulder and there was a presence about him. He wore simple clothes of wool and leather. His hair was black streaked with silver like the wings of a jackdaw. His beard was a jutting white and black thatch. He looked ancient to her young eyes, much older than her father. But he was no wizened greybeard. No gum-sucking old man, who sat staring out to sea on long summer evenings. This man was powerful, the way a waterfall or the sea in a gale has power. The instant he entered the clearing, the dog fell silent.

The man's cool gaze took in everything in an instant. He must have been running to keep up with the dog, but he appeared to be barely out of breath.

"Well, girl," he said, his voice gruff and clipped, "who are you?"

Aedwen could not speak. She opened and closed her mouth, but no sound came.

"You'll not be needing that knife," the man said, indicating the blade in her trembling hand. "I think you would just anger him, if you prodded him with it anyway."

Seeming to sense her distress, the massive dog, quiet now, edged forward. She let out a whimper of alarm.

"Odin," snapped the man. "To me." His tone was commanding, but the dog ignored him and padded closer to Aedwen. She tried to push herself away from him, but the tree prevented her from moving further. She was crying uncontrollably now, tears flowing, mouth open and panting in terror.

The man frowned.

"Do not fear," he said. "Odin won't hurt you. Will you, boy?"

As if in answer, the dog licked her hand. Looking down, she saw the knife still clutched there. The dog looked up at her with its one, deep brown eye. It nuzzled its snout into her, inviting her to stroke it perhaps. Shakily, she sheathed the knife and reached out to caress the soft fur of the dog's ears. Odin sat down contentedly and once again nudged her with his head, encouraging her to continue.

Could the man be one of the heathen Norsemen to have named his dog thus? she wondered.

"By Christ's bones," said the man. "Disobedient and soft."

She noticed then that he had in his large hand a long seax. The blade of the knife glimmered dully as he moved. For an instant, her fear returned with a sudden icy chill. But as she watched, he slid the weapon into a scabbard that hung from his belt.

"Now," the old man said, "who are you and what are you doing in my forest?"

"I—" she stammered, her voice catching, "I am Aedwen, Lytelman's daughter."

"And where were you headed?"

"To find my father…" she swallowed, not wishing to put words to what had occurred. "He— He was attacked."

The man ran a callused hand over his face and beard. His eyes glittered, chips of ice in the crags of his face. She wondered if he ever smiled. His was a hard face, unyielding and unsmiling, so unlike her father's. He always appeared content with his lot in life. She recalled his screams and shuddered.

"You will come with me and Odin. My home is not far. We will rest there and then, tomorrow, we will go to Briuuetone."

"No," she replied, "I must go to my father. He might need me."

"He does not need you now, child," said the man, his voice as cold and hard as granite. "Your father is dead."

Three

Dunston stretched his feet out towards the fire. The flames had died, leaving writhing red embers that lit the small hut with a ruddy flickering glow. By Christ, he was tired. And yet he knew he would not sleep for a long while. He sipped the strong mead directly from the leather costrel. It was soothing, and he felt his shoulders relaxing.

He looked over the coals of the fire to where the girl lay. She was exhausted and he had needed to halt frequently on the journey through the woods. He wasn't sure how old she was, he hadn't thought to ask, but she was somewhere in that awkward time between a girl and woman. Something about her reminded him of Eawynn. Perhaps it was her determination. She had shown great strength when he had led her to the site of her father's murder.

"You do not wish to see your father as he is," he had told her.

She had argued, but he had been adamant, sending her to the cart to find something they could use to cover the man's corpse. He'd ended up using the man's cloak and the leather cover that had been on the cart. He had made her wait with Odin by the handcart and had set about tending to the girl's father. It was a terrible task, as he had known it would be, and after a time he was covered in sticky gore.

Aedwen's eyes had widened when she saw him step from the glade, arms and hands besmeared in blood. He had led her with him to the stream, where he had washed himself as best he could in the bitterly cold water, picking up handfuls of sand and rubbing away the grime. Then he had filled the girl's bucket and carried it back to the glade.

"Wait a short while more," he had said when she asked if now she could see her father.

He had wrapped the butchered man tightly in the leather and cloth, shrouding his body from view. He left his face visible, using a scrap of the man's kirtle dipped in the bucket to wipe his cheeks, chin and forehead clean. Then he cut a long strip of woollen cloth from the cloak and bound it about his head, over the crown and beneath the chin to hold the mouth shut.

Only then, when he was sure he had done all he could to make Aedwen's father look at peace, had Dunston heaved the man's corpse up and carried him to the cart. They had cleared the bed of the cart and Dunston had laid the man down as softly as he was able. The girl had gazed at her father's face for a long while.

Dunston had been nervous, peering into the forest and listening for any sign that the men who had done this thing might be returning. But they had disappeared and now that he had found the girl, he did not regret letting them be on their way. Nothing he did would bring Aedwen's father back. And men capable of this kind of violence would meet a bloody end themselves one day, of that he was certain. Sweat-drenched and breathless from his exertions, Dunston drank cool water from the bucket while Aedwen cried silently.

They had piled the goods from the cart around Lytelman's corpse, even placing a couple of sacks, one of feathers and one of smoked mackerel, on his chest. Dunston had said they could leave the contents of the cart hidden and return for it, but Aedwen would not hear of it.

"This is all that is left of my father's dreams," she had said, sniffing. "I will not leave it or throw it away."

Dunston had not replied, merely helping her to arrange the sacks. The cart creaked and groaned and was difficult to coax along the root-snarled paths to his hut, but Dunston understood Aedwen's anxiety at leaving the things untended in the wood. He had asked about her kin and found she had none. She was an orphan now, and this was all she owned. It was not much, but it was better than nothing at all.

Taking another swig of mead, he looked down at the girl where she slept in the fire-glow. In sleep, her face was soft, trouble-free. How would such a young child survive in this world? Well, that was no concern of his. He would do his duty and take her to Briuuetone. Let Rothulf there find a home for the orphan. Not for the first time, Dunston wished he had not left his hut that morning. Nothing but trouble had come his way. Everything had changed when he'd stumbled upon the blood-soaked corpse of the girl's father. Well, as Guthlaf had so often told him over the years, there were only two things you could ever be sure of in life: the passage of time and the unexpected. Today, he had been reminded of both. He twisted his head around and his neck gave an audible click. He grunted, feeling his age of close to fifty summers.

Odin let out a suppressed growling bark, dreaming of the shade of some woodland creature no doubt. His legs twitched as he ran in his slumber. The animal was stretched out beside Aedwen and one of his huge paws rested on her arm. Dunston snorted and sipped again from the costrel. He had never seen the hound take to someone in this way. The dog was friendly enough with him, and fiercely loyal, but he usually slept alone beside the fire, or curled up close to the door. He never came close to Dunston's bed at the rear of the hut.

The foolish beast would miss the girl when they left her at Briuuetone. All the more reason to be done with it. At first light they would set out. He could not have the poor girl weeping and complaining around the place.

Dunston awoke with a start. He yet sat in the high-backed chair he had carved many years ago. He made to rise and his spine cried out in agony at having rested so long against the hard oak of the seat. The half-full flask of mead toppled from where it had perched atop his belly. Cursing, he lunged for the falling costrel, sending fresh stabs of pain down his back and neck. Too slow, his fingers brushed the leather and it fell to the packed earth floor.

"By all that is holy," shouted Dunston, angrily heaving himself to his feet and snatching up the flask before all the mead had been spilt.

Light streamed in through the hut's open door and at the sound of his voice, Odin padded inside to gaze up quizzically at his master. The sun had risen long ago and Dunston could scarcely believe how long he had slept. The exertions of the day before must have taken their toll on his body more than he had imagined. Thank you, Lord, for yet another reminder of how old he was becoming.

Beside the hearth knelt Aedwen. She had rekindled the flames and was now placing oatcakes on a griddle. The smell of cooking brought saliva rushing into his mouth. They had been too tired to prepare food when they had arrived the previous night and his stomach grumbled now at the prospect of eating.

Odin nudged Dunston's hand with his cold wet snout. To Dunston, it looked as though the dog was grinning at him.

"What are you looking at, fool of a dog?" he growled.

Aedwen looked up from where she was cooking. Her eyes were red-rimmed and sparkling. Dunston noticed that she had brushed her hair, and it shimmered in the morning sunlight from the doorway.

"You're awake," she said. "The oatcakes are almost ready."

"You should have woken me," Dunston said, pushing himself up from the chair and stretching. He winced as his body protested. "I wanted to be gone long before now."

"You looked tired."

"There's strength enough in these old bones to get you and your father to Briuuetone."

She cast her gaze down to the griddle, poking at the cakes with a stick to check whether they were done.

"Well, I thought it best if I fed you first. Neither of us ate yesterday, and you'll need to keep that strength up." She decided that the cake closest to the flames was ready and prised it from the metal and scooped it onto a wooden platter. Dunston recognised the plate as one he had made. She handed it to him and, after a slight hesitation, he accepted it. The oat cake smelt good. He broke a piece of it off and the warm fragrance wafted up to him. He tested it with his tongue. It was hot, but his hunger got the better of him and he popped it into his mouth. The crisp outer shell broke under his bite, exposing the steaming soft centre. Gasping, he breathed through his mouth, waving his hand to indicate he was burning.

Aedwen smirked and handed him a wooden cup of ale.

He filled his mouth with the cool liquid, sighing as it lessened the scalding and dissolved the mouthful of oat cake.

"You've certainly made yourself at home," he said, frowning.

"I thought you would be happy for me to cook. It is the least I can do. You have been kind to me."

Dunston grunted and took another bite of the cake.

"These are good," he said grudgingly, taking a second draught of ale.

"My mother taught me," said Aedwen, before falling silent. She busied herself with the griddle, flicking more of the oatcakes onto another plate.

"I'll have another," Dunston said, suddenly awkward. "And I thank you."

Aedwen beamed and slid two more cakes onto his plate. Then she nibbled one herself and nodded, seemingly content with her handiwork.

"Do you live here alone?" she asked.

Dunston nodded.

"Just me and Odin." At the sound of his name, Odin raised his head. Dunston glowered at the dog for a moment, before breaking one of the cakes in two and tossing half to the hound. Odin caught the offering and in a heartbeat the food had vanished.

Aedwen watched the dog, a small smile tugging at her lips despite the horror and loss she had suffered.

"You have no kin?"

For a moment, Dunston chewed in silence. He glanced over to where the girl had laid out the cooking utensils neatly beside the hearth. Everything was just so, ordered and tidy. How long had it been since a woman had been in this hut? It seemed like a lifetime. His gaze flicked to Eawynn's silver plate, hanging on the far wall, where it reflected the light from the fire.

"I have a brother," Dunston replied at last. "But I have not seen him since Michaelmas this past year."

"Nobody else?"

"No. No one else, damn your nosiness, girl." He crammed the rest of the oat cake into his mouth and chewed sullenly. The girl said nothing, but her eyes brimmed with tears as she finished her food and set about clearing the things away.

"I am sorry," Dunston said. "You are right, I was tired. And hungry."

"It is no matter. Father was always ill-tempered in the morning before he broke his fast."

"Ill-tempered, am I?" he said, unable to keep the smile from his face. "I suppose I am at that. I am not used to having company." He wiped his hands through his beard. "And what of you, do you have kin…" he hesitated, "… beyond your father?"

The girl's face crumpled, her lower lip quivering. She stood, picking up the soiled cooking things.

He felt a pang of guilt at her reaction. Damn his clumsiness. He understood as well as anyone the anguish of grief.

"I do not wish to cause you more pain," he said, stumbling over the words, unsure of himself. "I have never been good with words." He held up his hands. They were thick-fingered and callused. "I only have skill with these," he said. "It has ever been so. Whenever I speak, I cause offence."

"What do you make?" Aedwen said, her voice small.

Dunston was confused. He grunted, leaning his head to one side. Surprisingly, Aedwen grinned.

"What is so funny, girl?" Dunston said, suddenly annoyed once more.

Aedwen bit her lip.

"I beg your pardon, it is just…" her voice trailed off.

"Just what?"

When she did not reply immediately, he continued. "You had better tell me. One thing I like worse than waking up late are secrets."

Aedwen took a deep breath, but still she hesitated.

"Well?" he said, his voice taking on an edge of iron.

With a sigh, Aedwen said, "The way you looked at me just then, with your head to one side, you looked just like Odin."

For a long while Dunston stared at the girl. To his surprise and her credit she held his gaze, until at last, he allowed himself to smile.

"Like Odin, you say?" The hound looked up at him and cocked its head at an angle. Dunston let out a guffaw and he was pleased to see that Aedwen was laughing too. "Well," he said, through his chuckles, "it would seem I have been too long in the company of this hound. As we walk to Briuuetone you will have to teach me once again the ways of mankind."

They laughed together as they cleaned the plates with some of the water from a barrel by the door. For a moment it was almost as though the previous day, with its blood and terror, had never happened. But when they returned to the hut, they both looked upon the shadowed shape of Aedwen's father, wrapped in the makeshift shroud.

"Have you any inkling of who the attackers were?" he asked, unable to avoid returning to the dark subject of her father's murder.

"No," she said, "I thought they must be wolf-heads."

Dunston nodded, saying nothing of the cart laden with goods that had been left behind.

"But I have been thinking about that," she continued. "Men living outside the law would be desperate for anything of value. They would never leave the cart."

Dunston said nothing. The girl impressed him. She was sharp and thoughtful.

"In answer to your question," she said, "I have no close kin. My father had two sisters, but they married and moved away before I was born. I know nothing of my mother's family. She never talked of them."

"It seems we are both alone," he said, feeling a stab of pity. It was one thing for a man of his age to look at a future devoid of companionship and family, but for one so young... Aedwen must be terrified of what her life would be now.

"You are not alone," she said. "You have Odin."

Dunston grunted.

"And I am not truly alone," she said. "While I was hiding in the forest, I prayed." Aedwen's voice grew wistful. "I prayed to the Blessed Virgin." Her eyes burnt with a new passion. "And the Mother of God answered me. She sent me you."

"I don't know about that, girl," said Dunston, uneasy at the thought of being part of some sacred plan.

"The Virgin Mary sent you to help me."

"Well," he said, lifting up one of the sacks that belonged to Aedwen and carrying it out to the waiting handcart, "I am happy to help you to reach Briuuetone. You will not be alone there. The reeve will know what to do with you. His wife is kindly and he has daughters too. Perhaps you can stay with them."

She followed him out into the warming daylight.

"I do not wish to go to Briuuetone. I have been praying and I believe you were sent to me for a purpose."

Dunston did not like the sound of this, or the direction that the conversation was headed. He returned inside for another sack. Aedwen followed him.

"And what purpose would that be?" he asked, unsure that he wanted to hear what this child would answer.

"You are adept at following tracks in the forest, are you not?"

He dropped the sack into the bed of the cart and its timbers creaked.

"I am a hunter. I can see where beasts or men have trod," he allowed.

"And you are clearly a strong man. A warrior."

Dunston bridled, not liking one bit the turn this morning had taken.

"I am no warrior," he spat and stalked back inside.

Aedwen ignored his protestations.

"I think you are," she said, "and I think the Virgin answered my pleas by sending you, and in the night, while you slept, I understood what we should do next."

"We?" he said, his tone incredulous. "There is no 'we', girl. I will take you to the reeve at Briuuetone and then you can pray to the Virgin all you want. But whatever you pray for, think not that I will be part of your prayers."

"I do not believe you are a man who would allow something like the brutal murder of my father to go unpunished."

"It is not my place to seek justice. I am not the reeve and I am no warrior."

"And yet you have not denied my words. You would see the men who killed my father punished."

Anger began to bubble within Dunston. The girl's words raked through the embers of his ire at seeing her father's ripped and savaged corpse.

He bent to lift the heavy form of the dead man onto his shoulder. He noticed how blood had soaked through the cloak. The burden was cumbersome and his back once again cried in pain, but he wrestled the corpse up and walked stiffly towards the sunlight and the cart.

"Of course I would have the men who did this thing brought before the moot and tried," he gasped, breathless from the exertion. "But I am but one old man." The words threatened to catch in his throat, but he knew the truth of them. He knew that years before, he would have swung the corpse up and onto his back with barely a thought. Now his bones and joints screamed out in protest. "What would you have me do?"

Aedwen placed a small hand on his burly forearm. He halted and looked into her limpid eyes.

"I would have you track the savages who did this to my father. You say you are a hunter. I want you to hunt them. And when you find them, I want you to kill them all."

Four

They walked in sullen silence.

Aedwen watched as Odin bounded before them, flitting into the trees and then returning sometime later, tongue flopping, tail held high. She wished she could be as carefree. It would be wonderful to be content to run through the forest, in and out of the pools of sunshine that dotted the path beneath the trees. But her mind was a turmoil of emotions. After the initial fear and horror of her father's death, she had set to thinking and praying. She had awoken deep in the darkest part of the night and had been sure she had the solution. She had lain there and listened to Dunston's snoring, comforted by the sound that reminded her of her father. She had tried to turn her thoughts away from her father's body, shrouded, still and stiff in the hut, but no matter how hard she prayed, her mind kept on going back to her father's corpse. She had cried then, silent tears rolling down her cheeks in the darkness, but when the first light of dawn drew a grey line beneath the door of the hut, she had been resolved. She knew what she must do and she had been certain that the grey-bearded man who had found her would accept her challenge.

How wrong she had been.

They had barely spoken since his refusal to seek out her father's killers. He had said that her idea was foolish. He would stick to his plan to take her and her father to Briuuetone and then he would leave. She had felt the fury building within her, like the tension in the air before a thunderstorm. She had been about to scream her anger at Dunston, but something in the set of his jaw and the furrow of his brow, gave her pause. She recalled the last time she had raised her voice to father. She could barely remember what she had been angry about, but her ire had been sudden and terrible. When she had calmed down, father had said something she would never forget, and she thought on those words now.

"I am your father, and I love you. But make no mistake, if you speak to others the way you have spoken to me today, things will go badly for you. Only kin will put up with that kind of foolish rudeness and even then, a father's patience has its limits."

And so, rather than scream and yell at Dunston, she had fallen into step behind him, sour and bitter resentment washing off her like a stink. For his part, he had seemed to be pleased not to speak, conserving his energy for pulling the heavy cart that creaked and groaned over the rutted ground.

More than once, she had needed to help him, lending her small weight to his considerable bulk to heave the cart over a thick tree root, or around a boulder jutting into their path. Not once did she say a word to him, instead doing what was necessary, and then resuming her brooding; an ill-tempered shadow trudging in his wake.

They saw nobody else all that morning. The forest was teeming with wildlife. Magpies chattered and wood pigeons cooed in the canopy and once Odin frightened a partridge from where it rested in the bracken. The bird burst from the undergrowth in a fluster of beating wings and narrowly avoided becoming the hound's meal. But despite the numerous animal denizens of the woods, no humans crossed their path.

Dunston led them unerringly through barely visible deer tracks until they eventually reached the road. Aedwen began to understand how lucky she was that Dunston had found her. Without his aid she would have surely been lost forever in this dense world of twisted trees and clinging brambles. Again she thanked the Virgin for sending him to her, and like someone going back to scratch at an annoying nettle rash, she once more pondered how to have the man do her bidding.

The sun was high in the sky when they came to a fast-flowing brook that the road crossed over by way of a simple timber bridge. The cart clattered over the mossy boards of the bridge and on the far side, Dunston eased the cart's shafts down and stretched, reaching his hands to the small of his back. He grunted as he massaged at his aches and he winced as he bent his right knee to sit with his back to the cart wheel. His forehead was beaded with sweat, but he seemed hale enough. She produced the remainder of the oatcakes from where she had stored them in a bag and handed him one.

He nodded his thanks, broke off a piece and chewed for a time before washing it down with water from a leathern flask. She ate in silence, and accepted the flask from him. The day was warm, and she was thirsty.

Odin gnawed contentedly at a bone he had found somewhere in the depths of the wood.

"I understand that you are filled with anger at the men who did this to your father," Dunston said, breaking the hush that had fallen over them. "But it would be madness to chase after them as you wish." He took back the water bottle from her and drew another deep draught.

"I cannot bear the thought of those men roaming free."

"If I could track them, what then? A girl and an old man against four men."

"You are not so old," she said, a glimmer of mischief in her eye. "You look like you would be able to defend yourself in a fight."

Was that a slight smile nestled within his beard? He snorted.

"Defend, perhaps. But to seek out a fight with men like that would be foolhardy. As I said, I am no longer young and I am no warrior."

She had been watching him closely all that morning, the way he carried himself. Walking lightly on the balls of his feet, his blue eyes never missing anything. She had noticed that his muscled forearms bore many scars, a pale cross-hatching of lines against the tanned skin. She tried to imagine how he might have come across such wounds and could only conclude they were from cuts delivered by enemies standing against him in a shieldwall. Then there was the large axe he had picked up and placed into the cart before they had left his hut. It was a broad-headed, wicked-looking thing; a weapon more than a tool used by a woodsman, she thought. The axe's dark iron head was swirled with intricate patterns of silver, which had been cunningly forged into the metal, and the long ash haft was carved with runes and symbols. The lower end of the shaft was tightly bound in old, worn leather.

He had said nothing when he had fetched it from a trunk. It had seemed almost as an afterthought. But he handled the hefty weapon as if it weighed nothing and as he had strode from his hut, axe-head gleaming in the morning sun, a sudden chill had run through her. He was certainly not young, but he looked like a warrior to her.

More than that, he looked like a killer.

She reached out her hand for the water flask again and he tipped it up to show her it was empty. Pushing herself up, she made her way down to the water's edge. It was cool in the shade of the bridge and the water was clear and cold. Silver daces darted and snaked languidly beneath the surface. She plunged the flask's neck into the water and watched the stream of silver bubbles gurgle up from the opening.

"I understand," she called back to Dunston. "This is not your fight. Why would you put yourself at risk for me..."

"Do not besmirch me as a craven, girl," the old man growled. "To what end would we hunt these men? To slay them, you say. Even if we could do such a thing, you will find no peace from revenge." He heaved himself to his feet with a grunted groan of pain. He tested his knee, flexing it and grimacing at what he felt. "Trust me on this. No," he said, once more lifting the shafts of the cart and setting off again southward. "We will go to Rothulf, the reeve. He is a friend and a wiser man than me. He'll know what to do. Besides, justice is his job."

Aedwen drank deeply, the cold water doing nothing to dampen the anger she felt. Refilling the flask, she hammered the stopper back in place with the heel of her hand and followed behind Dunston, once more too upset and disappointed to speak.

Five

They barely spoke for the rest of the day and the sun was low in the sky when finally they saw the cluster of houses known as Briuuetone. They had followed the course of the River Briw as it wound its way towards the settlement. As it progressed downhill, the river grew ever faster, its water changing from a burbling stream to a churning torrent. The Briw was ever fast-flowing, but after the recent rains, it was a raging, white-frothed deluge by the time it reached Briuuetone.

A few times during the afternoon Dunston glanced at Aedwen and was unsurprised to see her face set, her lips pressed tightly together in an expression of disapproving anger. If her situation had not been so dire, her childish rage might have amused him. As it was, he was saddened. He understood her desire for vengeance. She must feel lost and impotent in a world that had suddenly become frightening and more violent than she had ever known. But he was sure of his decision. To chase after the men who had slain her father would have been madness and almost certainly would have spelt his and Aedwen's deaths.

For his part, he did not mind walking in silence. The path grew smoother as they approached the village, but it was still hard work to push the cart over the rutted track and he had little inclination to talk. Besides, he was accustomed to the hushed voice of the forest. The creak of tall linden and oak when the wind caught their highest boughs. A far-off cry of a sparrow hawk. The chatter of sparrows and finches. Odin's panting breath when he ran past, flitting in and out of the undergrowth. All of the natural sounds of woodland life calmed him, giving him time to listen to his own thoughts. He pondered again who might have done this thing. He was convinced now that it could not have been Norsemen. It made no sense for such a small band to be here, deep within the kingdom of Wessex. But then why mutilate the man's body in such a horrific fashion? What sort of men committed such an act if it were not in the name of their heathen gods?

Dunston walked on, brooding on that, his mind filled with dark memories of blood and screams. He knew all too well what sort of man took pleasure from torture and killing. He had believed he would never again need to face such men. Well, after he'd got the girl and her unlucky father to Rothulf, he would return to his home and try to forget this fresh horror he had witnessed. He knew Aedwen's father's blood-slathered and broken body would plague his dreams, just as so many other corpses did. Each pallid face of the dead had its own place in his nightmares. Lytelman was another innocent to join their ranks.

Aedwen stumbled. She was tired. It had been a long, hard day.

"We are almost there," he said, making his tone soft.

The girl glared at him, still refusing to speak. With a flick of her hair, she turned away and strode with renewed determination down towards the smoke-wreathed settlement.

Despite himself, Dunston smiled. Eawynn would have liked the girl. They were both haughty and stubborn as mules when angered. With a grunt of effort, Dunston set the cart to moving faster to keep up with her. He thought about calling for her to slow her pace, but thought better of it. He would have to shout over the roaring rush of the river that flowed alongside the path. And anyway, she was heading in the right direction.

The road twisted around an outcrop of rock up ahead. Without looking back, Aedwen disappeared from view. Dunston felt an unexpected twinge of anxiety. Foolishness, he told himself. They were almost in the shadow of the thatched houses of Briuuetone. He could smell the woodsmoke from the haze of cooking fires. These were Rothulf's folk. Good people. Nothing could befall the girl here. Surely.

As if he too felt nervous to have lost sight of the girl, Odin burst from the brush beside the path and sped past Dunston, running around the bend in Aedwen's wake.

The Briw, fast and deep, churned and crashed over boulders. Dunston could hear nothing over the river's rocky roar.

The cart's left wheel caught on a protruding chunk of flint. Aedwen's father's shrouded body began to slip. Dunston lashed out a strong hand, hauling the corpse back onto the bed of the cart, where it nestled amongst all of Aedwen's possessions. Dunston spied the leather-wrapped haft of DeaÞangenga and briefly he placed his hand upon it. He wondered what had made him pick up the great axe. He had scarcely touched it since Eawynn's passing. Whenever he saw the weapon, it reminded him of why he had never been good enough for her.

"In love with your king and killing," she had said to him once. He'd argued with her, unable to accept her words. But now, looking back across the dark frontier of time, he admitted she had been right.

He frowned. Pushing aside his memories, he turned his attention once more to the cart and with a great heave it was over the stone that had impeded its movements and was once again trundling on.

At last he rounded the bend in the road and brought the cart up short. It was quieter here, the outcrop and its encompassing blanket of sedge, nettles and butter dock muting the river sound to a rumble. Before him, several stocky kine were lumbering down the lane. The cattle lowed and rolled their huge bovine eyes at Odin, but the hound seemed oblivious to their unease, and he trotted along beside them, ignoring their baleful stares.

Behind the cows walked a slender man with a hazel switch that he used to goad the beasts forward. Aedwen walked close by and it appeared the two of them were deep in conversation.

"Hail, Ceolwald," said Dunston, raising his voice more than he'd intended.

The slim drover turned and stared at Dunston. Placing his hands on his hips, he halted, waiting for him to catch up. The cart was cumbersome and it took Dunston some time to reach them. Neither Aedwen nor Ceolwald offered to help him.

"It's early in the season for you to be down this way, Dunston," said Ceolwald. "It's not even St Vitus' Day yet."

"I know what day it is, and what day it isn't," growled Dunston.

The drover nodded, as if that explained everything.

"Well," he said, "this young lady tells me she is walking to Briuuetone. I was just saying as to how she has just about reached there. We don't often get visitors unless it's a holy day. Funny you are walking that way too. I suppose we might as well all walk together." He looked disappointed.

"The girl and I are travelling together," said Dunston.

"Oh." Ceolwald looked from Aedwen to Dunston and back again, as if he were trying to understand something unfathomable. After a moment, his gaze settled on the cart and its gruesome burden. His eyes widened, and he snatched off the woollen cap he wore, wringing it in his hands. "What's this then?" he asked.

"The girl's father."

"Oh," the drover said and made the sign of the cross. "You taking him to Godrum for a proper burial?" Before Dunston could reply, Ceolwald looked over his shoulder at the cows that were now some distance away. "Whoa there, girls," he called, but the animals ignored him and continued trudging along the muddy path.

Shaking his head, Ceolwald said, "They know the way to the Bartons right enough. If we stand here dillydallying they'll be there long before me and they won't be happy. This time of year they need milking before they're put out for the night. They'll make a devil of a noise if they don't get milked sharpish."

He set off to hurry after the beasts. Dunston sighed and pushed his weight into the cart, getting it rolling again. His knee ached and a fresh pain lanced down his back. He grimaced, but said nothing. He would be there soon and he could be done with this burden and the troublesome child. Let her talk to the idiot drover all she liked.

But Ceolwald had only walked a few paces when he halted and came back to Dunston.

"Let me help you with that," he said. "Otherwise, you'll still be pushing it down the path come nightfall and all the kine've been milked."

And you would have missed the gossip about the dead man and his daughter, thought Dunston. He offered the drover a thin smile of thanks and moved to one side to allow him room to add his weight behind the cart. With the two men shoving the creaking cart along, the going was much smoother and Dunston was pleased for the easing of the pressure on his joints.

After a brief spell, Ceolwald asked, "Well, are you?"

"Am I what?"

"Taking him," he indicated with his chin at the shrouded corpse on the cart, "to Godrum? It's a good time for a burial. The ground is soft and easily dug."

Dunston glanced over at Aedwen and noted her downcast gaze. Her eyes shone.

"Have care with your words," he snapped. "You are talking about the child's father."

"I beg pardon," Ceolwald replied, bobbing his head and swallowing. "Well, are you?"

Dunston sighed. He rarely visited Briuuetone and when he did he barely spoke to its inhabitants. Save for Rothulf and his family, he had no friends in the village. They liked him well enough to accept his furs and knives in trade, but he didn't think they missed him when he went back to his solitary life in the forest. At times, when the winter wind bit the skin, and food was scarce; when the nights were long and the days short and brittle with ice and snow, Dunston would ask himself if he had chosen the right path for his life. Wouldn't he have been better off finding a new wife to tend to his needs? At moments like that he yearned for the company of others. Now, listening to Ceolwald's inane and incessant chatter, he was sure he had chosen wisely when he had made his home amongst the trees of Sealhwudu.

They pushed the cart along and Dunston did not reply. Perhaps it would have been better to have pushed the cart alone.

"Well?" Ceolwald asked again.

At last, Dunston capitulated.

"He will need a Christian burial," he said, pausing to wipe the sweat from his forehead with the back of his hand. Ceolwald nodded, as though he had been proven right in his answer to a particularly twisted riddle. "But," continued Dunston, finding himself increasingly irritated by the drover's demeanour, "I do not plan to take him to the church first."

"Well, you'll not be burying him anywhere else than in holy ground," he laughed at the idea, before growing suddenly grave. "Or is he such a sinner that he cannot be laid to rest with the good folk of Briuuetone?"

"My father was a sinner, like all men," said Aedwen, wheeling on the drover, her eyes ablaze. "But he was a good man and he will be given a Christian burial."

Ceolwald swallowed, unable to meet Aedwen's glare. Again Dunston thought how the girl reminded him of Eawynn.

"Of course, maid," Ceolwald said, "I meant nothing by it." They walked along in silence for a few moments before he spoke again. "So what is it you plan for him?"

"I am taking both Aedwen and her father to Rothulf, that he may determine the correct course of action. The girl is without kin now, and her father was slain most cruelly. The killers will need to be caught and brought before the moot."

Ceolwald was looking at him with a strange expression. He opened his mouth to speak and then snapped it shut once more.

"What is it, man?" asked Dunston.

Again the drover made as if to speak, but then hesitated.

"Speak, man," growled Dunston. "You want to say something, so say it. God knows until now nothing has stopped you from uttering the first thing that pops into your thought-cage."

"Well," said Ceolwald, his voice uncertain now, sweat beading his brow, "it's just that you won't be taking him to Rothulf."

Dunston gave the man a sharp look. He felt a scratch of unease down his spine.

"Why is that?" he asked.

Ceolwald's throat bobbed as he swallowed.

"He is dead. That's why."

Six

Aedwen could see the tidings of the reeve's death had rocked Dunston. Tears welled in her own eyes. She was angry that he had not chosen to do her bidding and seek revenge on her father's killers, but in that very act of defiance to her, Dunston had shown her he was in control. He had a plan and she had fallen into step with him, allowing him to lead. She had argued at first and then shown him her displeasure with her stubborn silence, and yet she had been comforted by his commanding presence. In response to her ill temper, the old man had ignored her, marking a fast pace through the forest without offering her a word. She could cope with his brooding silence. But now, she saw his face contorted in confusion and grief and this show of weakness frightened her.

The sun was touching the top of the trees across the river now. The thatch of the buildings was aglow with the golden light, stark shadows heightening the details in everything in the last rays of the day.

"How?" Dunston asked.

"It was the damnedest thing," Ceolwald said, seemingly torn between the need to maintain a dour expression at the dire news he was imparting, and wishing to grin at bearing that most compelling of gossip: a death. "He was drowned."

"Drowned?" asked Dunston, his tone incredulous.

"Yes, sir," Ceolwald said, again tugging off his cap and screwing it up in his bony hands. "They found him in the river, down by the mill. White as a fish, he was. Nobody saw what happened, but there had been a frost that morning. It seems he must have slipped, maybe banged his head. Still, when God calls your name, it's your time, and that's that."

Dunston frowned and Aedwen could see him thinking hard, pushing the dismay at his friend's death to one side and fighting to understand what had happened; regaining control.

"When did this happen?" he asked.

"Not two months ago."

"And he was alone? Nobody saw him fall?"

"No. But it was just his time. Bad luck, that's all. We held a hall-moot with the new reeve and all these questions were asked, and answered."

"New reeve?"

"Oh yes, Lord Ælfgar appointed one not a week after Rothulf's passing. Can't be long without someone to uphold the law, he said."

Dunston, face devoid of emotion now, started pushing the cart again. After a moment, Ceolwald joined him and they continued along the path in the last warm rays of sunshine.

Aedwen was silent. Odin padded close to her and she placed a hand on his head, running her fingers through the warm fur of his neck and ears. Despite the warmth of the sun on her skin, and the peaceful gold-licked beauty of the village before them, she pulled her cloak about her and shivered. The river flowed deep and fast beside the road. Its dark waters were high, lapping halfway up the trunks of some sallows that grew on the river's banks. In the distance she could make out a watermill, its great wheel still now, but able to revolve with the power of the water alone. To think that those same chill waters could grind corn for life-giving bread and also drown a man, pulling him down away from the air and the light until he was forced to take in great lungfuls of liquid, slaying him as surely as a knife to the heart. For a moment, she fancied that she had been caught in the swirl of some invisible river's flow. Her life had careened away from all she had known and now, here she was, in a village she barely knew, surrounded by strangers.

"What of Rothulf's goodwife, Gytha?" Dunston enquired. "And the children?"

"They are back at Gytha's family's farm. Up Ceorleah Hill way."

Dunston nodded absently.

"The new reeve has taken up in the hall then?"

"Yes, sir." They were almost at the first buildings of Briuuetone now. As Ceolwald had predicted, his cattle knew the way and they were trotting towards a gap between two thatched houses. Beyond the houses, cloaked in the smoke of the cooking fires, loomed the shingled roof of a stone building. A crucifix projected from the apex of the roof. A group of horsemen came into sight, trotting their mounts between the cows.

"There were many in the village," Ceolwald went on, "who were not happy with the treatment of Widow Gytha and her daughters. Rothulf was barely in the ground and they were turfed out and sent packing to make way for the new reeve and his household."

Dunston said nothing. He stopped pushing the cart, and stepped to the left, all the while watching the approaching riders with his cool blue eyes. Aedwen noted that his right hand rested on the haft of the great axe that was hidden beside her father's body amongst the sacks on the cart. Ceolwald watched Dunston in confusion for a moment before following his gaze and finally noticing the riders. He gripped his cap tightly before him, fidgeting uncomfortably.

The horsemen had almost reached them now. There were five of them. They came on fine horses, the animals' Harnesses clanking and jangling, gleaming in the fiery light of the setting sun. The men wore colourful, expensive clothes and boots of supple leather. Their jackets were trimmed with intricate embroidery and their cloaks were held in place with large silver brooches. At the head of the band rode a young, handsome man. His cheeks were shaven and his fair hair was brushed so that it glimmered in the ruddy sunlight like metal heated on a forge. His mouth was partially hidden by a lustrous moustache. He reined in his mount, a well-muscled, dappled grey stallion, and stared down at them for a moment.

Odin growled, low and deep, like distant thunder.

"Odin, hush," said Dunston, his tone quiet but firm. The hound grew silent, and sat protectively beside Aedwen.

The lead rider raised an eyebrow at the dog's name.

"So, what have we here, Ceolwald?" he asked, his voice smooth and friendly.

"This... this is Dunston," stammered Ceolwald. "He lives nearabouts. I was just bringing my cows down from the pasture for milking when I came across them on the road." After a pause he added, "We are not together." He looked longingly to where the last of the cattle had disappeared between the buildings. Their lowing came to them faintly on the breeze. "I really must be after the foolish beasts. They will make a terrible fuss if they are not milked soon." The rider looked down at the drover imperiously. "If it please you, lord," Ceolwald said, dipping his head and twisting his hat so much Aedwen thought he might rip it. The horseman waved his hand. Without looking back, Ceolwald scampered past the riders and ran after his cows.

"Well, well, well," said the horseman, shifting his attention to Dunston, "so you are the famous Dunston."

"Dunston is my name," the old man said. He stood, legs apart and shoulders set. His hand yet rested in the cart's bed.

Aedwen did not think she had seen him standing so tall and straight since she had met him.

To Aedwen's eyes there was more communication going on between the men than the words spoken. They were weighing each other up, assessing and gauging the threat posed by the other.

"You are modest," the rider said, smiling beneath his moustache. "Are you not the one known as Dunston the Bold?"

"I have not been called that for many years."

"No. I can see many years have passed since you were a bold man. Not so much bold now, as old, eh?"

One of his men, a swarthy-skinned fellow, gaudy in blue jacket and red breeches, laughed. The others took up the laughter dutifully. Dunston did not laugh.

"Well, you have me at a loss," Dunston said, his voice cutting through the riders' mirth like an axe through soft flesh. "You know my name, and I know not yours."

The rider's nostrils flared and he glowered down at Dunston for a moment before replying.

"Ah, yes. I am Hunfrith, and I am the new reeve of the Briuuetone Hundred."

Seven

"It is not right, Hunfrith," said Dunston, his voice raising in anger. "I will not allow it."

Just when Dunston thought this day could get no worse, now the fool of a new reeve was demanding to see Aedwen's father's corpse.

"You will show me the body," said Hunfrith. "I would witness with my own eyes the truth of what you say." He had dismounted and handed his steed's reins to the dark-bearded rider in the garish attire. The reeve strode towards Dunston. He was tall, a head or more taller than Dunston. The man's youth and height only served to further anger Dunston.

The sun had set now, and the sky was a deep pink. The shadows of the buildings grew deeper and cooler. Soon it would be dark.

"Listen," Dunston said, softening his voice with a force of will. "I will show you the corpse, but not in front of the girl." He stepped close to the reeve and lowered his voice to a whisper. "I went to much effort to conceal the true nature of her father's wounds from her. The man was butchered."

Hunfrith glanced back at the mounted men behind him, as if assuring himself he had the strength of numbers to push his demands.

"Conceal the truth, you say?"

"Only from the child. His passing must have been awful."

Hunfrith waved his hand, swatting Dunston's words away. "I would see the wounds you mean to hide from the girl."

"By the love of God, no!" For an instant, Dunston imagined leaping back to the cart for DeaÞangenga. In a past life, when he had been known as bold, he might have done so. But it would have been folly then, as it would be foolish now. He had nothing to hide, and this man was the reeve. He had a right to see the crime that had been committed.

Sighing, Dunston walked slowly back to the cart.

"Quickly, man," said Hunfrith. "While there is still light."

Dunston ignored him.

"Aedwen," he said, staring into the girl's eyes. They were wide and dark. "Do not look."

She held his gaze for several heartbeats before nodding and turning her back on the cart.

Satisfied that she would not see the destruction of her father's body, Dunston turned to the task of unwinding the shroud. He could not risk Aedwen's father slipping to the ground so, taking a deep breath, he pulled the corpse half out of the cart and onto his shoulder. His back screamed at him, but he did not acknowledge the pain. As carefully as he could, he lowered the shrouded figure to the grass that grew at the verge of the path.

Unwrapping the corpse was not easy. It was stiff now, and the cloak and leather he had used to swaddle the body were sticky and rigid from blood and ichor. Dunston suppressed a shudder as his fingers brushed the man's face, revealing the blotchy pallor of the cheeks that he had wiped clean in the clearing where he had been murdered. The poor man's eyes were open, staring accusingly at Dunston in blind reproach for disturbing him.

"Turn him over."

Dunston flinched. He had not noticed Hunfrith coming so close. The young reeve leaned over the cadaver, eyes gleaming, mouth open with expectation. A couple of his men had also dismounted and crowded around to witness the grisly spectacle.

Dunston drew in a deep breath. This was wrong. The man should be left in peace, not stripped and uncovered for men to gawp at.

"Do it," snapped Hunfrith.

Dunston sighed. There was nothing for it. Perhaps when they saw the terrible wounds the man had suffered, they would feel compelled to seek justice.

Reaching out, Dunston gingerly rolled the man's corpse over onto his front. One of the men gasped at the horror of Lytelman's back. Dunston had made no effort to close the wounds, but he had bound the shroud tightly about him, and now, released from the constraining material, the split ribs yawned open slowly, like the maw of some unspeakable beast of hell. The butchered lungs and innards oozed and seemed to writhe as the body settled. Someone let out a nervous laugh. Another swore, turning away to spit.

Dunston gazed down at the ruin of the girl's father and felt anew his anger at the man's killers being allowed to roam the land after committing such an atrocity. It had been folly to think of pursuing them with the girl, but perhaps he could help Hunfrith and his men to track them. He had wished to return directly to his hut and be done with the girl and her troubles, but looking down at her father's corpse he knew that he could never turn his back on Aedwen. He could almost hear the sound of Eawynn's shade laughing at him for even considering such a thing. She had always known him better than he knew himself. And she had always seen the best in him.

"By God," said Hunfrith, his voice breathy, "you truly did a job on the poor bastard, didn't you?"

"I did my best to shroud him with what I had to hand. I knew not what else to do."

"Shroud him?" replied Hunfrith, taking a step away from the gore-smeared corpse. "Oh, I am sure your wrapping of his corpse was good enough. I was talking about the blood-eagle. To rip the man's lungs out like that. You must be a true savage."

Dunston's mind reeled.

"I did not do this thing to him," he said, his tone flat and shocked.

"What murderer admits his crime?"

"I am no murderer!" Dunston took a step towards the cart. Two of the reeve's men blocked his way. Their hands rested on the hilts of their seaxes. He halted. "Why would I do such a thing? It is madness."

"Most would call this madness, it is true," replied Hunfrith. "But what about one who worships the heathen gods? Would not a man who names his own beasts after the father of the old gods also require blood sacrifice? And look, the man is killed in the manner of the Norse."

Dunston looked at the shadowed faces of the men around him. Was this some form of jest? How could they think he had done this? But their faces were sombre and serious, with no sign of humour.

"I did not do this," he said, and he was angered to hear the note of panic in his own voice. "Ask the girl." He looked over to where Aedwen yet stood beside Odin. She had turned to face them and her features were pale in the gathering gloaming. Dunston was pleased to see that the cart blocked her view of her father's corpse. That was something at least.

"Well, child," said Hunfrith, walking towards Aedwen, his countenance and voice soft with compassion. "Did you see your father's killers?"

For a long while Aedwen looked from Hunfrith to Dunston.

"Tell me the truth, child," Hunfrith encouraged her. "Did you witness your father's slaying?"

"No," she answered at last.

Dunston let out a breath.

"And so it could have been this man who killed him, could it not?"

Tears trickled down her cheeks.

"But he helped me. It makes no sense."

Hunfrith stepped close to her. Odin snarled, his hackles raised.

"Odin, no," said Dunston, acutely aware of how his use of the name would sound to the listeners. "Lie down, boy."

The dog grumbled and growled, but slouched down to lie beside Aedwen.

"You are safe now, child," Hunfrith said, reaching a hand out to touch the girl's shoulder.

"Do not fear, Aedwen," said Dunston. The look of abject dismay on her face filled him with sadness. "All will be well. You know I did not do this."

"But it seems she really knows no such thing," said Hunfrith.

"Well, I know it, and there are many here who will vouch for me; who know me to be a man of my word. Men will swear oaths for me."

"Good. I hope for your sake things are as you say. But you will need to appear before the moot and there you can explain how it is you came to have the butchered sacrifice to a heathen god on a stolen cart."

Dunston's rage boiled up within him. His eyes narrowed as he took in the positions of the men around him. He could disarm the man closest to him, taking his seax and then moving on to the next. From there, he could snatch up DeaÞangenga and lay about him. With only a small amount of luck he would put an end to this madness and be done with it. But after that? What then? He would become a wulfeshéafod, a wolf-head, cast out from the law, to be hunted and shunned for the rest of his life.

Many years ago, he had been one of the feared Wulfas Westseaxna. He could become a Wolf of Wessex once more; dispatch these fools and be gone into the forest. But why do such a thing? To not stand before the men of Briuuetone and declare his innocence? Surely enough men would come forward to swear oaths to his good character. There was no plaintiff after all. Nobody could speak against him and his word was respected. All he had to do was attend the moot and declare his innocence and all would be well.

But what if he were made to face the ordeals? He had seen enough of them in his time to know they did not rest in any divine power. A chill ran through him.

Hunfrith, perhaps sensing Dunston's building anger, put his arm about Aedwen's shoulders. Dunston noted how the reeve's other hand dropped to rest on the handle of his seax. The threat was clear.

"I cannot have you free to flee from justice or to commit any further acts of violence, Dunston," Hunfrith said, almost apologetically. "You understand that, I am sure. So will you surrender your weapons and yourself without causing trouble?"

Dunston glowered at the man, for an instant imagining how easily DeaÞangenga would split his pretty skull. And yet he knew he would not risk Aedwen's life, even if he wished to risk his own. Besides, what of the promises he had sworn to Eawynn? He could not throw away his oaths so easily. He let his shoulders slump. Pulling his sharp seax from its scabbard, he tossed it without warning at the closest man. Caught unawares, the man fumbled the catch, dropping the blade to the ground with a curse. As the man stooped to retrieve the knife, he sucked at a finger where the blade had nicked him. Dunston smiled grimly at the small victory.

"I will go with you, Hunfrith, but this is wrong. While you waste your time with me, the real killers are free and surely travelling further from Briuuetone as we speak."

"We shall see," said Hunfrith. "We shall see."

And with that, the reeve went to his horse and swung effortlessly into the saddle.

Dunston left it to Hunfrith's men to deal with the cart and the corpse and in the closing gloom of dusk he looked to Aedwen. She walked along behind the horses. Her head was lowered and she moved like a beaten cur, defeated and broken of spirit. He knew how she felt.

She did not look at back at him.

"Do not fear, girl," Dunston called to her, as the men herded him towards the village. "All will be well."

The wind picked up, whispering secrets in the trees and Dunston shuddered. He wished he could believe his own words.

Eight

Aedwen lay in the absolute darkness and listened to the night sounds of the house as it settled its wooden bones. There was rustling in the thatch somewhere above her and she wondered whether there were mice dwelling in the roof. She was warm, but she found herself shivering beneath the blankets Gytha had placed over her and the other girls. Either side of her, Gytha's two daughters, Maethild and Godgifu, had finally fallen asleep. They were friendly and had welcomed her into their home and even their bed, and Aedwen had basked in the warmth brought by unexpected kindness. The world was a place filled with evil and despair, and yet, here were complete strangers treating her as one of their own family.

When the reeve's man had brought her to the widow's door, the woman had been wary, fearful of what might bring one of Hunfrith's bullies out to the farm after nightfall, but when she had heard the girl's tale and seen Aedwen standing there, pale and trembling from shock and exhaustion, she had shooed the man away and pulled the girl into the cosy interior of the cottage.

Despite the shroud of sadness that wrapped about her, Aedwen smiled to recall the meal that had followed.

"Where are you from?" Godgifu, the younger of the widow's daughters had asked, watching with wide eyes as Aedwen hungrily spooned the pottage into her mouth. Despite everything, she was ravenous and the stew, thick with onion, cabbage and peas and seasoned with parsley and sage, was deliciously warming and hearty.

"Let the poor girl eat," Gytha said.

"I don't mind," Aedwen said, dipping some dark bread into the dregs in the bowl and mopping up the last drops. "I am from Langtun."

"Where is that?" asked Godgifu.

"You don't know anything," snapped Maethild, who must have been the same age as Aedwen.

"Well, if you're so clever, where is it then?"

Maethild frowned at having been caught out by her younger sibling and Aedwen smiled at the bickering rivalry between them. She would have liked to have had a sister, she thought, someone who had always known her, and she had always known. If she had a sister, she wouldn't be alone now.

Godgifu was taunting her sister though, making Aedwen quickly re-evaluate her idea.

"You don't know! You don't know!" sang Godgifu, twisting her face into the contorted features of a simpleton.

"Girls! Enough," said Gytha in a tone that brooked no argument. "Aedwen has been through enough, without having to listen to your silliness." The girls fell quiet as Gytha fixed them with a stern stare. "You both know what it is to lose your father," she said softly. "Remember, Aedwen's father was killed only yesterday morning. Think about how you felt when you heard the news about father." The girls looked aghast and Godgifu sniffed, tears welling in her bright eyes.

"I beg your pardon, mother," muttered Maethild.

"It is not from me that you need to seek pardon," replied Gytha.

Maethild sat in dejected silence for a time, but Godgifu seemed to forget her self-pity soon enough.

"Is it true that old Dunston found you?"

"Yes," said Aedwen. Her mind had been in turmoil ever since Hunfrith had accused Dunston of her father's murder. It was true that she had not seen the killers, but she was sure she had heard many of them. And if it had been Dunston, why would he then tend to her father's corpse, feed her and bring her here? No, there was no sense to it, and she was certain that Hunfrith knew as much.

When she had seen the reeve, a tremor of fear had run through her. She could not say why, but the man frightened her. And the strangest thing was that she had recognised him. When they had passed through Briuuetone, her father had sought him out. It had been drizzling and she had been tired and so, as she had often done before, she had curled up to snooze beneath the leather cover of the handcart. Her father must have believed she had drifted off to sleep and so he had not disturbed her when he had approached the reeve. From beneath the leather sheet, she had watched as her father had asked to speak to the reeve. She'd heard him say he had urgent tidings for him. From her hidden vantage point in the cart, she had seen the handsome face of the reeve when he came to the door of his hall to listen to her father's words, though what he'd had to say, she could not imagine. Her father was but a poor peddler after all. Perhaps this was one of his schemes, a new way to get rich quick, she'd thought. But she'd never found out. With a glance back at the cart, her father, seemingly content that she was dry beneath the cover, had entered the hall. The steady drumming of the rain had lulled her to sleep then, and she'd awoken to the movement of the cart as her father pushed it up the hill out of the village.

When the reeve had approached her and Dunston she had recognised the man immediately. And yet, she was equally certain he did not know her. Indeed he seemed to have no knowledge of her existence. She had thought it strange that he had not mentioned to Dunston that he had known her father, that they had conversed at length just a couple of days before. And something had made her keep silent about what she had witnessed. But the more she thought about the events of the last days, her certainty grew that her father's death was not a random savage act perpetrated by wolf-heads. And after seeing Hunfrith, and hearing the man so quickly accuse Dunston of murder, she was sure the reeve had some part in it. But what, and why, she had no idea.

"They say he eats raw flesh," said Godgifu, voice filled with terrified wonder. "That he chews on children's bones in the forest."

"Who says such things?" asked Gytha, her disapproval clear in her tone.

"Everyone. Wulfwyn's mother told her that if she didn't go to sleep when she was told, old Dunston would come down from his forest lair and eat her!"

Gytha shook her head.

"Wulfwyn's mother was always a foolish girl. Dunston is no monster of the woods. He has never been anything but good to us. He was your father's friend."

"His dog scares me," said Maethild.

At the mention of Odin, Aedwen had begun to weep.

Now, lying in the hushed darkness, with the body warmth of Maethild and Godgifu pressing either side of her, tears rolled down her cheeks again as she remembered what had befallen the merle hound. The dog had padded beside her, every now and then glancing over its shoulder at its master. Dunston, flanked by a couple of the reeve's men, had trudged along head down and silent. They had been some way behind the mounted Hunfrith.

They passed houses, their shadows puddled cold around them like dark skirts. Ceolwald's cattle lowed from the animal pens she could just make out in the gloom. The village had the mingled scent of cow dung, woodsmoke, roasting meat and boiling vegetables.

Upon reaching a grand hall, Hunfrith had dismounted, throwing the reins to one of his men. Aedwen had needed to trot to keep up with the reeve and she was puffing. Odin matched her pace, mouth agape and tongue dangling between sharp white teeth.

"We cannot have the girl stay here, Raegnold," Hunfrith said to his mounted companion. "I don't want my rest interrupted by her snivelling. Take her to Widow Gytha. She will take the child in." He looked sidelong at Aedwen. "Until we get to the bottom of all this."

Raegnold, the tallest of the riders, with hair of crow black and a face as sharp as a seax, dismounted. He shot a furious look at Hunfrith's back, but quickly seemed to resign himself to becoming the child's escort. Snatching up a spear that stood propped by the hall's entrance, he set off southward, using the spear's haft as a walking staff.

Aedwen, dazed and shocked at the recent revelations, mutely followed the tall man up the hill as the dark drew the night about them. Odin seemed to have decided he would be her protector, and he shadowed them as they walked past gloomed houses and the silent mill, leaving the silhouette of the church and the moaning of the cows behind them.

"Get away," Raegnold shouted at the dog, angered by the animal's attention or perhaps taking out his annoyance at Hunfrith on the dumb beast. Odin flinched, turning its head askance to better see with his one eye. After a moment, the dog continued to follow them.

The man grew angrier and scooped up pebbles from the road. He flung one at Odin, but the stone missed, skittering away into the shadows. His second stone found its mark, hitting the dog squarely on the snout. Odin cried out in anguish, shaking his head against the sudden pain. But he was soon once more walking in their wake.

"I said get away," shouted the man, throwing another stone, which made Odin jump back a pace, wary now.

Aedwen could not bear to see the beast hurt any more.

"Go home, Odin," she said. At the sound of her voice, the dog cocked its head to one side, gazing at her with its one deep thoughtful eye.

The man used the moment of distraction to leap forward, lunging with his spear. The thrust would have spitted the hound, had it not been for the speed of its instincts. Odin jumped to the side and the sharp blade tore a gash down his flank. The animal yelped and snarled, snapping its jaws towards the spear that had caused him such pain. Blood ran down its side and soaked its fur black in the dusk.

"Odin!" Aedwen cried out.

The dog locked its great maw on the spear's ash haft and shook its head with all the strength of its muscled neck. The man clung onto the spear with difficulty, unable to dislodge the animal.

"Odin, no!" Aedwen screamed. "Run, boy! Run!"

For the merest moment, the dog's eye looked directly at her. And then, as if it understood her words, it heaved the spear out of the man's grasp. An instant later it dropped the weapon with a clatter and darted into the shadows of the trees that grew further up the slope. The hound did not look back and it ran effortlessly, as though it were the start of a new day; as if it had not been wounded. It did not cry out as it ran, and Aedwen began to wonder if the cut was shallower than she'd imagined. Surely it had just been a scratch.

But when Raegnold retrieved his spear from the ground the blade was smeared dark and Aedwen had seen splashes of blood in the mud of the path.

The house grumbled its timbered thoughts around her and Maethild muttered something in her sleep, rolling over and then becoming still. Aedwen's tears soaked into the blanket the way Odin's blood had soaked into his fur. By the Blessed Virgin, she prayed the dog was safe; that it had found its way back to its home in the forest.

But what of the dog's master? The last she had seen of Dunston, they had been leading him to a barn near the cattle pens. What would become of him? She could not dispel the image of his bearded face from her mind. He had taken care of her since her father's death and she was sure he was not his killer. And what was Hunfrith's part in all this? What did he gain from locking Dunston away and bringing him before the moot?

Her confused thoughts beat inside her head, as ever-changing as a murmuration of starlings. She wiped away the tears that had grown cold on her face.

For a long while she lay there, hoping that sleep would claim her. Perhaps she would awaken and find it had all been a nightmare. But the warmth and the soft sounds of the night did not lull her to slumber. She could not escape the terror of having to face the morning alone once more. Her mother and father had both been so cruelly snatched from her. And now, when she had found someone to guide and protect her, he too had been taken away. Gytha and her daughters had been good to her, but Aedwen knew she could not stay here. She could work for her keep, but even if they were able to spare the food, would she just begin a new life with these strangers?

Why not? What else could she do? She was young and alone. If Gytha would have her, to live here in Briuuetone on this steading would be better than almost anything she could have imagined.

And yet her thoughts kept on returning to Hunfrith. What had her father told him? And why had he kept his knowledge of Lytelman silent? And what did he hope to gain by accusing Dunston of this crime?

At last, resigning herself to a night of wakefulness, she rolled out of the bed, careful not to wake the girls who yet slept peacefully.

The cottage was cool now that the fire had died down and Aedwen picked up her cloak from where she had left it. Wrapping it about her shoulders, she tiptoed towards the hearth, hoping to glean some heat from the embers. As she neared the fire, small flames flowered and the coals glowed as someone blew life into them. The light flickered red on Gytha's face where she sat at the edge of the hearth, a blanket wrapped about her shoulders.

"You couldn't sleep either?" the widow asked in a whisper. The shadows from the flames contorted her features. Aedwen could not make out whether she was smiling or scowling in the gloom. "Come, sit," Gytha continued, patting the stool near her. Aedwen sat.

"I am not surprised you are unable to find peace," Gytha muttered. "You have been through so many trials these past days. Poor child."

"I cannot stop my thoughts," replied Aedwen. Her voice threatened to choke her, and she fought back the tears that suddenly welled in her eyes.

Gytha smiled sadly.

"Whosoever could do such a thing as keep themselves from thinking would be able to find peace indeed," she said.

Aedwen frowned in the darkness. It seemed to her only death would release her from the burden of her thoughts and fears. But she had no desire to join her parents.

"I keep asking myself questions. Questions about the reeve. About my father's murder. About Dunston. Questions that I cannot hope to answer."

Gytha gazed at her in the darkness, unspeaking for a long while, her flame-lit face haggard.

"I too have been pondering how all of this makes sense. Something is not right. I feel like the world shifted when my Rothulf died and now I do not stand on steady ground." Gytha's voice cracked and Aedwen realised they were not so different. Separated by many years of age, but they both grieved and the two of them were sitting awake and confused in the dark marches of the night.

Aedwen took a deep breath then and told Gytha about her father's meeting with Hunfrith and how the reeve had kept the meeting secret.

Gytha stared at her, the embers reflecting red in her dark eyes. After what seemed a long while, she spoke.

"We need to talk," she said.

Nine

Dunston tried to make himself comfortable. But no matter how much he stretched and turned, he could not find a position that would allow him to rest. His back was stiff and despite the hay and straw he had piled up to lay upon, his spine cried out if he lay flat on his back. When he turned on his side, his knee was agony, twisting if he bent it, and seizing up if he straightened it. In the dark of the barn he sighed to himself, a grim smile playing on his lips at the irony of his predicament.

He could almost hear the voice of Guthlaf speaking to him through the veil of time.

"The best trait of any warrior is to be able to sleep anywhere and anytime," the grizzled warrior had said to him. "You, Dunston, are deadly with a blade, but your ability to sleep in an instant makes you a truly great warrior." They had been resting beside a cracked old Roman road. They'd marched for two days already and Dunston had been exhausted. It had seemed as nothing to sleep on the verge, even as rain fell and thunder rolled over them.

Now, despite the relative comfort of the straw beneath him and the shelter provided by the barn's roof and walls, he was unable to find the relief of sleep. Guthlaf would have not thought him such a great warrior if he could see him now. But

Guthlaf was long in his grave, and it had been many years since Dunston had considered himself to be a warrior.

He had never thought of himself as great.

Sighing, he rolled over onto his back, staring up into the blackness of the roof space.

Again he regretted finding the corpse and the girl. If only he had chosen a different path, he would now be asleep in his hut, far from here and the machinations of men. And yet, would he truly wish for Aedwen to have been left, alone and defenceless in the great forest of Sealhwudu? She might have survived, he supposed. Perhaps she would have even found her way back here, to Briuuetone. But then what? What would have become of her?

He snorted in the darkness. What had become of her anyway? Yes, he had seen her safely here, but she had been taken away and here he was, locked inside a barn, with no prospect of freedom for at least three weeks.

Three weeks!

He ground his teeth in the gloom as he recalled Hunfrith's words.

"You will remain in my care until the next meeting of the Hundred-moot," he'd said.

"When will that be?" asked Dunston.

"The next meeting will be on the feast of Saint John the Baptist."

"But that is nearly a month from now," Dunston had raged.

"Indeed. Do not fear, you will be fed. No harm will befall you."

Dismissing him then, Hunfrith had left three of his retinue to lead Dunston to this barn. They had opened the door and ushered him inside, and after a moment's hesitation, he had entered without further complaint.

He had already begun to think of ways in which he could prove his innocence. Who would swear oaths for him before the moot? Would Aedwen speak out in his favour? Would anyone listen to her. She was a stranger and a child. If he was found guilty, he would need to face the trials by ordeal. Which did he believe he might survive? He had shuddered to recall others tried by the ordeal of iron, forced to grip a rod of glowing hot metal. This was then wrapped and, if after three days the wound was not healing well, the tried man was found to be guilty. Dunston was a smith of some renown and worked his forge on most days, so he had suffered many burns. But he doubted there was justice to be had from seeing how quickly such wounds healed or whether they became elf-shot.

Still, fire and iron he could face. The ordeal of cold water, where the accused was thrown into the river after drinking holy water, terrified him beyond anything he had ever confronted. If the accused floated, he was deemed to be guilty. If he sank, he was found innocent. Dunston was no swimmer. He imagined the cold water washing over his face, his breath running out and his lungs burning, while he prayed frantically that he would be dragged from the water and saved.

No, he must prove his innocence. He was no coward, but the thought of facing the ordeals filled him with dread.

Left alone in the dark, Dunston's mind had turned to Hunfrith's last words to him. He had not thought that he was in any immediate danger; that he had weeks to think of the means to secure his release and prove his innocence. That was until he heard those words. Now he was not so sure.

"No harm will befall you."

Why say such a thing? Unless...

By the bones of Christ. Three weeks cooped up in here. And what of Odin? The dog had gone with Aedwen. Dunston hoped she would feed him. Still, the hound could take care of himself. He was a good hunter. But what would happen to Wudugát, his goat? He had left the poor creature tethered. There was plenty of food and water for her for the time being, but he had never intended to be gone for more than a couple of days at most. Dunston's mind turned then to the snares left untended in the forest. His heart twisted to think of the animals that would be caught, only to die lingering deaths and then have their carcasses consumed by foxes and other carrion feeders. What a waste of good skins.

Dunston shifted again in the straw and groaned at the ache between his shoulder blades. The pain was in just the place where Lytelman had been hacked open.

What was happening here? Dunston felt like a child watching a game of tafl being played. He knew strategies were in place, could feel the shift and slide of the pieces, but he did not understand the rules of the game.

There was some dark contest afoot here, something that he was not aware of. Nothing else made any sense. The manner of Lytelman's slaying, and then Hunfrith's instant accusation. And what of Rothulf? Was his death somehow connected to all this? Perhaps there was no link. Dunston could certainly see none. But he was sure that the recent events he had become embroiled in held some dark secret.

He could barely believe that Rothulf was no longer alive. The old reeve would have known how to approach this problem. He was an astute man, able to unravel the most tangled of problems. Dunston sighed. By God, he would miss him. He had looked forward to their meetings. They would sit up late into the night drinking and talking of the past. And yet, while much of their chatter had been reminiscing over years gone by, they often spoke of the present and the future. Rothulf travelled widely and he listened wherever he went. And so he had become Dunston's only source of tidings of the lands beyond Briuuetone and Sealhwudu. Dunston had chosen to hide himself away from the day-to-day life of Wessex, but it would not do to completely shut himself off from the world.

He wondered now at the state of the kingdom. He had heard from Rothulf of the increasing frequency of raids from the Norsemen in their dragon-prowed ships. As the king's ally in Frankia, King Louis, had become embroiled in a vicious civil war with his sons, so the Frankish ships had ceased to patrol the waters that surrounded Britain. This had soon led to the Norse becoming emboldened, and not a year went by without some of their number striking along the coast, snatching what treasures and slaves they could, and then fleeing before the fyrd could be assembled and brought to the defence of the realm.

Only two years previously, Rothulf had recounted to Dunston how thirty-five Vikingr ships had landed at Carrum. The king had gathered his hearth warriors and the fyrds of the local hundreds and set upon them. The men of Wessex had been crushed, the king fleeing westward leaving the heathens to sack the lands there about with impunity.

Dunston had been saddened by the tale. Could this be the same King Ecgberht who had defeated the Mercians at Ellandun? The proud and wise man who had expanded Wessex to encompass the people of the Centingas, Éastseaxe, Súþríeg and Súpseaxe. Who had even taken the oath of Eanred, king of the Northumbrians, making Ecgberht the ruler of all of the Anglisc?

Dunston pulled up his knee and massaged it, wincing as his probing fingers pressed into the joint. No man remained young for ever. Even kings grew old.

Even warriors who once basked in battle-fame and were renowned as being bold.

From outside the door, came the muffled sound of voices. Earlier, one of the reeve's men had brought him a bowl of pottage and a hunk of dark, gritty bread. Perhaps he had been just outside ever since and was now, halfway through the night, being relieved of his duty.

The barn was stoutly built from planks of oak and the door was barred from without. But it seemed Hunfrith had taken the extra precaution of having his men guard the exit. Dunston thought on his situation for a moment. Would he attempt to flee if he could? Again his mind turned to the trials he might face, and the uncertainty of being judged by this new reeve and the people of Briuuetone without the guiding hand of Rothulf who was not only wise, but as honest as any man Dunston had known. Yes, Hunfrith was probably right to guard against his escape. Dunston knew he could survive in the forest for the rest of his days, he was not so sure of the outcome of the moot.

Perhaps his chance to run had already passed; the moment when he could have yet fought his way out, standing face to face with the reeve and his men. He was old and stiff, it was true, but armed he was still dangerous. He could have slain them and fled, he was certain. But Aedwen had watched on and she might have been hurt.

And he was innocent.

He had only ever fought his king's enemies. He was, or had been, a warrior, not a murderer. No, he would face the justice of the moot and pray that the people of Briuuetone would vouch for him.

The voices outside became louder. One laughed, a jagged harsh sound in the stillness of the night. Dunston strained to hear what was being said.

"... sliced the great bastard open like a..." The voices became muffled once more, then louder again. "... almost bit me... got my spear instead. Jaws like iron." Dunston didn't breathe, waiting for confirmation of what he was hearing. After a few more words that he was unable to make out, the louder of the two said, "No. The one-eyed beast was as fast as the Devil. It ran off, but I cut it good."

They must have moved further from the door then, for their words became unintelligible.

Dunston lay in the darkness and thought of interpretations of the words he had heard. He could think of none save that the bastards had cut Odin, and badly from the sound of it. He wondered whether the dog had attacked them. Had he been trying to protect Aedwen?

For a long time Dunston imagined the many ways he would hurt the man who had struck Odin. Whatever secrets were being hidden by the death of the peddler, and no matter the outcome of the moot, Dunston swore a silent oath in the darkness that he would make the man pay for hurting his dog.

At long last, with thoughts of vengeance spiralling in his mind, the fatigue from the day finally took its toll, pulling him down towards the welcome respite of sleep. His eyes closed and he was beginning to snore, when a sudden loud shouting woke him with a jolt.

"Fire!" screamed a woman's voice, splintering the still of the night.

Dunston pushed himself up with a groan. Through the cracks between the planks that made up the barn's door, the crimson flicker of flames was clear.

Ten

"I cannot believe Dunston is a killer," said Aedwen. Her voice quavered as once more the pain of her father's death washed over her.

Gytha gently placed a small log onto the fire, careful not to disturb the embers. The fire-glow painted her features the hue of fresh blood.

"Oh, he is a killer all right." She sat back in her chair and gazed at the tongues of flame that licked hungrily at the dry wood. "Or he was."

"He was a warrior?" asked Aedwen.

"One of the deadliest ever to walk the earth, Rothulf used to say. Though my husband was prone to exaggeration and he loved Dunston like a brother." Gytha fell silent for a time, perhaps thinking of the husband she had lost. "Still, Rothulf had seen the old man fight, years ago. They stood together in the shieldwall at Ellandun and Rothulf always said he had never seen a man so destined to slay others as Dunston. As men do when they are in their cups, he had boasted of how the corpses of the Mercians lay heaped before Dunston that day. How his axe had scythed through their ranks as if they were so many ripe heads of barley. To listen to Rothulf you would think nobody else had fought that day. But many brave men gave their lives on both sides."

Gytha looked wistfully into the fire, lost in the past and the sadness of remembered loss.

The flames and embers swam before Aedwen, and she cuffed angrily at the tears that brimmed in her eyes. It was as she had surmised when she'd seen Dunston standing beside the cart with his hand on his axe. If he was a great warrior, a slayer of countless foe-men, then surely he could have killed her father without a thought. She shuddered. Had she been so wrong?

As if the girl's movement had awoken Gytha from a dream, the widow started and turned her attention to Aedwen.

"Dunston may not have been the hero my Rothulf liked to brag about, but he was a killer. Of that there is no doubt."

Aedwen sighed.

"But make no mistake, child," Gytha continued. "I do not believe for one moment that Dunston slew your father. Woe betide any man who crosses him, even now, but the old man is no murderer."

Aedwen sighed again, but now with relief, not despair.

"Who do you think killed him?" she asked.

"I know not. But I think you are right to question Hunfrith's part in this. I fear that what your father spoke of with the new reeve was what led to him being killed."

"But what could they have talked about? My father knew nobody in these parts. This is the first time we have travelled this way." Aedwen didn't mention how she had argued against the trip. How she had warned her father against the folly of this new scheme of his. If only she had been more persuasive. But nothing could change the past.

"I do not know," said Gytha rubbing her fingers distractedly against her temples. "But I can only think that their meeting and his murder are connected in some way."

"Could it be that Hunfrith ordered my father to be slain?" Aedwen whispered, scared to voice her fear.

Gytha thought for a moment.

"I do not know," she repeated. "But Briuuetone has changed these past months. Nothing is as it was. It no longer feels safe."

"Why? What has happened?"

"Two things. First my husband drowned and then Hunfrith moved in as the new reeve."

Aedwen stared at the widow, sensing a deeper meaning in her words.

"You think Hunfrith murdered your husband," she said.

"Quiet, girl," Gytha hissed, as if the very sound of the words stung her. For a time, they were both silent. Aedwen watched as Gytha composed herself, smoothing her dress over her thighs. At last, Gytha nodded, the movement barely visible in the dim light from the embers. "I have no proof, and I have not spoken of this to anyone." She let out a long breath. "I fear for my girls."

"Why do you think Hunfrith would do such a thing? He is the reeve."

Gytha sighed.

"I have long thought on these matters. It is like a riddle that I cannot unravel." She looked down at her hands. She was rubbing them as if seeking to rid them of dirt. "Something had made Rothulf anxious, and he was not a nervous man. I asked him about it, but he said he would not talk of it until he had spoken to Lord Ælfgar."

Aedwen frowned.

"What tidings were so unsettling, so important?" she asked. "And why not tell you?"

"I know not," replied Gytha, her voice catching in her throat. "I like to think he was protecting us. He travelled to Ælfgar's hall, and then... I never saw him alive again."

Aedwen understood.

"You think his death was no accident?"

Gytha drew in a deep breath, as if girding herself for what she was about to say.

"I fear he was murdered." She sighed and smoothed her dress over her thighs. "There, I have said it."

"But why? What could Rothulf have said to Ælfgar that would have got him killed?"

For a moment, Gytha was silent, perhaps thinking whether she should continue.

"I have heard rumours," she said at last.

"Rumours?"

"That Hunfrith was born out of wedlock."

"I do not understand."

"Ealdorman Ælfgar appointed Hunfrith to be reeve of this hundred. Hunfrith is very young for such a post. He has no experience."

Aedwen thought for a moment, trying to deduce the meaning of what Gytha was saying.

"Ælfgar is his father?"

The widow nodded.

"That is what some say."

"You think Rothulf heard this rumour. That it was these tidings that he took to Ælfgar?"

"Maybe." She sighed. "But it makes no sense. Such a thing is not uncommon. There must be dozens of bastards in every hundred in every shire in the kingdom."

"But why then kill Rothulf?"

Gytha shrugged.

"All I know is that my husband went to Ælfgar with some news that had troubled him. The next day, he was dead. And then, Hunfrith came."

"What do you think Hunfrith will do with Dunston?"

"I know not, but I do not believe he means him well. Perhaps he will put him before the moot, as he says. But without you as a plaintiff, I see no point."

"But if Hunfrith killed Rothulf and my father. He could mean to slay Dunston too." The thought terrified her. Was it possible that a reeve could be so evil, so corrupt? A man trusted to dispatch justice by the lord of the shire and, through him, by the king himself.

"We have not one jot of evidence that Hunfrith had anything to do with my husband's or your father's deaths."

"But why not say that he knew my father then? Why keep that secret?"

Gytha shook her head in the gloom.

"And why," Aedwen went on, anger tinging her words, "lock up Dunston when he has shown me nothing but kindness?"

They went around and around these questions, circling and herding their thoughts the way dogs round up wayward sheep until there was nowhere else for them to go.

After a time, they grew silent and listened to the soft nighttime hush. The crackle of the fire; the quiet snoring of one of the girls; the creaking of the timbers as a gust of wind shook the house.

Gytha got up and walked silently to a chest that rested beside the small table where they had eaten. She opened it and brought something out and returned to Aedwen beside the fire. She carried a flask and two wooden cups. She handed a cup to Aedwen, unstopped the flask and poured liquid into each vessel.

Aedwen sniffed the contents and was surprised to smell the pungent bite of strong mead. She had only sipped mead before, at the end of the Crístesmæsse fast.

"I do not like mead," she said quietly, not wishing to appear rude to her hostess.

"Neither do I," replied Gytha with a bleak smirk. "But I think we could both use some fortification if we are going to do what I think we must. So drink it down, and let us get on with preparations, before I change my mind."

With that, the widow tossed the liquid into her mouth and swallowed it down with a grimace.

Confused, Aedwen raised the cup slowly up to her own lips and hesitated, unsure of whether to sip it, or just to swallow it quickly as the older woman had done.

"But what is it we are going to do?" she asked.

"It seems we have convinced ourselves of Dunston's innocence and Hunfrith's guilt, at least in keeping a secret, and at worst of having a hand in my husband's death and your father's murder."

"But what are we to do about that?" Aedwen asked, tentatively sipping a tiny amount of mead into her mouth. It was sweet and she was surprised to find it not unpleasant. It was warm as it trickled down her throat.

"Why, we are going to free Dunston, of course," said Gytha.

Eleven

Dunston snapped instantly awake. He pushed himself to his feet, his aches and pains forgotten as the sounds of alarm from outside grew more intense and increasingly insistent. A hollow clangour echoed in the village as someone beat on something, an empty barrel perhaps. Shouts and yells of anguish drifted to where Dunston stood. He bunched his hands into fists, forcing himself to remain calm, despite the blood rushing through his veins. He recognised the sensation of his skin tingling, his limbs thrumming with tension. This was how he had always felt before battle.

But was there a battle taking place outside? Or was this something less dire? An abandoned rush light, or a stray ember tumbled from a hearth on the dry rushes of a floor perhaps. He breathed deeply, taking in the night-cool air that smelt of straw and dust and the animals that had previously inhabited the barn. Underlying these scents, he half-imagined he could detect the slightest trace of smoke.

Just outside the barn door, his guard called out to someone. "What is that?"

Dunston could not make out the reply muffled as it was by distance, the barn's timber walls and the noise of many people hollering in the night.

Could it be that the village was under attack from the Norsemen? Was it possible that the blood-eagling of Aedwen's father had presaged the arrival of the sea wolves this far inland? Were the people of Briuuetone even now being slaughtered by savage heathens? By Christ, if that were so, what would befall Aedwen? And Gytha and her daughters?

Dunston trembled. How he wished he had hold of DeaÞangenga. The axe's sharp blade would make short work of this wooden gaol.

"What is happening out there?" he bellowed. No answer came to him.

He stumbled to the door in the gloom and placed his ear to its rough-hewn oak. Men and women shouted. Dogs barked, loud and insistent in the night. For a fleeting, sad moment he thought of Odin. There was no clash of metal on metal. The constant echoing drum beat had ceased.

He knelt and peered through a knot hole in the planking. Shadows flitted before the light of flickering flames. But he was unable to make out any details of the events beyond the door.

Standing, he beat on the door with a fist.

"Hey! Let me out of here. I can help."

He paused to listen for a reply.

To his amazement, he heard the bar being removed with a clatter. The door swung open, letting in the noise and light of the night. The cold air was redolent of smoke. Dunston blinked, trying to make sense of what he saw. Some distance away, in the Bartons, the alleys that led to the animal enclosures, a fire was raging. Long, dark shadows danced from the men and women who had flocked about the flames and were doing their best to douse them.

In the doorway, shadowed by the distant conflagration, stood two figures. After a moment, their shapes became clearer to him, their features limned by the silvery light of the full moon.

"Aedwen?" he said, bewilderment in his voice. "Gytha? What is this?"

"There is no time to talk," said Gytha. Despite the obvious urgency, Dunston could not help but notice how the woman had aged. She was, as ever, a handsome woman, and yet she looked as though a decade had passed since last they had met, rather than a few months. "You must flee," she said. "You are not safe here."

"What? Why?" Dunston felt stupid, unable to understand the meaning behind her simple words. The flames behind her seemed to be under control now, the shrillness of the voices in the darkness replaced with determined shouts and commands.

"There's no time, Dunston. You must run."

"I've done nothing wrong."

"I know that, but Hunfrith is keeping things secret. We think he means you harm."

"But why? I have done nothing." Dunston repeated the sentiment of his innocence, but even as he spoke, he could hear the shallowness of his words. Did he truly believe justice would be done here? He was being held for a crime he did not commit, by a man who would not listen to reason. And here was a girl and woman who had risked much to see him freed.

Gytha placed a hand upon his shoulder.

"That fire will not burn for long, Dunston. I must be gone from here and home with my girls before anyone suspects my involvement." She gripped his arm tightly for a moment. Her face was shadowed, but he could sense her terror of being found here. "You are a good man," she said, her voice hissing in the dark. "But you must go. Now. Godspeed." Without awaiting a reply, she turned and ran into the night, away from the now waning blaze. In an eye-blink she was swallowed by the darkness.

An instant later, his mind was made up. He trusted Rothulf's widow. She was a clever woman, honest and true, and if she had taken this action, there must be good reason. Casting about for his belongings, he saw none. That could not be helped. He would have to make do with what the forest provided. He wished he had a knife at least, but he would manage. He began to make his way around the barn, away from the noise and tumult surrounding the fire. Aedwen followed at his side.

Wheeling on her, he hissed, "You cannot come with me, child. Go after Gytha. You will be safe with her." He made to turn, but her small hand gripped his arm, pulling him back.

"No. I will go with you."

"By Christ's bone's, girl, do what you are bidden." He felt exposed out here. If someone should look in this direction they would see him arguing with Aedwen, lit up against the side of the barn by the dying flames of the fire.

"No," replied Aedwen.

By God, the girl was infuriating.

Dunston was about to snap an angry retort, when a large figure loomed in the darkness. It was a tall man, easily a head taller than Dunston, with a dark shock of hair and a mordant, angular face.

Without thinking, Dunston shoved Aedwen behind him. She was light and his strength flung her against the barn with a clatter.

"Well, well," said the newcomer. "If it isn't Dunston, the famous warrior. You don't look so bold now." He sneered, raising the weapon he held in both hands. The far-off fire gleamed from the familiar silver-threaded axe-head.

DeaÞangenga.

His eyes flicked towards Aedwen, who was pushing herself to her feet from where she had fallen. "Oh," he leered, "after I've cut you up, perhaps I can have some fun with the filly. I like them slim and tight."

If the reeve's man had expected Dunston to respond to his taunts, he was quickly disappointed.

Without a word, Dunston closed with the man. The man's eyes widened, but he was young and quick. He stepped backward and raised the great axe, just as Dunston had known he would. Dunston did not stop, instead he increased his speed, forcing the man to react. Dunston knew that most men will think twice before dealing a killing blow, especially against an unarmed man. He hoped to keep him off balance, but his adversary was no peasant and it seemed had no qualms about striking an opponent who bore no weapon.

He raised DeaÞangenga high in the air and swung a huge blow downward aimed at Dunston's head. If the axe had connected it would have killed the older man as quickly as lightning striking from a summer storm. But, Dunston was a veteran of many battles, and, unlike his enemy, he had used DeaÞangenga, the long hafted axe, in combat so often that he knew its heft intimately. He knew that such a powerful swing would slay any man, but he also understood that if it were to miss, the wielder would be unable to halt the weapon's progress.

Belying his advanced years, Dunston skipped backward, allowing the axe to slice the air a hand's breadth before him. His attacker was unbalanced. He stumbled as the axe-head struck the earth, burying itself deeply into the mud, Dunston sprang forward. Placing his left hand atop DeaÞangenga's haft, he drove his meaty right fist into his assailant's face. The man relinquished his grip on the axe's handle and staggered back, arms flailing. Dunston had struck him with all his weight behind the blow and was surprised that the man did not fall to the ground. He was a tough one, of that there was no doubt.

Shouts from the Bartons told of how others had seen the men fighting by the barn. There was no more time.

Tugging the axe out of the ground, Dunston swung it in a vicious arc, connecting with the blunt side of the iron head with a thudding crunch into the man's jaw. He dropped without uttering another sound.

Dunston scanned the gloom. His senses were sharpened now, the battle-fire flooding his body. He felt younger than he had in years. Several figures were approaching cautiously from where the fire was now almost completely extinguished.

Looking grimly at the collapsed man, Dunston prayed he would live. He had not meant to kill him, but perhaps he had hit him harder than needed. There was nothing for it now. His life was in Christ's hands.

DeaÞangenga was warm and comforting in Dunston's grip. Bending to the man's immobile body, he tugged the seax from the scabbard that hung from his belt. As he rose, his eye caught on a leather flask that was propped against the side of the barn. No doubt it held ale or mead that his guard had been drinking before the night exploded into fire and chaos. Without hesitation, Dunston snatched up the container.

Someone shouted out.

"Hey, you there!"

Quickly, Dunston decided which way he would run. He knew this land well and the night held no fear for him. He would make his way quickly down to the river's edge where the water's rush would mask any noise he made. Then he would head south for a time, away from his hut. In the opposite direction to that which the people of Briuuetone would likely expect. The thought of the tithing-men coming after him turned his stomach. The tithing-men would be simple folk of Briuuetone, doing their duty, as they saw it. Helping to bring a miscreant to justice. The villagers were known to him. He had no quarrel with them and did not wish to face them. He would flee deep into the forest where they would never be able to find him.

He sprinted into the darkness, the shouts of pursuers growing louder behind him. A moment later, he became aware of the slender shape of Aedwen, running along beside him. He halted and turned on the girl.

"You cannot come with me. It is too dangerous. You will become a wolf-head."

"I know you do not want me with you," she said, her voice high and trembling. "But think. The reeve's man saw me. If I stay, they will say I freed you. If I go, they will believe I acted alone and Gytha and her girls will be safe."

New voices had joined the shouting now. The crowd had found the fallen guard and from the sound of the yells and insults in the dark, the man's friends were not happy.

Dunston stared at Aedwen for a moment, her eyes glittered. She looked like Eawynn when he had first met her.

"Over there!" came the cry from one of the pursuers.

Dunston growled. There was no time to argue.

"Very well then," he said. "Try to keep up."

And with that, he sped into the black of the night and the willow-slender form of Aedwen followed.

Twelve

Dawn was not even tinging the eastern horizon and Aedwen's breath was ragged and wheezing. She was utterly exhausted, but she vowed not to admit weakness to Dunston. The grey-bearded man seemed not to feel fatigue as they trudged on into the night. Twice, soon after they had left Briuuetone, he had grabbed her shoulder and pulled her down, indicating for her to be silent. The first time he had done this, they had hunkered down beside the bole of a beech tree, hidden in the moon shadow beneath its boughs. They had remained there for a long time, but Aedwen was unsure of who it was that Dunston believed would hear them. The night was silent save for the breeze-whisper in the trees and the burble of the river, which ran broader and more slowly now they had moved south from Briuuetone. After a time, the light from the moon dimmed and, looking up through the branches, she had seen the darkness swallow up half of the great orb in the sky. She had trembled and when Dunston had followed her gaze, he had frowned.

"What is it?" she'd whispered, but Dunston had shaken his head and held a finger to his lips.

Moments later, the night had brightened once more and the moon was whole again.

They had waited so long like that, hushed and cramped beneath the beech that her limbs had become stiff and Aedwen had begun to fall into a doze. But then Dunston had pulled her roughly to her feet and was once again setting such a fast pace that she was barely able to keep up. Her legs were numb from the lack of movement and tingled unpleasantly as the blood flowed back into her abused muscles.

Dunston had appeared oblivious or uncaring of her discomfort.

The second time he had caught hold of her, guiding her into the lee of a stand of alder. She had shaken off his touch.

"What now?" she'd hissed, not wishing to again crouch in the cold and damp while her legs seized up. "And what happened to the moon?"

He had pulled her down roughly with an unyielding strength.

She opened her mouth to complain at his treatment, but before she could utter a sound, he clamped a large harsh hand over her mouth. She squirmed, but he held her tightly. She had been contemplating trying to bite his hand when she heard them. They must have been only ten paces from Dunston and Aedwen's hiding place.

Several men walked quietly past. From time to time one of them would whisper something, but they were travelling quietly, stealthily.

After a while, Dunston had released her, and they had both sat in silence for a very long time. Eventually, Dunston had been sure that their pursuers had moved on and he stood.

"Sorry," she whispered.

"Don't be sorry," he had replied, his voice the hiss of a blade being drawn from a scabbard. "Be obedient. Do what I say without hesitation and we both might live."

She had swallowed back a reply and merely nodded, unsure whether he could see her movement in the dark.

For the rest of the night they had walked in silence and had no further encounters.

Aedwen could not tell how Dunston was navigating. They were not walking on any roads or paths she could discern in the dark, and yet he appeared to be leading them with unerring conviction. Though to where, she had no idea.

She stumbled, her toe stubbing a root that ran across the track they followed. Dunston reached out with uncanny speed, grabbing the back of her dress and righting her. She could scarcely believe what she had witnessed in Briuuetone. Perhaps Gytha's husband had not been spinning tall tales about Dunston's prowess in battle. He had dispatched the younger, armed Raegnold in a heartbeat and it had all happened so quickly, she was hardly certain of what had occurred. One moment the tall man had been threatening them, the next he was slumped on the earth unconscious or dead. Dunston seemed to care not which.

"We will rest soon," he whispered in the darkness. She noticed with a start that she could make out his features. Dawn was not far off and the wolf-light that came before the sun was beginning to colour the land. Dunston had led them out of the dense woods and across some open grassland. It was colder here, the sky clear of clouds.

Aedwen's senses swam. Her legs ached as she climbed up an incline. She was barely awake and had been walking in a daze. Now, she was suddenly afraid.

"Will they find us?" she asked.

"Not where I am taking us," he replied. His voice was soft now, gentle. She nodded in the pre-dawn dark and stumbled along behind him. She believed him.

He led them to a cave. The entrance was scarcely wide enough for them to squeeze inside, and she felt a tremor of fear at being trapped in the earth. But she was too tired now to worry and so she followed Dunston in to the black gloom.

She sensed him moving, as he sat down, propping his back against the wall.

"You will be safe here, Aedwen," he said, his voice echoing quietly in the darkness. "Lie down and rest. Nothing will befall you here."

His voice was soothing, and the solidity of his presence comforting. She wrapped her cloak about her and sat down on the hard floor of the cave.

"You can rest your head on me," Dunston whispered. Without thinking, Aedwen did just that. She lowered herself down and placed her head on the old warrior's outstretched legs.

He patted her arm gently. She shivered.

Aedwen's mind was filled with visions of fire and blood and a moon being consumed by darkness. The face of her mother came to her as sleep embraced her, and in her dreams she was sure she could feel the warmth of Odin the hound stretched out beside her.

Thirteen

Dunston opened his eyes slowly, as if he were scared that the lids would ache like the rest of his body. Light lanced through the open doorway of the mound. He had not meant to sleep, but he supposed it had been foolish pride to think he would be able to stay awake for the whole night. Gone were those days of youth when he could ignore the desire for sleep and still be fresh and alert the next day.

During the night, he had sat for a time, the warm weight of Aedwen's head against his leg, and his mind running ceaselessly over recent events. Like Aedwen, he had been shocked at the moon partially vanishing in the sky above them. He had seen similar before, but had never understood the meaning of such things. Omens, he supposed. But of what, who could tell? Unable to answer any of the questions swarming in his mind, he had, at last, drifted into a deep sleep.

He looked down at where Aedwen slept. She had curled up on her side, resting her head on her arm now rather than his thigh. Her face was serene. Dirt smudged her cheek and her hair was dishevelled, but she slept with the carefree abandon of the young. At some point in the night she had placed her faith in him completely. He knew that she looked to him for protection and he felt acutely the weight of that responsibility.

She should have stayed with Gytha. By Christ's teeth, what had Rothulf's widow been thinking? Now both he and the girl were outlawed. He would never be able to return to Briuuetone. Still, he supposed there was not much for him there now that Rothulf was gone. He could find a new place to live, somewhere in the forest where nobody would find him. He would be content to live alone, with Odin for company.

With a pang of pain, he remembered that Odin was gone. He had wished to ask Aedwen about the hound the night before, but he had pushed the thought away. It was not the moment to converse. There would be time enough in the daylight for speaking, and waiting a while longer for tidings of Odin's fate would change nothing.

Aedwen stirred, mumbling something under her breath before growing still once more.

With an effort, Dunston pushed himself to his feet. His knee was a burning agony and his back popped and clicked painfully as he stood. To think that for a moment in the night he had thought he'd felt young again, able to fight and wield DeaÞangenga as though the last twenty summers had not passed. By God, who was he trying to fool? He gazed down for a moment at the sleeping girl. He had forced them to walk fast all night and she had done well, keeping up without complaint. Now, as his joints cracked and his muscles throbbed, he wished he had not pushed them so hard. If he was not careful, he would be the one unable to keep up the pace.

He snorted, looking to his side for where Odin usually stood. He stopped his hand as he reached for where the dog's head would have been. Stupid old man. It would take him some time to grow accustomed to living without the company of the dog.

Shaking his head, he moved silently to the entrance. He glanced back at Aedwen before he stepped out into the daylight. What was he to do with the girl? Perhaps he could take her to her distant kin. But where did the aunts she had mentioned live? And would they take her in if he found them?

Frowning, he held his hand over his eyes and scanned the horizon. The sun was high in the sky and the day was blessedly warm and dry. Thin trails of smoke rose in the distance to the north, but there were no other signs of men.

Setting off down the hill, he checked that the seax he had taken was still tucked in his belt. In his left hand he carried DeaÞangenga. His body's pains began to lessen as he walked. He would have to give some thought about what their next steps should be, but first, they needed water and something to eat. There was nothing to be gained from worrying about the problems of tomorrow.

Fourteen

Aedwen awoke to the smell of woodsmoke and for an instant she was back in Briuuetone in the dark, the fire Maethild and Godgifu had lit in the handcart spouting flames and billowing clouds of thick smoke. She sat up quickly, staring about her in fear. Where was she? It was dark, but sufficient light washed in from the entrance of the cave that she could make out the details of her surroundings well enough.

The walls and ceiling were too straight to be a cave. This was no natural cavern, gouged from the rock by aeons of rainfall and the flow of underground streams. The stone surrounding her was smooth, fashioned by man.

She saw Dunston then, looking much less like a warrior of legend and more like the old greybeards who sat hunched over their hearths in the long winter months. He was leaning over a small fire, feeding the flames with twigs.

Glancing over at her, he smiled. He looked tired, eyes dark-rimmed and skin wan.

"Ah, you're awake at last," he said. "We have much to talk about. But first, you should eat and drink. It isn't much, but better than nothing." He nodded to where a handful of cowberries glistened on a large leaf.

"How?" she asked, looking from the fire, to the berries, and finally to the trout Dunston was now skewering on a slender branch, which he had sharpened for the purpose.

"The land provides much, if you know where to look," he replied, with a twisted smile. "Everything seems better with a fire, and some food in your belly. It will be even better once this fish is cooked." He positioned the fish over the smoking fire and sat back, looking at her through the haze of smoke. "Drink," he said, handing her the leather flask he had taken from Raegnold at Briuuetone.

She unstopped it and sipped. It was water, with the faint tang of mead and leather. Aedwen suddenly realised how thirsty she was. She took several gulps of the cool liquid before handing the vessel back to Dunston.

"Eat," he said, nudging the leaf with the cowberries towards her.

She picked up a small red berry, nibbling it. It was good. Her stomach grumbled. The smell of the cooking fish made her mouth flood with saliva.

After she had eaten a few of the berries and Dunston had done likewise, he wiped his beard with his hand and looked at her with those penetrating ice blue eyes of his.

"First thing first," he said, "what happened to Odin?"

She told him of how Hunfrith's man had attacked the dog. She blinked back the tears that threatened to fall as she spoke.

Dunston sighed. Picking up a stick, he busied himself poking and prodding the fire. Not wishing to intrude on the man's grief, Aedwen looked down at the berries. They were the red of blood.

After a time, Dunston looked up. His eyes shone in the firelight.

"Now, why did you and Gytha see fit to rescue me from that barn?"

Aedwen recounted the conversation she had had with the widow; about her father meeting with Hunfrith but the reeve not mentioning it to anyone. She told him that Gytha believed Rothulf had been murdered, that he had unearthed something that had led to his death. She described how they had worried at the possibilities, going around the different reasons for the reeve's secrecy, Rothulf's drowning and her father's murder until they had become convinced that Hunfrith was somehow involved and, if that were the case, Dunston would not be safe in his custody.

Dunston turned the trout, holding the branch so that the other side of the fish would cook.

"So you think Hunfrith ordered your father murdered? And that he might have killed Rothulf too?"

"We don't know, but it seemed possible." Aedwen felt foolish, as if Dunston were judging her words and finding them wanting. It had all seemed so plausible in the black of night.

Dunston stared into the flames for a long time, his eyes pinched, looking beyond the fire. At last he nodded.

"I agree. It would make sense. But why? What did Rothulf and your father know? Even if the rumours Gytha spoke of are true, why kill for that? Bastards are as common as ticks on sheep."

"I know not," Aedwen said. It always came back to this. What reason could Hunfrith have for killing the old reeve and her father? "Father was but a peddler."

"Peddlers travel widely," said Dunston, his voice trailing off, perhaps lost in his thoughts. "Who did he trade with?" he asked after a pause. "Did you go to the houses of any ealdormen or thegns?"

She shook her head.

"No. We had only been on the road for a couple of weeks. Father had little idea of how to make money at the best of times. But he was a freeman and proud. And he had always wanted to travel." She wanted to say that she wished he had not been so proud. That he had been a fool to lead them north on dangerous roads with all of their goods on one small handcart. She longed to tell him of how she wished her mother had not died; that if she yet lived, her father would never have put his plan into practice and he would still be alive. But she said none of these things. Instead, she said, "He knew nobody of import. He was not important. A nobody." She felt ashamed at the words. Disloyal. He had been her nobody. Her voice cracked.

"You say he had not always been a peddler?" Dunston asked.

"No, until recently, he had worked the land."

Dunston nodded.

"An admirable labour. What changed?"

"My mother. She died." Aedwen could hear the tremor in her voice as the memory of her mother's passing rushed back, the pain as raw and sudden as a scab ripped off a graze.

Dunston turned the fish again, before adding a few fresh twigs to the small blaze. His firelit face did not give away his thoughts.

"I can only think of two ways to find out what your father spoke of to Hunfrith," he said after a time. "One would be to go back to Briuuetone and ask Hunfrith, but I think we can agree, that is not where we wish to be headed right now."

"And the other?"

"When you lose something, the best way to find it is to go back over the ground you have covered. I say we travel the route you took with your father and we speak with those he traded with. Perhaps one of the people he spoke to will give us the information we need to unravel this riddle."

Aedwen could think of no better suggestion.

"And then what?" she asked, wondering what Dunston hoped to do if he got to the bottom of the mystery of her father's murder.

Dunston squinted at her through the wafting smoke.

"If we find out why your father was killed our way will be clear," he said.

"Clear?"

"Of course," he said, lifting the trout and examining it to ascertain whether it was cooked. "I would rather not live out the rest of my days as a wulfeshéafod. I say we find your father's killers, and bring them to justice."

Aedwen stared at Dunston. Was he like her father? A dreamer. It was easy to have ideas, but quite another to see them through. She could see from the stern set of his jaw that he spoke in earnest. And this greybeard was not her father. She had seen Dunston fight, and he had brought them here to safety, finding food where they had none. No, Dunston was nothing like her father. And yet this was madness. How could an old man and a girl find the truth of all this? They scarcely knew where to start and they were outlaws, probably hunted even as they sat here in this cave. She looked about her again at the cut stone of the walls.

"Where is this place?" she asked. "I thought it was a cave, but these walls are shaped by man, not God."

Dunston busied himself with the fish that he had replaced over the fire.

"We are safe here," he said. "We'll rest for the remainder of the day, then set off south once again at dusk. I do not wish to meet travellers on the roads."

"But where are we?"

"Do you trust me?" Dunston asked, looking her squarely in the eye.

She thought for a moment. He was dour and irascible, but he was strong and honest, and she was certain he meant her no harm.

"Yes," she answered at last.

"Then trust me when I say we are safe."

"Very well, I believe you. But what is this place, if not a cavern?"

Dunston let out a long breath.

"It is a barrow."

"A barrow..." she repeated, the word not making sense for a moment. And then, cold claws of dread scratched down her spine and she sprang to her feet. "We cannot stay here any longer," she said in a hushed whisper, as if the sound of her voice might awaken the dead that slept deep within the crevices of the ancient burial chambers.

"Hush, Aedwen," Dunston said, but she noted that he did not move to impede her should she wish to leave. "I assure you that we are safer here than we would be out in the open. The day is bright and if anyone should be looking for us, they would likely find us up here on the hills."

"But the dead..." she stammered.

"Are long gone and still resting. They mean us no harm and I have oft slept in these places. No harm has ever befallen me."

Aedwen thought of his solitary existence, with only a dog for company, a dog that was quite probably dead. How he had been imprisoned by Hunfrith and was now a wolf-head, to be shunned by all men as outside the law.

He raised an eyebrow, perhaps reading the thoughts on her face.

"I have slept safely many times in barrows and the dead have never disturbed me. Now, sit, the trout is done."

She sat down slowly, unable to hide the fear that had now gripped her. She peered into the dark depths of the barrow, but she could not penetrate the gloom. She imagined the corpses of long dead kings lying there, listening to the echoes of the voices of the living, feeling the warmth from the fire. Smelling with dried cadaverous nostrils the delicious aroma of the sizzling fish. Did they miss being in the world of the living? Would they come crawling out of their ancient tomb, reaching for her young flesh with their skeletal, grasping fingers?

She shivered, and shifted her position so that she was closer to the fire and angled to be looking into the barrow and not towards the light. She would rather one of the tithing-men of Briuuetone found her than some nameless horror from the black interior of the barrow.

Dunston did not speak, and if he noticed it, he ignored her trembling fear. He placed the fish on a slab of wood he had cut to act as a trencher. With deft actions, he used the seax he had taken to pull the fish's meat from the thin bones. He offered her a piece of the trout. It was soft and succulent and tasted earthy and wholesome. The warmth of the food seeped through her, even as her skin prickled, the hairs on her arms rising as if she were cold. She could not shake the feeling that the dead were watching them, lying in wait for them to let their guard down.

"Are we truly safe here?" she asked.

"From the dead?" he asked.

She nodded.

"They will not disturb us," he said. "You know, the first time I stayed in one of these old burial mounds I was frightened too."

"So why did you go inside?"

"That is easy," he said with a shrug. "To remain outside would have meant my death. I had been caught in a terrible blizzard," he explained. "I was younger then, and less wise to the ways of the wild. I should have seen the signs in the sky, but by the time I realised the storm was going to catch me, it was too late to get home. Night was drawing in and the snow came down so thick I could barely see my hand in front of my face. I'd noticed one of the sacred mounds before the weather closed in, so I headed for it. They are dotted all over the land on the hills and the plains, but I'd never ventured into one before. I'd been too scared. But I knew enough about cold to know that if I stayed outside all night, I would not live to see the sunrise, so I swallowed my fear and I went inside."

She watched him as she savoured the fish. He prodded the fire and the flames jumped and danced.

"I trembled like a child," he said. He stared into the fire, lost to his memories. "As much from the fear of the ghosts that might inhabit the place as from the cold. And yet there was nothing for it. If I stayed outside, I would perish, so I entered the dark belly of the mound, praying all the while that the Lord would protect me."

"What happened?"

"Nothing." He laughed, looking up from the flames. "Eventually, I grew too tired to worry and I slept. When I awoke, the snow had stopped falling and it was day. The shelter of that barrow had saved my life and the dead did not seem to mind my intrusion." He scratched at his beard. "No evil befell me that night, but when I left, I made sure to place a silver penny in the barrow and I offered a prayer of thanks to the spirits of those who lived in this land long before you or I were born."

"You prayed to the spirits? Is that not blasphemy?" she asked.

"Maybe, but I don't think it does any harm to be respectful. Just in case. Whenever I've stayed in one of these old caves, I have always left a gift. And the spirits have never troubled me." He offered her a lopsided smile.

Did the dead truly live on in some way, she wondered? Her mother had been dead for nearly a year, and sometimes she could almost sense her touch or hear her voice. And yet she knew that her body lay deep in the earth, wearing her favourite blue dress and the necklace her father had given her as her morgengifu. Aedwen had placed the pendant around her cold pale neck herself.

"What will they do with my father?" she asked suddenly.

Dunston handed her another slice of fish and pondered for a moment.

"I daresay they will give him a Christian burial. They are good people in Briuuetone."

Aedwen thought of Gytha and her girls, but just as quickly recalled Raegnold lashing out at Odin, and then attacking them as they fled from the barn. She was not so sure.

"Godrum is a good man," said Dunston. "He will see to your father."

Chewing the fish she prayed to the Blessed Virgin that Dunston was right. Her father had been foolhardy and unsuited to the life of a peddler. And he had never been a good farmer, his mind was always on something else, far off in some half-imagined fantasy of his. But despite his faults he was not a bad man and he deserved to be buried correctly. A sudden searing anger ripped through her. She was taken aback by the ferocity of the rage that engulfed her. Her father deserved a decent burial, but more than that, he had done nothing to deserve torture and death in a lonely forest glade.

"I don't know how we can do it," she said, her voice trembling with the force of her emotion, "but you are right."

Dunston returned her gaze, sombre and unblinking.

"Right?"

"We must retrace our steps and try to find the truth."

Dunston's face was grim.

"Whatever your father knew, someone thought it was worth killing for," he said.

"Yes," Aedwen said, calm now that she had made up her mind, "and we must find out what that was and who his killers were. And then…" She faltered, unsure of the words she wanted to say.

"And then?"

Aedwen drew in a deep breath, conjuring up her father's guileless face in her mind's eye.

"And then," she said, staring directly into Dunston's icy eyes, "we make the bastards pay."

Fifteen

Dunston dozed by the barrow's entrance as the sun slid into the west. Aedwen had curled up once more, resting her head on her forearm. For a time she had turned and fidgeted, unable to sleep, casting furtive glances into the shadows at the back of the barrow, but Dunston had whispered that she was safe and eventually she had found sleep again.

Clouds had gathered all that afternoon, so as dusk approached, darkness was already creeping over the land. Within the barrow it was dark when Dunston woke Aedwen. He had only ventured out of the barrow to relieve himself and to find some more food. He didn't wish to risk discovery, so he had not returned to the river to fish, instead limiting himself to foraging for some more berries in a thick stand of alder and hawthorn.

He had also cut some linden bark and withies with which he fashioned a bag for any food they might pick up along the way. Into this bag he placed the leather flask.

Near the entrance to the barrow, Dunston pulled up some long grass. This, along with the fire-making materials that he had made earlier in the day, he wrapped in some of the linden bark and slipped the parcel inside his kirtle.

Finally, he had found a stout branch of oak, which he had cut to length and smoothed.

He handed the meagre handful of berries to Aedwen, who took them bleary-eyed and yawning.

"We will follow the road," he said. "We will make better time that way and it should be safe enough. Nobody will be abroad at night, save for outlaws and brigands." He smiled without humour.

He passed her the oak staff he had made.

"It will help with the walking," he said. "And, if we do run into any wolf-heads, that staff is thick enough to break a skull."

She accepted it without comment and together they walked into the gloaming.

As the night before, Dunston set a brisk pace, but he was careful not to push them too hard. His knee throbbed and he was already favouring his left leg, limping slightly. He would be of no use to Aedwen if he could not walk.

They stomped down the hill, through long damp grass, leaving the yawning black opening of the barrow behind them. Aedwen crossed herself as they looked back. Dunston had nothing to leave the spirits that dwelt there, but he vowed that if he were able to return, he would give them a small offering as a token of his thanks. Soon, the mound on the hill and the dark doorway were lost in the gloom of dusk.

When they reached the road, it was full dark and the rising gibbous moon cast but a dull glow through the roiling clouds.

Staring up, face pale in the moonlight, Aedwen whispered, "What happened to the moon last night? It looked as though it was being eaten." She shivered.

"I have thought long about what we saw," he replied. "But I have no answers."

"Could it be an omen?"

"Perhaps, but of what, I know not."

They walked on for a time. The stones of the road were cracked and pitted, ravaged by centuries of passing seasons. But the path was easy enough to follow, even in the darkness.

Without warning, Dunston broke the silence.

"Whatever the sign meant, the moon is whole again now, as it should be. It seems that if it was being eaten, it was quickly spat out again." She glanced up, perhaps to check that his words were true. "Put thoughts of the moon from your mind. We have more pressing matters to be concerned about."

A light rain began to fall, making the road slick and treacherous underfoot. They trudged on in silence, each lost in their own thoughts. Now that they had decided on a course, Dunston was calm and less concerned with what might happen to him. He could fend for himself and defend himself, and, if things went badly and the tithing-men came after them and caught them, he would be taken before the moot. Was that so bad? Even if they found him to be guilty of murder, the only thing he truly valued that would be lost would be his honour, and that was his alone. Should they take his life, that would not be so terrible. He was content enough with his existence of hunting, trapping and forging. But he had not been truly happy for many years. Not since Eawynn. No, the idea of death did not concern him. He had walked with death for so many years when he had served his king, it held no fear for him now.

But what of the girl? She was innocent in all this. As he had sat in the barrow during the quiet calm of the summer afternoon, his hands nimbly bending and softening the withies to tie up the edges of the bark bag, his mind had turned to Aedwen's father. For a moment he could only picture him as he had seen him, bloodied and broken, fish-pallid skin splattered with gore. But then he began to imagine the man Aedwen had talked about with such a mixture of emotions – grief, longing, sadness, exasperation, pity, but above all, love. And he had started to see Lytelman as he must have been in life. A man with desires and dreams, weaknesses and strengths, and with the responsibility for the life of a young girl. It seemed to Dunston that when he had stumbled upon the man's corpse, when he had looked into those unseeing, staring, horrified eyes, he had somehow taken on that responsibility. And he was not one to shirk from his duty.

"Very well, Lytelman," he whispered into the night, "I will keep her safe, or I will give my life trying. You can ask no more of me than that."

The rain fell heavily then in a squalling gust of wind that shook the boughs of the oaks that grew at either side of the road. Dunston shuddered before nodding at the dark sky. Aedwen glanced at him, peering through the darkness and the sheets of rain. Had she heard him? He could not tell, but if she had, she said nothing, merely pulling her cloak about her, lowering her head against the chill of the rain and trudging on.

He decided to make camp well before dawn. They were both wet, cold and miserable. Despite her cloak, Aedwen was shivering and Dunston had only his kirtle for warmth. It provided none, as it was sopping and plastered against his skin.

In spite of the season and the warmth of the previous day, the nights were cool, and the rain fell relentlessly, soaking them and leaching the heat from their bodies. Cold was a killer, Dunston knew. They needed a fire and shelter.

Leading Aedwen away from the road and beneath the dense canopy of the forest Dunston cast about in the gloom until he saw the familiar shape of a young sallow. The moon was high in the sky now, and some of its silver light filtered through the clouds and rain.

"We will make camp there," he said, pointing.

Aedwen did not reply. She was stooped against the cold, arms wrapped tightly around her in an effort to ward off the chill. Reaching the tree, Dunston pointed to its trunk, beneath the thickest foliage.

"Sit there. I'll make a shelter."

He went about constructing a rough shelter as quickly as he was able. First he used DeaÞangenga to cut several branches from the sallow. These he then piled up at an angle around the bole of the tree, using the branches there for support. In this way, very quickly he had a steep roof of branches and leaves, that whilst not affording complete protection from the rain, prevented most of it from reaching Aedwen where she sat against the tree's trunk.

"Now, help me collect bracken," he said, offering his hand and, when she grasped it, pulling her up to her feet.

Bracken grew thick around them and it didn't take them long to pull up an armful each of the stuff.

"Pile it up under the shelter," he said. "It will be our bed, so make it thick enough to keep us off the ground." She did as she was told. He looked at the small mound of bracken for a moment. "Fetch some more, while I start on a fire."

"Fire?" she asked, incredulous. "But how? Everything is so wet and we have nothing to provide a spark."

"It won't be easy in this weather," he said, "that's for sure, but with a bit of luck, I'll get a fire lit." I had better, he thought. Without the warming heat of a fire, they would get colder as their wet clothes drew the heat from their limbs.

She set to ripping up more of the ferns, while he took up his axe and quickly chopped into the lichen-covered trunk of a fallen alder. Within moments he had cut a few sizeable logs, splitting the trunk to get at the dry heartwood. Snatching up a couple of the branches he had cut for the shelter, he set to work on them with his stolen seax. It was not as sharp as he would have liked, but it would serve. His hands were numb with wet and cold, and in the dark it was clumsy work at best, but he worked with care. He knew that to rush would be to risk cutting himself, and so he went slowly, slicing into the wood of the branches and cutting along its length. Long curls of wood wound up from the seax blade. When he was close to the end of the branch, where the sliver of wood would be separated from the limb, he stopped, leaving the thin spiral of sap-rich wood exposed. He repeated the process several times until he had created something that resembled a wooden feather which would burn fast and well to get the fire going.

Aedwen carried over more bracken and placed it in the shelter. And then she sat on the leaves, out of the wind and rain and watched him. It was dark and he could not see her face, but her eyes glimmered in the moonlight.

Positioning himself in the wind shadow and partially under the sheltering branches, he reached inside his kirtle for where he had stored his fire-making items, wrapped in linden bark against the wet. He prayed they were dry enough. It would be nigh impossible to create a flame with wet tinder and wood.

Carefully opening the small packet, he withdrew the fire-lighting utensils he had fashioned the previous morning. He placed a sliver of wood on the ground and atop that, a larger flat piece of linden that would serve as the hearth. Then he took up a straight stick, as thick as his thumb and cut to a rounded point. He knelt, using his body to further protect the wood that would hopefully give them a fire. Holding the wooden board on the ground with one of his feet, he placed the dowel in the darkened groove that was already there from where he had created an ember to light the fire the previous day while Aedwen had slept. Placing the stick between the palms of his straight-fingered hands he began to rotate it rapidly. Rubbing his hands together with the stick between them, he pushed downward, forcing the dowel into the darkened depression.

The stick rotated against the wooden board as his hands descended. When they reached the bottom of the stick, Dunston quickly pulled his hands to the top and repeated the motion. Before long, his palms were warm. He carried on, more vigorously.

Was that smoke he smelt?

He knew not to stop too soon. This was a delicate process and on such a night as this, he could easily lose the precious ember after all his efforts. He continued until he was sure. A tendril of smoke rose from the depression where wood dust had accumulated and he detected a tiny glow, like a ruby in a distant cave. Quickly, careful not to lose it, he lifted the hearth block, discarded the stick and picked up the sliver of wood and its glowing ember and smouldering wood dust. With the utmost care, he gently tipped the ember onto the grass and lichen he had carried within the bark parcel.

Tenderly, he wrapped the tinder about the ember, like a father swaddling a tiny baby. Raising it to his lips, as if he were going to kiss it, he blew gently. Softly, he breathed life into the ember, blowing and then pulling the tinder ball away from his face. Then, blowing again, and a third time. The ball smoked profusely now and he knew the instant the flame would come.

After the fifth lungful of air that he offered the spark enshrouded in its grass and lichen, the ball of tinder burst into flaming life. The flames lit Aedwen's pale face. Her eyes flickered, reflecting bright tongues of fire. With haste he placed the burning tinder on the earth, positioning the first of the feather sticks over it. He held the stick delicately, dangling the wooden feathers into the hottest part of the new flame. They smouldered and blackened and for a sinking moment Dunston thought that perhaps the wood was too damp, that the tinder would not burn for long enough for the larger feathers of wood to catch. And then, just as it looked as though the tinder flame was about to die, a sudden brightness leapt up from the feathered wood. The flames crackled, giving off varied hues as the sap caught.

Dunston let out a long breath. By Christ, how a fire lifted the spirits.

He placed the second feather stick on top of the first, feeding the newborn fire's insatiable appetite. When it was burning hot, he carefully added some twigs and slivers of wood from the boughs he had cut down, before finally adding one of the logs. The fire was not large, but it was burning well now, and it would not be extinguished easily, as long as he continued to feed it.

Rising, he stretched, working out the aches from his back and rubbing his fingers into his stiff right knee. Being careful not to disturb the fire or to topple into the shelter's sloping roof branches, he slid in beside Aedwen. She was half asleep, but she moved enough to make room for him, and then rested her head on his shoulder.

Warmth from the fire washed over him. He had sat thus, enjoying the heat from a campfire in the wilderness countless times before, but it was something that always filled him with pleasure and wonder. To conjure the flames from nothing was a special magic and when it was cold a fire was not only a balm for strained nerves, it was life-giving warmth.

They sat in silence for a long while, staring into the ever-changing dancing tongues of flame.

Aedwen's shivering slowly abated.

"I am glad you know how to make fire from nothing," she said, her voice thick with sleep.

He gazed into the flames, enjoying the movement and randomness of them. Their vitality.

"So am I," he said at last. He recalled sitting in just such a shelter as this so many years before that he was uncertain whether he truly recalled it, or if he had created the story for himself, to think of on lonely nights. Still, the memory was vivid and it always pleased him. He remembered sitting beside a thickset man. Dunston had been a child then, and the man had placed his arm about his thin shoulders. They had sat in pleasant silence and watched the flames that the boy-Dunston had kindled. The man of his memories was grey-bearded and broad-shouldered; old, but wise and still powerful. Dunston smiled. He must look the same to Aedwen.

"My grandfather taught me how to kindle a fire," he said. He sighed, stretching out his hands to capture the warmth from the flames. Christ, he had loved that old man. "I could teach you, if you'd like."

Aedwen did not reply. After a moment he looked down at her and smiled ruefully. The firelight gave the girl's face a ruddy glow. Her eyes were closed and she was sleeping peacefully.

Around them, beyond the glow from the small fire, the night was impenetrable. The forest whispered and rustled out there in the dark. Somewhere far off, a vixen shrieked. A tawny owl lent its haunting voice to the forest music. Leaning forward he placed a fresh log on the flames and settled back next to Aedwen.

He was sure that nobody would be on the road now, and the glow from the fire would not be visible. But he knew that the smell of the smoke would be noticeable from quite some distance. Still, there was nothing for it. The fire would keep them alive. Tiredness engulfed him with its heavy, silent cloak and Dunston's eyelids drooped. He rested his right hand on DeaÞangenga's haft and offered up a prayer that nobody would stumble on them while they slept. Then, placing another chunk of wood onto the fire, he allowed sleep to overcome him.

Sixteen

Aedwen awoke when the sun was high in the sky. She stretched and was surprised to find she was warm. She had become so cold in the long wet miserable night she had thought she might perish. Her teeth had begun to chatter and her head had ached by the time Dunston had made the shelter in the shadow of the sallow tree.

She opened her eyes and saw that the fire was still burning and there were more logs piled nearby. There was no sign of Dunston. For an instant she felt panic rise within her. What would she do if he had left her? But just as quickly as the fear of being abandoned had come upon her, so it fled; dispelled by the warmth from the small campfire. She sat up and found that Dunston had covered her with a thick layer of bracken. The old man was surly at times, and he scared her, but no, she was certain he would not leave her to her fate alone in the forest.

The fire was burning low, so she took one of the logs and placed it carefully onto the embers. The rain had ceased falling but the sky was heavy and overcast. The day was hushed and the woodland dripped and murmured.

Aedwen's stomach grumbled. She hoped Dunston had gone in search of something to eat. He seemed to be able to

find food anywhere. She picked up a twig and poked at the
fire. She frowned to think of the cold nights she had spent
with her father on the road. If only they'd had Dunston for
a travelling companion, they would never have been hungry
or without warmth. She thought of his huge axe and how
quickly he had felled the man in Briuuetone. If Dunston had
travelled with them, she thought, her father would probably
still be alive. The questions around why he had been killed
still plagued her thoughts, but she pushed them aside with
an effort. She could not bear to spend the day gnawing on
the same bones of ideas. They had plucked all the meat
from them and they would glean no further information
by chewing over them again. She hoped they would learn
some useful piece of information when they spoke to those
who had traded with her father as they had made their way
northward. Until then, she vowed to try to think of happier
things than her father's murder.

Running her fingers through her hair, she felt tangles and
knots. When was the last time she had given it a proper brush?
Could it be only the night before last? Maethild and Godgifu
had both combed her long tresses, each plaiting her hair into
long braids. Aedwen had revelled in the soft touch from the
sisters' delicate hands, missing her mother terribly with each
pull of the antler comb. At some point in the nights and day
since then, the leather thongs they had used to tie her hair up
had worked loose and she had lost them. The hair fell around
her shoulders now in an unruly mess. She dreaded to think of
how she must look.

She smiled to herself. Her mother had always despaired at
Aedwen's lack of care with her hair and appearance in general.
She would fuss about her, rubbing Aedwen's face with a cloth
until her cheeks were red and smarting. And when she had
finished with her hair and face, she would go to work on her
hands and nails. Aedwen had always complained, trying to

escape her mother's clutches at the first opportunity, to flee out into the fields, or woods, or to run along the beach, where she would quickly undo her mother's work.

She sniffed at her kirtle. It stank of woodsmoke, sweat and fear.

How she longed for a bowl of hot water and a linen cloth with which to clean herself. And how she missed her mother.

A quiet rustle in the trees made her think that a breeze was picking up. But a heartbeat later, Dunston stepped into the clearing. She noted that his limp seemed less pronounced than the day before. He carried his axe in one hand and in his other there dangled the carcass of a squirrel.

He smiled at her through his wiry silver-streaked beard.

"Awake at last, I see," he said. "How are you feeling?"

"Well," she said, "thanks to you. I don't know what I would have done without you."

He shrugged, but said nothing. Pulling the seax from his belt he set about skinning and gutting the squirrel.

"You have brought us food again," she said, her voice filled with awe. "I do not know how you do it."

"I have learnt the ways of the forest. She will feed you well enough, if you know where to look."

"How did you catch the squirrel?"

He grunted as he pulled the skin from the animal, as though it were a tight-fitting jacket. The flesh that was left looked long and scrawny, but Aedwen's stomach groaned at the thought of roasted meat.

"I found where the animals travel and I placed a snare there. I did not have to wait for long."

Working deftly and with the alacrity that comes from many years of experience, Dunston tugged the entrails from the game and began threading the animal onto a spit of wood. Aedwen watched carefully, trying to remember everything.

"After we've eaten, we should carry on to Spercheforde," Dunston said. "I have been up to the road and know where we are. We will be able to reach the settlement before dusk."

"Do you think someone there will be able to help us?" she asked.

"I do not know," said Dunston, placing the spitted squirrel over the fire's embers. "But you said you and your father had travelled through, so someone might have spoken to him. Perhaps the meeting with Hunfrith was not the only thing he kept from you."

His words held no reproach or judgement and yet Aedwen felt a keen stab of an emotion she could not define. There was no doubt that her father had been holding a secret from her. A secret that might have got him killed. And the fact he had not told her hurt her more than she cared to admit, even to herself.

Dunston stood and inspected his handiwork.

"There is a stream down there, if you would like to drink or wash." He pointed beyond a copse of alder. "I'll keep an eye on this."

She must indeed look terrible if the old man who lived alone in the forest thought she should wash.

"Is it far?" she asked, anxiety gripping her.

"No, Aedwen," he replied, his voice softening, "it is not far. And that way is away from the road. You will encounter nobody."

She let out a breath and nodded.

Aedwen shook off the rest of the bracken that covered her legs and made her way past the alders. The stream was nearby. Fast-flowing, clear water flowed over a bed of shiny pebbles. She drank and the water was sweet and fresh. Then, scooping up handfuls of water, she scrubbed her face and did her best to wash the grime from her hands and arms.

When she returned to their camp, the smell of cooking meat was strong. Her stomach complained at its emptiness once more, and she swallowed the saliva that flooded her mouth.

"The meat will be ready soon," Dunston said. "Better?"

She nodded.

"Yes, I am," she said. "I can scarcely believe I slept so well in such a shelter."

"The body does not need much to be happy," Dunston said. "But it is the things we do not need that cause us most pain."

She pondered his words.

"What do you mean?" she asked, at last.

He turned the squirrel. Its flesh was dark now, sizzling and bubbling fat dropped into the embers making them flare and flash.

"Men always strive for what they do not have. But to reach the object of their desire does not make them content. When a man attains his goals, he merely looks further to the horizon, for the next prize. It is why men will never be happy and why we will never know peace."

Aedwen's brow furrowed. Dunston's bleak words made her sad.

"Do you truly believe that?"

Dunston nodded.

"The Norsemen see our lands and come to steal our riches, and so we fight."

"But they are pagans. They know not the love of the Lord. I pray that one day the Norse will become followers of Christ, and then surely we will know peace."

Dunston snorted and his amusement at her words angered her.

"Does not the Christian king of Wessex seek to control Mercia?" he said. "Do not the Christian Wéalas fight us Anglisc for our land and our livestock? No, the priests may say that Christ is the God of love, but He does not make men content with their lot in life. Perhaps one day the Norse will worship Him too, but if they do and even if they live in peace with us, others will come, seeking what the Vikingr once sought – land and riches. Just as our forebears came to these lands to take the land from the Wéalas."

He lifted the squirrel from the fire and cut a small sliver of meat. He proffered it to her, skewered on the tip of the seax. She took it, blew to cool it and then placed it in her mouth.

"It is good," she said, speaking around the food. She was glad of the change of topic away from Dunston's dark vision of the world. She could not believe in such a grim future, where nobody was ever contented and war would constantly ravage the land. She needed to cling to the hope that Christ and His mother, the Blessed Virgin, would bring happiness and tranquillity to all mankind.

They ate quietly. Dunston cut up the squirrel and shared out the pieces between them. The outside of the meat was dark and crisp, but parts of the flesh near the bone were almost raw, pink and still dripping blood. This was no matter to Aedwen. She had been ravenous and chewed the meat until the bones were clean. Then she sucked the marrow from the thicker ones.

They talked little as they struck camp. There was not much to do apart from see that the fire was safely extinguished. Very soon, with the sun beginning its downward journey into the west, they clambered up through the dense woodland and back onto the road.

Aedwen held the staff Dunston had given her. It already felt natural in her hand and she walked along beside him with purpose. Despite the cold and wet of the previous night, they were both rested and filled with renewed vigour.

"If we hear horses on the road, we will hide," Dunston said.

Aedwen said nothing, but nodded.

"Horses," Dunston explained, "can only mean trouble for us as far as I see it, so it is not worth taking any chances."

Aedwen nodded again and they walked on in silence beneath the canopy of beech and oak.

As it turned out, they neither heard nor saw any horses, or indeed anybody at all, until they left the shadow of the wood. The sun was well into the west now, but still high enough in the sky for them to have ample light left to reach Spercheforde.

The road led them down between ploughed fields and hedgerows. Strips of farmland stretched out before them. In the distance, a man was busy plucking weeds from between the rows of a crop of wheat.

A cluster of houses, barns and a small timber church nestled in the valley.

"I am known here," said Dunston, breaking the silence that had fallen between them. "I sometimes trade pelts and knives with the folk. We should have no trouble."

Despite his words, Aedwen noted how he seemed to grow in stature and how his gaze darted about, as if looking for threats.

The man halted his weeding, shading his hands to better see who approached the village. Then, he slung his weed hook and stick over his shoulder and set a course that would intercept theirs as they reached the houses. Dunston did not slow his pace.

For a time the man was lost from sight behind a hedgerow that was a-chatter with sparrows. Then, just as the path sloped down into the shallows of the river, he stepped from a break in the hedge.

Aedwen held her breath, ready to flee, but Dunston halted, lowering his axe's patterned iron head to rest on the earth.

The man was slender and wore a wide-brimmed hat woven from straw like a basket. His sinewy arms were bare, weather-beaten and smeared with mud.

"Well met, Snell," said Dunston.

The man peered at him and then at Aedwen from under the shade of his hat. He sniffed and wiped the back of his hand under his nose.

"I did not know you had any children," Snell said, nodding in Aedwen's direction.

"She is not my daughter," replied Dunston.

"New wife, is she? Got tired of cooking your own pottage? You must get lonely out in Sealhwudu."

"No," replied Dunston, an edge of annoyance in his tone.

"Thrall then?"

"She is not my child, my wife or my slave, Snell. Her father was killed. She has nobody."

Snell removed his hat and scratched his thatch of curly, greying hair.

"Oh yes," he said, replacing the hat and examining something he had found on his scalp, "I heard about that." He squeezed the nails of his thumb and forefinger together. He grunted, evidently content with the fate he had delivered to the louse.

"Heard what?" asked Dunston.

"That you killed a girl's father and then stole her away and fled justice."

Dunston stepped back slightly, perhaps to better swing his axe should it come to that, thought Aedwen.

"What you have heard is not true."

"P'rhaps," said Snell, looking askance at Aedwen, "but here you are, with the girl they spoke of."

"Dunston did not kill my father," Aedwen said.

Snell stared at her for several heartbeats, rubbing his chin. He sniffed again.

"P'rhaps," he said at last. "Mayhap he did, mayhap he didn't. Those that came here seemed to think he did." He turned his attention back to Dunston. "They had nothing good to say of you."

Dunston snorted and Aedwen was surprised to see Snell smirk.

"Who were they?" Dunston asked.

"Well, I didn't get all of their names, but they were a rum-looking lot. Said they were sent by the new reeve of Briuuetone. One of them had really been in the wars, looked like he'd fought a Mercian warband and lost. His face was a state – blue and black like a stormy day in January. Swollen too. Though it wasn't he who did the talking, seems someone broke his jaw when they were escaping."

"How many were there and when did they come through?"

"Five of them rode up this morning asking if I'd seen you and the girl."

"And what did you tell them?"

"Said I hadn't seen you since before Crístesmæsse."

"Good man," said Dunston.

"Well, it was the truth." Snell seemed awkward all of a sudden. He craned his neck, scanning the hills and woodlands surrounding the settlement, as if he expected the riders to return at any moment. "What shall I tell them if they come back?"

"You can tell them what you wish, but you have known me for many years, Snell and I tell you I am innocent of this crime. All we seek now is to find out who slew this poor girl's father."

"Well, I am sure it weren't nobody from Spercheforde. The closest to a killer you'll find here is Herelufu. Her ale is so strong you feel like death after drinking more than a cupful."

Dunston snorted.

"I do not think the man's murderer is from here."

"So what are you doing here?"

"We are looking for anyone he might have spoken to. We are hoping we might be able to find some indication of why he was killed."

Snell removed his hat again and scratched frantically at his head. He peered at Aedwen. He seemed agitated.

"What is it?"

"I remember the girl and her father now. They came through here a few days ago, but he had nothing that the likes of me or Herelufu needed, and so we sent him up to Beornmod's hall at Cantmael."

"That's right," said Aedwen. "I remember the hall at Cantmael." It had been the last time she had felt safe. "It was warm and they let me sleep in the bed chamber with the womenfolk. Father stayed up late drinking. He sold a bolt of linen, but he drank too much of the ale. The next day he was pale and we had to stop several times for him to rest."

"We will go and speak to Beornmod and see what he can tell us."

"You had best tread with care, Dunston."

"What do you mean?"

"The reeve's men asked the same questions as you. Asked who the girl's father had spoken to. I sent them to Beornmod's hall."

Dunston frowned.

"The hall is not far from here, and they are mounted. With any luck, they will be gone by now."

"I've been in the field all day and no riders have come back down the road."

Seventeen

Dunston knew something was amiss before they could see the hall. The sky was a flat, iron grey, but behind the clouds the sun was low in the sky. Long shadows trailed out from the ash trees that lined the path and the hill that dominated the skyline was huge and foreboding. Some long-forgotten men had sculpted out steps into the hillside, creating terraces in the grass and lending the mound a strange, unnatural quality.

Cantmael was not far from Spercheforde and so they had not tarried long there. There had still been enough light in the day for them to reach Beornmod's hall and so, after convincing Snell to give them a bowl of the pottage that he had left simmering over the embers on his hearth, they had set off once more.

Now, as they approached the steading in the lee of the looming, stepped hill, Dunston halted and held up his hand for Aedwen to do likewise. He shrugged off the hemp bag he now carried slung over his shoulder. He had persuaded Snell to part with it and also an earthenware pot in exchange for the promise of forging him a knife when all this was done.

Snell had smiled grimly, clearly wondering how likely Dunston was to be able to fulfil his promise, but he had agreed without quibbling. Dunston had thanked him. He knew it was no small thing to trust a man at his word, and he was grateful to the wiry ceorl.

In the cool shade of the great hill at Cantmael, Dunston sniffed the air. Smoke and manure, and rain somewhere far off. Nothing untoward. And yet...

He took a few more steps towards their destination. The hall and its outbuildings would be visible when they rounded the next bend in the path he knew. He halted again, listening, straining to hear anything that might suggest to him what to expect at Beornmod's hall. He crouched in the path, examining the furrows and tracks in the mud, turning his head this way and that in order to pick out anything unusual in the churned surface.

Several horses had come this way recently, and earlier in the day, oxen had pulled a cart with a wobble in the rear left wheel. There were prints from the shoes of ceorls going to and from the fields. He could clearly discern where the men had jumped over the numerous puddles, where they had placed their feet close to tussocks of grass, trying to keep dry. Two dogs, large ones, had padded along the path too, but unlike the men, they had cared nothing about muddying their paws.

He saw no indication of the horsemen returning along this path.

Without a word he handed the bag to Aedwen.

"Go there," he indicated a hawthorn that was flanked by huddled downy willows, "and hide. Wait for me to call or to come for you."

"What if you don't come back?" she whispered, terror in her voice.

For an instant he was going to lie to her, to tell her that of course he would be back. But then he thought of the girl's father, and all of the man's broken promises. He pictured Lytelman's back split open like a butchered boar. He would not lie to Aedwen.

"If I do not return, wait till nightfall and then make your way back to Snell. He is a good man and he would help you."

He could see she did not much care for his answer, but she merely nodded and scampered away into the undergrowth. After a moment, she was hidden from sight.

Glancing down at the muddy path once more, he saw again the indentations made from the clawed, padded paws of the two hounds. His breath caught in his throat and for a moment, he thought one of the dogs might be Odin. He bent to get a closer look and realised his mistake. These were not the tracks of his dog. Odin was surely dead somewhere in the forest where he had run after being injured.

Dunston set his jaw and, gripping DeaÞangenga tightly, he walked down the incline and around the bend in the path. The shapes of the buildings came into view. All was still and with a jolt Dunston realised what had alerted him that something was not right. This was the end of the day, when thralls and servants would be bustling about the steading, preparing for the evening meal. The last chores of the day should be under way. The small hall, barn and two outbuildings should be abustle with activity.

And yet there was no sound. No movement at all.

A crow croaked from where it was perched, dark and brooding, in the grizzled old oak that gave shadow to the ground between the buildings. It was the first bird he had heard or seen since arriving here, and its doleful call made his skin prickle.

And then he saw what the crow was resting upon.

Two men in simple clothing dangled from a high branch of the oak. Ropes had been thrown over the bough and secured around the bole. The men's faces were mottled, dark swollen tongues protruding from fish-pale lips. Their breeches were stained where they had soiled themselves in death. Dunston sighed and spat. Would he never be free from death and killing? He yearned to be left alone, to live out his days in peace.

The crow cried out again and to Dunston it sounded like a harsh bark of laughter.

The moment he had found Lytelman, his chance of a straw death, growing old and dying in his bed, had fled. Everywhere he turned now, he stumbled on more blood and murder. He felt his anger brimming within him. He fought to keep it in check, but he recognised the call of the old beast. It had been sleeping within him for such a long time that he had thought it was gone, but it seemed all it had been waiting for was the right food to give it strength once more.

Strength and purpose.

Skirting the hanging men, he moved stealthily towards the hall. There were no sounds from within. No smoke drifted from the hole cut into the thatch. The stillness was unnatural. This was the pure quiet of a tomb. All he might find here were ghosts.

Close to the hall's open doorway lay the corpse of a large tan-coloured dog. Its head had been almost severed from its neck, its mouth pulled back in a defiant snarl from its white, dagger-like fangs.

Hefting DeaÞangenga, Dunston took a deep breath and stepped through the dark maw of the hall's door. Inside was gloom-laden, the air stale. Cold soot, sour beer, the acrid scent of shit and, beneath it all, the metallic tang of blood.

Squinting and blinking against the darkness, he looked around the hall. It was a modest building, with a high table that would sit four and enough room at the benches for perhaps twenty men in total.

Three women and an elderly man lay dead on the floor near the cold hearth. They had been cut down by swords or long seaxes. Great gashes had opened their flesh and their blood had soaked the rushes black.

The other dog was dead beneath its master's feet. It must have tried to defend Beornmod, but it had been pierced by spears and then hacked into a mess of muscle, bone, sinew and fur. And blood, so much blood. The huge pools of the stuff mingled with the gore that had run from the board where Beornmod's corpse was draped.

Dunston instantly recognised the handiwork of Lytelman's murderer. Beornmod lay face down on the board, blood-splattered arms hanging down, flaccid and mottled in death. The man's kirtle had been torn asunder and it was the sight of his back that brought the gorge rising in Dunston's throat. The ribs had been shattered and wrenched apart and the man's entrails and lungs draped on his back, like wings of offal.

He turned away from the corpse. Beornmod would tell them nothing. They had come to this hall hoping for answers and instead they had found more death.

"Is that how my father was slain?" said a voice. It was small and empty-sounding, but it was loud in the complete still of the hall. Despite himself, Dunston started, letting out a tiny sound of alarm.

"I told you to stay hidden," he said, his voice harsh and as brittle as slate. "God, girl, you promised to do as I said." He grabbed hold of her shoulders, spun her round and shoved her out of the doorway, away from the mutilated remains of Beornmod. "It could have been dangerous."

Outside, she turned to face him. Finding an outlet for his anger now, his ire bubbled up and he jabbed a finger into Aedwen's sternum. She staggered backwards with the force of his stabbing blows. He was only using his thick forefinger, and yet she was unable to hold her ground.

"What if the men who did this were still here?" he asked, his finger prodding out the beat of the words.

Aedwen's eyes filled with tears, and they started to roll down her cheeks. She let out a sob, and as quickly as they had been kindled, so the flames of his anger were doused. After a moment of hesitation, he pulled the girl close to him with his left hand. In his right he held his great axe and all the while he scanned the other buildings for signs of danger. Aedwen shook and trembled against him.

"I need to know you are safe," he whispered to her, "or else I will not be able to protect you."

She sobbed and sniffed, and at last she pulled away from him. She swiped at her face, brushing away her tears.

She mumbled something under her breath. He could not make out the words. Perhaps she was apologising, but his anger still simmered.

"If you mean to say sorry," he hissed, "save your words. I need to know you will obey me. When I tell you to do something, you do it. No questions. No arguing. You just do it! Understand?"

Aedwen nodded, her face a mask of misery.

"Well, you have chosen to defy me, and now there is nothing for it. I did not want you to see such things, but maybe it is for the best that you do. Perhaps then you will comprehend what it is we are dealing with."

Aedwen's gaze flicked to the oak and its dangling corpses, then she peered, wide-eyed, into the darkness of the hall, as if she wished to see the mutilated corpse in more detail.

"You think the men who did this were the ones who killed my father?" she asked. Her voice was so quiet it was almost lost beneath the cawing of the crow.

"Who else?" Dunston replied. "Now, stay close and keep your eyes open."

They moved through the steading, searching every building, but the men who had massacred Beornmod's folk had left. They found two more bodies. A young man, and a girl. The man seemed to have come running from the fields. There was a hoe and two weed hooks near his corpse, but if he had tried to use them as weapons he had clearly been no match for the horsemen. Spear points had pierced his chest, and he had been left to wail and bleed out his lifeblood into the soil.

The girl had been dragged into one of the storerooms. Her clothes were ripped, exposing pallid skin. Beneath her dark staring eyes, her throat had been opened in a terrible wound. Dunston read what had happened inside the small shed as clearly as if he had been there to witness the atrocious last moments of the poor girl's life. After the men had done with her, they had cut her like a pig for slaughter. Blood had fountained, gushing and pumping as her heart fought to keep her alive. She had been young and vital and now she was no more than a carcass, cold meat on the packed earthen floor of a storeroom.

Dunston turned away, closing the door of the hut behind him. He sighed. Christ, to think he had hoped to be done with death.

Aedwen had grown very quiet and he noted the pallor of her skin. He placed a hand on her shoulder and for a heartbeat, he thought she was going to run from him. But then she trembled, letting out a strangled sob.

"Sorry," she said.

"Come," he said, ushering her towards one of the buildings that was devoid of corpses. "I'll light a fire and we can eat and rest."

"Here?"

"It will soon be dark and I don't think the men who did this will be back."

"Are you sure?"

"I cannot be certain, but the tracks of their horses lead south and west. If I am not mistaken, and I rarely am when it comes to reading sign, they are in pursuit of something. Or someone. They were riding hard, pushing the horses."

He led her into a small house. Like the hall its walls were whitewashed daub and its roof was thatched. Inside it was comfortably furnished. The small hearth was circled by stools and chairs. Chests lined the walls and ham and sausages hung from the rafters. To the rear, a curtain hung to separate the sleeping quarters from the main space. Thankfully nobody had been slain inside this abode and the riders had not plundered its contents.

Indicating to Aedwen to sit on one of the carved chairs, Dunston set about kindling a fire on the hearthstone. The ashes were still warm and there was dry wood in a basket. Dunston found a flint and steel in a small wooden box beside the basket of logs and in moments, he had a small blaze burning.

He placed the tinder box in the bag Snell had given him.

It was dark within the house, but the flickering light from the fire showed Aedwen's frown well enough.

"That is not yours," she said.

"You are right, of course, but we have more need of it than Beornmod's folk now, don't you think?"

Aedwen scowled, but said nothing.

"Make no mistake, Aedwen," Dunston said, "I am no thief. But I will take from these poor people whatever I can to help us. I think that is what they would have wanted. I know I would not begrudge someone taking my things after my death. Especially if they were hunting my killers."

"Is that what we are doing now then? Hunting these killers?"

For a while Dunston did not reply. He picked up a split log and placed it carefully on the flames. The truth of the matter was he did not know what they should do next. He was but an old man and Aedwen was a child. What could they do in the face of such ruthless barbarity? But what alternative did they have? If they could somehow unearth the reason for these murders and unmask the perpetrators, perhaps he could return to his life in Sealhwudu. Far from the evil of men. He had seen enough of that for a lifetime and more.

"What else can we do?" he said at last. "I would wager these are the same men who killed your father, and they are clearly searching for something. I think we will need to follow them. And, with luck, we can find out what they are about before they kill again."

"They told Snell they were the reeve's men," Aedwen said. "Surely that cannot be true. The reeve's men would not kill all of these people."

Dunston had been thinking about this, and he had his suspicions about what had happened here. He ran his fingers over his thick beard.

"Perhaps they lied to Snell, or mayhap they are Hunfrith's men."

"But how could that be so? To kill so many..."

"Maybe the first kill was an accident. But after that first one, the only way to avoid justice would be to kill everyone. I think that is what happened. From the marks in the mud outside, I believe the workers were speared first, then the horsemen, reeve's men or not, moved on to the others."

"And the girl?"

"Once such men are on the course of blood and killing, they would think nothing of taking their pleasure with an innocent."

Dunston glanced at Aedwen and saw she was staring into the flames.

"Why didn't they burn the hall with the people inside?" she asked after a time. "Surely that would have hidden the nature of their crimes. And people might have believed it to have been an accident. Fires happen all the time."

"True," replied Dunston, strangely proud of the girl for looking at the situation and analysing the possibilities. "But the smoke would have drawn neighbours, and they might have been caught here and found they needed to answer difficult questions. In this way, they must have hoped that when the bodies were found, nobody would be able to say who had done these foul acts."

"Just like my father, killed deep in the forest."

"Yes, Aedwen. If there are no witnesses to a crime, it is much more difficult to prove who did it."

Now it was Aedwen's turn to fall silent, as she pondered his words. After a time, she nodded, her face pale and doleful in the firelight.

"We should bury Beornmod's people," she said. "Before we go. We cannot leave them like that." She shuddered, and Dunston could imagine her thinking of the girl lying cold and alone in the store. The men, dark tongues poking from blue-tinged lips, swinging stiffly from the oak. The other corpses, brutally cut down by savage men. The bloody, mutilated butchered remains of Beornmod himself.

"There is no time for that," he said. "If we remain here, we will lose the men who did this. Worse, others will come and blame us for what has happened." He glowered in the gloom, recalling the madness of being accused of Lytelman's murder. But without witnesses or those to swear oaths for him, who knew what men would make of him being found in Cantmael surrounded by corpses?

"But it is not right to leave them…" she hesitated. "To leave them like that."

Before Dunston could reply, a mournful moan came to them from outside in the gloaming. It was a doleful sound, full of pain and torment.

Aedwen stiffened and horror filled her eyes.

But Dunston smiled.

"Do not fear, child," he said. "That is not a bad sound to hear. Listen."

Again came the droning moan and as Dunston saw the truth dawning on Aedwen's features, he stood and said, "Bring that bucket," indicating a wooden pail that rested in the corner.

Outside in the gathering dusk, the sound was louder and clearer. They followed it to its source, Aedwen trotting along beside Dunston. By the door of one of the barns they found the creature that was lowing pitifully as darkness draped the land.

It was a large cow with twisted horns and distended udders painfully full of milk. Inside the barn, Dunston found a stool and another bucket. He tethered the beast, and set down the stool.

"We will have fresh warm milk tonight," he said, smiling in the gloom.

He could not make out Aedwen's expression, but he was pleased when she sat and proceeded to milk the cow effortlessly, sending warm streams of liquid squirting unerringly into the bucket. It didn't take long until the first bucket was full. Dunston passed Aedwen the second pail.

"Poor girl," he said, patting the cow's shoulder. The beast had stopped lowing now, and was content to be milked, relieving the pressure from her udders. "Looks like we'll have more milk than we can drink," he said.

"Perhaps you could spare some for me then," said a voice from the darkness behind him.

Aedwen leapt up, overturning the stool and spilling the milk from the half-filled bucket.

Dunston spun around, dropping his hand to the small seax he yet carried in his belt. By God, how could he have been so foolish as to leave DeaÞangenga back in the house next to the fire? Pushing himself in front of Aedwen, he tried to discern the features of the newcomer.

The figure stepped closer and Dunston's eyes widened in surprise.

Eighteen

Aedwen sipped at the still-warm milk. Its creamy richness coated her mouth and throat. The flavour was comforting and she could feel her body relaxing in the glow of the hearth fire.

Across from Aedwen, face lit from beneath by the flames, sat a girl not much older than her. When she had approached them in the milk shed, Aedwen had been terrified that the men who had murdered the residents of the farmstead had returned. Dunston had pushed himself forward, crowding the girl who had stepped from the gloom and Aedwen had thought how lucky the girl had been that he had not thought to carry his huge axe with him. He was as taut as a bowstring and Aedwen wondered whether he would have been able to prevent himself from killing the girl where she stood, if he had borne the weapon in his hand. As it was, he soon realised this was no killer striding from the dusk, rather a timid, slender and frightened young woman. Her hair was dark and her face had angular cheeks and a pointed chin that reminded Aedwen of a fox. Her skin was smeared with mud and grime.

Nothgyth was her name and she said she was one of Beornmod's house thralls. They had made their way back to the house, where Dunston placed more wood on the fire. Aedwen noted how he positioned himself beside the door, but not with his back to the opening. He placed his silver-threaded axe within easy reach.

Nothgyth had quickly produced wooden trenchers, some cheese, hard bread and some ale from the shadows in the hut. She unhooked the ham from where it hung from a beam and sliced off thick slabs of salty, greasy meat. She clearly knew where things were kept and soon the three of them were seated around the fire, eating food that until that day had been destined for Beornmod's folk's bellies.

Dunston drained his cup of milk and then refilled it with ale. He took a deep draught, grimaced, and then emptied the cup again before pouring yet more ale. He sat back, stretching his legs out before him. He winced slightly as he straightened his right knee.

"So, Nothgyth," he said. "What happened here? How is it that you alone survived?"

Nothgyth stared into the fire for a time, chewing a morsel of bread which eventually she washed down with a mouthful of milk. Dunston waited patiently for her to answer, but Aedwen had begun to wonder whether the woman had heard the question by the time the thrall spoke at last.

"I hid. Under the store." The store shed where they had found the murdered girl was raised from the earth on wooden posts in an effort to keep rats away from the grain and food stored within. "I was round the back picking some fresh summer sætherie when I heard them come. The number of them and how they came on horses frightened me. I've never seen so many riders before in one place." She gazed wistfully into the flames. Her eyes glimmered.

"So you hid," prompted Dunston.

"Not at first," she replied, as if he'd awoken her from a dream. "I just stood there listening to start with. Wanted to hear who they were. Thought they must have been the king's men. Perhaps the king himself had come to the master's hall."

"There were so many of them?" asked Dunston.

"Oh, many riders. Must have been five at least."

Dunston frowned, but nodded.

"So what happened?"

"They talked for a moment to Frithstan. I couldn't hear what they said. Something about a peddler. It made no sense." She grew silent then. She nibbled on her bread, lost in her memories of that afternoon's chaos and violence.

"What happened next?" Aedwen asked.

"The men spotted Wynflaed. And they said things about her. Bad things. Frithstan grew angry and shouted at them, and one of them struck him. That is when Eohric and Tilwulf came back from the lower field. Eohric told the men to be gone..." Nothgyth's voice trailed off, as she relived the moment. "One of them speared him, without a word. As if Eohric was an animal. He didn't even have time to scream. He just fell into the mud and was dead. One of them laughed then, even though the others were angry with him."

"Angry?" asked Dunston.

"Yes. They said they weren't supposed to kill them. I couldn't hear much of what they said then though, because Wynflaed was screaming. A couple of them pushed her inside the store. For later, they said." Nothgyth's voice caught in her throat. "They bound her and left her there while they went to the hall. That is when I hid. I could see their feet and the hooves of their horses, and I heard how they hanged Tilwulf and Frithstan and the screams from the hall were so loud. But all the while I could hear Wynflaed crying just above me. I should have helped her," a sudden sob racked her. "I just hid there. Even while they..." Tears streaked through the dirt on her cheeks.

"No, girl," said Dunston, his deep voice soothing in the

darkness. "You did what you needed to do. You could not have saved her and what good would it have done for you to suffer her fate too?"

"Perhaps God kept you safe for a reason," said Aedwen.

"Truly?" asked Nothgyth, her tone pleading and desperate.

"Truly," replied Aedwen. Surely God and the Virgin must have some purpose in all this. To think otherwise was too much to contemplate. "We mean to find these men," she continued, "and see they are brought to justice. God must have spared you so that you can help us."

"Help you?" Nothgyth looked terrified. "How could I do that?"

"You can tell us all you know about them," said Dunston, leaning forward, so that his jutting beard shadowed his face from the firelight. His eyes shone in the gloom.

"I know nothing," she wailed. "I was hiding."

"Think, tell us all you heard. Did you hear any of their names?"

Nothgyth furrowed her brow and took another sip of milk. Slowly, she shook her head.

"I don't know. I just heard them shouting at my master. And then I heard them laughing while Wynflaed screamed." She shuddered.

"If I am able, Nothgyth," Dunston rumbled in the dark, "I will see these men killed for what they have done. Men who do such things do not deserve to live. Now," he reached over and gripped her arm. She flinched, but he held firm, looking directly into her eyes. "What can you tell us about who they were or what they were looking for."

And then, her eyes widened as a fresh memory came to her.

"I don't know who they are, but I know where they are going."

"Tell me," Dunston said, his voice cold and hard.

"They have gone after Ithamar."

Nineteen

Dunston forced himself to loosen his grip on Nothgyth's arm. The girl was frightened enough without her fearing him too.

"Who is Ithamar?" he asked.

"A monk," Nothgyth said, her tone implying that everybody knew who Ithamar was.

Dunston frowned.

"And what did these men want with a monk?"

"I don't know. One of them was shouting at my master over and over. They were both yelling, but I didn't really understand what they spoke of."

"What were they saying?" Dunston asked, willing his tone to remain calm.

Nothgyth took a sip from her cup of milk, lifting it to her lips with trembling hands.

"They were asking about the peddler."

Dunston glanced at Aedwen. Her eyes were shadowed, but she was staring intently at Nothgyth.

"What about the peddler?" Aedwen asked, her voice rasping in her throat.

"I couldn't hear. I don't know." Nothgyth hesitated and Dunston began to wonder whether they would learn anything of value from this poor, frightened girl. "It made no sense to me," she went on. "They just kept asking him how the peddler had known."

"Known?" said Dunston. "Known what?"

"I do not know," exclaimed Nothgyth. "I told you, it made no sense to me."

For a time they sat in silence, each thinking of what they had witnessed that day and of Nothgyth's tale of torture and murder. A log shifted on the embers and sparks drifted upwards to wink out amongst the rafters and the hanging meat.

After a time Aedwen spoke.

"And Beornmod told them that Ithamar was the one they sought?"

"I think he just wanted them to stop," Nothgyth hesitated, unsure now. "To stop what they were doing and he shouted that the monk had carried a message."

"A message?" Dunston asked.

But before Nothgyth could respond, Aedwen said, "I remember the monk. He too had stopped here at the hall for rest. He'd only meant to stay one night, but there was a sick traveller and Ithamar was tending to him. My father and the monk spoke together long into the night, after I had gone to sleep."

"That traveller died in the end," Nothgyth said, crossing herself. "We were all frightened it was the pestilence. The Lady had been terrified his illness would kill us all. She had me and Wynflaed burn all his belongings and Tilwulf and Frithstan buried him right out by the great elm in the top field. Far from the house." She sniffed. "It weren't the pestilence that got them in the end though. Goes to show."

Dunston thought on what the girl had said. Could it be that Ithamar and Lytelman had learnt some terrible secret from this sickly traveller?

Nothgyth was peering at Aedwen in the firelight.

"I remember you now," she said. "The Lady let you sleep with us in the back of the hall." And then her eyes widened. "Your father is the peddler they spoke of."

"That's right," said Aedwen. "He was."

"I thought this one was your father," said Nothgyth, nodding towards Dunston.

"No. My father's dead."

"Killed by the same men?"

"We think so," Aedwen said.

"But why?" asked Nothgyth.

"We do not know, child," said Dunston. "But we mean to find out. And when we do, we will make them pay." She was no fool this one, Dunston thought, and he could see her thoughts clearly on her face. First confusion, then inquisitiveness and then, finally, a sudden dawning fear.

"If they find that I am alive and I saw the things that happened here, they will return and slay me." She spoke in a matter-of-fact monotone. And there could be no arguing with the sense of her words.

"You must be gone from this place at first light," said Dunston. "And never speak of what you have seen here."

"But where will I go?"

"Do you have kin?" he asked.

Tears tumbled down her dirt-smeared face and she sniffed.

"These were my kin," she said, her voice desolate. "I have no others."

"Take what you can of value and head east. Make your way towards Witanceastre. The land is safer there and a clever girl like you will find a way."

Nothgyth stared at him, frowning in the ember glow of the fire. She swiped at the tears on her face with the back of her hands.

"And what of you?" she asked.

Dunston drained the ale from his cup and stood. His knee ached and his back was stiff. But he would walk around the settlement before he slept. He was sure the riders would not return and yet he could not shake the feeling that despite hunting these men, he too was their prey. Who would be first to bring their quarry to ground he could not tell. But of one thing he was sure. There would be more blood spilt before the end.

"We will continue with our quest to find the truth," he said.

"And how will you do that?"

"We must try and find this Ithamar before the others."

And with that he picked up his axe and stepped out into the cool darkness of the night, leaving the two grieving girls alone in the flickering firelight of the house.

Twenty

Aedwen was surprised that she slept so well. As she had lain in the quiet warmth of the hut the night before, her mind had thronged with the horrors she had seen. She had fought against sleep, fearing that her dreams would be filled with the swollen faces of the hanged men, the blood-streaked corpses of the bondsmen in the yard, the pale skin of the dead in the hall and the mutilated, butchered body of Beornmod. But worse than all of these fearful apparitions in her mind had been the sightless eyes of the girl in the storeroom, throat gaping like a hideous, monstrous, impossibly wide grin.

Aedwen had prayed to the Blessed Virgin for the girl's soul. And she had prayed for Nothgyth, that the girl would find a safe haven, far from all this tragedy. Somewhere she might find people she could call her kin once more. And, as Dunston had returned from his patrol of the steading, she had prayed for herself. She asked the Virgin that She might help them find her father's killers so that they would be able to avenge him and the poor people of Cantmael. Aedwen was not sure that the prayer was worthy of the Virgin, for surely the Mother of Christ would frown upon one of her own seeking vengeance instead of spreading love and forgiveness. But Aedwen could find no space in her heart for love. Her thoughts were dark and twisted, and so, she had thought, would be her dreams.

But she had dreamt of a warm summer's day. In her dream her mother, fit and hale and full of life, had embraced her and brushed her hair. Aedwen had awoken refreshed and relaxed. For a time she had lain silently with her eyes closed, clinging to the feeling of her mother's warmth against her. She could hear Dunston quietly rekindling the fire and moving about the house. But she did not wish to open her eyes, for when she did she knew that the world would be as it had been the day before, her mother would yet be dead, as would her father. And she was sure that her future would not be warm and full of light, but dark and filled with death.

The illusion of lying in her mother's embrace was shattered when Nothgyth, who had slept beside her and had wrapped her arms about her in the night, awoke and rose to her feet, coughing.

As much as Aedwen felt rested, so Dunston seemed all the more tired. The skin beneath his eyes was dark and bruised-looking and despite his broad shoulders and muscled arms, she thought his face looked slimmer, his cheekbones more pronounced.

He looked old.

Dunston had been up early and had already milked the cow, so they had fresh milk and the remainder of the bread and some cheese to break their fast.

"You must take the cow with you," Dunston said to Nothgyth. When she protested, saying she was no thief, he had raised up his hands and told her that without her to milk it the cow would grow ill. "You said the people here were your kin, or as good as." Nothgyth nodded. "So then," Dunston continued, "you are merely taking what your kin have left you. They would want you to do well with your life and I'm sure they would not want the cow to go un-milked and

abandoned. That animal has been well-loved and cared for."
Nothgyth acquiesced in the end and they waved her farewell
as she forlornly led the beast along the path back towards
Spercheforde.

Aedwen noted that the corpses no longer hung from the tree
in the yard. And the farmhand who had lain in the mud in a
pool of congealing blood was gone. It seemed that Dunston
had done more than merely tend to the cow that morning. He
said nothing of the dead and so Aedwen did not speak of them
either. But she was thankful that she did not have to face the
staring eyes of the corpses in the bright summer sun.

There were only the merest wisps of cloud in the eggshell blue
of the sky as they set off following the path to the southwest.
Dunston had picked up a few things from the house, stuffing
them into his hemp bag, and he had told Aedwen to fill a sack
with food from the house. From somewhere he had found a
good seax, complete with a tooled red leather scabbard, and
a belt, which he fastened around his waist. For Aedwen he
produced a small eating knife. It had a polished antler handle
and when she pulled it from its plain leather sheath, she saw
that the blade had been sharpened many times. It was a short
blade, but it was wickedly sharp and even though Aedwen
had no idea what she would do with it in a fight, wearing it
from her belt made her feel somehow safer.

When they had walked a short way from the steading
Dunston knelt over the path, gazing at the mud and grass that
grew there. After a long while he rose to his feet and set off
with a determined stride.

Aedwen trotted to keep up.

"What do you see in the ground?" she asked.

"The signs are confused," he said, a tinge of annoyance in
his tone. "The horses went this way, but I had hoped to be
able to see the sign of the monk. But I was unable to discern
anything for certain."

"Well, Nothgyth did say that Ithamar left two days ago," said Aedwen.

"And it has rained," he said. "It would be much to ask that I would find his tracks easily on such a busy path."

As they walked along the track, leaving the looming hill of Cantmael and Beornmod's hall behind them, Aedwen watched as Dunston continued to survey the ground. Sparrows and finches twittered in the bushes to their left and a crow flapped lazily overhead. Dunston glanced at the birds, nodding as if they too spoke to him, telling him what they saw from their lofty positions.

"How did you learn?" she asked.

"Learn?"

"To read the tracks of men and animals."

"My grandfather taught me first," he said. "And after him my father." They walked on for a time without speaking and when Aedwen looked at Dunston she saw a wistful glint in his eye. She supposed his grandfather and father must have died many years before. She wondered what it would be like for her as she grew old, when her parents would be nothing but a distant memory, half-forgotten ghosts that had at one time been her whole world.

Reaching the brow of a rise Dunston halted and lowered himself down onto his left knee with a grunt. His pale ice blue eyes were surrounded by wrinkled skin and yet they were clear and bright, showing no sign of age. They flickered as his gaze took in the hidden details strewn before him in the muck.

"There," he pointed to a twig that had been snapped and pressed into the soft earth of the track. "See," he said, "I'd wager that's Ithamar's print. A soft leather sole. See how the horse's hoof snapped the twig when the riders passed yesterday?" He touched the print softly, rubbing a pinch of soil between thumb and forefinger. "It is as the girl said. The monk is two days ahead of the riders. But he is on foot and he does not know he is being pursued. If he sticks to the path, or if they have a woodsman in their number, one who can read sign, they will run him to ground before we can reach them."

He heaved himself to his feet and set off once more.

"Much of what I have learnt, the forest has taught me," he said after a pause. "You can learn much if you watch and listen. With patience and time the woodland will give up its secrets. All learning comes from being patient and thinking what you can glean of use from what is around you."

"It is as though you can see things in the ground that nobody else can see," said Aedwen.

"Anyone can learn the things I know. Would you like to learn?"

"Would you teach me?"

After a brief hesitation, Dunston said, "I will if you would like. We cannot tarry if we mean to find these men, but I can tell you some things as we go. Would you like that?"

Aedwen thought for a moment. She tried to remember the last time her father had taught her anything of value. Nothing came to mind.

"Yes," she said. "I think I'd like that very much."

And so as they walked briskly southwest, Dunston began to point out things of interest. They passed a thicket of linden trees and he told her of how the bark could be used to fashion containers and the inner bark produced good string. Spotting a fallen beech just off the path, Dunston led her to the rotting wood and showed her where dark, smooth lumps of fungus grew. He collected some, telling her how the charcoal-like fungus could be used to hold an ember when lighting a fire. He pulled a tuft of straggly lichen from a branch, explaining that it would easily catch fire with the merest of sparks. He plucked leaves from a sorrel and nibbled at them.

"These are good eating at this time of year," he said, passing a handful of the leaves to her.

She sniffed them. They smelt green and fresh.

"Go on," he said. "Try one."

Taking a deep breath, she bit off part of the leaf and chewed. It tasted sharp and sour, but pleasant and refreshing. She smiled.

Every now and then, when tracks joined the path they followed, Dunston paused and checked for sign of the monk and his hunters. But now, instead of silently scanning the ground, he explained to Aedwen what he saw. The depth of a print. The tiny prints of insects, rodents or birds could show the age of the impressions in the earth left by man and horse. There were many details that later she could not remember, but in this way, the long tiring day passed quickly and she had little time to dwell on the evil that had been done to her father and to the people of Cantmael.

During the morning they saw nobody save for some shepherds, glimpsed through a stand of hazel far in the distance on the slope of a hill. But sometime after midday the track they followed joined a larger road that ran north and south. The sky was clear, the day was warm and it seemed that many had decided to take advantage of the fair weather to travel and so in the afternoon, they crossed the path of drovers, shepherds and several individuals walking about their business that took them onto the roads of Wessex. They even passed a waggon that was escorted by four mounted warriors in byrnies of iron. The cart was well appointed, covered with a frame from which hung patterned curtains. Aedwen imagined it must have carried a noble woman, hidden behind the fine drapes. She was desperate to know the identity of the lady who rode within the covered waggon, but Dunston hushed her and pushed her into the long grass and nettles that grew in a tangle on the verge. The nettles stung Aedwen's legs and she rubbed at the rash as they carried on their way.

Dunston grew tense and taciturn with each traveller they passed.

"I don't like it," he grumbled. "Too many people have seen us. We are not a pair to be easily forgotten. And travellers talk."

For a while she did not reply. Her legs itched and she scratched at them, until he plucked a large dock leaf and handed it to her.

"Rub this on where it stings," he said. "It will help."

She did as he said.

He was right, of course. They would be remembered. The young girl accompanied by the hulking brute of a man with a bushy greying beard, a great battle-axe resting on his shoulder. As if he was not memorable enough, the iron head of his axe, embellished with whorls and symbols in silver inlay, certainly drew attention as it glinted in the afternoon sunlight.

"At least there is something good that comes of being on this road," she said with a grin. Her legs were feeling better already.

"And what is that?" he growled.

"We can travel faster."

"And how do you propose we do that?" he said, frowning. "Unless I'm not mistaken, our legs have not grown since this morning. And I do not believe either of us are ready to run."

She chuckled.

"No, that is true. But we can still move more quickly."

"How?"

"By not needing to stop to look for sign," she said. And then, when she saw the blank look on his face, she continued: "We can ask the people on the road whether they have seen a group of riders. They may even have seen Ithamar, if they have been travelling for a few days."

For a moment, Dunston did not reply and then he smirked, his smile twisted behind his beard.

"I am glad you have been paying attention to my teaching," he said.

"But you have been telling me about tracks, fungus and eating leaves."

"Yes, that is so. But the most important lesson of all was the first one I taught you this morning. That you can always learn new ways of doing things, if you listen and pay attention to what is around you."

Twenty-One

During the rest of that long warm day, they did as Aedwen had suggested and spoke to some of the travellers they passed. One man, who was leading a heavily laden cart drawn by two oxen, seemed pleased at the chance to stop and talk. He was accompanied by two thickset men who looked like brothers, or maybe cousins. They both had the same small piggy eyes and massive shoulders almost as broad as the oxen. Each of them carried a stout cudgel and Dunston thought they would be deterrent enough against all but the most determined brigands. When the carter halted, the two guards slumped into the grass at the edge of the path. They said nothing, but their gaze did not waver from Aedwen and Dunston.

The carter offered Dunston a drink of ale from a costrel which he took from the bed of the cart. He didn't offer any to his escorts, who just glowered from the shade of the verge. It was good ale, fresh and cool and despite his reservations about being seen on the road, Dunston found he trusted the carter implicitly. Unlike the cudgel-bearing louts, the man had an open face, a quick smile and guileless eyes.

He was taking a load of salt and smoked fish to Bathum and had been on the road for two days already. When asked whether he'd seen a large group of riders he answered immediately.

"I saw the king himself riding out to hunt with his nobles. A fine sight it was, all those horses trotting high-hoofed in the sunlight." He looked wistful at the memory. "Like something out of a song."

"The king, you say?" Dunston asked. "When was this?"

"That was on the morning I left Exanceaster. The king arrived a week ago with so many hearth warriors and thegns, they must have eaten all the meat in the city by now. Perhaps that's why they went hunting." He laughed.

"Have you seen any other riders more recently? A band of them?"

The carter took back the costrel from Dunston with a nod.

"Oh yes," he said, taking a draught of the ale. "A group of horsemen galloped past and I called out to them. Asked them whither they were headed in such a hurry. I didn't really expect a reply. They looked a rough sort, if you know what I mean. But the last one shouted out to me as he passed. He looked even more vicious than the rest. I'll never forget what he said."

"What was that?"

"He said, 'Just be thankful we're not looking for you.' Then he laughed. It sent a chill right through me, I can tell you. I pity whoever it is they are after. They looked fit to murder someone."

Dunston didn't tell the carter how right he was. Instead he asked him about the men.

"I can't tell you much," he answered, lifting the cap he wore and scratching beneath it at his sweaty hair. "They were driving those horses fast and they were past us in a flash." He thought for a moment and took a swig of ale. "All I can remember really is that they carried spears and I'm sure at least a couple of them had swords. I wondered whether the fyrd had been called, I've heard nothing. Have you?"

Dunston told the man he did not believe that the levies had been called to arms.

"May God be praised," the carter said finally, pushing the stopper into the mouth of his flask. "I was worried that perhaps the heathens had attacked again." The man crossed himself then and the talk of Norsemen had spoilt his good humour. "Well," he said, "Godspeed to you and your granddaughter. I'd best be getting on my way. Come along, you two."

Grumbling, his guards climbed to their feet.

As the red-faced carter goaded his oxen forward once more Dunston called after him.

"Have you seen by chance a monk travelling south on the road?"

"A monk?" the man replied. "No, I can't say that I have. Good day to you both now."

Dunston pondered over the information the carter had given them as they had walked southward.

"Perhaps Ithamar has already reached his destination," Aedwen said.

"Perhaps."

They trudged on through the heat of the afternoon. When they passed settlements and steadings Dunston could see the longing for rest in Aedwen's eyes. But he felt too exposed to stop. It was too dangerous and so they pressed on, hurrying past hamlets and thorpes that Dunston did not recognise. He had seldom travelled this way before and he'd been alone in his forest home for many years.

They had just left a small settlement behind them and Dunston could sense the reproach from Aedwen. The sun was lowering in the sky and by not seeking shelter at the farm, he had consigned them to another night in the forest.

"Where do you think Ithamar is?" Aedwen asked suddenly.

Dunston sighed, wiping sweat from his brow.

"If nobody has seen him on the road, I don't know."

"Can't you track him?" she asked.

He snorted.

"I can read sign better than most," he said. "But I'm not a miracle worker. Ithamar is two days ahead of us and this road is too well-travelled to find tracks. No, unless we find something to lead us to him, all I can think of is to continue following the horsemen." Even as he said the words the idea sounded mad to him. Five armed warriors on horseback. Even if he was able to catch up with them, what then? What good could come of catching this mounted, murderous quarry?

They walked on without speaking. Dunston brooded. This was madness. If only he had never found Lytelman. He could have been sitting back in his hut, resting after a day of forging or hunting, Odin sleeping at his feet. Now Odin was gone and as likely as not he would be dead soon too. He glanced at Aedwen and for a moment, the shape of her nose, the sunlight picking out the delicate sweep of her eyelashes, reminded him of Eawynn when they had first met all those summers ago. She had been not much older than Aedwen he realised with a start. He sighed. God's teeth, he had been young then too. How quickly the years washed by, sweeping away loved ones and youth and leaving only fading memories.

He shook his head and cursed silently at his own foolishness. Not because of the course they now followed, but at his dwelling on the past and bemoaning his decisions. There was no changing the past, just as there was no holding back the water in a raging river.

The path sloped down into a shaded vale. Alders encroached on the road to either side and it seemed as though a mist hung in the still air. There was nobody on the road now. Nobody apart from the two of them. Anyone with any sense had already sought shelter for the night or had made camp, he thought, with a rueful smile. They should get off the road and find a place to make a fire. He looked up at the sky and the shreds of cloud that floated high, tinged with the pink of sunset. It looked to be a clear night, it would be cold, but they had brought blankets and cloaks from Beornmod's hall, so they should be comfortable enough.

They entered the shadows beneath the alders and Dunston wondered about the mist. Could it be so cold down here? Perhaps there was a stream running through the woodland. Mist often formed over cool water, though not on sunny afternoons. He frowned and sniffed the air.

His mouth slowly stretched into a grin. By the rood and all the saints, he must be tired not to have realised what it was that he saw in the valley.

"What is it?" asked Aedwen.

"If my nose does not deceive me, we will not be cold this night and we will not camp alone."

Aedwen lifted her head and scented the hazy air.

"Smoke? Do you think it is safe for us to camp with other travellers?"

"That is smoke," he replied, with a broad smile. "But not from a traveller's campfire. Now, there should be a path somewhere into the wood. Come. Quickly, before it is too dark."

He led her on at a faster pace. The gloom under the trees grew thicker, as did the haze of smoke. It drifted across the road in a fug.

"Here," Dunston said at last, peering down at the ground and looking at the tracks in the mud where a path led off from the road into the shadows of the forest. He stood, with a slight frown on his face. Could that print of a soft leather shoe be from the same wearer as the track he had seen at Cantmael? Possibly. But it was getting dark and he could not be sure. He stepped over the muddy patch.

"Careful," he said, "don't step there."

"Where are we going?" asked Aedwen.

"Quiet now," he said, holding a finger to his lips. He held DeaÞangenga before him, just in case he was wrong. "Stay behind me," he whispered. "And with luck we will soon enough have warmth and company for the night."

He saw her questioning look in the gathering dark, but chose to say no more. He turned and walked silently into the woods, towards the source of the billowing smoke that now stung their eyes, and filled their throats.

Twenty-Two

Aedwen followed Dunston further into the forest. The boles of the trees loomed in the smoke-hazed darkness like giants. She hardly dared to breathe as she walked behind the old man. He moved without a sound, like a wraith flitting through mist. Despite her youth and slender form, she felt clumsy. With each step she snapped a branch or her cloak snagged on a bramble.

It was dark under the trees, and a feeling of dread seeped into her as they crept stealthily away from the road. If only at that last steading they'd passed they had asked the goodwife for some food and a warm place to sleep for the night. The portly woman had been friendly and had waved to Aedwen as they passed. She had been taking in the clothes she had left to dry on the bushes outside her neat, thatched house. Aedwen thought they could have been cosy by her hearth for the night. But no, Dunston had made them carry on and now it was dusk and they were deep in the forest, surrounded by smoke. She had no idea where it came from. For a moment, she thought of a great wyrm, coiled and waiting in a forest glade, breathing out acrid clouds of smoke, its feral eyes gleaming in the darkness as it lay in wait for its prey to come to him, lured from the road with promises of warmth and shelter.

A sound came to her then. A strange sound, that for a time, she could not fathom. A lilting warble accompanied by a rumbling thrum. The noise rose and fell and seemed to echo all about them, as if it emanated from the very smoke itself.

Dunston had almost been swallowed up by the haze and the gloom and with a start she realised she had stopped walking. Quickly, she sped after him, uncaring now whether she made a noise or not. The thought of being alone and lost in this smoky darkness, surrounded by the eerie music, filled her with terror.

Music.

Yes, that is what it was. She suddenly understood the sounds, and all at once she could hear more than one voice. And there were words too. Words of love and loss. She caught up with Dunston. He turned to her with a grin.

"Listen," he whispered.

They stood still and silent there in the forest and listened to the song. She did not recognise the melody, but it was achingly beautiful, as if the forest itself was singing of its loneliness. There were deep, bass tones, and higher counterpoints, but against it all, there was the throb of a chanted song of lovers, destined to be ever apart and only united in death.

When the singing ended, she found her face was wet with tears. Dunston cuffed at his cheeks, and placed a hand on her shoulder, leading her forward. It was almost full dark now, but she fancied she could make out a glow between the trees ahead.

"Hail, the camp," said Dunston in a low voice.

After a brief moment of silence, a voice came to them.

"Who goes there?"

"Friends," replied Dunston. "Just me and my grand-daughter." Aedwen glanced at him, but he did not return her gaze. "We heard your singing. One of my favourites. I have always loved the lay of Eowa and Cyneburg. We seek shelter for the night."

"Not many know our songs or would spend time with us," replied the voice. "What is your name?"

"My name is Dunston, son of Wilnoth."

Whispers in the darkness.

"Approach," said the voice.

They walked towards the glow. As they stepped from the forest path into a wide, open glade, Aedwen saw that the light came from a small fire, upon which hung a metal pot from a wooden tripod. The fire was much too small to have created all this smoke. Around the fire were several figures. Beyond them were five huge shadowy mounds and for a fleeting instant she thought again of the great coiled dragon lurking, awaiting its prey. Perhaps the creatures around the fire were the dragon's servants. Nihtgengas, night-walkers, for surely they could not be men.

They were black-garbed and black-skinned. Their eyes and teeth flashed bright in the dark. She shuddered, a terrible fear gripping her. What were these beasts? Why had Dunston brought her here? Was he in league with these goblins of the forest?

Dunston stepped forward and offered his hand to the nearest of the dark-skinned creatures, who was standing before the fire. His teeth showed as he smiled and gripped Dunston's forearm in the warrior grip.

The firelight fell on the goblin's smiling features and, in an instant, she felt her face flush at her own stupidity. These were no monsters. They were but men, blackened and grimed with soot and ash. The glade was thick with smoke that oozed from the mounds and she finally understood. These men were charcoal burners, outcasts from the world. They lived together, in their hot, smoke-filled world, tending the charcoal piles. Charcoal burners had the reputation of being devils, stinking of smoke and living surrounded by fire, as if in their own personal hell on earth. She had never seen any charcoal men before, and she felt trepidation at being here at night, surrounded by them.

But Dunston was smiling and slapping the man on the back.

"You are well come to our glade," the black-smeared man was saying. "We have cheese and we have ham."

"Smoked!" shouted one of the others, receiving a roar of laughter from all of the men. Aedwen could not believe this was the first time they had made this jest, but they laughed uproariously and she could not help but chuckle too, feeling the tension draining from her.

"We don't get many visitors here," the leader of the charcoal burners continued, "and then we have two in as many days. If this continues, we will have to send someone in search of more food."

"Or start charging for the pleasure of sleeping here!" shouted the jester, again receiving riotous guffaws in response.

"We share our camp and our food freely, Dearlaf," said the leader, with a scowl of reproach. "Come, sit with us, and tell us your tale. We are ever hungry for tidings of the world."

"We thank you," said Dunston. "We carry a small amount of provender and will gladly share what we have. Tidings too."

The men shuffled apart, making space for them by the fire and Aedwen sat beside Dunston. Grubby hands passed them food and a cup was thrust into her grasp. She sniffed at the liquid, but could smell nothing over the all-pervading stench of charcoal smoke. She drank and found it to be ale, bitter, and with an unsurprisingly smoky flavour. It was good.

After they had eaten some of the offered food, Dunston said, "You said you had a visitor a couple of days ago? That wouldn't have been a monk, by any chance, would it?"

The leader of the charcoal burners, whose name was Smoca, gaped at Dunston, eyes wide and bright.

"How did you know? And how is it you know of our songs and are unafraid to sit, eat and drink with us?"

Smoca was wary now, as though he was afraid he had allowed a predator into a flock of sheep.

Dunston swallowed a mouthful of the smoked cheese. Aedwen had thought the charcoal man to be jesting about all the food being smoked, but it seemed he had been in earnest.

"Those are two different questions," Dunston said, after he had washed the food down with a mouthful of ale. "In answer to the second question, I have often spent time with the charcoal men in Sealhwudu, where I live to the north of here. They have ever been kind and have never seemed like devils to me." He gave a wry smile. "I know many consider you less than them, as you are blackened by your fires, but I know that beneath the soot you are but men. And I need what you produce for my work."

"You are a smith?"

"I have a forge, yes. I produce blades and tools for the folk around Briuuetone."

Smoca nodded at Dunston's rune-decorated axe, where it rested on the earth by his right hand. The firelight glimmered on the silver threads that ran through its head.

"Your work?" he asked.

"Alas, no," replied Dunston. "I took her from the dead hand of a Norse warrior."

"So you are a warrior, as well as a smith?"

"I was, once."

"What do the carvings mean?" Smoca asked, gazing in wonder at the intricate runes and sigils on the haft.

Dunston shrugged.

"I do not know and I didn't think to ask the original owner before I sent him on his way." He lifted the axe and Smoca tensed. Dunston smiled and patted the weapon. "I cannot read the runes, but I named this beauty, DeaÞangenga."

Smoca swallowed. His eyes never left the blade as Dunston turned it to catch the flickering light.

"An apt name," the charcoal burner said. "I am sure death never walks far from that axe."

One of the other charcoal burners, a cadaverous man with a bald head and skin as wrinkled and tough-looking as leather, leaned forward, peering at Dunston through the dancing flames of the fire.

"Are you *the* Dunston? The one they called 'The Bold'?"

"I have been called that," Dunston replied, with a sigh. "Long ago."

"You don't look so bold now," said one of the other men. He was much stockier than the rest, and younger. He was the loud one who seemed always quick to jest. This time none of the men laughed.

But Dunston let out a bark of laughter.

"No, I don't suppose I do," he said. "If I am honest, I am not sure I ever truly warranted the name. But once a name is given to you, it often sticks and is impossible to shake off."

"How did you come by it?" the jester asked.

"Ah, that is a long story. Perhaps I will tell it later."

The young charcoal burner looked set to press Dunston for an answer, but the old man glowered at him, his eyes shining from beneath his heavy brows and the man clamped his mouth shut.

For an awkward moment, they all stared into the fire. One of the men leaned forward and added a log to the embers. Another coughed. Out in the forest, a vixen shrieked.

"You knew our song. You must have spent a lot of time with our kind to hear them sing."

"Yes, I have spent many nights over the years with them. I consider them my friends." He fell silent and took another sip of ale. Aedwen thought he would offer no more about his time with the charcoal burners when he said in a quiet voice, "I owe them much. They gave me my best friend."

"Your best friend is one of us?" asked Smoca.

"No," replied Dunston, offering the man a sad smile. "He is – no – was, a hound. I called him Odin." A couple of the men crossed themselves and Aedwen thought it strange that people thought of these men as heathen devils.

"Odin?"

"He only had one eye, you see. Like the god of the Norsemen. He was the runt of a litter, a tiny thing. Somehow he had scratched one of his eyes and it had grown putrid, full of pus. His mother had left him to die. And he would have done, had it not been for the charcoal men. They nursed him and tended to his eye. One of them walked for a day to my hut to ask for milk from my goat." He smiled at the memory. "By God, we all loved that pup. We fed him milk from the corner of a cloth dipped in the fresh milk. He was so small, we never thought he would live, but there was something about him, a look in his good eye. We just refused to let him die. And in a few days he began to put on weight and grow strong. When I eventually made my way back home, he followed me." Dunston held out his cup and one of the men filled it with ale. "I hadn't known it, but I was lonely, and Odin made a wonderful companion. He grew strong and spirited. A great hunter and a faithful friend."

Dunston fell silent, gazing into the flames as he drank from his cup.

"He sounds like a worthy companion for Dunston the Bold," said the jester, his tone now reverential.

Aedwen thought of the rangy one-eyed hound, and could scarcely believe he had once been a sickly puppy. Looking at the taciturn, gruff old man who had led her southward these last days, she also found it difficult to imagine him tending to a defenceless animal. And yet, had he not done the same with her? Like Odin, she had been alone and in need of succour. It seemed that Dunston, beneath his hard shell, would not turn away from a lost orphan.

"He was the best of dogs," she blurted out, surprised that she had spoken. The black faces of the gathered men turned to her. "He tried to protect me, but was cut down by a bad man."

"Which brings me to the answer to your other question," said Dunston, not waiting for a response to Aedwen's comment.

"The monk who stayed with us killed your dog?" asked Smoca.

"No, but we believe he is being pursued by the same men who struck down Odin."

"Why?"

"He has information that they seek."

"What information."

"We do not know."

"And you are looking for him too?"

"We are. This girl's father was slain in order to keep secret what this monk knows. They tortured and killed the inhabitants of Beornmod's steading to find out where her father had learnt of the tidings that got him killed." Smoca was clearly shocked by these tidings of murder. His mouth hung agape for a moment. He seemed poised to ask something, but Dunston did not pause. "They found that the monk, Ithamar, carried a message." He held up his hand to halt the query on Smoca's lips. "We do not know to whom, or what the message says, but we are sure they mean to hunt him and slay him. We hope to find him first, if we are able."

Smoca drew in a deep breath and pondered Dunston's words for a long time. A log popped in the fire. The vixen called again in the night. Aedwen tried to hear Dunston's words as they would sound to these men. It was hard to make sense of what had happened. Would they believe him? There were so many uncertainties in his story. And yet he spoke with conviction.

"How did you know the monk had sheltered with us?" Smoca said at last.

"I saw the print of his shoe on the path that led from the road."

Smoca nodded.

"A smith, a warrior and a woodsman," he said, raising his eyebrows. "And you say these killers are on his trail? How far ahead of you are they? We have seen nobody else since Ithamar came to us."

"We are a day behind them, but we are on foot, they have mounts." Dunston thought for a moment, running his thick fingers over his beard. "If Ithamar was here, and you have not seen his pursuers, all I can think is that they missed his tracks turning off the road. It was only by chance that I noticed the print of his foot, and from horseback, it would be easy to miss the path to your encampment."

Smoca nodded thoughtfully.

"Ithamar was scared of being seen on the road, busy as it is. We just thought it was because he travelled alone and was fearful of brigands and robbers. There are wolf-heads that will even stoop to attacking a man of the cloth."

"When a man has nothing to lose, he is as dangerous as a savage animal," said Dunston, his face grim. Aedwen wondered if he was referring to himself or to the brigands who preyed on travellers.

Something in Dunston's tone made Smoca hesitate.

"How do we know you do not mean the monk harm?" he said. "Perhaps he was running from you. He was good to us. Puttoc had a carbuncle and Ithamar lanced it for him and prayed over him. He prayed with all of us." He squinted at Dunston, trying to weigh him up.

"I can offer you no more than my word that we mean him no harm," Dunston said. "But the word of Dunston the Bold has never been doubted before."

Smoca met his gaze for several heartbeats, before finally nodding.

"Anyone who knows the song of Eowa and Cyneburg and breaks bread with charcoalers cannot be too bad. If you are right about the riders that hunt for Ithamar, and they have lost his trail on the road, they must have ridden for Exanceaster."

"Yes," said Dunston. "That seems most likely."

"But," said Smoca, with a glimmer in his eyes, "we know that he was not headed towards Exanceaster."

Dunston leaned forward eagerly.

"Where was he going?" he asked.

"He was making his way to Tantun."

"But this road leads to Exanceaster."

"That it surely does," said Smoca with a grin. "But we set him right. We put him on a path that leads through the woods. It joins a road to Tantun not far from here. If he has walked fast, he might be there already."

"Do you know why he was heading for Tantun?"

"As a matter of fact, I do. He said he wished to see the priest there. Come to think of it, he said he had a message for him."

Aedwen wondered whether the Blessed Virgin had heard her prayers. To bring them to this glade and now to be put on the trail of the monk, the Mother of Christ must be smiling upon them.

"Will you show us the path to Tantun?" asked Dunston.

"In the morning, I will take you there myself," said Smoca. "But first, rest. You look like you could use the sleep. One of us is awake all the night watching that the mounds burn well. No harm will befall you."

Dunston gave the man his thanks, and rolled up in his cloak and a blanket beside the fire and was soon snoring.

Aedwen lay down beside him and stared into the coruscating embers. Dunston seemed to trust these soot-smeared men, but she could not shake the lingering terror that the forest was the home of a sleeping dragon, the charcoal men its servants and she and Dunston its prey.

For a long while she fought against sleep, despite the tiredness of her limbs and mind. A light breeze whispered through the forest. A night bird screeched in the distance. And then, all around her, the black-faced men began to sing again, softly this time, their voices calming and achingly beautiful in the smoke-filled darkness. The melody washed over her, soothing her, allaying her fears, and soon, her eyelids drooped and closed.

Twenty-Three

Dunston awoke with the first lightening of the sky. The air of the clearing was hazed with the smoke that oozed and drifted from the mounds. Beside him, Aedwen slept, her childlike face soft and peaceful.

Pushing himself to his feet, he stretched. His back popped like a pine cone thrown onto a fire and his knee was stiff as he straightened it. But he felt rested and when Smoca offered him a cup of water, he took it gratefully with a muttered word of thanks. He swilled some of the cool liquid around his mouth and spat into the long grass that grew at the edge of the clearing. His mouth was dry and tasted of ash and woodsmoke. The flavour reminded him acutely of the time he had spent with the charcoal burners near his home when Odin had been a tiny pup. He looked down at Aedwen, half-expecting to see the hound stretched out beside her. He snorted at his foolish sentimentality.

The girl stirred and looked up at him with a smile. Dunston grunted and walked away from the charcoal mounds to piss.

He was glad his instinct about the charcoal men had proven to be accurate. The truth was he had been too tired to stay awake. They had been on the run now for three days and when they had sat beside the fire the night before he had been exhausted.

But now he felt rested and, despite the aches of his ageing body, he was ready to recommence the hunt. He allowed himself a small moment of hope. It appeared they had stumbled upon Ithamar's path, while the horsemen had carried on towards Exanceaster. With some luck, it was possible they might even find the monk before the hunters did. Perhaps then, they would be able to discover once and for all, why so many people had been killed. What could be so valuable?

He wondered what they would do if they found the monk, but then dismissed the idea. There was no point in thinking so far ahead. First they must find the man, and then they could decide on their next move.

They ate a few mouthfuls of fresh oatcakes that had been cooked on a griddle by the campfire. Like all the food the charcoal men gave them, these too tasted of smoke, but they were warm and wholesome.

Aedwen walked about the clearing, studying the charcoal piles and even asking the men about their work. She seemed much more animated than the previous night. There was colour in her cheeks and her eyes were bright. Dunston was pleased.

He picked up his scant belongings, calling out to her to do the same.

Smoca was waiting to lead them to the path that Ithamar had taken. Dunston thanked all the men for their hospitality and promised he would return one day, if he could, in better times. The charcoal burners nodded back at them, faces dark and serious, as they followed Smoca out of the smoke-thick camp.

He led them through dense forest, past hazel, ash and beech. The foliage was so snarled and the path so infrequently travelled that Dunston did not believe he would have found it on his own. But after a time, he began to notice signs of Ithamar's passing. Broken twigs, a scratch on the bark of a wych-elm, a print in the soft loam of a hollow were rainwater had puddled. He recognised the shape and weight of the tread and paused a moment to point out the sign to Aedwen.

She was a good student and he'd discovered that he enjoyed imparting his knowledge to her. He recalled words that his grandfather and father had spoken to him and he heard his own voice echoing theirs all these years later. It was as if they talked through him and he wondered whether their spirits were somehow present in this forest, in the dappled shade beneath the canopy of linden and oak.

They picked their way along the overgrown path until quite suddenly, as Smoca led them past a dense tangled mass of brambles, they came out onto a more clearly defined path. It was by no means a main thoroughfare. The trees and shrubs that lined its verges were packed close and grew tall and overhanging in places. The ground was bare earth. Dotted along the track were knotted roots that, along with the low branches of some of the trees that encroached on the path, would make it difficult for anyone attempting to travel the path on horseback.

"So this leads all the way to Tantun?" he asked, signalling to their left, westward.

"It comes out onto the road from Exanceaster," replied Smoca. "You'll be able to see Tantun's church tower from there."

"How far?"

Smoca thought for a moment.

"The best part of two days walking," he said, gazing up at the clear blue sky through the gaps in the boughs that stretched over the track. "But the weather looks set to hold fair. You two take care."

"We will," Dunston replied, clapping the man on the shoulder. "And thank you."

Smoca nodded in acknowledgement, but did not reply. He turned and made his way back into the thicket, disappearing quickly from view. For a moment, they listened to him retreating through the woodland, and then they were alone once more, the only sounds the wind rustling through the leaves and the twitter of the birds.

Dunston dropped to one knee and was pleased when Aedwen did the same without comment. Together they surveyed the earth of the track.

"There," said Aedwen, pointing to a small indentation in a soft, shadowed portion of the path. "Is that Ithamar's tread?"

Dunston moved closer with a grunt as his knee made an audible cracking sound. He peered at the soil for a moment.

"Good," he said, forcing himself to smile for the girl's benefit, despite his misgivings about their quest. "You have a good eye. It is as Smoca told us. Ithamar passed this way a couple of days ago."

They set out westward, pausing only occasionally when one of them noted a print of interest in the earth. Aedwen was growing in confidence and had a keen eye for the details that most people would miss. When they stopped at a stream to refill their skins, she found the tracks and spoor of deer and boar.

"Are they fresh?" she asked, taking a sip of water. The day was warm, even under the shade of the trees and Dunston could feel sweat trickling down his back. He wiped his forehead with the back of his hand.

"Three deer and a family of boar all stopped to drink here this morning," he said.

Aedwen grinned, clearly pleased with herself. He returned her smile. He remembered how excited he had been when he had first begun to understand the sign left by the forest's animal denizens.

A little later, Aedwen called him over to inspect another set of prints in the mud.

"Are these from a dog?" she asked. There was a catch in her voice and he knew she was thinking of Odin. He was touched by her tenderness. Placing a hand on her shoulder, he glanced at the marks in the earth.

"No," he said, straightening his back, "these are not from any dog."

"What are they then?"

"These are from the paws of wolves." He saw her eyes widen. "Don't be afraid," he said. "They will not bother us." But he thought of the deer and the boar that roamed the forest, and pictured the pack of wolves that stalked them. And his mind turned to the men who pursued Ithamar. They were also after him and the girl and now those killers were behind them. As they walked on through the dappled light of that clammy afternoon, Dunston could not shake the feeling that they had become prey to a hunting pack of wolves that slathered and bayed at their heels.

They saw no other people throughout that long day, and it was plain from his footprints that Ithamar had continued following the path that Smoca had set him upon. They found an area of flattened grass, some crumbs of dark bread and a thin rind from a slice of cheese, where the monk had sat and eaten.

They were making good progress and Dunston could imagine the monk walking the path before them at a more leisurely pace. His confidence grew that they might be able to close with him even before he reached Tantun.

And then, as they were passing a huge oak with a twisted trunk, Dunston held up a hand for Aedwen to halt.

"What?" she asked. He hushed her with a sharp hiss and a cutting gesture with his hand.

The hair on the back of his neck prickled. What had unnerved him? He could hear nothing untoward. He sniffed the air. It was rich with leaf mould and loam, but there was no hint of smoke. He knew not what had unsettled him, but Dunston had lived for too long in the forest not to pay heed to his intuition. Grabbing Aedwen by the arm, he pulled her away from the track and dragged her behind the massive, gnarled bole of the oak.

"What is it?" she hissed.

He did not reply, but held a finger to his lips.

He strained to hear anything out of the ordinary. The murmur of the wind, high in the leafy canopy. The chatter of magpies someway off. Then the sudden, panicked flapping of a flock of wood pigeons, flying up from their roosts into the cloud-flecked sky.

A heartbeat later, the first of the horsemen rounded the corner on the path. Dunston pushed Aedwen against the rough bark of the oak. He did not risk looking, instead he listened carefully. They came from the east and were leading their horses.

"Are you sure this is the way?" one said, his voice tired and irritable.

"Do you really think he would have lied to me?" answered another, tone harsh, an edge of cruel laughter tinging his words.

The first man did not answer. Dunston counted the horses passing until five horsemen had led their mounts past the oak. Dunston stared into Aedwen's eyes and saw terror there. He could hear his blood rushing in his ears and his right hand gripped DeaÞangenga's haft so tightly that his knuckles ached.

Off to the west, the lead rider called out.

"The path opens out here. We can ride for a while."

Sounds of men climbing into saddles. The creak of leather and the jingle of harness. Then the thrum of hoof beats on the soft earth of the track, as the men cantered into the west towards the lowering sun that slanted through the limbs of the forest.

Twenty-Four

Aedwen could not be certain, but she thought she recognised the voice of one of the horsemen as that of Raegnold, the tall man who had taken her to Gytha's house. The man who had stabbed Odin and then attacked them as they were escaping from Briuuetone.

His voice was muffled and muted, the injury he'd suffered at Dunston's hands evidently making speech difficult. But the sound of his voice had filled her with dread, bringing back the terrible sadness she had felt at seeing Dunston's dog hurt, the bleak terror of witnessing Dunston, the man who had led her safely from the forest, locked up. And, even though she had not heard Raegnold's voice before that evening in Briuuetone, somehow, the sound of it sent her mind reeling back to that morning in the forest when she had lost her father. When she had sprinted blindly into the woods, fleeing from his attackers and his screams.

Perhaps, she wondered, as Dunston led her back to the path, she had heard his voice amongst her father's screams for mercy. Maybe there was something in his tone that her memory was able to latch on to. Whether she had heard him or not all those days ago, there was no doubt now in her mind that he had been there when her father was killed. Her rage at the thought threatened to consume her. Her fear of the man and the rest of Hunfrith's men turned her stomach. Oh, that she were a man! That she could take up a weapon and strike down these monsters who had caused so much misery.

Looking down at the earth, she could easily make out the five sets of horse's hooves and the heavy, booted feet of the five riders who had been walking beside their steeds. Dunston touched her arm and she flinched.

"They are gone," he said. "They are not aware we are on their trail. They are solely focused on Ithamar."

"What will…" she had been about to ask what they would do to him when they caught up with the monk, but bit back the question. It was foolish. She knew all too well what lay in store for him if the horsemen ran him to ground. "What are we to do?" she asked instead.

"They are ahead of us now, so we must be wary. But they are travelling quickly, and I doubt they will suspect anyone is following them. Perhaps in their haste they will miss Ithamar. Or maybe he has already reached the priest and delivered his message. If he has, they will be able to do nothing to prevent it. I say we press on." He lifted his axe so that the sunlight caught its sharp edge. "With caution."

Aedwen took a slow calming breath and nodded. Her hands were shaking, but she grasped the staff Dunston had given her and set off in the wake of the riders.

They walked on in silence with none of the relaxed companionship they had enjoyed earlier that day. They were wary now, uninterested in the tracks of animals. All they cared about was that they were on the correct path and that they did not stumble upon Hunfrith's men.

The sun was low, glaring in sudden flashes from between the trees, when Aedwen saw the track. She might not have noticed it, if not for the angle of the sunlight. All that afternoon they had followed the fresh, deep prints of the horses, and there had been no other sign to follow. Any impression Ithamar's light tread might have made in the earth was trampled and obliterated by the passing of the five horsemen.

But just as they reached the top of a steep incline, where a lightning-shattered elm stood, she saw a strange shadow in the corner of her vision.

"Dunston," she whispered, still afraid to speak out loud, lest the horsemen might hear. She knew it was foolish, as they were surely far away by now, but fear had gripped her since the men had passed them. The old man halted and returned to her. "Is that Ithamar's print?" she asked, pointing at the slightest of marks in the mud.

Dunston squinted at the ground and then whistled quietly.

"You will be a better tracker than I soon enough," he said with a twisted smile. "The lowness of the sun has cast a shadow in it. I doubt either one of us would have noticed this at any other time." She wondered at that, and thought fleetingly again about the Blessed Virgin and her prayers.

"Look there," Dunston said, pointing at something on the elm. He plucked at the splintered trunk and showed her a thin thread. She took it and held it up to the light. Wool. And it was dark, like a monk's habit.

"It looks as though our friend left the path here," Dunston said, the thrill of the chase colouring his tone with excitement. "Let us see what he was about."

They followed the monk's tracks to a clearing some way from the path, but still within sight of the lightning-felled tree. Away from the churned mud of the track it was much easier to see where Ithamar had been. The snakeweed that grew thick on the floor of the glade had been crushed by his feet. Most of the leaves had sprung back, but his path was still clear to Aedwen, now that she had trained her eyes to look for any sign of disturbance on the ground.

Dunston cast about the clearing.

"Look, here," he said. "Ithamar did not leave this glade and go further into the forest. He retraced his steps back to the path."

Aedwen saw the tracks that Dunston was pointing out. She nodded, as she gazed about the clearing absently, unsure what it was she was looking for.

"Could he have come here to… you know?" she asked.

"To take a piss?" asked Dunston. "Or a shit?"

"Yes," she said, feeling her cheeks grow hot.

Dunston circled the clearing, sniffing and scrutinising the ground all around.

"There is no evidence he did anything here apart from walk about. And then go back to the track." He frowned, again moving about the clearing until he stood before a tree. There was nothing remarkable about it, as far as Aedwen could tell, and yet Dunston was staring at it.

"What is it?" she asked.

"An oak," Dunston replied, with a smirk, and despite herself, Aedwen laughed. Some of the tension ebbed from her. "He stopped here for a time," Dunston said.

She looked down at the ground, but she could not decipher the slight markings there that told Dunston that Ithamar had paused by this tree. And yet something did call out to her, snagging on her sight the way the unusual shadow had back at the path. Stooping down, she stared at the ground where the oak's roots rose from the earth. There was a large stone there, lichen-covered and almost buried in the loam. But some of the lichen had been scratched from its surface. The bright scrape of bare stone is what had caught her attention.

Bending down, she placed her fingers under the edges of the stone and tugged. It was heavy, but it came away from the ground easily. Much more easily than it should have, if it had not been prised from the earth recently.

Aedwen set aside the stone and Dunston dipped his hand into the insect-crawling space where the rock had been. He stood, holding something in his hands and turned to Aedwen.

"What is it?" she asked.

He showed her. It was a rolled up piece of thin calf's leather. The material had been scraped and stretched until it was smooth and thin enough to be written upon. It was tied up with a cord. Dunston untied it, letting the vellum fall open, exposing line after line of densely crabbed writing, scratched into the skin with the nib of a quill.

"What does it say?" asked Aedwen. The priest back in Langtun had taught her the letters that spelt out her name, but that was the sum of her knowledge of writing and reading.

Dunston looked back at her, bemused.

"I know not, child," he said. "I cannot read. I was a warrior in my youth, not a clergyman."

For a moment, they were both silent, gazing at one another. And then, despite the gravity of their situation and the blood-soaked journey they had travelled, they began to laugh. Deep belly-shaking guffaws racked Dunston and he bent over, resting his palms on his knees as he struggled for breath. Aedwen's eyes streamed with tears of mirth and she too found herself gasping for air, such was her merriment.

When at last, their laughter subsided, Dunston wiped his face with his hands.

"Well," he said, "whatever is written here, I suppose this must be the message that has got so many people killed."

His words were sobering and Aedwen stared at the sheet of vellum and wondered what on earth the words etched there might say.

But before she could reply to Dunston, a new sound came to them on the late afternoon breeze. All of their good humour was leached from them by the noise. It was a chilling sound that she had heard before. She had hoped never to hear its like again.

From the west, through the snarled undergrowth and moss-clad trunks of linden and oak, came the anguished, agonised wails of a man being tortured.

Twenty-Five

Dunston's breath rasped in his throat. Crouching behind the broad bole of an ancient oak, he tried to breathe silently, but was all too aware of his wheezing panting.

A howling scream. Loud. Harsh. Terrible. The forest was still all around them, as if it had been shocked into silence by the poor monk's pained cries.

Gruff laughter followed the piteous wail. Voices, but the words were muffled by distance and the woodland.

Dunston signalled for Aedwen to join him in the lee of the oak. Pale-faced and wide-eyed, she hunkered down beside him. She was trembling, but her mouth was a thin line, jaw set. She was not out of breath.

With a start, Dunston understood that his own laboured breathing was not from exertion, but from the horror of what he was hearing. The horrific sounds of the dying man's last moments conjured up dark memories. Often the faces of fallen enemies would come to him in his dreams. At such times, he would stoke up the fire in his hut until the flames burnt away the darkness. He would gulp down strong mead until at last he could no longer remember the faces of those he had seen die; no longer recall their screams and pleas for mercy.

But here, there was no escape from the cacophony of Ithamar's agony.

With an effort, Dunston slowed his breathing, taking long, drawn out breaths of the warm loamy air. It tasted verdant and full of the life of the forest.

Someone shouted. This time, the words were clear.

"Where is it?"

A pause. A sob. A mumbled answer. Then, another excruciating scream of pain.

Dunston wished Aedwen and he had not come closer. They should have run into the forest in the opposite direction, away from these murderers. But Aedwen had grasped his hand and stared up at him, eyes brimming with tears and compassion.

"We must help him," she had said.

And so, even though he knew there was nothing they could do for the monk, Dunston had led her through the dense foliage towards the sounds of torture. If only Ithamar had fallen silent in death before they had come so close. Then it would have been an easier matter to lead the girl away. And yet it seemed the man's tormentors had some skill in inflicting pain without causing death. For the monk yet lived, though there was no doubt in Dunston's mind he would join Lytelman, Beornmod and the rest in death as soon as he had given his torturers what they wanted.

The man he assumed was Ithamar screamed, and then groaned a reply. Louder now, more emphatic.

"Hidden!" he said, his voice rising into a shout. "Hidden, you sons of Satan!"

His angry answer was cut off by his renewed screaming, as one of his captors performed some unspeakable act of cruelty on the poor man.

Dunston half rose to his feet, hefting Deaþangenga. By Christ's bones, he could stand this no longer. He would creep to where they were torturing the wretched monk and he would slay them all. He could not bear to hear the man suffer further. Aedwen gazed up at him as he stood. Her eyes were bright, her face expectant.

"Will you rescue him?" she asked.

In the distance, the monk's cries had dwindled to sobs and coughing. Harsh laughter echoed in the forest.

Slowly, Dunston lowered himself back down beside the girl. He placed a hand on her shoulder.

"I cannot," he whispered, fearful that any sound they made might be overheard in the preternaturally silent woodland. She open her mouth to reply and he held up a hand to silence her. "There are too many of them." As he said the words he heard the truth in them. There were five of them and he was but one old man. He might be able to kill a couple of the bastards, three with luck and surprise. If he had been alone, he would have taken his chances. It would not be a bad death to die trying to free an innocent monk from five murderers. It would be a death he would be proud of. Eawynn would have been proud of him too, he thought, despite the oath he had made to her long ago.

"I love that you always seek to defend the weak," she had told him once.

But as he looked at Aedwen's youthful, terrified face, he knew that his path had already been set. He would not rescue the monk. For if he fell in the attempt, what fate then would await Aedwen?

"Who else knew of the message?" came the sudden, furious shout from one of the torturers. "Who knew?"

"Nobody! Only the peddler…" Ithamar's words trailed off and were lost for a time. And then, with vehemence he cried out. "Forgive me, oh Lord, for speaking to the man, for his death is on my hands!"

"We cannot leave him at the mercy of these people," hissed Aedwen. Tears streamed down her face now, but she seemed oblivious to them. "We cannot."

When Dunston made no move to stand, Aedwen started to rise. He gripped her arm and yanked her down to the ground again. He longed to be able to act, to save the poor monk, but it would be folly.

"We must," he whispered. "We should never have come here. But now we know enough. We must take the message to someone able to read it."

Aedwen's expression changed from anguish to anger in a flash. She tried to shake off his grasp, but he was too strong.

"Let me go," she hissed, more loudly now. "We have to do something even if you are too craven!"

Her words stung, but he held her firm and would not allow her to move.

From the distant site of Ithamar's torment there came a strangely calm voice. After a moment, the words became clear.

"*Fæder ure þu þe eart on heofonum; Si þin nama gehalgod…*"

The voice must belong to Ithamar, but gone was his crying wail of pain, instead replaced with a tranquillity Dunston could scarcely believe. And he was reciting the prayer to the Lord. The man must have been incredibly strong of will.

"Stop that!" came a screeching scream and anger. "Answer me. Where is the message? Where have you hidden it?"

But the Lord's Prayer droned on and Ithamar did not miss a word.

"… *to becume þin rice, gewurþe ðin willa, on eorðan swa swa on heofonum.*"

It seemed the monk was done speaking to the men who had cut and tortured him. He had commended his soul to God and would pray until his demise.

Aedwen shuddered in Dunston's grasp. Sobs racked her frame and her face was wet with tears.

"Coward," she cried, her weeping making her voice catch in her throat. "Coward," she repeated and Dunston knew there was nothing he could say that would change her mind.

"Quiet," he hissed, shaking her. "Would you have us both killed too, foolish girl?"

His tone was sharp, and his words cut through her distraught anguish, for she bit back a retort and he could see her forcibly seeking to control her crying.

She stared into his eyes, unspeaking and unblinking, as they both listened to Ithamar's last moments of life.

"... *and forgyf us ure gyltas, swa swa we forgyfað urum gyltendum...*"

Ithamar continued chanting the words of the prayer, exhorting God to forgive him as he would those who did him ill. But before he could complete the prayer, his words were cut off.

"If you will not speak," came the coarse voice of Ithamar's tormentor, "then I will make you sing the song of the blood-eagle. Sing, you bastard. Sing!"

Whatever savagery was being dealt to Ithamar's body became too much for him to bear then, and he let out a moaning, keening squeal of pure agony.

This was a man they had known by name only. Hearing his howling cry cut off in a strangled gasp, Dunston knew they would never know the monk in this life. And yet in a short time of hearing him facing his attackers Dunston knew Ithamar was a brave man. He had been defiant till the end and had died as a true, devout follower of God.

Aedwen gazed up at him, her face contorted with fear, grief, anger. He shook her again, more gently this time.

"We must flee," he said in a hushed murmur, his mouth close to her ear. "We cannot have Ithamar's death be for nought." He touched the vellum that lay in the bag slung over his shoulder. "He gave his life for this message, we must carry it now."

"What can we do?" she said, her voice terribly loud in the stillness of the wood. "These men are monsters."

"Quiet, Aedwen," he whispered. "They might hear you."

Aedwen's eyes widened in sudden, abject terror and she pulled back from his grip, as though she thought he might be about to strike her. For a heartbeat, he was confused. Then he followed her gaze. She was no longer looking at him, but over his shoulder. Dunston's skin prickled as he heard a twig snap behind him.

"Too late," said a deep, husky voice. It held an edge of cruel humour. "One of them has already heard you."

Twenty-Six

Aedwen could not pull her gaze from the man's face. She recognised him as one of those who rode with Hunfrith. He was young, with a wispy beard and cheeks marked with the memory of the pox. But what caught her attention and would not allow her to look away, was the line of dots that ran all the way across his neck, chin, cheek and forehead.

The points were bright, red and glistening in the last light of the sun that filtered through the forest.

Her stomach lurched as she understood what she was seeing. Blood. Ithamar's lifeblood that must have sprayed up in a spatter of droplets as this man and his companions tortured and murdered him.

At last, she cast her eyes down, following the blood-splatter down the man's chest. In his right fist he held a long sword. The blade was clean; polished and deadly. The metal of the blade caught the sunlight. It glimmered with the patterns of a serpent's skin or the ripples of waves on the sea.

He gestured with the blade, twitching it, so that the point lifted.

"Well, old man," he said. "We've been looking for you and the girl for days. You've led us quite a merry dance."

Dunston did not reply. He fixed Aedwen with a steady look and gave the slightest of nods. She saw his hand tighten its grip on his great axe. The weapon was hidden from the swordsman's view.

"Come on, greybeard," the man said, stepping closer. "On your feet."

Without hesitation and with a speed that belied both his age and his bulk, Dunston surged to his feet and spun around in one fluid motion. At the same instant he swung his axe, flinging it at the young man's face. The axe was heavy and sharp and the throw was true. If it had connected it would have surely killed or mortally wounded the man. But the swordsman was fast and stood a few paces distant from Dunston. Moving nimbly to the side, he batted away the spinning axe with the flat of his sword.

But Dunston had never intended for the axe to slay the man. Using the momentum from turning around and standing, he threw himself forward, pulling Beornmod's seax from the scabbard at his waist.

The swordsman had not anticipated the old man's speed or his second attack. He was caught off balance, with his sword pointing to one side. Dunston did not slow his advance. He clattered into the slimmer man, knocking him from his feet. They landed heavily. The man grunted. Dunston made no sound as he plunged the seax into the man's guts. The blade came up bloody, droplets of gore flying from the wound. Again he hammered the seax into the man's stomach.

Aedwen watched on in amazement as Dunston grasped the man's throat in his meaty left hand. Dunston squeezed and the man's eyes bulged. Fighting for air, he struggled against the old man's grasp. In his panic and agony, he dropped his sword and fumbled at Dunston's wrist. It was like watching someone trying to prise the roots of a tree out of frost-hard ground. Dunston's grip was too strong. His fingers squeezed tighter. Two more times he drove the blood-drenched seax into the man's body.

With a juddering sigh, the light fled the man's eyes, and he grew limp. Blood bubbled and pumped from the savage rips in his midriff.

Dunston let out a long breath and he rose to his feet. Blood now flecked his face and stained his beard.

"Come, we must be gone from here," he hissed. "Now."

He retrieved his axe and the man's sword. Tugging off the dead man's belt, Dunston quickly fastened it about his own waist. He sheathed the sword, and spun to Aedwen once more.

She had not moved. She stared at him, eyes wide. She was not breathing. He had killed the man. It was all over so quickly, she could barely take in what she had seen. Her whole body trembled. She felt her gorge rising and feared she would puke.

"Come," he said again. "There is no time to waste." He reached out a hand to pull her to her feet.

She stared at the hand. It was large; thick fingers and callused palms. And it was covered in the brilliant crimson of the man's hot blood. She could not bear the thought of touching it. It would be warm and sticky, she knew. The scent of it was everywhere in the glade now. Metallic and hot on the back of her tongue.

"Come on!" Dunston implored. The sudden sounds of men calling out for their dead companion made Dunston rush forward, reaching for her with his huge hand. "We must flee!"

The sound of the monk's murderers' voices and Dunston's movement broke her moment of inaction. She did not wish to touch his blood-soaked hand, so she pushed herself to her feet.

"Follow me," Dunston said. "We need to be fast and silent."

She nodded, swallowing back her terror and the bile that burnt her throat.

Close by, on the path, the horsemen were approaching.

"Osulf," they called. "Where are you?"

Without waiting for her to reply, Dunston turned and ran southward, away from the path and deeper into the woods. For an instant, Aedwen glanced down at the dead man. Blood pooled in the gashes in his body. His mouth hung open in shocked silence. His unseeing eyes stared upwards into the canopy of the trees.

The men on the path were nearer now, their calls more urgent.

Leaving the bloody corpse of the young man behind her, Aedwen rushed into the forest following Dunston into the failing light.

It would be night soon.

Twenty-Seven

The night was quiet, the forest hushed, wrapped in the night-time cloak of darkness. Dunston was a shadow within the shadows; his footfalls silent on the leaf litter.

Through the trees, a campfire flickered, its light brilliant in the near absolute darkness of the forest. Even without the light to guide him, Dunston would have had no difficulty locating the men. They were whispering, their sibilant hisses strident in the stillness of the night. Despite not being able to make out the words, Dunston could hear the anxiety in their tone. The death of their comrade had unnerved them.

He smiled grimly.

These men had pursued them for some time as the sun went down. They had shouted and hollered, screaming abuse and threats after them as he had dragged Aedwen through bramble-choked gullies and bracken-thick ditches. There had been no time to cover their tracks or to attempt silence, and so he had decided his only option was to make their path impossible for horses, and difficult for men, to follow.

Thorns had scratched and snagged at their clothing. Nettles had stung them. For a time, their hunters had sounded very close behind and Dunston had feared he might need to stand and fight. But night had finally fallen and the forest was plunged into a darkness that reminded him of the depths of the barrow. They had stumbled on for some time, but when they had finally paused for breath, they could no longer hear the men.

Aedwen's face had been pallid, her eyes glistening in the gloom. Her cheeks were streaked with tears. Awkwardly, he had reached for her, meaning to offer her comfort. The girl must have been terrified after what they had heard and witnessing his killing of the man who had found their hiding place. Aedwen had shied away from his touch and Dunston had been shocked at the strength of emotion her reaction had caused in him. He felt powerless in the face of her sorrow. And her judgement.

He recognised the fear and revulsion Aedwen felt at seeing what he was capable of. Eawynn too had been terrified of the man he became when going into battle. Before her passing, he had promised her that he would die a peaceful death in their forest home. She had closed her eyes as he'd gripped her emaciated hand. He knew she worried that when she had gone, he would take up his axe and return to the ranks of the warriors who defended Wessex. She'd been scared that the darkness that brooded within him would engulf him, burying the light that had come from their love for each other. As he'd looked down at the once-beautiful face, Dunston had been filled with an all-encompassing feeling of terror. Perhaps if he swore the oath she wanted from him, promising to leave DeaÞangenga in the chest where he had hidden it, to never fight again, to not become the killer that frightened her so – perhaps then she would recover from the sickness that cruelly ate away the flesh from her bones. And so he had babbled pledges of peace to her, as tears streamed down his cheeks, soaking into his thick beard.

She had died the following morning.

But he had kept his oaths to her. All these long years.

Until now.

When they had recovered from their headlong run through the forest, he had pulled out from his bag a piece of cheese that Smoca had given them and a hunk of the ham they'd taken from Beornmod's hall. They had eaten in silence, each lost in their own troubled thoughts.

Now, with Aedwen secure in the dark sanctuary of the forest, Dunston crept closer towards his enemy's camp, threading his way wraith-like and silent between the ghostly shades of the trees. The men had camped close to the path, and he could make out the silhouettes of their mounts where they had tethered them in a widening of the track.

It had taken him a long time to make his way back here and he hoped that Aedwen would be all right where he had left her. She should be safe, he told himself. She was wrapped in their cloaks and blankets and covered by a layer of bracken. There could be no fire for them that night, but she would be warm enough. He had given her strict instructions not to move from where he had placed her.

He had explained what he planned to do, and all the while she had said nothing. But she had grabbed at his sleeve as he'd made to leave. Her touch had brought him up short.

"Promise me you will return to me," she had said then, her voice small, tremulous.

"I will return," he had said, and a chill had run down his spine. He knew he could not make such a promise. He recalled again his oaths to Eawynn. He would break at least one promise in the darkness that night, it seemed. Why then was he heading out into the night? Would it not be safer for them both to rest and then to press on away from the men who pursued them? He had thought much on this as he had stalked through the night and he had convinced himself that this was a sound course of action. If he could weaken the men further, they would be less of a threat to Aedwen. This is what he told himself, but if he was truthful, he did not believe this was his main reason for seeking out their camp.

What he had heard of Ithamar's last moments of life had filled him with a terrible rage. He thought about Lytelman's mutilated corpse. The man was just a peddler, a man of no consequence, but he had been Aedwen's father and not a bad man from what she had spoken of him. Then Dunston recalled the butchered inhabitants of Cantmael and the tale of rape and murder told by Nothgyth.

Perhaps it was true that to weaken the force that followed them would prove useful, but more than that, Dunston knew that now, despite his words to Aedwen and his promises to Eawynn, he sought revenge for what these men had done. With their acts of savagery they had awoken something in him he had believed long banished, and the realisation filled him with dismay.

He wanted to make them pay.

One of the men coughed and a horse stamped a hoof and snorted. The night air was cool on his cheeks. The flickering firelight and the sounds of the night brought back memories from long ago. For a moment, he could almost have believed he was a young man surrounded by his brother warriors, Guthlaf and the rest. Wulfas Westseaxna, Wolves of Wessex, they had called themselves. Many times they had sneaked up to enemy encampments, as silent as ghosts. He could not count how many men they had slain over the years. Norse, Wéalas, Mercians, Eastseaxna. Wherever their king had sent them, the Wolves would hunt. They had become feared by all of the enemies of Wessex. Some had thought them Nihtgengas, night-walkers, creatures of legend. Others had scoffed at the idea, saying they were but men. But wherever they were mentioned, people would cross themselves, and make the sign to ward off the evil eye, for the Wulfas Westseaxna, just like the hungry wolves in winter, would descend upon their prey and leave only bloody, ripped carcasses behind them.

Dunston drew in a deep breath of the forest air, tasting the smoke and the faint coppery tang of blood, whether from the man he had killed, or from Ithamar, or both, he could not tell.

He was the last of the Wolves now. But this Wolf, grey though its beard might be, still had teeth.

Stealthily moving closer to the fire, careful to avoid making any sound to give himself away, Dunston pushed all thoughts of Aedwen, Eawynn and his past out of his mind. The girl would be safe, and if she was not, worrying about her would do him no good. He took a deep breath, offering a silent prayer for Eawynn's forgiveness. He must not be distracted. He was a wolf stalking its quarry and he sensed that the moment to strike would be upon him soon.

He was very near to the fire now. So close that he could smell the dusty coat of the horses and the leather of the beasts' harness. He stood for a moment, pressed against the trunk of an oak, listening and watching. In his right hand was the familiar weight of DeaÞangenga. He had smeared mud from the bank of a stream over its silver-decorated head. He had rubbed more of the dark muck over his face and into his beard. If anyone had looked in his direction, they would have seen nothing but a shaded tree.

For a long while he stood thus; silently observing the men. Their whispers were loud in the night, but his hearing was not what it once had been and he could not discern their conversations. His right knee was stiff and when he shifted his posture, he was surprised to notice that his right elbow ached. He must have jarred it when stabbing the man, or perhaps when throwing DeaÞangenga. But these pains were as nothing to him. He had once fought with a spear jutting from his shoulder and still managed to take down four foe-men. The aches of old age would not slow him enough to blunt this Wolf's bite. This grey Wolf would still kill.

Three men sat close to the blaze. One threw a branch onto the fire and sparks flew high into the night sky before winking out. The sudden flash of light picked out the shape of the fourth man. He was some way off, outside of the fire's glow. He stood closer to the tethered horses and Dunston assumed he was supposed to be guarding them.

Dunston bared his teeth and, as silent as thought, drifted towards the guard. He propped DeaÞangenga against a wych-elm. And covered the last dozen paces to the unsuspecting man. Dunston was so close that he could smell the man's sweat and the sour stink of ale on his breath. It seemed that this Wolf still knew how to move silently in the night.

Clamping a hand over the man's mouth, Dunston plunged his seax into the small of his back. The steel penetrated the man's kidney and he went rigid in Dunston's grasp. He clung to him tightly. The man struggled as Dunston pulled out the seax, then shuddered when he slid the seax blade effortlessly into the man's throat. After a few moments of trembling, he at last grew limp. Dunston lowered the man to the ground and glanced over at the campfire. The three men still sat there, whispering and chuckling over some jest.

Dunston made his way to the horses. They stamped and blew at his approach. One whinnied. The smell of fresh blood always spooked horses. The element of surprise would soon be lost, so Dunston flitted quickly between the animals, using the bloody seax to slice through the ropes and reins with which they'd been tied to the trees that lined the path.

One of the horses, a large black stallion, tried to bite him, its white teeth snapping close to Dunston's face as he pulled back from it. Regaining his balance, he punched the steed hard on the snout and the animal shied away, whinnying angrily.

"Hey, Eadwig," came a voice from the fire, "what in the name of Christ are you doing?"

There was no time for anything more now. Dunston hurried back towards the wych-elm where he had left DeaÞangenga. As he passed the jittery horses, he prodded them with the sharp tip of his seax. They reared and kicked and the night was filled with their cries of pain and fear. In an instant, the path was a chaos of furious horseflesh.

One mare skittered in a circle, blocking Dunston's way. He slapped it hard on the rump, jabbing it with the seax for good measure, and the animal bounded away, galloping eastwards along the path.

The men from the camp were on their feet now, lending their shouts and calls to the madness that had descended on the small glade. All was confusion and Dunston grinned to himself in the darkness as he snatched up DeaÞangenga from where it lay. He watched for a moment as they tried to calm the horses, shouting insults at the man who had been set the task of watching the beasts.

He listened to them calling to each other in the darkness, as he slid back into the night. He did not worry about making noise now and he hurried away, sure-footed despite the black beneath the forest canopy. He heard their voices raised in fear and alarm as they found their fallen companion, and he grinned despite himself. For too long these men had believed themselves above justice, able to torture and kill as they pleased. And for what? A sheet of vellum that bore Christ knew what message.

Their voices receded and as he made his way unerringly back to where he had left Aedwen, Dunston was unable to suppress the warm feeling that flowed through him. What would Eawynn have thought of his actions? he wondered. She never understood him or the sheer joy and exhilaration that fighting could bring. But she had understood that sometimes the strong must stand up to defend the weak. And in killing one of their pursuers and scattering their horses, he had evened the odds against Aedwen and him.

That was so, but as he retraced his steps through the dense undergrowth of the wood towards the girl, there was one thing that troubled him. And he knew that it was this, more than the breaking of any vow, that would truly have upset Eawynn.

It had felt good to allow the long-sleeping Wolf out of its cage to kill once more.

Twenty-Eight

The forest whispered and murmured around Aedwen in the darkness. From where she lay under the thick blanket of cloaks and bracken she could make out a small patch of sky through the boughs of the great linden tree that spread its limbs above her. The light from the quarter moon silvered the leaves as they waved in the light breeze. Far beyond the tree, in the infinite expanse of the sky, the spray of stars was bright against the deep purple of the night's shroud.

Staring up at the moon, she wondered whether she would see it swallowed up before her eyes, as she had when they had fled from Briuuetone. But its light remained constant and cold in the sky.

An owl hooted far off. Aedwen half-imagined she heard the plaintive call of a wolf on the wind, but perhaps it was just a dog in a farmstead somewhere nearby. She recalled the prints that Dunston had told her belonged to a wolf and shuddered, despite feeling snug in her hiding place.

Something rattled and cracked out in the blackness of the woodland and she started, clutching tightly the small knife Dunston had given her. She shook her head. What use would such a weapon be should a wolf come upon her in the darkness? The thought of slavering jaws, full of drool-dripping sharp teeth filled her with terror.

She tried to push the thoughts away. No wild animal would attack her. No, she thought, it should not be the animals that frightened her. There were worse things in the woods that night.

She had watched in rapt silence as Dunston had daubed mud over his shiny axe and rubbed the mire on his face and beard. She knew he had once been a warrior, and she had watched him fight at Briuuetone, but now she had seen the true nature of the man. He had killed without thought, and then, painting his face so that he seemed more beast than man, he had slunk off into the night to kill again.

The sounds of Ithamar's torture had ripped at her soul, terrified her. After witnessing the aftermath of these men's tortures in Cantmael, she could well imagine what they had been doing to the monk.

When she had finally found the courage to ask Dunston what he meant to do, he had turned to her and she was sure there had been a savage gleam of hunger in his eyes.

"I am going to even the odds," he had said.

He had promised to return, but as she lay there in the darkness, she trembled to think of him coming back for her drenched in blood and stinking of death.

She tried to push such thoughts from her mind. It was unfair of her, she knew. He had shown her nothing but kindness and he was risking his life for her. And yet there had been something in his gaze since he had slain the man that unnerved her.

She awoke, surprised that she had slept at all. She was more shocked to find that the grey tinge of dawn illuminated the clearing. The clouds that drifted high in the sky above the linden were painted pink by the rising sun.

A rustling movement made her reach for her knife.

"Hush, Aedwen," said Dunston. "It is I. Here, drink some water." He handed her a flask. "We must be away from this place."

Gone was the blood and mud from his face and hands. He must have scrubbed himself clean in one of the many streams that trickled through the woods. His kirtle was stained. She chose not to wonder what substance had made the dark marks on the wool.

Shoving into her hand a piece of the hard cheese the charcoal burners had given them, Dunston rose and busied himself picking up their few belongings. She watched him as she chewed on the smoky cheese. He was moving with none of the grace and fluidity she had seen when he had faced their enemy. He grimaced as he bent to pick up his bag, pushing his hands into the small of his back and groaning as he straightened. With the grime and blood removed from his face his skin appeared sallow, his eyes bruised and tired. She could scarcely believe she had been so fearful of this old man.

She swallowed the cheese and drank the water. He turned to her as she sat up and his eyes seemed to glow in the dim light of the dawn. For a heartbeat she could not breathe under the force of that cold glare. She rose, mumbling that she needed to relieve herself. He did not move, merely nodding.

"Hurry," he said, his voice rasping like a blade drawn along a whetstone.

No, she had not imagined the savage fire that had consumed Dunston the night before.

When she returned, she had made up her mind about him. Dunston frightened her, but he had treated her well and she could think of nobody she would rather have at her side as they fled from Hunfrith's murderous men.

"How did you do? In the night?" she asked.

"Well enough," he replied, heading into the dense forest. She could not be certain, but she believed they were heading away from the path that led towards Tantun.

"Did you…" she hesitated. "Did you kill any of them?"

"One more," he answered without pause, as if slaying a man meant nothing to him. "And I dispersed their horses. It should take them a while to be after us. If we keep off the roads and paths I doubt they will find us."

"Did you sleep at all?" she asked.

"I closed my eyes for a few moments. I will sleep when we reach Exanceaster."

She had been right; they were heading south. She felt a flush of pride at keeping her sense of direction despite the rush in the darkness through the trees and foliage.

"Exanceaster?" she said. "Why should we go there?" She had never been to the place, but knew it to be the seat of power of Defnascire.

Dunston paused at the foot of a steep rise, peering upward into the dawn dark. The earth beneath the slope was boggy and clogged with sweet gale. A thin mist hung there, like webs of forgotten dreams. Evidently having made up his mind as to the best way to ascend, Dunston set off up the incline, using the slender trunks of birch saplings to pull himself up.

"Whatever is written on the vellum," he said, his breath ragged from the exertion of the climb, "it is something worth killing for." His foot slipped in the leaf mould and he cursed under his breath, catching hold of a sapling and hauling himself up. When he reached the summit, he turned and reached out his hand to her. She gripped it without hesitation and he pulled her slim form up to him easily.

"What do you mean to do with the message in Exanceaster? Tantun is closer and there would be priests and monks there who could read it."

"That is true, but those bastards know that Ithamar was heading to Tantun, and maybe they will believe we mean to carry it in the same direction. Besides, we must see that it gets into the hands of someone not only able to read, but also to see justice done."

They pushed on through a more sparsely forested area of sallow and elder. Aedwen welcomed the sense of openness, of air between the widely spaced trunks. To her left, the rising sun shone its rays deep under the leafy forest roof. She turned to the east, revelling in the warmth of the day on her face.

"You seek the king's reeve then?" she said.

"No," said Dunston. He let out a sigh and shook his head, as if to clear his thoughts. "I seek the king."

"The king?" she blurted out, unable to hide her incredulity. "Even if we could get to speak to him, why would he listen to us?" The thought of even seeing the king of Wessex seemed like madness to her. She glanced at Dunston, to see whether he was jesting. Perhaps this was his misguided way of trying to lift her spirits.

"He wouldn't listen to you," he said, raising an eyebrow. "But by God, he'll listen to me."

He picked up his pace and for a moment she looked at him, her head full of questions. She wanted to call after him, to ask him how he could be so sure that the king would grant him an audience. But as she opened her mouth to shout, the thought of the horsemen on their trail came to her. Her voice would carry far in the quiet dawn, cutting through the chorus of birdsong and leading their enemies to them, if they were near. She clamped her mouth shut and ran after Dunston.

Twenty-Nine

They made good progress as they trudged southward. Dunston had for a time contemplated setting snares and traps for their pursuers to stumble upon. He could rig traps that would injure them with sharpened stakes and sprung branches whipping forward when triggered by a clumsy footfall. But he quickly dismissed the idea as a waste of effort. To fashion such traps would take time and there was no way of knowing whether the men who followed would encounter them. He had seen nothing that made him believe they knew how to track them through the forest. And, encumbered by their valuable mounts, which would impede their progress through the foliage, he believed they would more than likely head to the main north–south road.

For a long while, Aedwen had walked beside him in silence. Whenever he glanced at her he saw her face set in a determined mask. Something had changed between them, he knew, but he could do nothing to alter that. He thought of Eawynn and how she had always said he was a better man than others saw.

"They see the great warrior," she had said. "I see the true man who hides behind his axe and fearsome face."

He smiled to himself at the memory.

"Fearsome am I?" he'd laughed, grabbing hold of her. She'd squirmed, pliant curves soft under his firm grip.

Giggling, she had kissed him.

"I do not see what frightens others," she'd said. "I only see my lovely bear of a man."

As always when he thought of Eawynn, the memory of her stirred and warmed him, but all too soon, the bitterness of her loss returned and he frowned.

Aedwen had seen in him what others had always seen. The warrior. The killer. The Wolf. He wondered whether the girl would ever believe that there was another side to his nature that only Eawynn had been able to coax from him.

"Do you think they are close behind us?" Aedwen asked, breaking the silence between them and bringing him back to the present.

They had walked for a long while. Dunston looked up at the sky that was visible between the limbs of the trees. The clouds had thickened and the warmth that the day had promised with the dawn had fled, replaced with a greying light and the scent of rain.

"They might be," he replied, "but I do not believe so. They won't be able to bring their horses this deep into the woods and they will not wish to leave them." He paused, listening to the sounds of the forest. There was no indication they were being followed. "No. I think they will have gone on towards Tantun, or at least the road that leads from Exanceaster to Bathum."

"If they have not followed us into the forest, how can they think to catch us?" she asked, hope of escape colouring her tone.

"They might send men along the road in both directions, hoping to hear news of our passing or to spy us when we leave the woodland." He set off once again, wincing at the constant ache in his knee. It hurt more when he was still, but all the same, he longed to sit and stretch out before a fire. Not much chance of that any time soon. Aedwen trotted along beside him, her youthful energy bringing the hint of a wistful smirk to his lips. By God, he missed being young.

"Won't they head towards Tantun?" she asked.

"They may well do that. But I think that they will soon fathom out that we have gone south and there is only one reasonable destination for us in this direction. After all, they must know we either have the message or know of it, so we need to take it somewhere. Knowledge is useless if it is not shared."

"And so we just plan to walk to Exanceaster and pray for the best?"

He shrugged.

"I would rather trust to our wits than rely on God to see us safe. We should head south of the town until we reach the River Exe. Then we can follow the river back to the walls of Exanceaster. In that way, with a bit of luck, we can avoid any prying eyes on the road."

They walked on for a time, following the course of a small river until it widened into a broad expanse of water. Aedwen held her oaken staff as if she had been born with it in her hand and Dunston smiled as he watched her halt for a moment to casually inspect the tracks of an animal in the mud beside the lake. Days ago she would not have noticed the small marks. She turned to him, eyes bright and inquisitive.

"What are these tracks?"

"Look about you," he answered. "What animal do you think might have made them?"

She gazed around her, forgetting about the men pursuing them, focusing solely on the matter at hand. Dunston lowered himself down, leaning his back against the trunk of a sallow. He turned his head this way and that, grunting as his neck popped. They needed to rest for a while and this place was as good as any. He pulled the ham and cheese from his bag, cutting off a slice and watching Aedwen as she thought.

She knelt on the earth and inspected the tracks carefully and methodically, before looking back at him.

"I don't know," she said. "I've never seen anything like this before. It looks as though a creature has dragged something behind it through the mud."

He grinned and took a drink from his leather flask.

"And so it has."

"But what?" she asked, confused.

"Animals do not only leave their prints in the earth," he said. "Look about you and take the time to really see. Think carefully and you will find the answer."

She got up and went close to the pool. A dense tangle of spearwort grew at its edge, the yellow flowers bright against the green of the leaves.

"Careful not to touch that plant," he called. "It will cause your skin to blister."

Moving warily past the flowering spearwort, Aedwen looked about her.

A large alder had fallen and its leafy boughs trailed into the still waters. Dunston broke the last of the smoked cheese into two pieces and ate his half. He was enjoying watching the girl discover the truth for herself. She moved to the toppled tree and touched the bright, fresh wood where its trunk had been split. Then she gazed out at the water, at last taking in that which Dunston had seen immediately.

She turned, pointing to a mound of branches that rose from the water.

"Is that where it lives?" she asked. Her face glowed with childish excitement.

"It is," he said, returning her smile. "So what left the tracks?"

"It is a beaver," she said. "The thing it is dragging behind is its tail."

When he nodded, she clapped her hands with delight.

After they had eaten, they continued on, leaving the beaver's dam and lodge behind them. Aedwen had been pleased with herself and Dunston had revelled in her simple pleasure. But their spirits were soon dampened when the rain that had been threatening to fall all morning finally began to waft down from the sky in a light, yet soaking drizzle. For a time, the tree cover kept them dry, but soon, the water trickled down to drench them. All about them the forest was dank, gloomy and wet. The birds that had filled the morning with song and cheer fell quiet and the only sound was that of the rain, pattering and dripping from leaf and limb. Where there were patches of open ground, the earth squelched underfoot.

There was still no sign they were being followed, but their conversation of that morning nagged at Dunston. They had followed the course of the river for a time, but now they had left it behind. Dunston pointed to a hill in the distance.

"Let us take a look at the land about from up there," he said, wiping the rain from his eyebrows and forehead.

The hill was bare, save for a stand of yew on its crown. If he judged rightly, the Bathum to Exanceaster road would lie someway off to the west.

"If we approach the rise from the east and head to the trees," he said, "we should get a good view of the road and the land to the north. Careful now, let us not be out in the open for too long."

It was steeper than it had looked and they both slipped and slid on the wet grass. All the while he worried that they might be seen. He felt exposed and began to question his decision to climb up here. Too late for that now. There was nothing for it but to press on. As they got higher and could see the rain-swept wooded hills of Somersæte rolling away to the north, he was relieved to see no movement.

Their clothes were sodden by the time they reached the shelter of the trees. After the exposed slopes of the hill, it felt almost warm beneath the branches.

"We will rest here awhile," he said, panting from the struggle up the hill.

They settled down under an old yew, beside the twisted skeletal remnants of a dead juniper bush. Old, brown needles crunched beneath them. They were wonderfully dry and it was good to be out of the rain even if only for a short time.

Below them, they could make out the unnatural straight line of the road, a shadow like a spear haft plunged through the undulating verdant curves of the forest. They sipped at the water from their flasks and watched, each silent and anxious. As if to speak would somehow give away their presence on the hill.

Thin trails of mist formed over parts of the woodland, like wisps of lamb's wool caught on thorns. Dunston drew in a deep breath, finally allowing himself to relax. He was rummaging in his bag, looking for the last of the ham, when Aedwen touched his arm. He followed her pointing finger. Far in the distance, where the road ran between two steep-sided hills, a great flock of birds was flapping into the misty sky, pale against the dark of the rain-slick leaves of the wood. His eyes were not as good as they had once been, but he thought the flock was a mixture of wood pigeons and doves.

As he watched, he noticed that the air was clearer now, making it easier to pick out details from afar. The rain had stopped and the wet land shone in a sudden blaze of golden afternoon light.

A croaking cry split the silence of the hill as half a dozen crows flapped into the sky from where they had been roosting on the branches of the yew trees.

Cursing silently, Dunston peered up and saw that the clouds had parted, sending brilliant sunlight down upon the trees and hills of Wessex. A flash of silver, as bright and flickering as distant lightning, drew his gaze back down to the road. He squinted.

"What is it?" he asked.

For a moment, Aedwen did not speak.

"I'm not sure how many," she replied at last, "but there are at least two horsemen down there on the road. The sun caught their horses' harness, I think."

Dunston spat.

"Riding south?"

"Yes," Aedwen said without hesitation.

By Christ's bones, he should not have brought them up here. He reached for her arm and pulled her back into the shade beneath the trees.

"Come, we must leave this place."

He led her through the copse, and then they proceeded to slip and slide down the southern slope, putting the hill between them and the riders on the road.

"You think they saw us?" she asked, her breath coming in ragged gasps.

"I do not know," he said. But he could not believe anyone could have missed the black-feathered crows that had taken to the wing above their vantage point. He hoped they were more foolish than he thought, but they would not have to be woodsmen to understand that something or someone had disturbed the birds from the trees.

He glanced at Aedwen and could see from the set of her jaw that she was thinking the same thing. She did not protest when he urged them into a trotting run southward, away from the hill and back under the canopy of the forest.

Thirty

They ran into the humid shade of the trees. They were both out of breath, but Dunston did not slow until they were deep within the woods once more, sheltered from the hill and the road by dense thickets of hazel and hawthorns. They pressed on. When Aedwen tried to speak with him, Dunston merely grunted. She wanted to say that it had not been his fault. He could not have known the men would ride into view at that moment, or that the crows would take wing, giving away their position. But after a time she kept quiet. Her words would not change how he felt. He was tense and irritable and clearly angry at himself for leading them up to the hilltop.

And so they walked in silence, and soon her sweat mingled with the damp from the rain as she struggled to keep up with him.

Such was the pace he set that soon her legs were burning and a blister on her left heel had burst, stabbing her with a jolt of pain at every step. She was on the verge of asking Dunston for a rest when he held up his hand, signalling her to be silent. He dropped into a crouch. She copied him, her aches and pains forgotten momentarily.

For a long while they remained thus, hunkered down on their haunches. She was about to ask him what was happening, but one glower from his blue eyes and she snapped her mouth shut.

A moment later, a skinny, dirt-smeared man stepped into the clearing. Aedwen had not heard him approach until the instant before he walked into sight. How Dunston knew he was coming, she had no idea.

Over his shoulder, the man carried a brace of pigeons and a plump hare. He held a bow in his hand, and a sheaf of white goose feather fletched arrows were thrust into his belt.

Dunston stepped from their hiding place. The man started, dropping the game to the leaf mould and snatching an arrow from his belt.

Before he nocked the arrow, Dunston stepped close.

"You'll not be needing that," he said, his voice deep and rumbling like far-off thunder. The man's eyes were wide and shining in the forest shadows, but Dunston moved back a pace, placing his axe on the ground. "I mean you no harm."

For a moment, Aedwen thought the man might run, but then he seemed to relax. Glancing past Dunston, he grinned at her, his teeth bright and surprisingly whole in his weathered and begrimed face.

Dunston asked him whether he had seen anyone else in the forest.

"Not since I left home yesterday morn," the man said, flicking his attention back to Dunston. "Not a soul. The only folk I ever see in these woods are wolf-heads." He looked at them askance then, and Dunston fixed him with his icy stare.

"Wolf-heads, you say?"

"Yes, but not today. Nobody today. Just the animals and me."

"And you have not seen us," said Dunston.

The man swallowed.

"Well, I have now," he stammered.

Dunston bent down and lifted his huge, besilvered axe. He swung it to rest upon his shoulder where the blade caught a ray of sunlight that lanced through the trees.

"You have not seen us," he repeated, his words slow and pointed.

The hunter's throat bobbed. He could not pull his gaze from the massive head of the long hafted axe. At last, he nodded.

"I haven't seen you."

Dunston waved his hand and the hunter snatched up the pigeons and the hare and hurried on, his shadow stretching out before him as he headed towards his home somewhere to the east.

When the man had disappeared and they could no longer hear his footfalls, Dunston strode off into the forest once more. Aedwen stumbled after him, her blistered foot squelching and rubbing with raw agony. She longed to be able to halt, to pull off her shoes, perhaps to bathe her feet in a cool stream. And yet she remained silent, not wishing to further anger Dunston.

The meeting with the hunter had done nothing to quell his nerves.

They walked along a barely perceptible path that had been made by some woodland creature. For a moment she paused, trying to discern what creatures' passing had worn this trail, but Dunston did not slow. Fearing she would be left behind, she abandoned her search for sign and limped after him. The track led south and east and Dunston seemed content to follow it as the sun fell. The shadows grew darker and colder, the light that filtered through the boles of the trees golden and blinding. The sun would soon set and they would be plunged into darkness. Aedwen shuddered. Her foot screamed in silent anguish.

"We should make camp soon," she offered.

Dunston ignored her. His pace did not falter. Aedwen did not like the thought of spending another night in the forest with no fire. She hurried after him, wincing and hobbling on her bleeding foot.

"Did you hear me?" she asked, raising her voice. "We should make—"

Dunston spun to face her, raising his hand. For the merest instant she thought he meant to strike her, such was the anger in his eyes. She flinched. Dunston's features softened and he pulled her in close and whispered.

"We cannot halt here. We are being stalked. Keep your eyes open and," he shook her shoulder, staring directly into her eyes, "no matter what happens, do exactly as I say."

Without waiting for an answer, he turned and continued along the path. She rushed after him, panicked thoughts tumbling in her mind. What did he mean? Who was stalking them? She had seen nobody.

They walked on without speaking. With every tree they passed, Aedwen found herself peering into the shadows, staring into tangles of brambles. They passed a holly tree, its leaves glistening in the sunset. A breeze shook the branches as the travellers drew near and Aedwen jumped back, certain that an unseen assailant was about to leap upon them from the mass of spiny leaves. Nobody sprang out of the undergrowth and Dunston did not slow. With her breath ragged from the exertion and the building fear, Aedwen ran after him.

When the men who hunted them finally showed themselves, they did not come crashing out of the foliage, but seemed to materialise from the shadows, like wraiths. The sun must have still been just above the horizon, but here, deep within the forest, little of its light penetrated. Without warning, Dunston halted and Aedwen almost collided with his broad back. Her eyes widened and panic rose in her throat as she saw three men had stepped into the glade before them. Glancing behind, she spotted the shadowy forms of three more.

Her breath came in short gasps and the blood pounded in her ears. How had their pursuers managed to follow them here, into the darkest part of the forest? Her stomach twisted as she thought what the men would do to them both. They would be furious at the old man. He had killed two of their own. And these men had tortured and slain for much less. Would they rip Dunston's lungs from his back? She trembled. Would they torture her too? Her mouth was dry and she felt faint.

"I told you before," said Dunston, "you do not need your bow."

The central man before them stepped into the failing light and she immediately realised her mistake. These were not the horsemen who had killed her father, raped and murdered the people of Cantmael and tortured to death the monk, Ithamar. The man confronting Dunston was the thin hunter. Relief flooded through her. They were safe. They would not be tortured and killed. The dirt-streaked hunter grinned at her with his unusually white teeth. There was something feral and disquieting in that smile. In his hands he held his bow, an arrow on the string. The wicked point of the hunting arrow was aimed squarely at Dunston's chest. As quickly as the relief had come, so it was washed away on a fresh tide of fear. There was no welcome in this man's eyes, only the wild hunger of a man who has nothing to lose.

"I suppose it is not surprising that you said you only saw wolf-heads in the forest," said Dunston, "as you are a wulfeshéafod yourself."

"You know nothing of me, or my friends of the greenwood," snarled the hunter.

"Well, that is not so, is it?" asked Dunston, taking a step towards the men who blocked their path.

"What do you mean, old man? You do not know me."

Dunston nodded and took another pace forward.

"I do not know your name, but I know much about you."

The archer raised his bow, pulling back on the string so that the yew wood creaked.

"Not another step," he hissed. Dunston halted. Swinging his axe down from where it rested on his shoulder, he grasped it in both hands, holding it across his body. The dying light of the sun made the silver threads in the blade glow in the gloaming.

"What is it that you think you know?" asked the archer.

"Why, I know that you are a wolf-head. Outside the law. I could kill you as I would a wolf and nobody would seek to take me to a moot. There would be no weregild to pay. Your life has no price."

"You know nothing of what I have done," said the archer, a cunning gleam in his eye. "Being a wulfeshéafod is a curse, but it is a blade that cuts both ways. My life has no worth to freemen or reeves, so I have nothing to lose. I could slay you where you stand, old man."

"You could try," growled Dunston, raising his great axe menacingly. "Do you truly believe your puny arrow could slay me before I could bury DeaÞangenga here in your skull?"

Aedwen could scarcely believe Dunston's words. Terror gripped her in its icy fist. She could barely move and yet Dunston seemed not only unafraid of these men, he appeared to be goading them into a fight. As she watched, she saw the bowman's gaze flit to the weapon in Dunston's massive hands and she realised she was not the only one frightened. Glancing past Dunston, the leather-faced wolf-head met her eyes for a heartbeat. Gone was the quick smile of before.

"Drop your axe," said the archer, "or we shall see just how deadly my arrows are." He tensed the string once more, the arrowhead aiming unerringly at Dunston's heart.

Dunston did not move.

"I will say this only once, boy," he said, his voice low and rasping. "Walk away now. Lead your friends away back to wherever you call home. If you threaten me or the girl again, you will regret it." He paused, glowering under his grey brows, his blue eyes flashing like chips of ice. "But not for long."

"Why not let them go, Strælbora?" said the man to the archer's left. Younger than the bowman, he was just as dishevelled, with the gaunt, wary look of a stray dog about him. "They have nothing of worth. They are probably fleeing from tithe-men. Perhaps they are being followed. It will be just our luck to have them bring the reeve down onto us."

"Silence, Wynstan," snapped the archer. "That axe of his is worth something. And when was the last time the camp had a young girl? That is worth more than a little."

Wynstan looked at Aedwen and licked his lips. She shuddered. She was sure this was how the hare must have felt before the man's arrow pierced its flesh.

"Drop the axe," repeated Strælbora, his tone harsh.

Dunston's shoulders slumped and with a sigh, he let the huge weapon fall to the loam at his feet.

With a smile of triumph, Strælbora said, "Wynstan, fetch that axe."

After a moment's hesitation, Wynstan scurried forward. Dunston stood, head down as if in defeat. Aedwen wanted to scream. These men would surely kill him and after that... She could not bear to think of what would become of her.

Wynstan bent quickly to lift the axe, clearly meaning to hurry back to Strælbora's side. But in the instant when he took his eyes from Dunston to retrieve the weapon, the grey-bearded warrior pounced. If she had not witnessed it with her own eyes, Aedwen would never have believed one so old could move with such speed. Like a striking serpent, Dunston's right hand lashed out and grabbed Wynstan by the neck of his grimy kirtle. Surging forward and stooping, he gripped the man's groin with his left hand. Wynstan let out a pitiful yelp.

For a heartbeat, nobody seemed able to move. Apart from Dunston. He hoisted Wynstan off the ground at the same moment that the unmistakable sound of an arrow being loosed sang out in the shadowed glade. The arrow thudded into flesh and for a terrible instant Aedwen believed Dunston had been struck. And yet it was Wynstan who howled in pain. Strælbora had let fly his arrow into his friend's back, and now, using the man's body as a shield, Dunston surged forward. He did not attempt to pick up his axe, instead he ran towards Strælbora, holding Wynstan as if he weighed little more than a child.

Suddenly, the clearing was filled with chaos. Men yelled and shouted. Somebody grabbed Aedwen roughly from behind, a strong arm encircled her chest and the stench of stale sweat and woodsmoke enveloped her.

Despite the horror that threatened to overwhelm her, Aedwen could not tear her gaze away from Dunston. He flung Wynstan's injured body at Strælbora. The archer was trying to free another arrow from his belt, and Wynstan clattered into him, sending him reeling backwards. Both men collapsed in a heap on the forest floor. Dunston did not slow his advance, instead speeding into the man who had been standing to Strælbora's right. The man had pulled a rusty knife, but Dunston seemed unperturbed by the blade. Catching the man's wrist in his left hand, he thundered a right hook into his jaw. The man fell to the ground as if dead. Perhaps he was, Aedwen thought, such was the power behind that punch.

"Halt!" shouted the man who held Aedwen. As if to reinforce his command, he shook her and pressed a cold blade against her throat. Aedwen felt her strength leaving her. She could barely breathe. Her legs trembled and she feared she might fall. "I'll kill her!" yelled the man, his voice hoarse and ugly. His warm breath, sour and stale, wafted against her cheek. His left hand was clamped over her chest. His touch made her want to squirm away, but even if she could have summoned the courage to move, his wiry strength would have held her firm.

Dunston showed no sign of hearing the man's threats. He did not turn or falter, instead he flung himself onto Wynstan and Strælbora. Wynstan screamed as the arrow was pushed further into his body before snapping from the pressure of Dunston's bulk. Strælbora was pinned beneath his injured comrade.

"You whoreson!" he bellowed, trying in vain to pull himself out from under Wynstan's stricken form and Dunston's considerable weight. "I will cut your eyes out and piss in your skull! I will cut off your manhood and—"

Dunston hammered a punch into his face, silencing him. Strælbora's head snapped back against the loam, his eyes vacant and unfocused. His mouth opened and closed like a beached trout, but no sound came. Dunston looked down at him for a moment, before thundering another blow into his nose. Blood blossomed, bubbling and flowing into Strælbora's dirty beard. His eyes rolled back and he lay still.

With a sigh, Dunston shoved himself up from the earth and the tangled forms of the wolf-heads. He rose to his feet with a grimace and turned to Aedwen and the three remaining outlaws.

As if remembering his role in this confrontation, the man who held her tightened his grip. The knife pressed against her throat and she gasped.

"I'll kill her," he said. Did she hear an edge of panic in his tone now?

Dunston ignored the man. He moved to his axe and lifted it from the earth.

"I will!" shouted the man, desperation in his voice now. Aedwen readied herself for the pain of the cut. How quickly would she die? She had seen plenty of pigs killed with their throats slit and they didn't seem to suffer for long after their initial squealing terror. Without being aware of what she was doing, she began to recite the prayer to Maria, Mother of God.

"If you harm her," said Dunston, his voice as cold and menacing as the huge axe in his grasp, "it will be the last thing you do on this earth. Even if you think you could kill me, I promise you I will take you with me. Death holds no fear for me. What about you, boy? Do you truly wish to stand before God in judgement of your sins before this day is out?"

Behind Dunston, Wynstan whimpered and panted.

For a long, drawn out moment, nobody spoke. Aedwen was aware of the man who held her wavering. She could almost hear his thoughts as he looked at the grey-bearded axe man and his three incapacitated companions sprawled on the forest floor. Could the three wolf-heads who remained standing defeat the old warrior? Was the prize worth the risk?

Dunston did not move. His cool eyes were unblinking as he glowered at the wolf-head. There was no doubt in Aedwen's mind that this was no idle threat. Dunston was prepared to kill them all, even if he died in the battle.

The tight grasp around her chest loosened. The wolf-head, it seemed, had decided to release her. Aedwen let out a ragged breath. Without warning, the blade was removed from her throat and the man pushed her away with such force that she stumbled and fell.

"Kill him!" he screamed.

The three wolf-heads surged forward, and Dunston widened his stance, swinging his war axe up to meet their attack.

Aedwen watched in horror from where she lay on the damp leaf mould. Death was in the late afternoon air and all that remained to be seen was who would survive. Surely Dunston could not hope to stand before the three outlaws and live.

The instant before the men met, a new voice rang out in the clearing.

"Halt! Put up your weapons!" the voice bellowed. It was loud and clear and carried the power of command in its tone.

Aedwen could not see who it was who spoke. The voice came from the shadows beneath the trees.

The wolf-heads evidently recognised the voice, for they responded by stepping back and lowering their blades. Dunston did not step after them, instead he lowered his axe and peered into the gloom of the forest, a quizzical expression on his face.

"Aculf?" he asked, his tone incredulous. "Is that you?"

Thirty-One

"Time has caught up with you, I see," said Aculf. He sat across the fire from Dunston, the flames lighting his face with a ruddy glow. It was full dark now, the forest black, the grey boles of the trees surrounding the camp crowding about the gathered band of wolf-heads.

Dunston offered a thin smile that didn't reach his eyes.

"Time is the hunter that always catches its prey," he said.

Beside him Aedwen leaned against his shoulder. The eyes of the outlaws glimmered in the gloom. All of the men were dirty and thin, with skin ravaged by the weather and years of living outside. Off to one side, Strælbora glowered at him. Huddled around the archer were the rest of the men Dunston had fought. Aculf, who had always been skilled with the ways of healing, had removed the arrow from Wynstan's back and now the injured man lay in a feverish doze. He had cried out like a child when Aculf had drawn the arrow point from his flesh, but despite the man's complaints, Aculf said he would more than likely live.

Strælbora's nose was broken, his eyes dark-ringed and bruised. The other man Dunston had punched had lost one of the few teeth he had left. The five of them did not cease to glare at Dunston and Aedwen, and he wondered whether he would be able to sleep that night.

"You may be old, but you are still as strong as an ox," said Aculf with a grin. "I cannot imagine any other man lifting Wynstan the way you did."

Dunston grunted. He did not feel strong. His back ached terribly and the pain in his elbow was worse than ever. You are not young any more, he rebuked himself after the fight. Lifting Wynstan was foolish. The moment he pulled him from his feet, Dunston had regretted it. His back screamed with the effort, but what else could he have done? He would not stand by while they raped Aedwen. You should have just killed them, a small, dark voice whispered deep within him. Perhaps he should have. They were outlaws, men who had lost their place in society. Why not simply strike them down with DeaÞangenga? It would have been faster and the chances were that if he had killed a couple, the others would have run. And yet he recalled slaying the man by the horses in the night, and how the thrill of the kill had coursed through him. He had made a solemn promise to Eawynn, he did not wish to forsake that vow. He had clung onto it for too long. He did not wish to admit to himself that he would resort to killing so effortlessly, as if the promise had never been made. Or that it meant nothing to him.

Looking over the fire at Aculf, Dunston felt his world shift about him. For a moment it was as if he had stepped back into his past. So easily had he returned to a life he'd believed gone forever, and now, to add to his discomfort and unease, ghosts were returning to the land of the living.

Aculf was thinner than he remembered him, his forehead bore a long scar Dunston did not recall, and his beard was dusted with frost, but the power of the man's character still shone in his dark eyes.

"I thought you long dead," said Dunston.

"I have come close," replied Aculf. "And now," he waved a hand to encompass their surroundings and the couple of dozen wolf-heads that were dotted about the clearing, "I am as good as dead to all but those outside of the law."

"What happened?" asked Dunston, accepting a leather flask from one of the other men sitting nearby. He took a tentative sip and was surprised to discover it was mead. Good sweet mead. He filled his mouth and passed the skin to Aedwen who took a small gulp, grimaced and handed it back, shaking her head.

"What always happens," said Aculf. The shadows from the flames danced and writhed about his features. His eyes were black in the darkness. "Bad luck. War. And the accursed Norsemen."

Dunston took another mouthful of the mead, feeling his body relax and the warmth of the liquid sliding into his tired and aching limbs. Handing the flask back to the wolf-head with a nod of thanks, Dunston waited for Aculf to continue.

Aedwen moved to rest her head in his lap. Her eyes were closed. She was exhausted. Aculf had given his word that no ill would befall either of them in the camp that night, but did Dunston truly know him? It must have been close to a score of years since he had last seen the man. They had been brothers in the Wulfas Westseaxna then. They had stood shoulder to shoulder in the shieldwall and they had walked together into the darkest of nights where the only certainty was death. Dunston remembered Aculf as a formidable swordsman and a man of honour. To find him here, outcast and living amongst brigands in the forest, filled him with pity. He snorted. Was he too not a wulfeshéafod? Who was he to judge this man he had long ago considered to be his friend? He would have trusted his life to Aculf once, he at least owed him the benefit of hearing his story.

"How is your woman?" Aculf asked. "Eawynn, isn't it?"

Dunston sighed. He did not wish to speak of Eawynn; of his loss. His expression must have been answer enough, for Aculf held up a hand. "I am sorry, my friend. How many children?"

Dunston shook his head.

"We were not so blessed."

Aculf raised his eyebrows and glanced down at the sleeping girl.

"I thought she was yours." He gave a twisted smirk. "Or your granddaughter, perhaps."

Dunston shook his head.

"She is not my kin, but I will not let any harm come to her."

Aculf nodded.

"You were always a good man," he said.

Dunston frowned, thinking of all the men he had killed. Had all of those men deserved death?

Aculf picked up a stick and prodded the embers of the fire.

"We had three, Inga and me," he said. "Two girls and a boy." His voice had taken on a distant, haunted tone. He poked at the fire and sparks drifted into the darkness. "All gone now."

"It is a terrible thing to lose loved ones."

Aculf sighed and threw another log onto the fire in a spray of embers and winking motes.

"I found my boy and Inga," Aculf said. "They had fought as best they could." He stared into the fire for a moment, his mind walking along the shadowed paths of memories. "I should have been there. I sometimes wonder what would have happened if I had been."

Dunston did not know the full tale of what had befallen Aculf's family, but he knew the folly and pain of such thoughts.

"You cannot change the past, old friend," he said, his voice barely a whisper. "To rake over those old coals will only cause you pain."

"You sound like Guthlaf," said Aculf. "He would always tell me how to think."

"I meant no harm."

"I know it. The pain is there whether you speak of it or not. I will never be rid of it, I fear."

Dunston said nothing.

Aculf sniffed, then reached out for the flask of mead.

"I never found my daughters," he said. He took a long draught from the skin and wiped his mouth with his hand. "I wonder if they are still alive somewhere. In Denemearc or Íraland. Perhaps they married strong Norsemen."

Dunston watched his old friend, but said nothing.

As if his memories had been held within a cask that had now been split, allowing its contents to pour forth, so Aculf's tale rushed out then. He spoke in a soft, distant voice of how he had been chopping timber in the woodland near Cernemude, the village where he had settled with his family, when he had seen smoke rising above the settlement. He had sprinted back through the trees, leading the other young men who had been with him. All of them desperate, all terrified of what they would find when they reached their homes. The Norsemen had left nothing behind except corpses and burning buildings.

He was not the only man bereaved that day. But the other men had not been of the Wulfas Westseaxna. They had wept and buried their dead and slowly rebuilt their homes and lives as best they could. Not Aculf. He had been filled with an all-consuming rage and a feeling of such helplessness that he had not been able to remain there, living the life of a farmer where all that remained for him were the memories of his dead wife and son and the daughters who had been snatched and borne away on the sleek sea-dragons of the Vikingr.

"We had become soft," said Aculf, his voice beginning to slur from the mead. "It had been years since the Norsemen had raided the coast. But when the Frankish ships stopped sailing the Narrow Sea, it was only a matter of time before the bastard Vikingrs returned. It was my bad luck that some of them spied Cernemude from the sea."

Dunston watched him through the flickering flames. He could hear the despair in Aculf's words. He recognised the feeling of impotence he felt at losing his family. For a man used to fighting, to cutting his way through the obstacles before him, it was a terrible thing to be powerless to protect those you loved. Dunston had sat and watched as sickness consumed Eawynn. The memories plagued him and he recalled the anger that had filled him after her death. But where should he direct his ire? At God? At the disease that had destroyed his beautiful wife? Such thoughts were foolish. Aculf knew there was an enemy responsible for his pain. He would never have been able to return to a life of peace while those men still lived.

Aculf continued with his tale and Dunston noted that many of the wolf-heads had fallen quiet, listening intently, their eyes glimmering in the dark as they watched their leader speak. He wondered whether this was a story he seldom told. Perhaps they had never heard it before. But now that he had started, he did not appear inclined to stop.

Unable to rest, and filled with the burning need for vengeance and the desperate hope of finding his daughters, Aculf joined the crew of a ship bound for Íraland. When they were attacked by a band of Norsemen aboard a dragon-prowed wave-steed, he had revelled in the fight, cutting them down and screaming the names of his daughters at them. But none of them knew of the attack on Cernemude, so they had been killed and thrown overboard. It was after that first trip that he began to realise that the men he travelled with were no better than the Vikingr he hated. They would set upon smaller vessels, killing the occupants and stealing their cargo.

"I was a fool," Aculf whispered. "I thought I could find my girls and bring them back. In the end, I knew I would never find them." He spat into the embers of the fire. "If I did, they would not recognise the man I had become." He sighed and took another drink of mead. He could not meet Dunston's gaze. "I left the ship, but on land I fared little better. Soon I had to come here, into the forest. Any reeve in the land would see me hanged for what I have done, so this is my life now."

Dunston stared at him for a long time.

"What happened?"

Aculf shook his head and waved his hand, dismissing the question.

"Bad luck," he said. "And not always just for me." He met Dunston's gaze for a moment and his meaning was clear. "I do not wish to speak of it any further. I am here, and this is my family now." A murmur came from the listeners. Strælbora and his knot of friends glowered at Dunston. "Now, Dunston, you must tell us how it is you have come to spend the night in our humble encampment."

Dunston sighed. He reached out and someone handed him the mead. He took a mouthful. Swallowing the liquid slowly, he pondered how much to tell. He cleared his throat, unable to think of a good reason not to tell Aculf everything. They were at his mercy after all. Dunston might have been able to kill three more in the fight that afternoon, but he could not hope to stand against two dozen.

And so he told them the whole story, leaving nothing out. At the mention of how Lytelman had been killed, Aculf glanced over at Strælbora, but it wasn't until Dunston described finding Beornmod's blood-eagled corpse and then how they had heard Ithamar tortured in the same way, that Aculf spoke.

"This sounds like the work of Bealowin, don't you think, Strælbora?"

"You know him?" asked Dunston.

Strælbora nodded, still scowling at Dunston.

"An evil whoreson," he said.

"With a taste for torture and inflicting pain," said Aculf. "You know the type."

Dunston nodded. Every group of fighting men attracted those who enjoyed the act of killing. Some such men became monsters, worse than any warrior they would have to face in battle.

"Bealowin travelled with us for a time," Aculf said. "I never knew his story, he would not speak of it. But his love for the ritual of the blood-eagle was unholy. Unnatural." Aculf stared into the flames and seemed to suppress a shudder. "We are wolf-heads, not animals. There are things even we will not abide."

"You turned him out?"

"Yes," Aculf said, smiling. "I can be quite persuasive, you know? I thought he would have got himself killed years ago, but if he yet lives, he is as deadly as a snake." He traced a finger along the puckered scar that ran across his forehead. "If you meet him, perhaps you could repay him for this."

Dunston thought of all the suffering the man had inflicted.

"He owes many for what he has done. I will collect the blood-price for what he did to you and much more besides."

Aculf stared at him for a moment and then laughed.

"I believe you will at that!" He chuckled. "This is Dunston the Bold, men! And he is even more persuasive than me!"

They spoke little of anything of import as the fire died down to embers. They reminisced over past battles and escapades and, despite their situation, Dunston found himself enjoying Aculf's company. It had been so many years and it was good to speak to one who had shared much of his youthful days of strength and battle-fame. Their mood seemed infectious, and soon, even Strælbora was smiling.

As the thin archer laid out his blanket on the ground, preparing for sleep, Dunston called out to him.

"There is no bad blood between us?"

Strælbora's face was dark in the ember glow. His eyes glinted and then his white teeth shone as he grinned.

"Very well, axe man," he said. "You can sleep easy."

"Good," replied Dunston. "I would hate to have to kill you before I break my fast."

Some of the men laughed.

"You have my word that no harm will befall you in my camp," slurred Aculf. "If any one of you touches him or the girl, and Dunston does not kill you, I will. Understand?" A rumble of assent. Dunston ached and was tired beyond anything he had felt for years. He hoped Aculf held sway over these outlaws, for he was sure they could slit his throat without him even waking.

Wrapping himself in his blanket, close to the fire and beside Aedwen's slumbering form, Dunston could feel sleep descending on him quickly.

"You seek the king tomorrow then?" asked Aculf, dragging Dunston from the welcoming embrace of sleep.

"I do," he replied, propping himself up on his right elbow and instantly regretting it, as it stabbed with pain. "I hope he will remember me and know what to do about all of this."

"Ecgberht will remember you, Dunston. Of that there is no doubt. We will see you safely to the edge of the forest. From there, it is a short walk to Exanceaster."

"I thank you," Dunston said, lying back.

"You have done no wrong," whispered Aculf in the darkness. "Perhaps old Ecgberht might pardon you."

Dunston had not thought so far ahead. He just wished to deliver the message and Aedwen safely to Exanceaster.

"Perhaps," he said, his voice softened by approaching sleep.

"Give me your word you will not speak of me," hissed Aculf, his whispering voice tinged with urgency. "Of us, here."

"Speak of you?" answered Dunston, confused with drink and tiredness. "In what way?"

"I know you could track a mouse across the forest. You could lead them to us."

"I would not do that. You have aided us. You are my friend."

"We were friends, weren't we? Long ago, in a different life."

"We each only have one life, Aculf. Perhaps I could speak of how you have helped us. The king would remember your service." A thought came to him. "He might pardon you."

"No!" hissed Aculf. "Promise me you will not speak to him of me. I would that he remembers me as the great warrior I once was."

Dunston sighed in the darkness, wondering what atrocities Aculf had committed in his past. But he knew he would not ask. He too would prefer to remember him as he had once been, full of power and honour.

"You have my word," he said.

Aculf said no more and soon the sounds of snoring and the soft whispers of the forest pulled Dunston into a deep and dreamless sleep.

Thirty-Two

"Look at that," said Aedwen, awe in her voice.

The River Exe was a wide thread of silver before them. Wherries and cogs dotted the water as fishermen and merchants plied their trades. To either side of the river were broad flat meadows of lush grass and summer flowers. Butterflies and insects fluttered and droned in the air. Nearer the water, the muddy banks were festooned with birds. Dunlins, sandpipers and redshanks dipped their slender bills into the dark muck in search of food. In the distance, to the northwest of their position, reared the walls of Exanceaster. They were crumbling in places, having been built many centuries ago by the long-vanished Romans, but the city was still an imposing sight to behold. And yet this was not what had excited Aedwen so. The sky above Exanceaster was a muddle of grey clouds, still heavy with rain, and before that drab backdrop, in a brilliant display of God's power, there arced a perfect rainbow. It reached high into the sky with one end seeming to touch the ground within the city's walls.

Dunston paused for a moment, but seemed unimpressed by the spectacle. He took the opportunity to scan the horizon for sign of any of their pursuers. Across the river, on the hills that rose there, sheep and goats grazed the slopes. All appeared calm. Aedwen sighed.

"It must be a sign that God is watching over us," Aedwen said, gazing raptly at the rainbow. It was so beautiful. After all the ugliness of these last days, it almost hurt to look at it. Her eyes prickled with tears and the vision of the vibrant colours swam.

Dunston grunted, he pressed on, walking determinedly along the meadow, the wet grasses soaking his leg bindings.

They had started the day dry. The rain had held off for much of the night and after her initial fear of the wolf-heads, Dunston's presence, the warmth from the outlaws' fire, and the drone of voices as the men spoke had lulled her to sleep. She had thought she would never be able to rest, with the hungry gaze of Strælbora and the others on her, but to her surprise sleep had found her quickly enough. As she had closed her eyes, her head resting on Dunston's thigh, Aedwen had begun to feel less frightened of what the future might hold. The rumble of his voice soothed her nerves. The way he had fought the wolf-heads filled her with awe. Dunston still frightened her, but she knew he would do anything, even risk his own life, to protect her.

She had awoken with a sense of wellbeing she had not felt for days. But that was as nothing when compared to the rapturous feeling she had now, looking upon the colourful arch of light in the sky.

Aedwen hurried to keep up with Dunston. She knew that he was nervous, more so now that they had left the cover of the forest and their destination was so close. The outlaws had led them to the river and then, with the briefest of farewells, they had vanished back into the gloom of the forest, like so much smoke.

Fear still scratched its fingers along her back and neck when she thought of the men who chased them, but she could not believe that the rainbow was not a good omen.

"The tale of Noah is my favourite story," she said. "Father Osbern told it often and he told it well."

Dunston said nothing.

"I always liked to think of all those animals in that great ship," she said. "I would picture the horses, cows, dogs, cats, chickens and such, but Osbern also spoke of other creatures. Lions and camels and other things I can't recall. Do you know what they look like?"

Dunston shook his head.

"I've never seen a lion or a camel," he answered gruffly.

They walked on. The clouds had once again drifted over the sun and the land was suddenly darker and cooler. Aedwen shivered.

"You know what the best part of the story is?" she asked.

Again, Dunston shook his head. His attention was elsewhere, and he reminded her of a sheepdog watching the land about its flock for wolves.

"It's when God placed a rainbow in the sky and promised never to send another great flood to kill His people."

"There are many other ways to die," Dunston said, his tone flat.

She did not know what to say to that. The old man had grown morose and looked more tired than ever.

"You know what the Norse call the rainbow?" he asked.

Now it was her turn to shake her head.

"I spoke to a captured raider once," he said. "I don't remember his name now." He snorted derisively at his bad memory. "How can I not remember his name? Anyway, it is no matter. Most of the Norse we captured shouted and spat at us until they were beaten senseless. This one, a great red-bearded giant of a man, was talkative. He'd sailed from Dyfelin with two shiploads of Vikingrs. They made the mistake of landing at Tweoxneam."

He fell silent for a moment, clearly remembering the events of years past.

"Mistake?" she said.

"Well, Tweoxneam is a rich port, with a wealthy church, so it was a good place to attack. But what the red-bearded bastard and his crews didn't know is that the king was there with his hearth warriors to celebrate the wedding of the son of Tweoxneam's ealdorman. Bad luck for the Norsemen. Good luck for the king."

"Or perhaps God helped the Christian king of Wessex to defend the land against the heathen."

Dunston gave her a strange look that she could not interpret.

"We met them on the beach, shieldwall to shieldwall." He grimaced at the memory. "It was a bloody business."

"You were in the shieldwall?"

"Oh yes, I was there all right. Got this scar on that beach." He pulled back the stained sleeve of his kirtle to show a long, thin white line running down the corded muscle of his right forearm. "It bled like a stuck pig," he said. "Looked worse than it was really. It stung like the Devil himself though. Funny that I can remember that so clearly but still cannot recall the name of that Norseman."

He scratched at his head, as if that might help him to remember. They were covering the ground leading to Exanceaster more quickly than she had expected. After the days of threading around trees, brambles and bushes, to walk in the open, with the wind and sun on her face, was a relief.

"Was Aculf there too?"

Dunston shook his head.

"No, he had left us before that." He paused, turning to face her. "When we reach Exanceaster, you are not to mention Aculf or the others. I gave my word." As if he needed to explain himself, he added, "We were friends, once."

She nodded, uncertain of what had been said in the night; what bonds connected the two old warriors.

"You have my word too," she said. Whatever Aculf had done to see him cast out from the law, he had helped them and he was a friend to Dunston. She thought he probably didn't have many. He held her gaze for a moment, then, seemingly satisfied, he continued walking through the long wet grass.

"Tell me of the Vikingr and the rainbow," she said.

Dunston looked up at the colourful arch of light against the rain-laden clouds, adjusting his huge axe on his shoulder.

"We drank ale together the night after that battle, that red-bearded warrior and I. As the sun went down, there was a rainbow over the Narrow Sea and he told me that his people called it Bifröst." Dunston let out a guffaw. "By God, I can remember that! What was the man's name? I should remember. Ah, it will come to me, I'm sure. I haven't thought of him for years. He said that Bifröst was the bridge that led to the afterlife, or to the kingdom of their gods, or some such nonsense."

They walked on, and Aedwen noted that Dunston had grown grim once more.

"He said that seeing the bridge was an omen that he would die and that his spirit would depart and travel to the feasting hall of the gods."

"What happened to him?"

Dunston sighed.

"The following morning, the king came to where we held the captives." Dunston stared up at the sky.

"What did the king do to the Vikingrs?" she asked, unsure whether she truly wished to hear the answer.

"He ordered them all hanged." Dunston spat. "They begged to be allowed to hold a weapon as they were killed. They said otherwise they would not go to the feasting hall of Valhalla."

"Did the king allow them their request?"

Dunston glanced at her.

"No," he said.

She pondered what he had told her as they continued across the meadow.

The men the king had ordered to be killed had attacked Wessex, had sailed intent on murder and theft. Was it not right they should be hanged? And yet she could sense Dunston's sadness at the memory of the death of the red-bearded Norseman and his Vikingr crews.

The rainbow had gone now, vanished as quickly as it had appeared. She watched Dunston stomping across the meadow, his great axe on his shoulder and his beard bristling from his jutting jaw. He looked more marauding Norseman than Christian. She would never look upon a rainbow with unbridled happiness again.

In the distance, a flock of green plovers burst from the grassland, filling the sky with flapping and squawking cries.

Dunston halted, raising his hand to shade his eyes, peering to see what had disturbed the birds.

And then, beneath the angry screeches of the birds, she heard something deep and resonant, like a far off peel of thunder. But this thunder did not dissipate, it grew until it was a thrumming rumble. She could feel it in her feet. The earth was shaking.

Dunston grabbed her shoulder.

"Run!" he shouted.

She could not make sense of what was happening. And then, in an instant of crashing terror, she saw what was making the thunderous roar. From beneath the swarming birds in flight came a line of some ten horsemen. Her eyes were young and keen and she picked out the glint of buckles on the mounts' bridles, the shine of sword blades slicing through the air. They came at a gallop and great clods of soft earth flew up behind them as they trampled the flowers and grass of the meadow. In an instant she recognised Raegnold, his sharp face mottled and swollen from where Dunston's axe had smashed into his jaw. At the sight of him she knew these men had only one purpose: to slay them; to silence them before they could deliver the message and its secrets to Exanceaster.

Dunston was shaking her, pointing away from the river. A copse of alder stood a spear's throw away.

"Run!" he repeated, thrusting his bag into her hands and shoving her towards the trees. "Climb a tree. I will fight these bastards."

"But… they are so many."

"Enough!" he bellowed and the strength of his voice alone spurred her into action. "Do as I say, or it has all been for nought."

She sprinted towards the trees, not looking back until she was in the shade beneath them. Her blood roared in her ears. As she ran she slung Dunston's bag over her shoulder. When she reached the trees, she leapt for the first low branch she saw and swung herself up. She could not carry her staff, so she let it fall. She still had the knife at her belt though. She prayed the horsemen did not have bows, and climbed as fast as she could, scrambling higher and higher. Her hands were raw and cut from scrabbling at the rough bark. Lichen and moss stained her pale soft skin.

When she was more than two men's height above the ground, she looked back at the meadow. She stifled a scream at what she saw.

The wall of horsemen were almost upon Dunston. They had not slowed and they bore down on him with weapons raised. Some carried spears, others swords, two wielded axes. The men screamed and shouted.

Before them, alone in the meadow, damp grass hiding his feet, stood Dunston. As immobile and resolute as a rock awaiting the incoming tide. His legs were set apart and in his strong hands he held DeaÞangenga. How could one old man stand before so many mounted warriors? It was folly. But what else could he do?

She offered up a prayer to the Blessed Virgin.

"Mother of God, please protect him," she implored.

And then the riders were upon him with bone-crunching force and Aedwen's tears prevented her from seeing clearly any more.

Thirty-Three

Dunston felt no fear as the riders charged towards him. There were too many of them for him to defeat alone, of that he had no doubt and he felt a pang of terrible sadness as he thought what they would do to Aedwen once they had finished with him. Hefting DeaÞangenga before him, he rolled his head, causing his neck to pop and crack. He would make them pay dearly for his life. Perhaps she would find a way to escape if he could hold them long enough. He knew that the idea was foolish, but he clung to it. He could not think of what might befall the girl. All he could do now was to kill as many of these bastards as he was able.

Glowering at the horsemen as they galloped towards him, he was filled with rage. Fury at his failure to protect Aedwen. Ire at the atrocities these men had performed on innocents. And anger at having to break his oath.

They were nearly upon him now, and he had already chosen the man he would kill first. A broad-shouldered man with blue cloak and a long, deadly spear. The spears were the most dangerous weapons in that first pass, so he would slay the largest spearman first.

"I am sorry, my love," he whispered, wondering whether Eawynn's shade could hear him. Well, they would be together soon. "I know that I promised, but I must break my oath to you once more, for it seems I will die fighting."

He thought she would have understood. What else could he do? He had to try and defend the girl. Surely that is what Eawynn had seen in him all those years before; what set him apart from other killers of men.

There was no more time for thinking. The thunder of the horses' hooves enveloped him. He stared into the eyes of the beast that carried his first target. It was a roan stallion, muscled and strong, but this was no warhorse. Its eyes were white-rimmed with terror as its rider urged it forward. The men screamed abuse at Dunston, but he ignored them all. There was nothing now save for the stallion and its rider. The man's spear dipped towards Dunston. In a heartbeat he would be skewered on the sharp steel point of the weapon. But in the last instant, he stepped to the right and raised DeaÞangenga high. The spear whistled harmlessly past his face, and the rider was powerless to adjust his aim. Even if he had been fast enough to do so, the horse's head and neck were in the way.

With a great roar that caused the horse beside the spearman to shy away from the axeman, Dunston swung DeaÞangenga in a great downward arc. Its silver-threaded head bit deeply into the roan's neck, splattering gore in the summer air. The animal let out a pitiful scream and collapsed, turning over itself in a flail of legs, hooves and mud. The rider was thrown.

But Dunston did not pause to see how the spearman tumbled into the long grass. Instead, he used the momentum from his great axe's swing to spin around and, crouching to avoid any strikes from the horsemen, he swung DeaÞangenga low. With a sickening splintering, and a jarring force that almost knocked the axe from his hands, DeaÞangenga's blade hacked into a second horse's forelegs. Bones shattered and the beast added its cries to those of the first animal. It ran on awkwardly for several paces, before toppling forward into the earth. Its rider leapt from the saddle, landing badly and sprawling on the ground.

The remainder of the horses rushed past, with no blow coming near Dunston.

In the time it took the horsemen to wheel their steeds around, Dunston ran past the first dying horse. The spearman was rising, half-dazed, from the long grass. Dunston's axe hammered into his neck. Blood fountained and the man fell back, to lie almost hidden from view in the meadow.

The second rider fared momentarily better. He clambered to his feet, sword in hand and advanced on Dunston. Perhaps he expected to be able to take the older man easily, while Dunston fought his comrade, but the axeman spun to face him a heartbeat later. Bright gore dripped from DeaÞangenga, and the man hesitated.

Dunston did not.

"Now you die, boy," he hissed and he sprang at his assailant.

The young warrior raised his sword, but Dunston batted it away with his axe before burying the blade into his opponent's chest. The young man collapsed to his knees and his eyes filled with tears. His face took on a look Dunston had seen countless times before: a dreadful mixture of despair and disbelief at how quickly death had come when moments before life had pumped hot and vibrant in his veins.

Dunston tugged his axe, but it was held fast between the man's ribs. The man keened. Wrenching harder, DeaÞangenga made an obscene sucking sound as it came free. Dunston kicked the man over and turned to face the rest of his attackers.

The riders had regained control of their mounts and were gathering for another charge now. But Dunston did not wait for them to come. He sprinted towards them, giving them no time to gain any momentum. Several of the riders' horses turned away, refusing to attack. Perhaps they were frightened by the screaming man rushing towards them, or maybe from the smell of fresh blood in the air. Dunston cared not, all he knew was that he had to keep moving, keep killing. To give them a moment to organise themselves would spell his doom.

Three of the men managed to spur their mounts forward. Dunston ran straight towards them. Only one, the man on his right, had a spear, the other two brandished swords. They built up speed, but they only reached a fast trot before Dunston was upon them. He laughed, filled with the glee of blood-letting, all thought of his broken oath now forgotten. The Wolf was no longer the hunted. This is what he had been born to do.

Feinting towards the spearman, Dunston swerved to the left, making it impossible for the man to bring the spear to bear without fear of striking his companions or their horses.

One of the swordsmen swiped at him, but Dunston dodged the blade easily. Reaching for the man with his left hand, he grabbed hold of his kirtle and hauled him from the saddle. The man's left foot caught in the stirrup and he was pulled away from Dunston. The horse, scared and confused by the unusual burden, bucked and shied, dragging the man away from the fight.

The second swordsman was evidently an accomplished rider, for he spun his mount around and aimed a strike at Dunston's neck. Dunston caught the sword's blade on DeaÞangenga's iron bit. The two weapons clanged together and Dunston half-expected the sword's blade to shatter. But despite the terrible blow against the axe's head, the sword was well-forged. Its patterned blade sang from the impact, but it did not break.

The man's steed reared, pawing the air with its hooves. Dunston jumped back and was surprised to see his assailant sliding from the saddle. He smacked his mount on the rump and the horse bounded away, happy to be distanced from the battling men.

"What are you doing?" called a heavy-set man on a splendid grey mare. He was richly dressed in fine linen and wool. A garnet-studded clasp held his cerulean cloak and a golden chain hung at his throat. He was older than the rest of the men and Dunston took him for their leader and clearly a man of worth. Dunston did not recognise him.

The dismounted warrior however was known to him. The man had been with Hunfrith at Briuuetone. It was impossible not to recall those ridiculous red breeches. The man swung his sword before him and grinned, his teeth white in his swarthy face and black beard.

"Just kill him and be done with it, Bealowin," shouted the leader. "We cannot tarry here. We are too close to Exanceaster."

So this was Bealowin. The torturer. The defiler. The murderer.

The swordsman was stepping lightly through the long grass and Dunston circled to follow his movement, unwilling to take his eyes off him for even a moment.

"I will slay him soon enough, lord," Bealowin said. "But this bastard has taken too many of my men. His life is mine. You would not deny me vengeance, would you?" He smirked at Dunston then, as if they were both party to some secret jest. The leader of the men was silent.

From the edge of his vision, Dunston could still make out the lord and the clump of horsemen gathered about him. He would have to hope that the man who had been pulled along by his stirrup had been dragged too far away to pose a threat.

Dunston took in a deep breath and swung DeaÞangenga in a wide arc, flexing the bunched muscles of his shoulders. Droplets of blood, as brilliant and red as the garnets in the lord's brooch, sprayed up in the sunlight. Sweat trickled down Dunston's forehead and stung his left eye.

"Feeling your age, Dunston the Old?" sneered Bealowin.

"At least I have grown old, boy. Just like Aculf. We both yet live. You must ask yourself how that is so."

If the mention of the wolf-head registered, Bealowin did not show it on his face. Without warning, he leapt forward and lashed out with his sword. He was fast and Dunston was barely able to step back from the attack. He felt the wind from the passing blade on his face. He recovered quickly. Taking advantage of Bealowin's lunge, he swiped across the man's chest. Bealowin's speed and agility saved him, and he danced away from Dunston, giggling.

"You are so slow," he chortled. "Just like Aculf. How you managed to kill so many of my men, I will never know. They say you were once one of the fabled Wolves of Wessex, but I cannot believe it. You are so very old now."

Dunston was out of breath, but willed himself to appear calm and poised. He could feel the sweat running in rivulets down his back.

"You will find out soon enough how easily I can kill," he said. "I am Dunston the Bold. Son of Wilnoth. I am yet a Wolf of Wessex, boy. And I will take your life."

"God," said Bealowin, stifling his laughter with difficulty, "how I wish I could have more time with you, old man. Your bleating amuses me. I would have liked to make you sing a merry song beneath the blood-eagle."

Dunston said nothing. The time for words was over.

This was the man who had performed the atrocious acts of butchery on Lytelman, Beornmod and Ithamar. Dunston thought of Nothgyth and the corpses at Cantmael. Who knew how many others Bealowin had tortured or killed? Dunston had met his kind before. Bealowin was one who took pleasure from the pain of others. And Dunston knew something with absolute certainty: Bealowin would die here today. Whatever the cost, Dunston would not allow the man who had inflicted such pain and misery to live.

As the thought hardened like tempered steel in his mind, Bealowin's expression changed, as if he too had come to the chilling notion that he might die here.

Without a sound, Bealowin sprang forward once more, slashing and scything his sword in a frenzied attack. It was all Dunston could do to parry and dodge the blows. All the while he was pushed back. Sweat drenched him now. His eyes smarted and his breath came in gasping wheezes. Step after step, Dunston retreated. DeaÞangenga was heavy in his grip now, and with each parry he seemed to be growing weaker and slower. Damn Bealowin. He had the one thing that Dunston could never regain: his youth.

A savage swing at his head made Dunston stagger, barely catching the sword's blade on his axe haft. Splinters flew from the rune-carved wood. The watching men let out a ragged cheer. But Dunston saw an opening in Bealowin's defences. The young man had over-stretched, leaving himself open to attack. Shifting his weight, Dunston sliced DeaÞangenga towards Bealowin's unprotected midriff.

Too late he saw the gleam of triumph in Bealowin's eyes. Dunston cursed himself for a fool. His mind must be growing as old and slow as his body to have fallen for such a ruse. For, in the instant that the axe swung towards Bealowin, the swordsman, clearly anticipating the attack, parried the blow, and then followed up with a vicious riposte. His sharp patterned blade scored a deep cut along Dunston's arm, following almost exactly the scar that a raiding Norseman had given him all those years before on the beach of Tweoxneam.

Dunston staggered back. His sleeve was in tatters and blood welled in the long cut.

Bealowin laughed.

"Finish him now, man," shouted the mounted lord.

The gathered horsemen jeered at Dunston, taunting him. They could see his death looming; imminent.

Dunston shook the sweat from his eyes. He could feel his strength sapping from him as the blood pumped from the wound. His arm throbbed with each beat of his heart.

"Come and finish it then, boy," he said to Bealowin. He opened his arms wide, holding DeaÞangenga out to the side in his bloody hand. This had to end now, he could not afford to grow any weaker. "You think you could make me sing? See if you can make me scream like those you tortured, you worm," he goaded. "Is that the only way you can make someone moan with your blade? To tie them up and cut them? Not man enough to make a woman moan with the weapon between your legs?"

With a bellow of anger at the old man's insults, Bealowin rushed in, lunging, jabbing, slicing with his blade. Dunston gritted his teeth against the burning pain in his arm and parried and dodged as Bealowin pressed his attack. Dunston's right hand was slick with blood and he could feel his axe slipping in his grasp. This could not go on much longer, and so, grasping the haft in both hands, Dunston smashed Bealowin's sword away and then followed with a powerful downward arc. If it had connected, it would have surely cut Bealowin from the crown of his head to his belly. But the blow did not make contact. Instead, Bealowin stepped back and Dunston's axe bit deeply into the soft earth.

Again the gleam of victory was in Bealowin's eyes. His foe was unarmed, his great axe embedded in the loam of the meadow. Bealowin roared and sprang at Dunston. He lunged with his deadly blade, meaning to spit the axeman on his sword.

But Dunston had not survived all these years and countless battles by strength alone. He knew when to bludgeon and batter an opponent, but sometimes guile was the way to win a fight.

Dunston released DeaÞangenga's haft, leaving the axe buried in the soil, as he had known it would when he'd made the swing, inviting Bealowin to believe him defenceless. Dunston spun, with the speed of a man half his age and Bealowin's sword did not plunge into his guts to deliver a death blow. And yet Dunston did not avoid the sword's bite altogether. The sharp blade ripped open his kirtle. Blood instantly streamed, hot and stinging, from a long slicing cut.

Dunston ignored the pain of the cut. It was not a killing wound. He gripped Bealowin's right wrist in his left hand, tugging him forward. At the same moment he pulled Beornmod's seax from the scabbard at his belt and drove it into Bealowin's stomach. He felt the younger man tremble in his grasp and he twisted the blade, pulling it out of the sucking wound and plunging it back into his flesh. Again he stabbed, and again, all the while watching the comprehension dawn in Bealowin's dimming eyes.

The man's blood gushed over Dunston's hand, mingling with his own that pumped from the wound on his forearm.

"Aculf sends you greetings," whispered Dunston, his face close to Bealowin's. "And now you understand."

"What?" the dying man gasped, lost confusion on his face.

"How I killed your men. Even an old wolf has fangs."

Bealowin let out a rattling, rasping breath and slumped. Dunston released him and let him fall to the ground.

Blinking away the sweat from his eyes, Dunston turned to face the horsemen. His kirtle was sodden with blood now, his stomach and arm a stinging agony.

"Who's next?" he shouted at the gathered men, disappointed that his voice cracked in his throat.

"What in the name of all that is holy is wrong with you all?" screamed the gold-chained lord. "He is but one old man!"

Dunston spat. He wished he had some water, but his flask was in the bag he had given to Aedwen.

"I would find some new men if I were you," he said, grinning despite the pain in his arm and stomach. "These ones are more like lambs than warriors."

"Kill him now!" yelled the men's leader. Spittle flew from his lips and his horse flinched at its rider's strident voice.

For a heartbeat, Dunston thought the man was giving the order to the riders around him. But then the thrumming of hooves reached his ears and penetrated through the rushing sound of his blood. The lord was not looking at Dunston, but behind him.

Dunston spun to face the new danger that came from his rear.

All was a blur. The glittering tip of a spear blade flickered towards Dunston. Instinctively, he leaned backward, allowing the steel to pass a hand's breadth from his face. But he was too slow to avoid the charging horse. The spearman who had passed him earlier spurred his steed onward and it hit Dunston with the force of a storm wave buffeting against a cliff.

Dunston was thrown into the waving grass. He tumbled over until he lay on his back. For a moment, he could not draw breath. He barely knew what had happened. The sky above him was grey. Was it growing darker? Sounds of a horse and a man shouting, muffled, as if from a great distance.

With a huge effort, Dunston finally sucked in a deep breath of the earthy air. His chest screamed out. A sharp stabbing agony made him groan, as he slowly climbed to his feet. He attempted another breath. The same searing pain engulfed him. The spearman had dismounted and was coming towards him. For a moment, Dunston's vision blurred and he thought he might faint. Then the man's features became clearer. It was Raegnold, the man he had fought outside the barn in Briuuetone. Raegnold's face was swollen and bruised.

Clenching his jaw against the pain, Dunston reached down and retrieved DeaÞangenga from the grass. Tears pricked his eyes from the pain. He could barely stand. Had his ribs pierced his lungs?

Raegnold was almost on him now. None of the other men came to aid him to dispatch Dunston. He was not surprised. He must have looked as though he might die soon anyway, soaked in blood and mud, and barely able to rise to his feet. He shook his head in an attempt to clear it. Judging from the intensity of the pain, he might well succumb with no further injuries, if he was given time. But Raegnold was clearly not going to allow that to happen.

"Come to let me finish what I started back in Briuuetone?" Dunston asked. His voice rasped, his breath scratched in his chest.

"You're dead, old man," hissed Raegnold through gritted teeth, unable to open his mouth any wider due to his broken jaw.

Dunston willed himself to stand upright.

"Speak up, I can barely hear you," he taunted. But he had heard the words well enough. And what was worse, he knew them to be true. He would die here, now. His body was aflame with pain and even if by some miracle he was able to defeat Raegnold, there were still six men here, hale and strong. He could not survive against them all.

Raegnold pulled his sword from its scabbard, but did not reply. Evidently speaking hurt too much. Dunston understood that feeling.

"Well, Eawynn, I will be with you soon," he whispered. "I hope I did not disappoint you too much by breaking my promises."

He hoped that Aedwen had run from her hiding place. Perhaps she would be able to reach the safety of Exanceaster before these brutes could capture her. He prayed it was so. For there was no more that he could do now.

"Come on then," he said, lifting his great axe in both hands. "Let's see if I can't improve that ugly face of yours."

Raegnold growled and rushed forward.
Dunston moved on leaden legs to meet him.
To meet him, and to die.

Thirty-Four

Aedwen clung to the branch and watched Dunston's stand against the riders with a mixture of awe and horror. She cuffed away bitter tears, smearing her cheeks with the green of lichen and moss. Despite the terror that she was about to witness the old man's death, she could not look away.

More than once she was certain that Dunston would be struck down, but each time he had emerged from the press of horses and weapon-wielding men. She watched in a daze of disbelief as the grey-bearded woodsman killed two of the riders in that first attack and left two mounts screaming and kicking in the grass. The sound of the animals' distress scratched at her nerves, echoing her own anguish. But she did not scream. She gripped the alder tightly until her muscles cramped while she willed Dunston on.

Surely he could not hope to face so many foe-men and survive. And yet, as some of the horses wheeled about, she gasped. The old man was rushing at them! His bellowing cry reached her and she shuddered. He pulled one rider from his saddle and the man was sent careening away over the meadow towards Exanceaster, dragged from his stirrup.

And then one of the horsemen dismounted. His sword flickered in the sunlight as he circled Dunston. The man was young and fast and Aedwen was certain that she was about to see the death of the man who had kept her alive these last days. She felt a hollow emptiness; was unable to think. She knew she should take advantage of the fact that all of the remaining men were watching the duel. She could slip down from the tree and sprint to the path that ran alongside the river. With luck, she could be at the woods the other side of the path before anyone noticed her. Perhaps then she would be able to make her way carefully and invisibly to Exanceaster. She patted the bag that was slung over her shoulder. The message was yet there. And surely that is why Dunston fought, so that she might have time to escape. He could not hope to live. She must flee. She knew it.

And yet she did not move. She shifted her position slightly so that she might see more clearly through the tree's leaves and she watched.

The two warriors, young and old, were speaking, but she could not hear the words from this distance. She held her breath as the dark-bearded warrior leapt at Dunston without warning. The clash of their blades reached her a moment later and she was shocked to see Dunston had avoided the man's attack.

Along with all of the riders, she watched raptly, unable to turn away as the two men fought. She let out a whimper when Dunston was cut, and wept with relief when finally he slew his younger and faster assailant.

But Dunston was wounded now, bleeding and struggling. She could barely imagine the fatigue and exhaustion he must feel, and yet she saw it in his gait, in the droop of his head and the slump of his shoulders.

Against all the odds, Dunston remained upright and Aedwen cursed herself for not running. He had bought her this time with his blood and his suffering. And, she was sure, with his death, which must come soon enough. And yet still she did not climb down from her vantage point.

She screamed out a warning when she saw the horse bearing down on him from behind. Perhaps this was how she repaid him, by saving him from a craven attack from the rear.

Dunston turned, but too slow and she could not stop her tears now as the horse clattered into him, sending him tumbling and sprawling to the soft earth of the meadow.

She sobbed, willing him to rise. And when he did, pushing himself painfully and slowly to his feet, her heart clenched. He was barely able to stand, his body broken and clearly in agony. The horseman who had hit Dunston dismounted. Despite the distance, she recognised him instantly and cursed at the cruelty of it. That the man who had slain Odin would now kill the dog's master.

The circle of horsemen watched on, anticipating the end of the great Dunston the Bold. Expecting to see his lifeblood pumping into the meadow grass here, beneath the crumbling walls of Exanceaster.

Aedwen watched too. Like the riders, she was entranced, unable to turn away. But from her lofty position in the alder she caught a movement in the corner of her vision. A stealthy rippling in the long grass. A grey shadow, slipping between the waving sedge and golden marigolds of the meadow.

Raegnold was close to Dunston now. The old man, holding himself awkwardly against the pain, said something to the advancing man, but she could not hear what it was.

Her blood rushed in her ears and she looked back for the approaching shadow in the grass, thinking she must have imagined it.

It was still there, creeping ever closer. Could it be a wolf? Her mind could make no sense of it.

And then, in an instant, all became clear.

For, at the moment that Raegnold rushed at Dunston, ready to hack him down, the grey shape sprang forward, abandoning stealth for speed.

Thirty-Five

Dunston blinked, unsure for a moment what he was witnessing. Had he lost his senses? His body screamed at him, his chest a burning agony with each breath, hot blood running in rivers down his arm and belly. He had seen men lose their minds at the end, delirious from the pain as their spirits fought to cling to life for just a few more heartbeats.

He shook his head to clear it.

He was not dead yet. His vision was clear.

And now there could be no doubt. The grey shape that had leapt from the tall grass was Odin, his great merle hound. The dog's snarling jaws snapped onto Raegnold's wrist and the tall man, completely taken by surprise, let out a wail of fear and pain and fell into the grass. Odin was a frenzy of snarling and growling. Raegnold screamed as the two of them rolled, half-hidden by the foliage.

Regaining his wits, Dunston staggered forward. He would not allow the bastard to kill his dog. Evidently he had not slain Odin in Briuuetone, Dunston was not about to let him now.

He had only taken a couple of steps, when Raegnold's screams abated suddenly. Odin rose, panting, chest heaving. Raegnold was still. The dog's tongue lolled and its maw was stained crimson. Dunston almost laughed to see the dog's grin, but then he saw the long, blackened wound that ran the length of Odin's body and his stomach tightened. No hair grew along the cut that appeared to have been stitched and then burnt to staunch the bleeding. Someone had tended to the dog's injury, but Dunston feared the mystery healer's work would be undone soon.

The leader of the riders was the colour of a ripe rosehip now, as he screamed at his remaining men.

"Kill him! Kill him! Kill him, you incompetent fools!"

Goaded on thus by their master, the men spurred their horses forward. Dunston saw fear in some of their faces. Much blood had been spilt in a matter of moments, and the old wolf still stood. And yet, there was resolve in his enemies' expressions too. The warriors urged their mounts closer. Their eyes were hard and their weapons' steel glimmered dully in the sunlight.

A light rain began to fall and Dunston welcomed its cooling touch on his brow.

"To me, Odin," he called.

The hound padded to his side. Dunston's hand dropped to the dog's head and scratched behind his ears affectionately. It was good to see the old boy one last time, though how he had come to this place Dunston could not guess.

The riders were hesitating now, unsure how to proceed. They were grim-faced and determined, and yet it seemed they had not contended with the prospect of attacking an armed killer and his huge hound, both covered in the blood of their fallen comrades.

"What are you waiting for?" yelled their leader. Dunston noticed that despite his anger at his men's ineffectiveness, he did not ride forward with them.

A horse snorted and stamped. Its rider sawed at the reins, struggling to keep the beast from galloping away.

Dunston scanned the men's faces. Their jaws were set and they still had the benefit of overwhelming numbers. They would attack soon enough, goaded on by their lord.

"Just you and me again, old friend," he whispered and patted Odin's head. The fur was wiry and wet. Odin gazed up at his master with his one eye and licked his hand.

Above the riders, a rainbow appeared in the cloud-embroiled sky. Dunston smiled, wondering at the sign. He drew in a deep breath. By Christ, his ribs hurt.

Well, whether the rainbow was God's promise or an omen from the Norse gods, he would find out soon enough.

Hefting DeaÞangenga before him, Dunston raised himself up to his full height. His teeth ground together and he winced at the pain. But he would not let it show on his face. He would meet these murderers standing tall, not cowed and broken like some old washer woman.

"Come on then, if you are coming, you cowardly whoresons," he bellowed without warning. The steeds shied at the volume of his voice. He grinned, his teeth flashing wolfishly. "Or are you too craven to kill an old man and his dog?"

He would die now, he knew, but he had resigned himself to that reality and had made peace with breaking his oaths to Eawynn. The thought of death held no fear for him.

"Come on then, you curs," he yelled, ignoring the agony in his chest and raising DeaÞangenga into the air so that the sun caught its silver-threaded blade. And at last, their leader's commands and Dunston's taunts made the men move. As if at some unspoken signal, they all touched their spurs to their horses' flanks as one, and approached him and Odin with a deep-throated growl rather than a roar of defiance.

Dunston lifted his axe and prepared to take as many of them with him before death claimed him.

"Goodbye, Odin, old friend," he said.

The riders were almost upon them when a sound cut through their ire-filled shouts and the thrum of their horses' hooves. It was a piercing wail of a hunting horn and it came from the direction of Exanceaster. The riders reined in their mounts, clearly pleased for an excuse not to attack the blood-soaked greybeard, with his death-dealing axe and his fanged companion.

They halted a few paces from Dunston and turned towards the sound of the horn.

Riding from the town, sending up more angry green plovers into the sky, came a large group of men. Their cloaks were bright and polished metal glittered from their clothing, weapons and horses' harness.

One of the men who had been about to attack Dunston cursed and spat. He wheeled his horse about and trotted back to his lord. A moment later, the other horsemen followed him.

The golden-chained lord who led Dunston's assailants had lost all of his bluster. He was pale now where he had been crimson with rage moments before.

Dunston placed his hand on Odin's head once more and let DeaÞangenga's blade rest on the earth. Smiling, he looked up at the many-coloured arc of the rainbow that still hung in the air. He wondered again at its meaning. Whichever god had sent it into the heavens, it would seem it was a good omen for him.

He leaned on DeaÞangenga and patted Odin as the new group of horsemen approached. The horses splashed through puddles, sending up showers of tiny rainbows into the air. He counted close to thirty men coming from Exanceaster. They rode good horses, and the men wore colourful cloaks. Spear-tips glinted. Silver and gold glistened at throats, shoulders and fingers. Dunston noted that several of the men bore bows. None were armoured.

Dunston watched as his erstwhile attackers drew together. They were agitated and there was much hushed conversation. Dunston could not hear what was said and he did not much care. His body screamed at him with every breath. He longed to slump down, to rest in the long wet grass. And yet he willed himself to remain upright. He did not know who these newcomers were and he would not face a potential enemy sitting down, not while he yet lived.

They came at a canter and once again the horn sounded, piercing and loud. Moments later, the large band of riders was reining in around them. Dunston met the gaze of the men who looked down from their well-groomed mounts. Most were young, fresh-faced and arrogant, with combed and trimmed beards and moustaches. Their expressions of disdain withered under the glare of his ice blue stare.

One of the riders, an old man, with full, grey beard and wolf fur trimming his cloak, despite the warmth of the day, nudged his steed forward. Two dour-faced, younger men, with swords at their belts, pushed forward to accompany him.

"So," said the old man, taking in the dead and dying men and horses scattered about the meadow, "this is what prevented you from joining me for the hunt, Ælfgar."

The gold-chained leader spurred his steed forward.

"My lord king," he said, "I thought you were planning on hunting to the north."

"I was drawn to the commotion to the south. I may be old, but I yet have eyes in my head and great flocks of birds taking to the wing seemed like good prospect for hunting." He paused, casting his gaze about, taking in each of the bloody corpses strewn about. With each passing moment, his expression grew darker. For several heartbeats, his eyes lingered on Dunston, blood-streaked, wounded and leaning on his gore-slick axe. "By all that is holy," the king raged suddenly at the ealdorman, causing the horses to stamp and blow. "What is the meaning of this?"

"My lord king," said Ælfgar, raising himself up proudly in his saddle. "This man fled imprisonment. He has broken your peace, as you can see." He waved a hand about him as evidence of Dunston's wrongdoing. "He has slain several of my men."

Ealdorman Ælfgar's voice trembled with barely contained emotion. "He is a killer and he must be punished."

The king shifted in his saddle. The leather creaked. He narrowed his eyes beneath his bushy brows and held Ealdorman Ælfgar in his stare. For a long while, he did not move. Men jostled and shuffled. Someone coughed. The ealdorman swallowed and, after a moment's hesitation, dropped his gaze. Seemingly satisfied, Ecgberht turned his attention to Dunston.

He peered down at him for a time. With an effort, Dunston stood straighter and met the king's gaze. Ecgberht nodded.

"Well," he said as last, "I know that this man is a killer."

Relief washed over Ælfgar's face.

"You are wise, lord king. Have your men take him and we will have him hanged forthwith."

"Do not presume to give your king orders, Ælfgar." Ecgberht's tone was as hard and sharp as a blade.

"No, lord," stammered Ælfgar, "of course not, I merely meant—"

Ecgberht cut him off.

"I said that I know this man is a killer," he said. Ælfgar nodded, uncertainly, waiting now for the king to elaborate. "But I have never known this man to slay any but the enemies of Wessex," the king continued. "What do you say on the matter, Dunston, son of Wilnoth?"

"But lord…!" blurted out Ælfgar. "The man is a murderer."

"Silence, Ælfgar," snapped Ecgberht and, despite the pain that racked him, Dunston could not help but smile thinly to hear the steel in the king's tone. The man had grown old, but this was the same Ecgberht who had led Wessex to so many victories over the years. Age had not diminished his spirit.

The ealdorman seemed about to continue to protest, but another glower from the king silenced him.

"I would hear the telling of this tale from the mouth of one I trust," Ecgberht said. "Dunston, speak."

And so, in spite of the pain throbbing in his arm and the burning agony stabbing his chest with each intake of breath, Dunston told the tale as best he could. When he mentioned Hunfrith the reeve, one of Ælfgar's sworn men, the ealdorman could keep himself silent no longer.

"Lord king, you cannot listen to any more of this wolf-head's lies. He is outside the law. He has no voice."

Ecgberht turned to the granite-faced man to his right.

"If the ealdorman speaks again without my permission, you are to bind and gag him."

The guard nodded.

"With pleasure, lord king."

"Continue, Dunston."

Dunston did his best to tell the story of how they had fled from Briuuetone, their plan to find out why Aedwen's father had been murdered, discovering the slaughter at Cantmael. He did not mention Nothgyth, instead saying he had picked up the tracks of the riders and followed them. He told of the torture of the monk and how they had found the message and decided to head for Exanceaster in the hope of finding the king.

"I thought that only you could bring justice, lord," Dunston said. "I am but a simple woodsman, but it seemed clear to me there was more to this whole affair than banditry and wanton thirst for blood."

"Indeed. If what you say is even half-true, then there is the stink of conspiracy and treason about it. Though to what end, I cannot fathom. Where now is the message? Without it, your word is pitted against that of the ealdorman's."

"The girl, Aedwen, has it."

"And where is she?"

"I sent her to hide in those trees," Dunston said. "I do not know if she remains there."

"Well, call her hither, man, and let us see if we can put an end to this."

Dunston raised his arm, wincing at the pain and waved towards the stand of trees. For a long while there was no movement and he began to think Aedwen must have fled, as he had hoped she would only moments before.

He waved again.

"Aedwen," he called, his chest screaming from the effort. "Come, all is well."

Still no sign of her. He sighed. His mouth was dry. The gathered men were growing impatient, no doubt imagining that his whole tale had been nothing but lies.

"Where are you, girl?" Dunston whispered. Sweat mingled with the blood staining his kirtle.

He raised his hand for a third time and was about to shout once more, when the slender figure of the girl stepped silently from the shadow of the trees.

At the sight of the girl, Ælfgar tensed. He seemed ready to ride away, but the king's stony-jawed guard rode forward and grabbed the ealdorman's reins.

Aedwen walked slowly towards them. Her eyes were wide as she scanned the mass of mounted men.

"Do not fear, child," said Dunston. "This is the king." Her eyes widened yet further.

"And you are Aedwen, daughter of Lytelman, I take it?" asked Ecgberht.

She nodded, but seemed unable to speak.

"I am sorry for the loss of your father," Ecgberht said. "Do you have the letter that Dunston has been telling us about?"

She nodded again.

"Yes, lord," she managed at last.

"I would read it," said Ecgberht, holding out his hand expectantly and clicking his fingers.

One of the young men jumped from his horse and moved to Aedwen's side. She glanced at Dunston.

"It's all right, lassie," he said. "The king must read it."

She rummaged in the bag and pulled out the rolled up vellum. She handed it to the man, who in turn carried it to the king.

Swaying on his feet from the effort of standing, Dunston shook his head. He blinked against the blurring of his vision and clutched tightly to DeaÞangenga's haft. The carved patterns and runes in the wood dug into his palms. He watched as Ecgberht read from the flimsy sheet of stretched calf hide. As the king's gaze drifted over the scratched markings, his face grew dark and thundery. Nobody spoke as he read. Ealdorman Ælfgar fidgeted uncomfortably in his saddle, glaring at the man holding his reins.

When he had finished reading, the king frowned and handed it to one of his retinue, a hawk-nosed man, with a prominent brow. The man read it more quickly than the king. On finishing, he lowered the vellum and looked with incredulity and scorn at Ealdorman Ælfgar. Without a word, he handed the note back to his king.

"Well," Ecgberht said, shaking the sheet of writing so that it flapped and snapped like a banner, "now I understand why you chose not to ride on the hunt with me. Retrieving this message was much more important." He shook his head sadly. "What a fool you are! For surely only a fool would commit treason and then have scribes put quill to vellum setting out that very treachery in ink for anyone able to see."

Without warning, Ælfgar tugged his reins free of Ecgberht's man's grip. Kicking his heels into his mount's flanks, he sought to gallop away. But, the grim-faced warrior had only been momentarily surprised and before Ælfgar could pull away from him, he reached out and took a firm grip of the ealdorman's cloak. The lord's horse bounded away from under him and he tumbled backwards, landing hard on the soft earth. As quick as a diving kingfisher, the warrior leapt from his own saddle and was beside the ealdorman, deadly long seax unsheathed and at his throat.

Ecgberht sighed.

"You really are a fool," he said, still shaking his head. "The rest of you," he said, looking at the face of each of the ealdorman's men, "drop your weapons. You will be judged in accordance with the dooms of Wessex and, if you are innocent, you have nothing to fear." Two of the men tossed their swords into the grass and held out their hands. The remaining three evidently did not think much of their chances of being found innocent. They swung their horses' heads to the south and spurred them into a gallop.

The hawk-faced man barked orders and several of the huntsmen galloped after them.

"Lord king," said Ælfgar, his tone pleading. "Show me clemency, I beseech you."

"Clemency?" spat Ecgberht. "I would no more offer mercy to an adder. You sought to conspire with my enemies, to see me slain and the kingdom invaded. And for what?" Spittle flew from the king's lips, and his face was crimson, such was his sudden fury. "For wealth? For power? What riches did the Westwalas promise you in exchange for your treachery?"

"Lord," whimpered Ælfgar, "let me explain."

"Silence him," commanded the king and his man cuffed the ealdorman about the head. Hard. "Gag him, I would hear no more of his villainy. I have enough here, in writing and his guilt is plain on his face for all to see."

The warrior who held Ælfgar pulled off the noble's belt, shoved it in his mouth and tightened it, so that the man could do nothing more than grunt and moan.

Ecgberht turned away from the scene as if it disgusted him. Slowly, with the careful movements of the old, he swung his leg over the back of his horse and slid to the ground. Dunston's head spun. How young he had been when he had first met

Ecgberht. The king had seemed old to him then. God, he must have been close to Dunston's age now. By Christ, the man must feel tired and stiff. It didn't seem all that long ago, since they had ridden into battle side by side, both strong and full of life. Hungry for glory and battle-fame. Not long ago. But a lifetime had come and gone since then. Many lifetimes. He thought of Eawynn. She had never liked Ecgberht. She had been overjoyed when he had left the king's service.

Strange that now, all these years later, he should be with Ecgberht once more, and Eawynn long gone.

"It's been a long time, old friend," Ecgberht said. He took in the blood that soaked Dunston's clothes, the tatters of his sleeve. "You look terrible."

Dunston laughed.

"I only came back for the compliments," he said, wincing as the pain in his chest intensified.

The king laughed too.

"By Christ, it is good to see you, even if you have grown old."

"We all grow old, lord king," replied Dunston. "At least I will always be younger than you. You must be over sixty summers now!"

"I don't need you to remind me of that." The king smiled ruefully and Dunston chuckled. His laughter promptly turned into a cough that sent paroxysms of pain through his chest. Ecgberht placed an arm about his shoulders until the coughing subsided.

"It seems," he said, "that as is usual with you, you come to my aid when I most need it. You know," Ecgberht said, shaking his head, "I had thought you dead long ago."

Dunston grimaced with each stabbing breath. His vision darkened. Ecgberht's voice sounded distant, echoing and strange, as though he were in a great cavern. Dunston tried to focus on the king's face, but he could not see him clearly.

Behind Ecgberht, the rainbow was still bright and vibrant in the grey sky.

"I'm not dead yet," Dunston said, and collapsed into the long, lush meadow grass.

Thirty-Six

Aedwen looked down at Dunston and whispered another prayer to the Blessed Virgin. Dunston's skin was grey and his cheeks hollow. The wounds he had sustained in the fight beneath the walls of Exanceaster had taken a cruel toll on his body.

"He is not a young man," Abbess Bebbe had told Aedwen when Dunston had been carried to the monastery and placed under her care. The abbess was a tiny woman, with a bird-like air of fragility about her. And yet she brimmed with energy and bustled about the wounded man, cleaning and binding his cuts, tying tight strips of linen about his ribs and probing with her twig-like fingers to ascertain how deep the damage was. Like Dunston, she was not young and to Aedwen, she seemed as old as the crumbling Roman walls of the town. But the woman was kindly and had set up a pallet for the girl in the room beside Dunston's. Aedwen had asked whether she might be allowed to sleep in the cell with the old man. She felt safe when she was near him and she could not bear the thought that he might die. At the suggestion, the abbess had tutted and shaken her head so vigorously that Aedwen had thought her wimple might fall off.

"That would not do," the elderly woman had said. "No, no, no. You are not even of his blood. It is not seemly."

The morning after they had arrived at Exanceaster, Aedwen had woken at dawn. She had gone outside to the courtyard where the nuns and monks were going about their tasks, trudging through the mud in a thick, drenching drizzle that fell relentlessly from an iron sky. Gone were the bursts of rainbow-bringing sunshine of the day before, replaced with this incessant, dreary downpour. Odin had been curled up in a doorway, half-sheltered from the rain, but wet and cold all the same. He'd stood on stiff legs and shaken himself, gazing up at her with his single brown eye. Abbess Bebbe had forbidden the hound's entry into the monastery, but Aedwen could not allow the animal to remain outside in the rain. He had been lost for so many days, alone and hurt. Yet he had still found them. Her eyes filled with tears whenever she looked at his blackened, cauterised wound, and the pain he must have felt. She wondered whether they would ever know who had saved him and tended to his wound.

Aedwen had brought the hound inside and led him to Dunston's bedside. There they had sat vigil together. The abbess had found them there and had shooed them out of the room.

"That beast cannot be in here," she had complained, but it seemed to Aedwen without much conviction. And the old woman seemed to have forgotten her own rule about the dog when she had changed Dunston's bandages and Odin was lying patiently outside the room beside Aedwen, waiting to be allowed back in to sit with his master. The old woman clucked her tongue disapprovingly, but later, when one of the young novice nuns, a pinched-looking girl called Agnes, whose nose reminded Aedwen of a weasel's, brought Aedwen some soup and bread, she also carried a ham bone that she tossed onto the rushes by Odin's paws.

That was four days ago and each day had passed in the same way. Aedwen had sat with Odin watching over Dunston, searching for some sign of improvement in his condition. Each day the abbess would come to clean the old warrior's wounds and to bind them with fresh linen. Every day the old nun would usher the girl and the dog out of the small cell, impatiently clapping her hands for them to hurry. And every day when Aedwen and Odin returned to Dunston's side, Aedwen would enquire about his state.

For the first three days, the abbess had shaken her head.

"He is not young, but he is strong. If it is God's will, he will live."

But to Aedwen's eye, with each passing day Dunston had looked more feeble, older, more fragile.

Closer to death.

She clung to Bebbe's words, taking comfort from the scant encouragement in them. Surely such a godly woman would only speak the truth. So Aedwen prayed and dozed. And when she slept, her dreams were filled with visions of death; the screams of horses, thrashing in long grass; Ithamar's heart-rending wails of agony in a forest glade. She longed to see the soft, smiling face of her mother in her dreams, but it seemed as though the horrors she had witnessed had burnt her mother's memory from her mind.

On the fourth day, something had changed in the atmosphere of the monastery and for a moment Aedwen lay on the straw-filled mattress and listened, trying to ascertain what was different. Bright light streamed through the small window, spearing the gloom of the room, the lance of light illuminating motes of dust that danced in the air.

That was the change: it had stopped raining. The day had dawned bright with the promise of warmth and sun. She felt her spirits lift. But, just as she was rising from the pallet, she heard sobbing from a nearby cell. Such sounds were not uncommon here. Many of the young novices were homesick and sad, and weeping was often heard, especially at night.

But now, the sounds of sadness struck Aedwen like an ill omen.

She rose, crossing herself and whispering the words of the prayer to Maria, Mother of God, under her breath. She hurried to the courtyard, to allow Odin in to the building. Abbess Bebbe's good nature had not stretched so far that she would permit the animal to sleep in the monastery overnight. Odin was not where he usually waited for her. She whistled, but he did not appear. Her unease grew. Could it be that he had fled, or been hurt somehow? Perhaps one of the monks or the city guards had beaten him, or worse, killed him. She had seen the corpse of a small dog in the river on the day they had arrived and ever since, she had worried that Odin might meet the same sad end.

Panic rising in her chest, she whistled again and called the dog's name, ever more urgently. After several heartbeats, the hound came bounding into the courtyard. His tongue dangled from the side of his huge maw and her fear disappeared in an instant. She laughed at his expression, for he seemed to be grinning. The warmth and sun must have pleased him. The beast seemed full of puppy-like energy.

She was still chuckling and scratching Odin's ears when they arrived at Dunston's cell. Unusually for this time of day, the abbess was there, and the slender woman's bleak expression sent a chill through Aedwen.

"Is he...?" she could not bring herself to voice her fear.

Bebbe shook her head and took one of Aedwen's hands in hers. The old woman's skin was cool and dry.

"He yet lives," she said. "But you must prepare for the worst, child. There is nothing more I can do for him. He is in the Lord's hands now."

Aedwen bit her lip and closed her eyes. Taking a deep breath, she thanked the abbess and entered the room.

She immediately sensed the change. The air was dank and Dunston's skin seemed to glow in the shadowed cell. She sat beside him, taking his huge hand in hers. His skin was hot. Odin sniffed at Dunston's face and licked his cheek, before whimpering and curling up on the rush-strewn floor.

Taking a clean piece of linen, Aedwen dipped it in a bowl of water. She used the wet cloth to drip cool water on Dunston's lips, then, wringing out the linen, she moistened his brow. He made no movement. Her heart lurched, suddenly certain that this was one fight too many for the old man, that he had given in to his wounds and left this world.

And yet his skin still burnt and, when she looked closely, she could see his chest slowly rising and falling.

She prayed to the Virgin, Christ and all His Saints, that they might spare Dunston. She babbled in her prayers, caring not for the words. She clutched his hand tightly and wept. Tears streamed down her cheeks and soaked into the blanket that covered Dunston.

"You cannot die," she sobbed. "You got me safely here, but it is not enough. I am alone. Would you just leave now? Leaving me alone to my fate? I do not wish to be a nun." She sobbed, uncaring that her words were unfair. Her anger swelled within her and she let it burst forth in an outpouring of ire directed at this frail, dying man. She was furious at her mother for her sickness, for leaving her alone with her father. Enraged at her father for leading her into peril and for allowing himself to be killed. For his inquisitiveness that had led him to discover the plot against the king and then for his sense of duty that had seen him tell the secret to one of the conspirators. Tears washed down her face and the words tumbled from her in a cataract of anguish and anger.

"I want to see the forest and learn your skills. You said you would teach me. Would you die now and break your promise to me? You are no different from my father. All promises that you never meant to keep." She sobbed, dragging in ragged lungfuls of air.

Dunston's leathery fingers pressed against her slim hands. She started, sniffing back the tears and the rage that had consumed her.

"Dunston?" she whispered, terrified now that this was his body's last convulsive movement before his spirit departed. Would the last words he heard in this life be hers rebuking him for having the temerity of succumbing to his wounds?

"I—" his voice croaked in his throat. She could barely hear him.

"What?" she asked, leaning forward, placing her ear over his mouth. "What is it?"

"I have broken enough promises," he whispered. "I will not break this one. Stop your crying and let me sleep, girl. I need to rest."

Scarcely believing her ears, she sat back and looked at him, but he was quiet once more. She stared for a long while at his chest. Was his breathing deeper than a moment ago? Yes, she was sure of it.

Leaning forward, she placed a soft kiss upon his brow. He was warm, but the feverish glow of sickness had fled.

He slept.

It seemed he would keep his promise to her after all.

When Agnes brought a bowl of pottage sometime after Terce, she found Aedwen standing by the window and looking out to the trees and the wide, silvered waters of the river. Aedwen turned to greet the young nun and saw that her face was blotched, her eyes puffy. Had she been the one weeping that morning?

Aedwen took the bowl from her with a broad smile. For the first time in many days, she felt as though she had come out of the darkness and chill of a cave, stepping from the cool, black shadows of a barrow and into the bright sunshine of a summer's day.

"Do not be sad, Agnes," she said.

Thirty-Seven

Dunston awoke slowly. With each passing moment, as he clawed his way back to consciousness, he wished that death had claimed him. For as his senses returned, so did the pain. His chest was a dull throb, then stabbing in agony with each breath. He raised his arm to touch gingerly at his ribs and found them bound tightly. His arm, too, was bandaged, and the sharp pain there as the skin stretched reminded him of the deep cut he had received from Bealowin. He let his arm drop back to the bed. He was so weak. That one motion made him gasp with the effort, sending fresh waves of pain through his chest.

Turning his head slightly, he observed his surroundings. He was in a small, plain room. The walls were whitewashed and blue sky gleamed through a single narrow window. Sitting on a stool by his bed was Aedwen. Despite the torment of his body, Dunston smiled. The girl's head was slumped forward to lean on her arms which rested on the mattress beside him. Her hair tumbled over her face and arms, leaving only one smooth, pale cheek visible. Relief and a strange calm came over him at the sight of her. So young. So alone. Brave and resourceful. He fought the urge to reach out and caress her face.

With a stifled grunt, he shifted his position a little and saw the shape of Odin, stretched out on the floor beside the bed.

Dunston sighed, as the memories of the journey south and then the confrontation on the water meadows came back to him. Images and thoughts flooded his mind and, as he lay there, staring at the pale sky outside the window, he tried to make sense of what had transpired. But his thoughts were muddled and all he knew for certain was that he had not broken his promise to Eawynn. And he had seen Aedwen to safety. With those thoughts bringing a contented smile to his lips, sleep engulfed him once more.

When he next awoke, the room was darker and the sky outside was the hue of fresh blood.

"Thank the Virgin and her holy son," breathed Aedwen, as Dunston opened his eyes. "I had started to think you would not live."

Dunston offered her a smile.

"It takes more than a dozen mounted men to slay me," he said. His words rasped, dry and cracking in his throat.

"There were but ten of them, I recall," Aedwen answered with a smirk.

He chuckled, but quickly his laughter changed to coughing. He grimaced at the pain as each cough felt as though a seax was being thrust between his ribs.

"Sorry," said Aedwen, lifting his head and offering him some water. He drank a few sips. The cool water tasted better than the finest wine, such was his thirst. The liquid trickled down his throat and he could feel it running down inside him, replenishing him like rainfall soaking into a field of barley after a drought.

"How long have I been here?" he whispered. He didn't attempt speaking normally for fear of starting the cough again.

"Four days." Aedwen offered him more water, and he drank again. "Not too much," Aedwen said after he had taken several mouthfuls. "Abbess Bebbe says you must drink and eat sparingly to build up the balance of your humours."

"We are in a nunnery?"

Aedwen nodded.

"The monastery in Exanceaster. Both nuns and monks live and worship here. The abbess has tended to your wounds. She is very skilled."

Dunston touched the wrappings about his chest and winced.

"I must thank her," he said. He knew he owed his life to this Abbess Bebbe whom Aedwen spoke of and yet all he wanted was to be whole again, to leave Exanceaster and return to his home. He was as weak as a newborn lamb, but he longed to be able to stride away up the path and into the forest. He was done with the lies and conspiracies of nobles. He frowned. He had ever been thus. Eawynn had said he was a dreadful patient, always keen to undo what those nursing him had done to make him well. He supposed some things never changed. Just like the mendacity of some ealdormen and the ever-present plots that swirled around kings.

"You can thank the abbess soon enough," said Aedwen. "I will fetch her and bring you some broth too. You must be terribly hungry."

Odin rose from the rushes, stretched with a whining yawn, then nuzzled at Dunston's face. Dunston pushed Odin's snout away and scratched the hound's ears.

"I missed you too, boy," he said.

Dunston's stomach grumbled and he realised that he was ravenous. His belly felt drawn and painfully empty.

"Food would be good," he said, but, as Aedwen made to leave the room, he called her back. "But first, I would know of the message. What was in it, and what has our lord, King Ecgberht, done in these four days I have been abed? We carried that message for so long without knowing its meaning, and so many died to keep it secret, I must know. I wonder if I didn't die so that I wouldn't go to my grave without discovering the truth."

Aedwen's expression darkened, but she sat once more on the stool.

"It would seem that the message was from one Ealhstan to Ealdorman Ælfgar."

"The Ealhstan? Bishop of Scirburne?"

"The same."

Dunston whistled softly.

"But what of the message itself? What did it say?"

"I do not know exactly, but from what I have heard from the novices and the guards at the gate, the bishop and the ealdorman were discussing ways in which Ecgberht could be distracted away from the southwest of the kingdom."

"To what end?"

"So that a combined attacked between Norsemen and Wéalas could strike from Cornwalum."

"The Westwalas of Cornwalum have allied with the Norse?" Dunston asked, amazement in his tone.

Aedwen nodded.

"Such a thing goes against God," she said. "I know the Westwalas are our enemies, but I believed they were good Christian folk all the same."

"Greed has no honour and prays to no god. Both the Norse and the Westwalas are our enemies and they have their eyes set on the rich lands of Wessex. Together, a well-organised host could take Defnascire and Somersæte, especially if the king's forces were weakened in some way."

He scratched at his beard. It felt greasy and matted.

"Where is the king now?" he asked.

"Gone. He gathered his hearth warriors and the warbands of the ealdormen from these parts and sent out riders to call the fyrd. They have ridden west into Defnascire. The letter gave the date of the attack as the feast of Saint John the Baptist." When she saw Dunston's blank expression, she added, "Only a week ago."

Dunston's head was spinning. Ecgberht had been right. The men must have been fools to write such treason.

"What of Ealdorman Ælfgar?"

"Imprisoned, along with his men. They will face the king's justice when he returns."

If he returns, thought Dunston, but he merely nodded. Even now the king and his men might be facing a horde of Norsemen and Wéalas. Dunston could well imagine the scene, the fluttering banners and standards, the thickets of spears. He could almost hear the screams of anger and pain and the clash of the boards in the shieldwall. Men would be slaughtered and their blood would turn the earth to a quagmire, and for what? If the bishop and the ealdorman had succeeded in their treachery, the host of Wessex's enemies would have marched into the land unimpeded, plunging them into war and chaos. And all in the name of greed. For surely it must have been gold and power that they had been promised should Wessex fall and a new Norse or Wéalas king be seated on the throne of Witanceastre. Dunston sighed. Sadly, the men's avarice did not surprise him, but their lack of guile did. Ecgberht had governed Wessex for well over thirty years. He had expanded the borders of the kingdom and repelled enemies from all sides. While he lived, Wessex would remain strong. But even as he thought this, he recalled hearing of Ecgberht's defeat at Carrum two years previously. And the king was old now. He had seen as much with his own eyes. And an old, weakened king opened the doors to plots and emboldened the kingdom's enemies.

The room had grown silent, and with a start, Dunston opened his eyes. Slumber had sneaked up on him, stealthy as any hunter.

The sky was dark now, and the room was lit with guttering rush lights. The warm glow caught in Aedwen's eyes, softened the lines of worry that had formed on her brow. She smiled to see him awake once more.

"I have some soup. It will be cold now, but I did not wish to wake you. The abbess said it was best to let you rest. She is pleased with your progress."

"I will have to thank her tomorrow, it seems," he said, returning her smile.

He longed to snatch the spoon from her hand, to sit up and feed himself, but he allowed her to prop pillows beneath his head and then to spoon the cold broth into his mouth. It was thin, with the vaguest taste of meat and a hint of salt, but he could feel it restoring his strength by moments.

When the bowl was empty, Dunston belched and was glad that action did not hurt his ribs.

"Where is Odin?" he asked, noticing that the dog was not at his side.

"The abbess does not allow him to sleep inside at night."

He raised an eyebrow.

"How is he?" he said. "His wound had been tended by someone. Stitched and burnt, it looked to me."

"Yes," she said, and he noticed her eyes gleaming as tears welled there. "He seems well enough. Though he will be scarred there forever, and no hair grows now around the wound."

"Poor boy," said Dunston. "It must have been agony. I can think of few people Odin would allow near him when injured and fewer still he would let treat him so. And two of them are in this room." He felt his own eyes prickle with the threat of tears at the thought of the dog's suffering. He blinked them back. "Perhaps one day we will find out who patched him up. I would like to reward them somehow. Kindness is all too often accepted and not repaid. Whoever they were, they might not have done a pretty job, but they did a good one. The boy can still hunt." Dunston grinned wolfishly, recalling how Odin had leapt out of the grass and slain Raegnold. "And he can fight."

For a time, they were quiet, each lost in their memories. Finally, the pressure in his bladder made Dunston break the silence.

"I need a pot," he said.

Aedwen looked embarrassed.

"There is one beneath the bed," she said. She rose. "I'll leave you to relieve yourself."

"Aedwen, I do not think I can climb from the bed unaided."

She hesitated, then moved to help him up. He groaned as his ribs twisted, but he thought the pain was less than it had been earlier that day. After a few moments, he had his feet on the floor. Aedwen pulled out the earthenware pot and placed it beside the bed.

"Can you manage?" she asked.

"Yes, Aedwen," he answered, and smiled at her sigh of relief. "Thank you. I will call you when I am done."

She left the room and Dunston soon realised he was not certain he could cope unaided. His body ached and he felt so weak he was worried that he might fall. Grunting with the effort, he was at last able to position himself in such a way that he could piss into the bowl while half-sitting on the bed. The liquid gushed from him, foul-smelling and dark, and he wondered how he could have so much piss in him when he had barely drunk in four days. When he was done, he fell back into the bed, too tired to worry about the jolt to his ribs.

"I am finished," he called out. His voice was feeble, the weakness of it filled him with dismay and shame. He might be younger than the king, but by God, he was old and weak.

Aedwen came in and took the bowl away without comment.

"Sorry," he muttered as she carried it carefully from the room. Though what he was sorry for, he was not sure.

When she returned a short while later, replacing the empty bowl beneath his bed, Dunston had regained his breath and was as comfortable as he could be.

"You never told me you knew the king," Aedwen said, as she sat on the stool once more.

"You never asked," he said.

"He likes you."

Dunston grunted.

"I don't know if I would go that far."

"Was it the king who gave you the name of 'Bold'?"

Dunston cast his thoughts back all those years. He could barely remember the events that had led to the title he was famous for. The tale had been told so many times, first by those who were there, and later by men who claimed to have been there, and then just by anyone wanting to tell a good yarn. He himself had heard the story many times and with each telling the story was different. And as the years went by, his memories became blurred and confused, as if the weft of the truth had been woven with the warp of the fanciful tales, so that it was impossible to tell which was which.

"I never liked the name. I was just a warrior, like any other. I did my duty, nothing more."

"But for the king to name you 'Dunston the Bold'," she said, her tone full of awe. "It is an honour."

"It does not feel like an honour." He gazed at the flickering flame of the rush light. Sometimes, the name the king had given him that day, all those long years before, felt more like a curse.

"But why did he call you that?" she asked. "What did you do?"

Dunston remembered the man he had been: strong, reckless, hungry for battle-glory and fame. And then he recalled how, moments before, he had trembled and moaned to fill a pot with stinking piss.

"Perhaps you should ask the king," he said. "I am tired now. I must sleep."

"Of course," she replied, and the sound of her disappointment stung him.

He closed his eyes and listened to her blow out the flame of one of the rush lights and then, carrying the other for guidance, leaving the room. With Aedwen gone, the room felt cold and lonely and Dunston lay awake for a long while, looking at the darkening sky outside the small window.

He listened to the sounds of the town and the monastery that came to him through the window. A dog barked from the distance, and he wondered whether it might be Odin. Somewhere far off a baby wailed. A bell rang and soon after came the thin voices of the holy men and women of the monastery singing Compline.

Dunston lay there, willing himself to find the solace and peace of sleep, but it refused to come for a long time. He thought of Ealdorman Ælfgar and Bishop Ealhstan, of Hunfrith, Raegnold and Bealowin, who had tortured and slain all those people. Who would bring themselves to do such things? To betray their people for greed, to torture and kill? What manner of men were they?

And a small voice within him whispered a question that had often kept him awake in the darkest reaches of so many nights throughout his life.

What manner of man was he?

Thirty-Eight

Aedwen went down to Exanceaster's western gate to watch the king and the fyrd return. She hadn't really wanted to, but Agnes had begged her to go.

Ever since she had shown the girl some kindness, the novice nun would often seek her out, sneaking into her room long after she was supposed to be asleep. There, hidden beneath the blankets, the two girls would whisper and share their secrets and fears. Agnes was sad most of the time. She missed her brothers and sisters and felt so lonely in the monastery. When she had heard that the king had called the fyrd to arms she had grown certain that her brothers would join the defence of the realm. Her family's steading lay to the southwest and so, as the two were old enough to bear shield and spear, it seemed likely they would join the levies of their hundred and march to stop the Norse and Wéalas force.

She had become convinced that they would either be dead or return in glory, basking in the favour of the king, and so had begged Aedwen to look out for them when the men came back to the city.

Aedwen had pointed out that she did not know what Agnes's brothers looked like and also that they would more than likely have returned to the family farm, as they would pass it on the way back to Exanceaster, but Agnes would hear none of it.

"The abbess does not permit any of us to leave the monastery," she had whispered, her breath hot against Aedwen's cheek in the cool dark of the room. "So you must be my eyes. Twicga looks just like me, but taller, and a boy, of course." Agnes giggled. "Leofwig is broader and shorter and looks more like my father."

When Aedwen had commented that she had no inkling of Agnes's father's appearance, Agnes had waved her hands in annoyance.

"You will recognise Twicga sure enough," she'd said. "We are like two beans from the same husk. And Leofwig will be with him."

Aedwen had been very doubtful she would see the young men, or even that they would enter Exanceaster, but Agnes had been so insistent, that in the end, she had relented and joined the crowds awaiting the fyrd's triumphal homecoming.

It was a warm day and the sun was high in the sky when the mounted nobles and their hearth guards splashed across the wide expanse of the Exe. The people had gathered, awaiting the moment when the tide would make the crossing possible, and now the horses sent up great sheets of spray as the thegns and ealdormen trotted their mounts through the shallow river. They rode up the dry slope and clattered between the stone columns of the gate into the city. The streets were thronged with people. Tidings of Ecgberht's victory over Wessex's enemies had reached Exanceaster two days previously and the town had been abuzz with thankful chatter and bustling with preparations for the fyrd's return.

The smells of cooking and brewing hung over the settlement like a cloud, and now the women who lined the streets held out bread, cakes and pies to the men who had defended their land. Young women smiled and looked through their lashes at the dashing thegns, bedecked in iron-knit shirts, riding proudly in the king's retinue. Many of the warriors returned the smiles of the girls and called out to them suggestions of how they might repay their bravery in battle. Flirtatious laughter rippled amongst the young women.

Aedwen did not understand the attraction of these men. They had the hard faces of the horsemen who had attacked Dunston. They were younger versions of Dunston himself, she thought. Tough, unyielding, dour and steadfast.

These past few days, the old warrior had regained much of his strength. He was able to rise and walk for short distances. He revelled in the fresh air and had taken to walking around the walls with Odin. Each day he managed to go a little further before he grew tired and needed to rest. The abbess had been dismayed at his stubbornness, telling Aedwen that she needed to ensure that Dunston did not overexert himself. One grey drizzled day, Dunston had set out to walk with his dog and the abbess had confronted him.

"Would you undo that which the Lord has repaired?" she had asked. "You will catch cold. If it goes to your chest, then what?"

"Then the Lord will have to heal me again," Dunston had said. The abbess had trembled and it seemed as though the old lady might scream with fury, but Dunston had placed a hand on her shoulder and looked directly into her eyes. His ice-chip blue eyes glinted. "Lady Abbess," he'd said, holding her gaze. "Bebbe. You know that I am indebted to you for healing me. But I will surely die if I am not allowed to feel the fresh wind on my face or the rain in my hair. I will be well."

He had stepped out into the rain, wrapping his cloak about him.

The abbess had wheeled on Aedwen, as if Dunston's behaviour were her fault.

"The man is insufferable!" she hissed. She was flustered and smoothed her habit with nervous strokes of her bony hands. "You must talk sense into him. If he grows sick and dies, I will not be held responsible. But I would not be sorry to see the end of the cantankerous fool."

But Aedwen had noted the frequency of the abbess's visits to check on Dunston. She had seen how the old lady's face lit up when he spoke to her. Once, Aedwen had even heard Bebbe giggling at something Dunston had said, like one of the girls who mooned over the returning thegns. No, Aedwen thought, the abbess would be very sorry if anything were to happen to Dunston. And yet, despite her warnings that he would fall ill once again, Dunston did not cease in his activities, and with each passing day, his strength grew. He would be ready to leave soon, she knew, and a shiver of anxiety ran through her at the thought. She was alone now, and did not know what the future would hold for her. The thought of losing Dunston terrified her. He may be an ill-tempered old man, but he had protected her and had proven himself a man of honour.

Carts and waggons, pulled by oxen and mules, were trundling into the town now. The mood of the crowds altered. These were the wounded; those too badly hurt to ride or walk. The onlookers grew sombre. Many wept at the sight of so many injured men. As the waggons passed, Aedwen glimpsed pallid skin, blood-soaked linen, vacant, staring eyes.

One woman, her eyes dark and cheeks flushed, rushed forward, calling out the name of her man. The carters shook their heads and waved her away. After a moment, another woman pulled her back, away from the wounded. The first woman sobbed, clearly convinced her husband had been slain. Aedwen scanned the faces of the other women gathered there. All were pinched and guarded. Some wept, but most held on to their hope with dignity.

After some time, the fyrdmen, bedraggled, dirt-smeared, wet-legged from their crossing of the river and leaning tiredly on their spears, made their way into the city. Soon the air rang with the happy laughter and joyful weeping of women being reunited with their loved ones. Aedwen watched as the woman who had been inconsolable moments before now laughed with abandon, clinging to an embarrassed-looking man who patted her head awkwardly. Aedwen looked away, suddenly angry with the woman. She had someone to worry about, a man to hold and to fuss over.

Nearby, a plump woman called out to a warrior she clearly recognised.

"Hey, Bumoth. What of Edgar?"

Bumoth's face was ashen and he would not meet the woman's gaze. He looked down at the worn Roman cobbles of the street and shook his head. His meaning was clear, and the woman wailed, her face crumpling in grief as tears washed over her cheeks.

Aedwen turned away. It was too much. She didn't know what she had expected when she came to witness the return of the Wessex fyrd, but she had not been prepared for this outpouring of emotions. She had her own grief and sorrow that weighed on her heavily enough without watching others learn of the deaths of their kin.

Pushing through the crowds, she wandered the shadowed streets, her head teeming with dark thoughts. The sounds of the people at the gate receded and she found much of Exanceaster quiet and strangely peaceful. Most of the populace had gone to welcome the triumphant men home. She gave little thought to where she walked, but after some time, she found her way back to the monastery.

She could hear the sound of singing coming from the chapel and she prayed that Agnes was at Vespers. Aedwen could imagine how she would react when she told the novice she had not seen her brothers. She could not face the girl and her weeping.

Aedwen's stomach growled and she wished she had asked one of the goodwives for a pie or some bread. She could have shared it with Dunston. Perhaps they could find some food and eat together. She would like nothing more now than to sit quietly with the old man and his dog. She felt safe when she was with them. Perhaps the time had come to broach the subject of her future.

But when she arrived at Dunston's small cell, she knew she would find no peace any time soon. Two grim-faced warriors, cloaks and boots still muddy from the road, stood in the room. Their bulk all but filled the space.

"Ah, Aedwen," said Dunston, noticing her. "It is good that you have come."

Aedwen said nothing, but she knew her expression must have been one of anxiety. Her nerves had become as taut as a bowstring.

"It is nothing to fear," the old woodsman said. "The king has returned, victorious from Defnascire. And we are summoned."

"Summoned?"

"To an audience with the king. We are to attend him at the great hall."

The thought of an audience with Ecgberht and his nobles in the grand hall filled her with dread. In the silence, her stomach grumbled noisily.

Dunston smiled.

"I am sure the king will be hungry too after his journey. There will be food in the hall, no doubt. Come, let us go. The sooner we have spoken to the king, the sooner we can be gone from this place."

The warriors led the way out of the cell and Aedwen followed behind Dunston. She knew he was keen to be gone, to return to the forest and his old life. But what of her?

Walking behind the two broad-shouldered guards, she wondered for how much longer she could avoid confronting her next steps.

Thirty-Nine

Dunston looked over to where Aedwen sat surrounded by young women of the court. These were the daughters and wives of the king's retinue. Aedwen's features were tight, skin pale with flourishes of colour high on her cheeks. A beautiful raven-haired girl tittered at something. She was about the same age as Aedwen, but with silver pins glinting in her coiled plaits and a silken girdle of the deepest red around her slender waist. Aedwen smiled, but Dunston could see she was even more uncomfortable than he felt.

He had thought nothing of the girl's clothes and hair as they had been led to the hall. Aedwen was clean enough and wore a simple dress of drab brown that Bebbe had given her. But when they had entered the hall, which was lively with rushing servants and already filling rapidly with men and women come to celebrate the king's victory, Dunston had felt a needling of guilt. He could almost hear Eawynn rebuking his thoughtlessness, bringing a girl to a royal celebration without seeing that she had something finer than coarse-spun wool to wear.

He sighed. There was nothing for it now. He thought longingly of the peace of Sealhwudu. The forest was simpler. The trees and the animals cared nought for what clothes people wore.

Nevertheless, he recalled that Eawynn had always brushed her hair until it shone and had adorned her clothes with trinkets and jewels, even though they rarely entertained anyone in their woodland home. He had never understood why she wasted time on such things, though he could not deny that he enjoyed to gaze upon her when he came home from a day's work.

Pushing his fists into the small of his back, Dunston stretched. He winced. His chest still troubled him, but less so with each passing day. His daily walks were restoring his strength and the constant aches of the knitting bones and mottled bruises were receding. It was when he was sitting that his healing ribs bothered him the most. And he had been seated now for a long while. He reached for the cup before him. A servant, a comely, round-faced woman, had just refilled it with a delicious Frankish red wine. Dunston did not miss his previous life in service to the king. He was not made for great halls, small talk, speeches and the conniving plots of court. No, he thought, taking a sip of the rich, spicy wine. He did not regret living his simple life in the forest, but he did miss the wine.

With a thin smile playing on his lips, he looked about the great hall of Exanceaster. It rang with the hubbub of celebration. Conversations, laughter, the clatter of trenchers and cups. It was a large hall, roofed in wooden shingles, and painted in bright patterns without. Inside, it was spacious and well-appointed. Embroidered tapestries hung along the walls, depicting scenes of hunting and what Dunston supposed were stories of Christ's life and miracles. Most of the images he did not recognise, but one in particular was clear. A figure, head crowned in light, walking on the blue threads of a sea, while a sinking man reached out pitifully from the waves.

It had been many years since he had sat at the board in such a fine hall. From the awe in Aedwen's eyes as they had entered the building, he presumed the girl had never been in such a grand place and again he felt the stab of guilt at not having thought of her comfort. It could have been worse, he told himself, taking another warming mouthful of wine. They could have been in Witanceastre. Now there was a lavish hall that would have truly intimidated Aedwen, with its paintings, carvings and stone-flagged flooring. Even the seats there were finely carved with the intertwining images of animals and plants. He had never been in a finer hall than that of Witanceastre, and he had been in many halls. Several had been larger and richer than this one. He thought of the hall of Baldred of the Centingas. And the long, dark hall of Sigered of Éastseaxe. He shivered, pushing those distant memories from his mind and signalling to a passing servant to replenish his cup.

Yes, he had been in many halls over the years, and they all had some things in common. They were always filled with too many people and too much noise. And no matter how high the rafters, or how long the benches of a hall, it always felt to Dunston that the walls were slowly pushing in on him. The pretty servant returned to him and poured fresh wine into the cup he held out for her. She smiled. He muttered his thanks and she was gone.

He sipped at the wine. He must be careful not to drink too much too soon. If he was not mistaken, this feast would go on for some time. But despite his good intentions, the afternoon slipped into evening and Dunston's cup was rarely empty. The servant seemed to have taken a shine to him, and saw that he had food and drink aplenty throughout the long feast.

Dunston had been seated at a linen-covered board near to the high table, where the king sat with his closest ealdormen and thegns. Ecgberht had raised a hand to him in welcome when he'd noticed him, but other than that brief recognition, Dunston began to wonder why he had been ordered to attend the feast. The wine was wonderful, it was true, but he would rather have taken a jug of that back to his room and drunk it by himself. Instead, here he was surrounded by loud-voiced men and women he did not know. He shifted uncomfortably, attempting to relieve the pressure on his bound ribs. However he sat, he could not get comfortable.

By his feet, Odin stretched out onto his back, opening his rear legs in an undignified display of absolute relaxation. It seemed the hound was quicker to adapt than his master. Dunston reached down to stroke the dog and immediately regretted the movement.

"Your wounds yet trouble you?" said the man to his left. They had spoken but briefly before when the younger man, a thegn of Somersæte called Osgood had sat beside him and introduced himself. Since then, Osgood, perhaps sensing that Dunston did not wish to talk, had directed his conversation at other diners.

Dunston winced and straightened. Frowning, he turned slowly to the man. Osgood was fair-haired, with clear skin and an honest face. His shoulders were broad, hands strong and Dunston had noted the grace of his movements when he had slipped down onto the bench beside him.

"Well, I am getting no younger," Dunston said, his tone gruff.

Osgood smiled.

"I fear that even the mighty Dunston cannot turn back the tide of time."

Dunston stiffened. Was the thegn making fun of him? He took another swig of wine. Perhaps he was at that, but the man's grin was open and seemed to hold no malice.

Dunston snorted and returned the smirk.

"I certainly do not feel mighty."

"But bold perhaps?"

Dunston groaned.

"Not really. I don't think I have ever understood why the king named me thus."

"Like most men, I have heard the tales," replied Osgood. "If they are even half-true, then you were bold indeed."

Dunston shrugged.

"Perhaps I was once. Long ago."

"The man I saw surrounded by the corpses of his enemies a few days ago looked bold to me."

"You were there? With the king?"

"Yes, and I think if you do not like to be known as bold, you must stop acting quite so boldly."

Dunston laughed. His chest tightened and he willed himself not to cough.

"That sounds like fair advice." Still smiling, pleased that the wine had softened his anxiety at being here, surrounded by strangers and the oppressive walls of the hall, Dunston asked, "You fought with the king?"

"I did," Osgood replied, and his gaze shifted, took on the glaze of memory.

"Tell me," said Dunston.

And so Osgood told him of how they had waylaid the approaching host of Westwalas and Norsemen at a place called Hengestdūn.

"Our scouts had come back with tidings of their movements and so we were able to position the fyrd across the path between the hills. Ecgberht ordered those of us who were mounted to conceal ourselves in the forest on the slopes overlooking the road."

Dunston nodded. When he had been in the king's warband, they had used a similar tactic on more than one occasion and it had served them well.

"How many were they?"

"There must have been well over a score of crews of Norsemen joined by the same number of Wéalas."

Dunston blew out.

"A war host indeed," he said, picturing in his mind the size of such a force, how they would sound, the crash and thunder of their shields, the roar of their battle cries.

"Yes, but they were poorly organised. They faced our fyrd, but before they could summon up the courage to act, Ecgberht ordered the Wessex men to attack. And the moment after the shieldwalls clashed, we galloped down from the woods and hit them hard."

Osgood grew quiet and took a long draught of ale. Dunston knew what it was to relive battles and so did not press the younger man for more detail.

After a time, as though he felt he owed Dunston further explanation, Osgood continued.

"We slaughtered many of them," he said, and his pale face and set jaw told Dunston much. "And then they scattered. We chased them, riding after them and cutting them down. When the sun set, we had killed more than half their number and the rest had fled like whipped curs."

Dunston patted Osgood on the shoulder.

"You did what was needed of you. They were marching to kill our people, to steal our land and riches."

Osgood nodded, but his eyes were dark and clouded.

They grew silent then, allowing the waves of the celebration to wash over them.

"Does it get any easier?" Osgood asked, suddenly.

"What?"

"The killing," said Osgood, his voice lowered to not much more than a whisper.

Dunston looked at him sharply.

"This was your first battle?"

Osgood nodded.

Dunston swallowed, casting his mind back to the first time he had faced armed foe-men. The first time he had plunged his blade into the flesh of a living man, watched the life ebb from him, as the hot blood pumped into the mud. He sometimes saw that man's pleading eyes in his dreams, heard his desperate wails for mercy.

"The taking of a life should never be easy." He thought of the ripped and rent corpses of Bealowin's victims, Ithamar's screams. "Killing in the defence of the weak is honourable, but it should never be taken lightly. And an honourable man must never seek to inflict pain and suffering, for that is the way of the weakly coward. But to answer your question, killing can become easy, but you will have to live with the memories of your actions forever. And God will surely judge you for them when you stand before Him, so make sure you are acting for the right reasons."

Osgood stared at him for a long while, his expression grave. At last, he nodded and raised his cup.

"I thank you for your honesty, Dunston," he said.

"It is all I have," he replied with a thin smile, lifting his own cup and tapping it against Osgood's. "Now," he said, "let us talk of happier things. This is supposed to be a celebration."

And so the evening passed more pleasantly than Dunston had expected. To his surprise he found Osgood to be good company and they talked of all manner of things. From time to time Dunston glanced over at Aedwen and was pleased to see her seeming to relax. Perhaps she too had drunk the wine, he thought and smiled. One thing that had been worrying her was soon dealt with when plentiful dishes of all types of delicacy were carried into the hall. There was roasted hare, succulent mackerel, glutinous stews and freshly baked bread. Dunston saw that Aedwen, whether she felt embarrassed or shy in the company of these rich nobles, had decided to eat her fill. Her trencher was heaped with food and at one point in the evening, as the lowering sun cast golden rays through the hall's unshuttered windows, Aedwen grinned at him, her mouth full of meat. To see her thus, smiling and contented, warmed him and he felt as though an invisible weight had been lifted from his shoulders. Whether from this lightening of his burden or the dulling effects of the wine, his ribs pained him less as the sun set.

Candles were lit and the feast continued, increasingly raucous, as the ale, wine and mead flowed. Laughter stabbed through the general hubbub from time to time, like flashes of sunlight through thick cloud.

Dunston rose stiffly with a groan and a grimace. His belly was full and so was his bladder. On his way outside, he passed Aedwen. She looked up at him.

"All well?" he asked.

"Yes," she said. "At least I am not hungry now." She smiled, but he could see there was more she wanted to say. He patted her arm. Now was not the time or place. They could speak about whatever was troubling her later, or on the morrow.

When he returned from the midden, he made his way to his place beside Osgood, who welcomed him back with a broad grin and a refilled cup of wine. The atmosphere in the hall had changed. Dunston looked to the high table.

Ecgberht, resplendent in a gold-trimmed purple gown, stood and surveyed those gathered in the hall. Slowly, a hush fell over the room.

"Friends," he said, his voice strong and carrying. "Country-men. Folk of Wessex. As you know, we have returned victorious from battle with a host of Wéalas and Norse."

"Praise the Lord," exclaimed a dark-robed priest who sat to Ecgberht's right.

The king glanced at the priest slowly and pointedly. His meaning was clear. Interruptions were not something he tolerated.

"The brave men of Wessex fought with the strength of wild boars. Many gave their lives, but it would have been much, much worse for us if we had not been forewarned of the treachery that had festered in our midst. There will be time for gift-giving soon. You know that I am a generous king and I reward those who stand by my side."

This received a loud roar of approval and the gathered men, intoxicated on drink and life, pounded the boards with their fists and stamped their feet on the ground until the hall reverberated as if with thunder.

Ecgberht smiled, seemingly happy with this interruption. The small priest pursed his lips and swept his gaze about the room, as if he were judging all those gathered there.

When the cheering abated, Ecgberht nodded.

"Yes, there will be gifts soon for my trusty thegns and ealdormen. But first I must give my everlasting thanks to one man, without whom we might well have been doomed." He held his hand out to indicate Dunston. All eyes turned to him and he glowered back. He could feel the men weighing the worth of him. They might well know his name, but to see him, old and grey, must surely have rankled some, who would begrudge him the king's praise. "You have my undying gratitude, Dunston the Bold," the king said. "Without the boldness of your actions, it is likely our enemies would have prevailed. Because of your warning, we were able to lie in wait and ambush them at Hengestdūn. If not for you, Dunston, Ælfgar and Ealhstan might very well at this moment have been accepting your new Norse or Westwalas king with open arms." The king's face was dark now. "And for what? Some extra land and gold? Am I not generous enough?"

The hall again echoed with the acclamation of their king's generosity, but Ecgberht did not seem to pay them heed. Instead he was staring fixedly at the figure seated to his left. A timber pillar had been blocking the man from Dunston's view but now he shifted to see who had so caught Ecgberht's attention. He started when he recognised the man. It was Ælfgar, grim-faced and dismal, but dressed in expensive linen and silks, with his gold chain at his throat.

The hall grew silent.

"Well," Ecgberht said, his voice dripping with venom, "was I not a generous enough lord for you, Ælfgar?"

Ælfgar said nothing.

"Answer your king," screamed Ecgberht, fury bursting from him.

"You have always been generous, lord king," Ælfgar said, his voice tiny in the silence of the hall.

"And yet this is how you repay me," said the king. "And now I expect you would seek mercy from me."

Hope lit Ælfgar's face.

"Lord king," he said, his tone pleading. "You have always been the best of lords. Wrathful in battle. Just and merciful in victory."

"Was it mercy you would have offered me when the Norse and Westwalas marched over the Exe?"

"Lord—"

"Shut your treacherous mouth," Ecgberht snapped. "Dunston, what would you do with Ælfgar?"

Dunston's mouth felt suddenly as dry as dust.

"Lord, it is not for me to say," he said. "He should stand trial."

"He is before the king. And we know of his guilt. Do you deny it, Ælfgar?"

The ealdorman looked from the king to Dunston, two old men with grey beards and piercing stares. He swallowed.

"I do not," he said.

"There you have it, Dunston," Ecgberht continued, his voice as cold and hard as iron. "He is guilty. What would you have me do with him?"

Dunston sighed. He met Ecgberht's gaze and saw the rage there. He had known the king for many years and knew there was one thing he despised above all else: disloyalty.

"I would have him put to death, lord king," he said at last.

Ecgberht grinned and nodded.

"Quite so," he said. "I hope you have enjoyed the feast, Ælfgar. For it will be your last."

Ælfgar had grown very pale, but he did not weep or whimper. He held himself rigid and listened as his king pronounced sentence over him.

"Tomorrow," Ecgberht said, his voice loud and clear, "Ealdorman Ælfgar will be hanged and his body left for all my subjects to see. It must be known that infamy and betrayal of one's king brings nothing but death."

Ælfgar lowered his head, but remained silent.

"His family," the king continued, "will be stripped of all titles and lands and they will be exiled from Wessex. If they should ever be found in the kingdom, they are to be treated as traitors and slain. Take him out of my sight."

Two guards, who had clearly been awaiting the order, stepped forward. The ealdorman stood and offered the slightest of nods to the king before he was led from the hall.

"What of Bishop Ealhstan?" asked Dunston.

Ecgberht turned to the priest who sat at his side.

"Yes, that is a good question, is it not, Inwona?" he asked. "The Church would not have the king try one of their number, Dunston. A matter for God, it would seem." The priest squirmed beneath the king's glare. "But I sent men to fetch him anyway. I would have liked to look the weasel in the eye. But alas, it seems that news travels faster than a horse can carry a man, for when my men arrived at Scirburne, the good bishop had fled. To Frankia, if one is to believe what Inwona here says, isn't that right?"

The diminutive cleric looked up. Dunston was shocked to see a glint of defiance in the man's eyes.

"That is so, lord king," Inwona said. "I have sent word that he is to be detained and he will receive the justice meted out by the Holy Father of Rome himself."

"I would rather a noose about his neck," grumbled Ecgberht, "but no matter. I shall have to bow to the wisdom of the Pope in this matter. So," he said, suddenly jovial, "what of you, Dunston?"

"Me, lord?"

"Your reward. I owe you my kingdom and perhaps my life."

"Seeing you hale and triumphant over our enemies is reward enough. I want nothing but to return to my home in Sealhwudu."

Ecgberht shook his head. Dunston was aware that every person in the hall was staring at him. Many would be thinking of what they would ask of their king should they be in the same position. But he had spoken the truth, all he wanted was to go home.

"No, Dunston," said the king. "I cannot allow you to go unrewarded. What would the people think?"

"I want for nothing, lord king. I merely wish to live out the rest of my days in peace."

"Ah, peace. Yes, that would be nice. But I fear we will not be so lucky, old friend. With Frankia forgetting her allies, our enemies are circling Wessex like flies around horse dung."

The thought of more enemies attacking Wessex, and warfare becoming ever more commonplace, filled Dunston with dread. If only he could return to Sealhwudu, he could be free of fighting, leaving the shieldwalls to younger men such as Osgood. He had played his part in the defence of the realm.

"I need no reward," he said, stubbornly refusing to acknowledge what he knew to be true. Ecgberht was determined and intractable. He was also the king. Dunston recognised the jut of Ecgberht's jaw and knew that when the king was in this frame of mind, it was impossible to dissuade him.

"Nonsense, man," the king said, laughing, as if he knew what Dunston had been thinking. "I have a gift for you, which I insist you will accept."

Dunston nodded.

"Very well, lord king," he said with a sigh. "What is this gift you would give me?"

Grinning, King Ecgberht told him.

Forty

Aedwen breathed in deeply, taking in the warm summer scent of the land. The sun had shone these past days and the air was redolent of lush life, verdant and brimming with energy. She'd felt it herself, the summer heat seeping into her body as they'd ridden northward. The dark days of pursuit, fear and death had vanished, replaced with a comforting sensation of safety and contentment. On the light breeze she could make out the distant lowing of the cattle that were being led down the path on the other side of the valley. There was a figure walking with the animals, too far to discern the features, but she thought it must surely be Ceolwald, leading the cows down to the Bartons for their evening milking.

The houses of Briuuetone were peaceful and inviting as the golden light of the late sunshine gilded the thatched roofs and hazed the smoke that drifted from dozens of cooking fires. The hint of woodsmoke reached her and Aedwen's smile faltered. For a moment, she recalled the last time she had been in this place. The night had been aflame and filled with screams. Raegnold had attacked Dunston and threatened her. The men of the village had chased them out into the night. A tremor of trepidation rippled along her spine. She shuddered. Perhaps she was wrong to have come back here.

Reining in her horse, a small, placid mare from the steward of Exanceaster's own stable, she glanced back along the road. Dunston raised his hand in friendly greeting. His presence settled her nerves somewhat. She knew he was not overly happy with the gift that the king had bestowed upon him. But the tension he had carried in his every movement seemed to uncoil the further they rode from Exanceaster. He spoke little as they travelled, seemingly lost in his own thoughts. When they halted to rest and when they made camp at night, he had resumed his teaching of her. He pointed out the signs of animals and set her challenges. Could she find leaves of sorrel? What about burdock? And each night he had insisted that she build and light the fire, while their escort looked on impatiently waiting for her to kindle a spark that would catch.

She returned Dunston's wave with a smile. He was a good man. If he was ready to bring her back to Briuuetone, it must be safe. He would not allow any harm to befall her.

Out of the bushes that grew in a jumble beside the road, bounded Odin. His sudden appearance caused one of the king's hearth warriors' mounts to shy and stamp. The rider, a stern-faced warrior by the name of Eadric, cursed.

"Keep your damned hound under control," he shouted, tugging at his reins in an effort to control his startled steed.

"Learn to control a horse," said Dunston. "After all, you are riding it. I am not seated on a saddle atop Odin's back."

Eadric scowled and the other men laughed. This was a long-running feud between the two men and it was well-meaning enough. The escort of six horsemen had been forced upon them by the king.

"We do not need to be protected," Dunston had said.

"Nonsense," Ecgberht had replied. "I will not have you set upon by brigands on the road. No, Eadric will go with you to Briuuetone, and that is the end of the matter."

Aedwen had seen the resignation on his face, and Dunston had not argued. He knew the king well, it seemed. They had an easy camaraderie when they spoke that told of many shared years of campaigning in the past. And what good would arguing do anyway? No man could challenge the king's will. But as they had ridden along the north road, Aedwen began to wonder whether the king had truly had their safety in mind when he sent the armed men to accompany them.

At night, when the moon rose and the land grew dark and still, Aedwen would look at Dunston and see him staring into the flames of the fire. The shadows danced and writhed about his face, his eyes glinting and haunted in the darkness. When she awoke in the cool of the mornings, Dunston would have risen before the dawn and be gone from the camp.

The first time this happened Eadric had grown anxious, pacing around the rekindled fire as his men cooked oatcakes. As the sun had risen high into the cloud-free sky, he had cursed Dunston.

"We'll never find him now," he'd said. "The king warned me he might do this."

"Do what?" asked Dunston, stepping from the shadow of the lindens and oaks of the forest, Odin at his side. Over his shoulder, Dunston carried a hare. The cut along its stomach showed where it had been gutted. "I thought I would catch us some meat for tonight's meal."

"We have been waiting for you for what seems an eternity," Eadric said. "By the nails of the rood, man, we have wasted most of the morning."

"I have wasted nothing," Dunston said, flopping the plump animal over the rump of his horse, where he secured it with a leather thong. "And you have rested. We are in no hurry to reach Briuuetone, are we? We will be there soon enough."

Dunston had called many stops on the journey.

"I am an old man, and I need to rest," he would say, with a wink to Aedwen. "And my wounds are not yet fully healed."

She was sure that his ribs still pained him, but she was equally certain that he was more than strong enough to ride without so many halts, that he was merely slowing their progress, prolonging the moment when they would arrive here, at the settlement on the River Briw.

She did not mind that the journey had taken them a day longer than Eadric had anticipated. She had enjoyed the sensation of riding, even though at the end of the first day her backside and thighs had ached terribly. She found the gait of the mare soothing, and the sure-footed steed needed little guidance, allowing Aedwen to stare out at the rolling hills and woodland that they rode through. She also relished the time spent with Dunston learning further secrets of the forest. After they reached their destination, she did not know how often she might be able to have his undivided attention.

The lowering sun glimmered on the fast-flowing waters of the Briw. Dunston caught up with her and turned his horse's head to the left, away from the river and along a narrow path leading uphill. Aedwen's mare did not wait to be steered in the same way. The beast fell into step beside Dunston's mount and together, with the armed escort riding at their rear, they approached the small steading that nestled at the knap of the hill. The sun was in their eyes as they rode up, the front of the hut shaded, and cool after the warmth of the afternoon.

Dunston was swinging himself down from the saddle when the door opened and Gytha emerged, wiping her hands on a rag and smoothing her apron over her thighs. Behind her, Aedwen could see the pale faces of Maethild and Godgifu. Godgifu waved at Aedwen, beaming.

Aedwen smiled back, but she could not halt the roiling sensation of anxiety in her gut. She had thought that she had been contented and relaxed as they had travelled from Exanceaster, but now she realised that in her own way she too had been dreading arriving here, at this door.

Gytha took in the mounted warriors with a glance. She held her face still, unsure of what was happening here. Aedwen thought back to the night she had fled from Briuuetone with Dunston. Gytha must live in fear of a visit from the reeve for her involvement in the woodsman's escape. Despite her anxiety, Aedwen let out a sharp bark of laughter.

Both Dunston and Gytha stared at her. She felt her cheeks grow hot. She dismounted to cover her embarrassment.

Gytha stepped towards Dunston, placing her hands on her hips and meeting his gaze.

"What brings you to my door, Dunston, son of Wilnoth?" she asked, her tone flat.

"I come bearing a gift and a request."

"Do you indeed?" she asked, glancing at the warriors who remained mounted behind the grey-bearded man. "The last I heard, you were a wulfeshéafod, having escaped from the reeve's custody, injuring one of his men in the process."

"That was a dark day," Dunston said. "When Rothulf died, justice died in this hundred. But I am no longer an outlaw."

Gytha looked thoughtfully at him, weighing the meaning in his words.

"So these men are not your guards?"

Dunston gave a crooked smile.

"Perhaps they are, in one manner of speaking. But I have been pardoned by the king himself."

Gytha could not hide her astonishment at this pronouncement. Such was the confusion on her face that Aedwen was unable to stifle another burst of laughter. For a moment, Gytha said nothing, and then, seeming to have made up her mind, she said, "In that case, you must come inside and tell us all of your tidings. It seems much has happened in these last weeks. You men," she indicated the mounted guards, "will need to stay without the house. There is not enough room for all of you inside. But if you wait for a moment, I will bring out some ale, bread and cheese for you."

Without awaiting a reply, she walked back into the house.

It was not long before they were sitting at the small table with plates of cheese, bread and some good ham in front of them. Godgifu and Maethild sat either side of Aedwen and for a moment she remembered the warmth of their bodies pressed against her comfortingly when she had shared the girls' bed. While their mother had prepared food, the two girls had chattered like finches fluttering around a bramble hedge in autumn, bombarding Aedwen with questions. She had told them of the journey to Exanceaster, deciding to leave out much of the story, but giving enough for Gytha's daughters to gaze at her, awestruck, as they heard tales of sleeping in a barrow, spending a night in the charcoal burners' camp and another with dangerous wolf-heads and then meeting the king himself in the great hall of Exanceaster.

All the while Dunston talked in hushed tones with Gytha and Aedwen noticed that the woman's gaze flicked in her direction several times. What she was thinking though, Aedwen could not tell.

As they had sat at the table, the girls had fallen silent. Godgifu stared with undisguised fear at Dunston until Gytha snapped her fingers.

"Dunston is a guest under our roof, girls," she said. "Show some respect."

Godgifu lowered her gaze and Maethild sniggered at her discomfort.

"Girls," Gytha said, after they had eaten in silence for a few moments. "I have some tidings." She paused, and looked at Aedwen for a moment. Aedwen's stomach clenched, but Gytha smiled at her and she quickly remembered the warmth of the widow's welcome when she had first come to this small house, lost and terrified in the dark of night. Gytha nodded in reassurance and turned to her daughters. "Aedwen is going to stay with us."

With the words spoken, Aedwen's eyes blurred. Her heart hammered and she feared she might weep. What would Gytha's daughters think of this turn of events?

"Oh, mother," said Maethild, "that is wonderful. Finally, I can have a sensible sister to talk to."

Godgifu leaned across and pinched her older sister, who slapped her hand in return.

"Girls!" Gytha's tone cut through their sport. "Aedwen will be treated as kin, and I will have no fighting. You must all learn to get along, or I will bang your heads together until you see sense. Is that clear?"

Gytha glowered at them in turn, and each girl nodded and bowed her head. Aedwen wondered for the briefest of moments whether she would have been better off with Dunston, but then, as if the two girls could sense her disquiet, each of them reached for her hands under the board. She grasped their hands and blinked at the tears that threatened to fall.

"Well, this is a gift indeed," said Gytha. "A new daughter."

"She is a good girl," replied Dunston. "But to accept Aedwen into your care was the request I had for you."

"And the gift then? What would that be?"

"Ecgberht has offered a gift of coin for Aedwen's upkeep. You will want for nothing."

Gytha was rendered speechless. This news was clearly a surprise and such was the look of amazement on her face, that the three girls burst out laughing.

Gytha wiped her eyes and then drank some ale.

Aedwen's hands trembled with the force of emotions that ran through her. Tears of joy rolled down her cheeks. She wished to dry her face, but did not want to relinquish the hold on the girls' hands. So she gripped them tightly, sniffing and blinking.

"Well," said Gytha, laughing. "What a fine to do. Now we are all crying. But still we do not know how it is that you both have returned to us. And not only free, but with the king's favour."

Dunston drained his cup of ale, wiping his mouth with the back of his rough hand. And in the warm gloom of the house, with the hearth fire and rush lights providing scant, flickering light, he told their tale. The womenfolk watched on, wide-eyed, as they heard tell of the pursuit through the forest and the hardships Aedwen and Dunston had been forced to endure. Dunston was no scop, not a poet from a lord's hall, but his words spun a stark picture of the terrible days they had spent in the forest. Unlike a tale-spinner, who sought to shock his audience, Dunston did not dwell on the moments when they had found corpses, or when he had stood and fought against their attackers. But somehow, the sparseness and simple nature of the telling made the tale more captivating. Gytha had grown pale. Godgifu and Maethild clung to Aedwen.

She shuddered as Dunston's words brought back the horrors they had faced. It was strange, she thought, that even though she had lived through the events he described, she found herself moved by the story, as one who is hearing it for the first time. Again she felt the bitter sting of the loss of her father. The terror of being caught by the savage men on the road. And then the breathless anxiety of seeing Dunston facing a line of charging, mounted men, as they threw up great clods of mud and sprays of water from the meadow. Dunston did not mention the rainbow that had shone in the darkened, clouded sky above Exanceaster, but she recalled its colours vividly and how the red of blood had been both darker and brighter than God's promise in the heavens.

At the end of the telling her face was again wet with tears. The girls at her side were snivelling and tears also streaked Gytha's face.

The widow reached out a hand and gently touched Dunston's shoulder. He started, as if woken from a reverie.

"You are a brave man, Dunston," she said, her voice quiet. He grunted.

"Aedwen owes you her life, and it seems the king owes you his kingdom." Dunston picked up his cup to hide his embarrassment and found it empty. Gytha lifted the pitcher and filled it, smiling. "Perhaps we all owe you our lives. For who knows what would have happened if the king had not learnt of the ealdorman's treachery?"

"I merely did my duty," he said, his tone gruff.

It was clear that the praise was making him feel awkward, so Gytha rose and fetched a small wooden box, which she placed upon the table. She lifted the lid and inside there was a parcel wrapped in linen.

"Would you care for a honey cake?"

Her daughters, tears forgotten now, sat up expectantly.

"Dunston?" Gytha said, peeling back the linen and proffering the box to him.

Dunston peered inside and plucked out one of the small cakes. Sniffing it, he grinned.

"Better than the fare from the king's own board," he said and took a bite. "And certainly better company." A few crumbs sprayed out of his mouth and he quickly rubbed at his beard, abashed.

But Gytha beamed at the praise and offered the cakes to the girls. They each took one. Maethild and Godgifu made short work of theirs, but Aedwen savoured hers. It was sweet and chewy and perhaps the nicest thing she had ever eaten. She thought then of her mother, and how she would sometimes bake honey cakes. They were not as good as

Gytha's, she thought guiltily, and once more tears threatened to fall.

"So, Dunston," Gytha said after she had finished her own cake. "I suppose you will go back now to your home in Sealhwudu?"

Was there a hint of sorrow in Gytha's tone?

Dunston washed down the last of his cake with a swig of ale and stifled a belch.

"I would like nothing more," he said. Did Gytha frown at his words? "But it seems my days of peace in the forest are over."

"But you said that Ecgberht King offered you a gift. Surely with gold you can live comfortably any way you please."

Dunston scratched his beard and looked sidelong at Aedwen.

"Ah," he said, a rueful expression on his face, "but it was not gold or silver that our lord king gave to me."

"No?" replied Gytha, surprised. "What then?"

"Why, for my sins he has made me his reeve of the Briuuetone Hundred."

Forty-One

Sweat dripped into Dunston's eyes. It was a hot day and he had set a fast pace along the familiar forest paths. Sunlight slanted down through the summer-heavy canopy, dappling the hard, root-twisted ground before him. Taking out his water skin, he took a long pull. The cool water soothed his parched mouth. By Christ's bones, how he'd missed being out in the woods, free from the troubles of the folk of Briuuetone, away from the concerns of upholding Ecgberht's many laws. Who would have ever thought there would be so many disputes over the boundaries between men's plots of land? Dunston longed to return to the life he had known before, where he was able to hunt, forage and forge as the whim took him.

He smiled at the irony of the king's "gift". The position of reeve was one of standing, which came with a stipend and status, and Ecgberht had also rewarded him handsomely with a bag of silver scillings so large that he doubted he would ever be able to spend all the money. And yet the very thing that had been gifted to him prevented him from leading the life he craved.

But he was a man of honour, and he had long ago sworn his oath to Ecgberht. So while the king yet lived, his word was his bond. And Dunston knew that, though he would rather not be given the task of upholding the law, the king's choice had merit. Dunston was diligent and honest. The people of Briuuetone and the surrounding hundred could rest easy that he would do the job to the best of his ability.

But how he pined for the quiet of the forest. The wind rustled the leaves of the lindens above his head and he drew in a deep breath of the heavy, loamy air. He was almost at his destination. Just past that fallen beech, then a short way until the mossy outcrop on the left and the clearing he had called home for so many years would open in front of him. His back was hot and drenched in sweat beneath the empty pack he carried there. Now, as he drew close to his old home, he wished he had brought a cart. There was so much he would like to carry back to his new house in Briuuetone. Well, there was nothing for that now. He would have to make do with just taking a few small items; Eawynn's plate, his favourite hammer, the small seax he had been working on for Oswold, perhaps a couple of the cheeses he had stored, if the mice hadn't got to them. He had worried that Wudugát, his goat, would have come to harm. He had left the poor girl tethered and had hoped she would have managed to chew through the rope easily enough. And yet, he had still fretted. There were wolves out here, and he had assumed the worst.

He still could barely believe he had found her hale and whole that morning roaming a small enclosure on the edge of the charcoal burners' encampment. These were the men who had helped him to raise Odin when he was a pup and they welcomed Dunston like a long lost son. They had slapped him on the back, which made him wince, as his ribs were still tender. They laughed to see him, their blackened, soot-smeared faces lined and wrinkled with their happiness. When Dunston had enquired about the effusive nature of their welcome, the response they gave him answered a quandary that had been bothering him for some time.

"We thought you were dead," said the oldest of the men. "Thought you'd gone the way of all things, these many weeks past."

Dunston had shaken his head, confused.

"People often make the mistake of thinking I am dead it seems," he'd said, with a crooked smile. "But what made you think such a thing?"

"Why, when old Odin limped in here with half his back hanging off and covered in blood, we thought perhaps a boar had got you and him. You weren't with him, so we figured as like you were mouldering in the forest somewhere. Botulf sewed up the cut on Odin and burnt the flesh so that the rot wouldn't set in. That hound is as tough as they come. He barely whimpered and didn't snap at Botulf, not one bit. I thought he'd as likely bite his hand off, but it was like he understood that Botulf was just trying to help."

"Botulf," Dunston called to a younger man. "I thank you for saving my dog. If you had not done so, I might be dead after all."

"Odin lives yet then?" asked Botulf. "I thought he must have surely died by now. For when we woke the next morning, he had run off into the forest and no matter how much we called, he did not return. Gone off to die in peace, we thought."

"He lives, all right. He is out hunting with a new friend. A girl."

"Oh, a girl," said Botulf, with a wink. "About time you took a wife again, if you ask me."

"I didn't ask you," replied Dunston. "And she is not my wife. She is not much more than a child."

He had told the charcoal burners of their adventures then. They thirsted for knowledge of the world beyond their smoke-wreathed clearings and it seemed the least he could do after they had tended to Odin. It transpired that, after Odin had vanished, fearing for Dunston, they had gone to his hut to see if he might be there and in need of help. Instead, they found Wudugát. Realising she would perish if left alone, they brought the goat back to their camp.

"She has been well looked after," said Botulf, "and we have been glad of the milk, I can tell you. But, of course, you must take her with you now."

"No. Wudugát is yours," Dunston had said. "You saved my dog and in doing so, you saved me and maybe the kingdom, so I would have you supplied with fresh milk."

He smiled to himself as he remembered the charcoal burners' delight at first finding him alive, and then learning that Odin was well. And after that, they were even more pleased that they could keep the goat when they had thought they would have to give her back. It is the simple things that bring the most pleasure, he thought.

Pushing the stopper back into his flask, he set off on the last stretch of the path that would lead him to his hut in the clearing.

He had looked forward to getting away from Briuuetone for several days now. He was staying in the hall that Rothulf had built. It was comfortable and spacious; much too large for his needs apart from one day each month when the hall-moot was held there. On the day of the moot, it became the centre of life of the people of the village and the surrounding area of the hundred. He had been prepared for the busy nature of the day, but had found himself unable to sleep the night before. His mind kept jolting him awake with dark thoughts that he might need to preside over a suit involving murder. He knew he could face an armed man in combat and take his life in an eye-blink, but to have someone stand before him, to speak with them, to listen to the charges made against them, and then to mete out justice, took a different type of bravery.

As it turned out, his first moot at Briuuetone was a tedious affair, with the most arduous of the suits being that in which

Eappa had struck Cuthbald over some drunken squabble. Eappa had broken Cuthbald's nose, and Cuthbald demanded restitution. Dunston had conferred with Godrum, the priest, who had read through the dooms and informed him of the weregild that must be paid. Eappa had grumbled and complained when he was told to pay Cuthbald three scillings, but Dunston had stood up, and glared at him until he had meekly nodded and left the hall. The rest of the day had been filled with petty disputes over land rights and some minor thefts. Dunston relied on Godrum to provide him with good counsel and to pore over the vellum sheets of dooms. He found the priest to be methodical and patient and, despite the tedium of the day, his initial fears had been misplaced. He was sure his concerns had been due in no small part to having witnessed the trial of the traitors in Exanceaster just a few weeks previously.

By God, that had been harrowing, and Dunston was glad that he did not have to deal with anything as dire as treachery and murder.

After Ælfgar had been hanged unceremoniously from the east gate of the city walls, Ecgberht had ordered the men who had ridden with the ealdorman to be brought before him. The king had insisted that Dunston attend the trial, as he was a witness to many of the acts the men stood accused of.

Most of the accused, certain of their fate, were sullen and refused to speak. But one, a lank-haired man with stooped shoulders, by the name of Lutan, had seemed convinced that he could escape his punishment by telling everything he knew of what they had done. The others glowered at him, and one spat in his direction and swore he would seek him out in the afterlife and cut out his tongue. A guard had beaten the man into silence, and the greasy-haired Lutan had been allowed to speak.

The king nodded and urged Lutan to tell them all he knew.

"If you tell me the truth, man," the king said in a quiet voice, "I will see to it that you are treated better than your comrades in arms."

Lutan had dipped his head, swallowing and grovelling pitifully, while his companions looked on. Hatred burnt in their eyes at his betrayal.

Prompted by questions from Ecgberht, Lutan told of more than the incidents Dunston knew of. Much of what he told, Dunston had already deduced. Lytelman had somehow learnt of the message from Ithamar and then sought to bring the news of treason to one in power. He visited the reeve of Briuuetone. But, unbeknown to Aedwen's father, Hunfrith was party to the plans of Ealdorman Ælfgar and so had ordered the peddler silenced.

"Why was Hunfrith involved?" Dunston had asked, interrupting Lutan's snivelling whine. "Surely Ælfgar did not take lowly reeves into his confidence."

Lutan had stared at him for a moment, a sly expression on his ugly face.

"You do not know?" he asked incredulously.

"Know what?"

"Hunfrith is Ælfgar's son. A bastard from a milkmaid in Wincaletone. When Ælfgar learnt of Rothulf's meddling, he sent Hunfrith to take care of it. If you know what I mean."

He had smirked then at Dunston, and it had been hard not to rush at the man and knock him to the ground. Dunston had clenched his fists at his side, holding himself rigidly still. So, the rumours Gytha had heard were true, but it was not this knowledge that had led to Rothulf's murder.

"Meddling?" Dunston had asked. "How so?"

Lutan's eyes had darted about as his mind worked, seeking some advantage for himself from his knowledge. At last he turned to the king.

"If I tell you of more crimes, it will go easier for me?" he asked.

Ecgberht inclined his head slowly.

"I give you my word."

Lutan licked his lips.

"Rothulf had somehow heard tell of the plans to attack Wessex," he said. "I don't know how. But just after Easter he came to see Ælfgar and told him what he knew. Ælfgar thanked him and sent him back to Briuuetone. But no sooner had he gone than he sent Hunfrith, me and the others after him. It was Hunfrith's idea to drown him. Wouldn't look like a murder that way, he said. Once he was dead, Hunfrith took over as reeve. That way he could help stop any more rumours. And we would all share in the spoils once war came."

Dunston had grown cold at hearing Lutan's words.

"So Hunfrith murdered Rothulf?" he asked, his voice barely more than a whisper, but heard by all in the great hall of Exanceaster.

"He did," Lutan answered. He sounded somehow pleased with himself.

"Where is this Hunfrith now?" asked the king.

"The last we saw him, he was still at Briuuetone," replied Dunston.

The king ordered riders to go with all haste to Briuuetone and to seek out Hunfrith.

"He must be held accountable for his crimes," he said, and his face was thunder. "Rothulf was a good man."

But when the riders returned a few days later, it was to tell the king that there was no sign of Hunfrith at Briuuetone. It seemed he had fled when word had reached him of his father's capture. The news had weighed heavily on Dunston. He had not truly expected Hunfrith to still be in his hall, awaiting his fate, but the idea that the man had evaded justice after committing such foul crimes was almost more than he could bear. He had told Aedwen that vengeance did not bring happiness, but since Hunfrith's involvement in Rothulf's death had been confirmed, he had prayed that the man would be found and that he might witness his death, for there could be no other sentence for such as him.

But Hunfrith had run and now he would never have to pay for Rothulf's murder, for ordering the slaying of Lytelman, for abetting his father's treachery.

Dunston had resigned himself to taking some consolation in the downfall of Ælfgar and his men. And yet, witnessing their deaths by hanging, their tongues swollen and black as they danced on the end of a rope, had left him feeling as empty as if he had watched animals being slaughtered before winter.

He had felt something akin to a twinge of grim amusement as Lutan met his fate. True to his word, the king had made the man's sentence easier than that of his cohort of traitors; instead of hanging, which could be long and painful, Ecgberht had ordered the man beheaded. There had been a twisted sense of justice at hearing Lutan's anguished cries as he was forced to watch his friends pulled, choking, kicking and strangling into the air, before he met his own, mercifully quick ending.

But none of the killing had provided Dunston with any release. He had brought Gytha the news that Rothulf had indeed been murdered, but Hunfrith had vanished, leaving Dunston bitter and angry. He now wished that he had not told Gytha the truth. She had suspected, but in time she would have made peace with her husband's death. Learning of the certainty of his murder and the lack of justice for his killer had sowed dark seeds of despair in her soul. Dunston felt responsible for Gytha's new sorrow, though he knew in truth he was not to blame; he had loved Rothulf as a brother.

There had been many dark days since they had returned to Briuuetone. The summer days were bright and warm, but the shadow of recent events still hung over them, as if a storm cloud had drifted before the sun. And yet, there was much to celebrate in his new life. He had invited Gytha, her daughters and Aedwen to live in the hall with him. He needed someone to run the place and Gytha had been the lady of the hall until recently. And, though sometimes he found the noise of the girls' chatter grated on his nerves, he thought the time for silence in the forest was over for him. Better to be surrounded by the laughter of youth than the silence of approaching decrepitude and death.

And yet, when the opportunity to head into the forest had arisen, he had not hesitated. Dunston knew that he would settle in well enough over time, but some days the constant companionship of Gytha, the girls and the ever-present folk of Briuuetone became too much and he longed for the peace of nature to embrace him.

Stepping out into the glade where he had built the stout house he had shared happily with Eawynn, Dunston paused to take in the scene. The grass was faded and dried as it often became in late summer. The ground was parched, and he noted how fissures and cracks had opened up in the earth due to the long dry spell. The lindens that overshadowed the house were thick with leaf and heavy with fragrant yellow blossom. The trees whispered, as if in greeting and their voice was as familiar as his own breath. Dunston sniffed the air. The summer would be on the turn soon and those glossy green leaves would become ochre and russet. They would fall, forming a thick blanket on the ground. The nights would grow longer. It was then, he knew, when he would most miss this place. Every year the summers seemed shorter and winter's icy fingers scratched over the land more quickly. With each passing year, time seemed to flow faster, and with a maudlin frown, Dunston wondered how many more passing seasons he would witness.

Shaking his head at such thoughts, he moved to the forge that stood under a lean-to timber shelter beside the hut. He looked about the grimy surfaces, the charcoal that nestled cold and grey in the fire pit. His gaze fell on a scrap of leather on the anvil. He could scarcely believe it was still there, but other than the charcoal men, who else would have come here? Picking up the greased leather, he let it fall open to expose what was wrapped within. He smiled. It was just as he remembered it, not even a spot of rust. It was the fine blade and tang of the knife he had been working on for Oswold. There was still some fine hammering to do, it was not sharp and was still a piece of iron without a handle, but it would be beautiful when it was finished. He had left it out here on the morning when he had found Lytelman and Aedwen, meaning to work on it when he returned from checking his traps and snares. He would take it back to Briuuetone and finish the knife there. He had just the right piece of antler that would serve as a handle. Wrapping the blade back in the leather, he tucked it into his belt and with a last longing look at the forge, he turned to the house.

He opened the oak door that he had fashioned what seemed a lifetime before. It creaked on the leather straps that held it in place. He had often contemplated forging iron hinges, but had never been able to justify the extravagance. He snorted. Now he had enough silver not to worry about such things, but he would no longer be living here to care about the door's hinges.

The instant that Dunston walked into the hut, he knew something was wrong. At first he was uncertain what had alerted him that all was not well. The air was not as still as it should be, the house less quiet somehow, though when he paused by the door to listen, there was no sound. He took a slow breath and then it struck him. A faint scent of sweat, wool, leather and sour mead. Someone had been there.

He moved to the hearth, holding his hand over the thick layer of grey ash. Still hot. How had he not smelt the smoke before? He had been too distracted reminiscing about the past to notice. Cursing himself for a fool, he stood, his senses sharp and alert once more. He had grown soft in just a few weeks living in luxury in a warm hall. This was still wild land. There were beasts that could kill a man in Sealhwudu, and as he well knew, there were outlaws who would not think twice about killing him to take the clothes from his corpse. His hand dropped to the seax sheathed at his belt and he regretted bitterly not bringing DeaÞangenga. But he had come to hunt and to visit his old home, not to battle. He was done with fighting and killing. It was time to keep his oath to Eawynn.

A rustle outside gave him an instant's warning, but when the door swung open with a rasp, Dunston started. The sound was loud in the small hut.

Without turning, Dunston looked up at Eawynn's silver plate where it hung on the far wall. Within the burnished metal he saw the reflection of the shadowed figure that hesitated in the doorway. It was a tall man, but Dunston could not make out his features with the light from outside behind him.

"Well, come in, if you are going to," Dunston said. "It seems you have made yourself quite at home in my house, so there is no point being shy now."

For a moment, the man did not move, then he stepped quickly into the hut. The light from the open door fell on his face and Dunston's breath caught in his throat.

"You!" he said, turning to face the man. For the second time he regretted not bringing his axe. It seemed even now it was not his wyrd to fulfil his oath to Eawynn and lay down his weapons. For sure as the leaves would fall from the trees in the autumn, there would be a fight here today.

Hunfrith, thinner and with sharper cheekbones than Dunston remembered, slowly pulled his long sword from the scabbard at his side.

"I could scarcely believe my eyes when I saw you come down the path," he said. His sword glimmered in the sunlight spilling in through the doorway. The metal was clean and polished. It appeared that Hunfrith had at least not forgotten to tend to his weapon. His clothing was a different matter. His cloak was threadbare and ripped, stained with mud and lichen. The kirtle he wore was streaked and filthy. His moustache and beard, once so well-tended and clipped, were now an unruly and straggled thatch. His eyes held a febrile glint. His smell was overpowering in the small confines of the hut and again Dunston could not believe he had failed to notice the man's presence earlier.

Holding his sword menacingly before him, Hunfrith took a step towards Dunston.

"You ruined everything, old man," he spat.

Dunston kept his hands loose at his sides, ready to react in an instant. He only had the seax he had taken from Beornmod. It would be difficult to fight against a sword, but he had no other weapon to hand.

"I did nothing, Hunfrith, save see a young girl to safety after you ordered her father murdered."

Hunfrith's eyes narrowed and Dunston knew that he would strike soon.

"I should have killed you when I had the chance," Hunfrith said.

"We all live with regrets," Dunston replied, edging around the hearth and away from Hunfrith.

Hunfrith sneered.

"Your time for living is over, old man."

He swung his sword at Dunston's head. Dunston ducked and, scooping up a stool from beside the fireplace, flung it at Hunfrith. The stool's leg's tangled with Hunfrith's blade and Dunston rushed out of the open doorway and into the bright light of the summer afternoon.

Blinking against the sunlight, he ran as fast as he could across the clearing. His ribs, still not fully healed, were already paining him. He could not keep this up. Besides, even without his recent wounds, Hunfrith was younger and taller and would catch him soon enough.

Behind him, Hunfrith roared and sped out of the hut.

Dunston slid to a halt only a dozen paces away. There was nothing to be gained from running. All that would happen is that he would be out of breath and struggling when he had to confront Hunfrith's sword. Better to stand now while he was fresh and had some small chance of victory.

Turning to face the younger man, Dunston slid his seax from its sheath. Hunfrith sped towards him, the long blade of his sword gleaming. Dunston could see instantly that the younger man was no novice with a blade. Facing a skilled swordsman, without a shield and with only a seax, Dunston's only chance would come from luck. Or a cool head, if he could only make his adversary lose his.

"Your father's corpse is decorating the gate at Exanceaster," Dunston shouted. "All his men are dead too. Some I slew, others were hanged by the king. You are the last one left. The pathetic bastard who doesn't know when he is defeated."

Dunston had hoped to goad Hunfrith into a reckless attack, but the erstwhile reeve slowed his charging pace before reaching Dunston. Crouching into the warrior stance, he spat.

"They may be dead, but you will join them soon enough. You may think me pathetic, old man, but like you say, I don't know I am defeated, because I am yet standing and I have a sword in my hand. That doesn't feel like defeat to me."

Without warning, and with none of the tell-tale signs Dunston had grown to expect from warriors who faced him, Hunfrith leapt forward. He feinted at Dunston's head, and as the old warrior brought up the short blade of his seax to parry the blow, Hunfrith altered the trajectory of his blade. Unarmoured as he was, the sword would have disembowelled Dunston, if it had connected. But at the last instant, Dunston threw himself backwards to avoid the blow. His foot sank into one of the deep clefts in the earth caused by the recent lack of rain and he tumbled to the hard earth of the clearing. Dunston grunted with the pain as the fall jarred his ribs.

Sensing victory, Hunfrith pressed forward, swinging his sword down. Dunston threw his seax up with nothing but instinct to guide his hand. He parried the strike, and sparks flew. His hand throbbed at the force of the collision and his fingers grew numb. He could not survive more than a few heartbeats, but he could see no way of saving himself. He scrabbled back in the dirt, and Hunfrith came on, grinning at the sight of his foe lying prostrate before him.

"Now you will die, cowering in the muck. Not so bold now, are you, old man? Who's the pathetic bastard now?"

Leering, he sliced his sword down at Dunston's exposed legs. Dunston twisted away from the attack and his ribs screamed from the effort. Hunfrith's blade bit into the earth. Dunston tried to regain his feet, but he was too slow; his old injured frame not as lithe as it had once been. Before he was able to rise, Hunfrith had recovered his balance and his wickedly fast sword flickered down again.

Again Dunston managed to intercept the swing with his seax, but as the two blades clanged together, the weight of the heavier sword sent a wave of shock up his wrist, numbing his hand completely and Beornmod's seax skittered out of his grasp. It fell in the grass a few paces away, but it might as well have been in Exanceaster, for all the help it would do him now.

Hunfrith raised his sword. Dunston could only watch in dismay. He was not afraid of death, but to be killed by this treacherous cur rankled. By Christ's bones, how he wished he had brought Deaþangenga with him. No matter his promise to Eawynn, he had never truly believed he would die without a weapon in his hand.

"Now you die, old man!" screamed Hunfrith.

A flash of inspiration came to Dunston then, as Hunfrith's blade glittered in the afternoon sun. With numb fingers, Dunston scrabbled at the leather-wrapped knife at his belt. He would yet die with a blade in his grasp.

Hunfrith's sword sang through the air as it sliced downward. Dunston roared and surged up, ramming Oswold's unfinished blade into Hunfrith's groin. The knife was unquenched and blunt, but it still had a point. Hunfrith's eyes opened wide as hot blood drenched Dunston's fist. With his left hand, Dunston grabbed Hunfrith's quickly weakening sword arm.

Aghast, Hunfrith stared down in confusion and disbelief as his blood pumped over Dunston's arm.

Dunston rose to his feet, grinding the bones in Hunfrith's right wrist in his powerful left fist. He shoved the younger man away from him and Hunfrith staggered, but did not fall.

"What?" said Hunfrith, stupidly. His eyes followed Dunston's movements, but he seemed incapable of action.

Dunston snatched up the fallen seax from the grass and advanced towards Hunfrith. At last, Hunfrith understood the threat and shook off his shock. He attempted to defend himself, to lift his sword. He stumbled back, away from Dunston. His face crumpled in agony; Oswold's knife yet jutted from his body. Again, he tried to raise his sword, but once more the effort proved too much. His breath was coming in wheezing gasps now. Blood gushed down his legs soaking his breeches.

Taking three quick steps forward, Dunston batted the sword away, slapping the flat of the blade with the palm of his left hand. His right fist punched forward and Hunfrith's eyes widened in horror. Dunston twisted the seax blade. It snagged on one of Hunfrith's ribs. The man juddered. Savagely, Dunston withdrew the steel from his flesh and then, without pause, drove it in again, probing with the point until it penetrated Hunfrith's heart. The man's stench filled his nostrils. Hunfrith let out a moaning, rattling breath, fetid with old mead and meat, and sagged against Dunston.

Stepping back, Dunston let his foe slump to the earth. Blood pumped from his wounds, staining the grass and the clover. Dunston was breathing heavily. His ribs ached and his hands shook. Looking down at Hunfrith's bleeding corpse, he thought absently how the grass would grow lush there, fed with the man's lifeblood.

The feeling slowly returned to his numbed right hand. His breathing came fast and ragged for a time and he slumped down in the grass, content to allow the afternoon breeze to cool the sweat on his brow. Eventually, his breathing slowed and he looked at the corpse in the grass. He could not tarry. Aedwen would be here soon. He had not been sure about letting her hunt alone, but in the end she had convinced him.

"Odin will protect me, won't you, boy?" she'd said, stroking the hound's ears.

Gazing at Hunfrith's crumpled form, Dunston felt a cold fear grip him. The forest was too dangerous for Aedwen alone, even with the dog. He would never allow such folly again. He stood with a groaning wince.

Dunston knew what he should do, but for a moment, he was filled with unease and uncertainty. He was the reeve now. It was his duty to uphold the law. Should he not take Hunfrith's body back to Briuuetone? Surely it was not right to merely leave him out here for the foxes, wolves and the woodland creatures to feast upon.

Dunston looked at his old house and remembered the day, only weeks earlier when he had set out one morning to check his snares and had instead found a mutilated corpse in a glade. He thought of how taking Lytelman's body to the village had sparked the dreadful events that followed. Of course, had he not found the man's body and taken it to Briuuetone, Wessex might now be overrun by Norsemen and Wéalas.

He sighed.

If there was a doom in Godrum's books forbidding what he meant to do, he did not know of it. Besides, Hunfrith was a wolf-head, his life forfeit. He would not be missed.

Hunfrith was a large man, and Dunston's ribs throbbed terribly as he dragged the corpse into the forest, far from the house.

Later, when he returned to the glade, smoke drifted from the hut's thatch and the smell of roasting game wafted to him on the warm summer breeze. As he drew near, he could hear Aedwen humming a tune to herself and relief flooded through him.

She was safe.

Her singing reminded him of Eawynn. Unbidden, tears filled his eyes. He stood there for some time, listening to her. The summer sun soaked into his skin and he closed his eyes, allowing himself to imagine, just for a moment, that the years had not passed. That he was not now an old man. That Eawynn yet lived.

Then, Odin barked and came bounding out of the hut. Dunston smiled at the hound and cuffed away the tears from his cheeks.

Stepping into the smoky darkness of the hut, he said, "Is that partridge I smell? Let's eat and then, let's go home. We have hunted enough for one day."

Historical Note

Novels often grow from the smallest seed of inspiration. So it was with *Wolf of Wessex*.

I stumbled upon the account in the *Anglo-Saxon Chronicle* for 21 June in the year 838. On that day King Ecgberht of Wessex defeated a joint force of Cornish and Danish at a place called Hingston Down (Hengestdūn). This got me thinking. How did Ecgberht know the enemy forces had gathered deep within Cornwall with enough time to muster his troops and march them all the way to the Tamar, where it is assumed the Danes had landed and the battle is traditionally thought to have taken place? I can't imagine the Cornish and Danish leaders would have amassed and then tarried for long enough to allow word of their impending attack to reach Wessex, so perhaps Ecgberht had been forewarned. We don't know where the Danes that joined the Cornish had come from, but it is very likely they were based in Ireland, which was by this time a Norse stronghold. But wherever they came from, if this was a planned joint assault, there must have been some communication beforehand that could have been intercepted. Now, it could well be that all communication had been verbal, but what if some of the missives about the attack had been written down?

And that was enough for me to start coming up with the plot of *Wolf of Wessex*.

Most of the characters in the novel are fictitious, but they are placed within the tapestry of real events and places. The very late eighth and early ninth centuries were years of upheaval after a period of relative stability for Britain. Following the first account of Norsemen landing on the coast of Wessex in 787, over the subsequent decade there followed a series of brutal raids all around the coastline of the British Isles. Infamously, the raiders, known now as Vikings (*vikingr* in the novel, the Old Norse word for people travelling to raid and seek adventure), sacked Christian monasteries such as Lindisfarne in Northumbria and Iona in the Hebrides. These Christian sites were situated in exposed locations, with access to the sea and no armed guards, and they also housed many rich artefacts which were ripe for the taking. These Scandinavian pirates were not Christian, so cared nothing for the supposed eternal damnation they might face for defiling the sanctity of monasteries and churches. And so it was that the Viking Age began. A time where the sleek dragon-prowed ships of the Norsemen were a constant threat to anyone living near the coast or navigable rivers in Britain and northern Europe.

For a time in the early ninth century, the number of attacks seems to have reduced, thanks in no small part to Frankish ships patrolling the English Channel. Like so many monarchs in the Anglo-Saxon period, Ecgberht had been exiled in his early life. He spent those years in the court of Charlemagne, the Frankish king, the greatest king of the age. There Ecgberht learnt much of how to be a statesman and how to govern a Christian country. This knowledge would serve him well and the alliance with the powerful Frankish royal family must certainly have aided him when he returned to claim his place as the king of Wessex.

Under Ecgberht, and with Frankish support, Wessex quickly became the most powerful kingdom in Britain. While the Frankish navy kept the southern coast relatively safe from plundering Norsemen, Ecgberht focused on conquest and expansion. In 813 and then again in 825 he led campaigns against the "West Welsh", conquering what is now known as Devon and subjugating Cornwall to the status of vassal state. Soon he had defeated the Mercians at the Battle of Ellandun (probably Wroughton in Wiltshire) and then swallowed up Kent, Essex, Surrey and Sussex. According to the *Anglo-Saxon Chronicle*, he even took the oath of Eanred, king of the Northumbrians, leading Ecgberht to be called the ruler of all of the English.

But as with all kingdoms, things didn't run smoothly for long. Mercia, Wessex's enemy number one, quickly regained independence in 830. And the Vikings posed an increasing threat along the coast of Wessex. This was due to a civil war breaking out in Frankia between the sons of Louis the Pious. As the bloody civil war raged, thoughts of protecting the Channel from Norse ships vanished, and the navy was disbanded.

So, with his continental European allies otherwise engaged and removing their support, Ecgberht found himself having to fend for himself. In 836, a fleet of thirty-five Danish marauders landed at Carrum (Carhampton). Ecgberht summoned his levies and they attacked the Vikings. But the Danes defeated the men of Wessex and "had the place of slaughter".

Ecgberht was getting old by this time and the threat of attack by Vikings must have been an ever-present worry for him. There was always the possibility of treachery from within too, of course. Which brings us back to the planning of the joint attack in 838. If messages were being sent to arrange times and places, perhaps they would be written down. This would be much more likely if Ecclesiastics were involved.

Perhaps they would be arrogant enough to think that so few people could read, their plots would not be found out.

There are several instances of bishops conspiring against kings for their own personal gain. Bishop Wulfstan in the tenth century, for example, switched allegiances between the Northumbrians and the Vikings as was expedient at any given time. Another example is Wulfheard, Bishop of Hereford. He had some very public spats with King Offa and went as far as to forge land grants to gain riches and power.

Ealhstan was the Bishop of Sherbourne in 838, but the only evidence for his duplicitous nature comes from Asser's *Life of King Alfred*, where he states that Ealhstan was involved in a plot to prevent King Aethelwulf (Ecgberht's son and Alfred's father) from regaining his crown when he returned from his pilgrimage to Rome.

As to nobles plotting against their kings for their own advancement, such a thing is all too commonplace. Even today the idea of powerful politicians betraying their nation for personal gain is met with resigned acceptance rather than outraged shock. One historic event that partly inspired Ealdorman Ælfgar and his bastard son, Hunfrith, is that of Huga (or Hugh), the Frenchman who had been made reeve of Exeter. In 1003 he betrayed the city to a great army of Danes led by Swein Forkbeard. The city was taken and destroyed and much of Wessex was invaded and plundered as a result.

Dunston is all fiction, but I liked the idea of a warrior looking back at the life he had led, believing he has served his purpose, only to find he still has a role to play, and perhaps a reason to strive for more than simply existing.

The location of his home, Sealhwudu (Selwood Forest), is real. In the ninth century the woodland covered the land between Chippenham in modern-day Wiltshire to Gillingham in Dorset. It was an important natural boundary between east and west Wessex. The name derives from Sallow Wood. Sallow is an archaic name for willow. A small part of this ancient forest remains to this day at Clanger Wood in Yarnbrook, Wiltshire.

Briuuetone (Bruton) gets its name from the river that flows through the town. Briw means vigorous and describes the fast-flowing water of the River Brue in spate.

The idea of a Christian of the ninth century having a dog named Odin, after the one-eyed father of the Norse gods, may seem far-fetched. However, the idea comes from my own family history. My paternal grandfather had a black Labrador called Satan, which I believe was named by my father (who incidentally went on to become a missionary and then a Baptist minister!). You can imagine the strange looks my grandfather would get in the 1960s and 1970s calling out for his dog.

The partial lunar eclipse of the full moon on the night of 11 June 838 was something I discovered while writing and seemed like a detail I had to include in the story.

The land of Wessex has been populated for millennia and is the home to Stonehenge and the larger stone circle of Avebury. It is also dotted with ancient burial mounds and barrows. The barrow where Dunston and Aedwen spend the night is loosely based on Stoney Littleton Long Barrow, which is maintained by English Heritage and open to the public. It can be entered free of charge.

Much of Dunston and Aedwen's story centres around the legal concepts of Anglo-Saxon Wessex. I have taken a rather loose approach to the legal system of the first half of the ninth century, incorporating elements that were not documented until later. However, I believe this leads to an authentic feeling of the legal process of the time, and does not detract from the novel or stray too far from the reality of what would have been.

The kingdom was broken down into areas called hundreds. These hundreds were probably comprised of a hundred hides of land. Each hundred was further broken down into tithings of ten hides each. The terms, hundreds and tithings, were first recorded in the laws of Edmund I in the tenth century, but they may well have been in use for much longer and I think they give a good framework of understanding for how the law worked.

Each hundred held a monthly hundred court (or moot) where legal disputes would be heard. Any case that could not be settled could be taken to the shire court. The reeve of each hundred was a powerful man and responsible for the administration of the law and keeping of the peace. When a miscreant fled justice, or someone was accused of a violent crime and needed to be apprehended, the men of the tithing where the criminal resided were responsible for bringing him in to face justice.

Above the hundred was the shire, and difficult cases could be taken to the shire reeve (where we get the word sheriff). The shire court was held less frequently, perhaps every six months. The highest court of the land was the King's court, where the king himself dispensed justice.

The Church had its own Ecclesiastical courts where cases against the clergy were heard.

The trial system was based on oaths being made. If a defendant could find enough people to swear oaths to their innocence, they would be exonerated. If found guilty, the accused could seek to face trial by ordeal to prove their innocence by divine providence. However, this must always have been a last resort, due to the grisly, painful and sometimes deadly nature of the ordeals!

Most crimes had a price, or weregild, that needed to be paid to the aggrieved party and sometimes the reeve and king too. These penalties were set down in lists of laws, or dooms. Alfred the Great of Wessex, Ecgberht's grandson, codified the laws of Wessex into a single book. *The Doom Book* or *Code of Alfred* compiled three previous lists of dooms – those of Athelberht of Kent, Ine of Wessex and Offa of Mercia. For the weregild in this novel, I have used the dooms of Ine of Wessex.

The concept of the wulfeshéafod, or wolf's head, or wolf-head (caput lupinum in Latin) referred to a person being outside the law, and, like a lone wolf, they were open to attack by anyone. A wolf-head had lost all rights and so could be harmed by anyone with impunity. Such outlaws must have been truly desperate individuals, as they could expect no quarter if captured.

Dunston's axe is inspired by the axe found in Mammen, near Viborg in Denmark. The head of the Mammen axe is iron with intricate patterns of silver thread inlaid. It is not as large as DeaÞangenga, and it is not known whether it was used in battle or merely for ceremonial purposes. DeaÞangenga means Deathwalker in Old English, and seemed a very apt name for Dunston's huge axe with which he has sent so many men to their deaths.

The crossing of the River Exe by the warriors on their return from Hingston Down may have surprised readers familiar with the area. There had been a Roman timber bridge over the Exe, but that would have decayed and washed away by the ninth century. However, before the later stone bridge over the river was built in the thirteenth century, there are accounts that the Exe could be forded at low tide.

The generally accepted location of the battle of Hingston Down is near the Tamar River, in Cornwall. However, there is another Hingston Down, in Devon. It seemed more likely to me that, rather than striking deep into hostile territory, Ecgberht would gather his troops and waylay the approaching host of Vikings and Cornish. The Devon Hingston Down is near Moretonhampstead and on the route from the Tamar, where the Vikings landed, to Exeter, so it seems like a perfect location for an ambush.

At the end of this story, Dunston has somewhat reluctantly accepted the mantle of responsibility gifted to him by his king and Aedwen has found people who have welcomed her as if she were kin. For the time being, they are at peace. But King Ecgberht is old and his reign cannot last much longer. And when a king dies, chaos often ensues. And when the ruler of a kingdom as rich as Wessex dies, war is never far away. The power of the Norsemen is on the rise and Britain will soon see itself beset with an ever-increasing number of invaders.

How will Dunston and Aedwen cope with the upheavals that will shape the island of Britain and the history of the English people?

That is for another day, and other books.

Acknowledgements

As always, my first thanks go to you, dear reader, for using some of your valuable time to read my writing. Without you, there would be no books. I hope you have enjoyed *Wolf of Wessex*. If you have, please consider taking a moment to leave a review on your online store of choice and spread the word to friends and family. In a world awash with content, with so many things vying for people's attention, it is hard to stand out from the crowd and word of mouth is everything.

As with every book, there are a lot of people who have helped in getting *Wolf of Wessex* into the finished, published product.

Thank you to my trusty friends and test readers, Gareth Jones, Simon Blunsdon, Shane Smart, Rich Ward and Alex Forbes. They always provide me with invaluable input that helps me to polish the manuscripts before anyone else sees them and I make too much of a fool of myself!

Special thanks to Christopher Monk for his help with the Old English.

Thanks to Robyn Young, for her ideas for a title (even though in the end, I went with something else!).

Thanks to Steven A. McKay for reading an early draft and giving me some extremely useful feedback. I'd also like to thank

Steven and the rest of the online community of authors for all their support. These include, in no particular order, Martin Lake, Giles Kristian, E. M. Powell, Justin Hill, Stephanie Churchill, Gordon Doherty, Angus Donald, Jemahl Evans, Ian Ross, Ben Kane, Sharon Bennett Connolly, Paul Fraser Collard, Christian Cameron, Simon Turney and Griff Hosker. This is not an exhaustive list of all the writers who have helped me in one way or another, and I apologise unreservedly to those I have forgotten to include here!

I am indebted to Chris Bailey, founder and administrator of the Bernard Cornwell Fan Club group on Facebook. Not only has he been extremely supportive of my writing efforts, he also produced my very own customised axe, based on the description of Dunston's DeaÞangenga. It is a thing of exquisite craftsmanship and beauty and there is nothing like holding a Viking axe in your hands to get you in the mood to write some rip-roaring fight scenes!

Thanks to my editor, Nicolas Cheetham, and all of the team at Aria and Head of Zeus for their hard work and dedication to producing great books.

And lastly, but certainly not least, extra special thanks to my wonderful wife, Maite (Maria, to her work colleagues!), and our daughters, Elora and Iona. They all have to put up with me every day and I know I can sometimes (often) be grumpy when the writing isn't going according to plan. But I also know that without loved ones to share my highs and lows, whatever I wrote would be meaningless.

About the author

MATTHEW HARFFY grew up in Northumberland, England, where the rugged terrain, ruined castles and rocky coastline had a huge impact on him. He now lives in Wiltshire, with his wife and their two daughters.